If Mistletoe Could Tell Tales

Jude Knight

Published by Titchfield Press at CreateSpace
Copyright 2017 Judith Anne Knighton writing as Jude Knight

ISBN 978-0-9951049-5-2

TITCHFIELD
PRESS

If Mistletoe Could Tell Tales

In this 2017 box set, you'll find Jude's four published Christmas novellas plus two Christmas-themed stories from her lunch-length reads collections. All together in one 97,500 word volume for your holiday pleasure.

Candle's Christmas Chair (A novella in *The Golden Redepennings* series)
They are separated by social standing and malicious lies. How can he convince her to give their love another chance?

Gingerbread Bride (A novella in *The Golden Redepenning* series)
Mary runs from an unwanted marriage and finds adventure, danger and her girlhood hero, coming once more to her rescue.

Magnus and the Christmas Angel (from *Lost in the Tale*)
Scarred by years in captivity, Magnus has fought English Society to be accepted as the true Earl of Fenchurch. Now he faces the hardest battle of all: to win the love of his wife.

Lord Calne's Christmas Ruby
Lalamani prefers her aunt's quiet village to fashionable London, its vicious harpies, and its importunate fortune hunters. Philip wishes she wasn't so rich, or he wasn't so poor.

A Suitable Husband
A chef from the slums, however talented, is no fit mate for the cousin of a duke, however distant. But Cedrica can dream. (first published in *Holly and Hopeful Hearts*, a Bluestocking Belles collection.)

All that Glisters (from *Hand-Turned Tales*)
Rose is unhappy in the household of her fanatical uncle. Thomas, a young merchant from Canada, offers a glimpse of another possible life. If she is brave enough to reach for it.

Dedication

To the ghosts of Christmas past, present, and future. And a merry holiday season to you and your family, whatever festivals you celebrate.

Table of Contents

Gingerbread Bride

Lieutenant Rick Redepenning has been saving his admiral's intrepid daughter from danger since their formative years, but today, he faces the gravest of threats—the damage she might do to his heart. How can he convince her to see him as a suitor, not just a childhood friend?

Travelling with her father's fleet has left Mary Pritchard ill-prepared for London Society, and prey to the machinations of false friends. When she strikes out on her own to find a more suitable locale to take up her solitary spinsterhood, she finds adventure, trouble, and her girlhood hero, riding once more to her rescue.

This sweet Christmas novella first appeared in the Bluestocking Belles box set Mistletoe, Marriage, and Mayhem.

Chapter One

"I don't run away. I run towards," she had told Rick the first time
he retrieved her for her father, the admiral. That was half his
lifetime ago, when she was nine, and he was a young midshipman
of nearly fourteen.

He sat on his horse for a moment, watching her trudging down
the meadow towards the village in the valley. The Mary of today
was slowed by a bandbox in one hand and a carpetbag in the other.
The earnest child of his memory—chasing after a dream through a
sunlit field in Spain, or Italy, or Jamaica—had never bothered with
such practicalities as luggage.

Rick hadn't seen her since she was sent home to relatives after
her father's death, but he couldn't mistake her. What was Miss Mary
Pritchard running towards today?

The immediate destination, he could guess well enough. He'd
seen the broken-down coach back around several curves of this
long, winding road, and not long ago, he'd passed the coachman
with a string of passengers grumbling along behind him. And pretty
rough sorts some of them looked, too.

Miss Independent Mary had undoubtedly struck out on her own
across country instead of sticking to the road, and would be at the
inn in the valley a good half hour before the rest of the coachload.

But what was the admiral's daughter doing on a coach in the first
place? The aunt she lived with was in London. Indeed, he had
dropped his card at the house. He had called three times before the
aunt had consented to see him, only to explain that the niece of the
Dowager Viscountess Bosville could expect better than a half-pay
navy lieutenant with a bad limp and few expectations. He wanted to

renew his friendship, not court her, but no doubt, the aunt knew Mary's mind better than he did.

Perhaps not, though. The aunt was, indeed, in London, but Miss Mary was definitely there below him, striding across the field.

He nudged the post horse into a walk. There must be a gate along the road somewhere. Yes. There. By the time he'd dismounted, led the horse through, shut the gate, and awkwardly mounted again, Mary had reached the lowest corner of the field and was opening a gate there.

What was that movement? Three men were creeping along her side of the field, careful to stay in the shadow of the hedge. Sneak up on Mary Pritchard, would they? He'd see about that.

He kneed the horse into a gallop. The men stopped at the noise, then spun round and hurried away uphill. Mary turned to face the horse.

She stood rigid, one hand creeping into her coat. So Miss Mary was armed? That didn't surprise him. He'd taught her to shoot himself, after the incident in the date grove just outside Tunis. He still got the collywobbles thinking about the danger she'd put herself in, running off to buy a present for her father's birthday.

The slavers were congratulating themselves when he caught up with them. They had left the sweet little red-haired girl bound and helpless, and were brewing coffee and boasting of the money she would fetch. Except she'd used the flip knife he'd given her, after the escapade in the Spanish church, to cut her bonds. When he arrived, Mary, bless the courage of her, had armed herself with the rifles they'd carelessly left slung on their camels.

When he attacked, they found themselves shot at from two directions, including from their own ramshackle weapons. They might have withstood his assault, but the sight of a child with an armful of guns gave them pause. Her first wild shot convinced them that she had no idea what she was doing, but was going to do it anyway.

With no way of predicting what would happen next, they decided discretion was the better part of valor. Rick teased Mary that he'd been tempted to flee with them, given her wildly inaccurate shooting. He had no idea how it happened that they stopped at the Tunisian market to buy a woolen klim for her father before he took her safely back to the ship.

He tugged his mind back into 1799. She'd recognized him. The tension remained, but she removed her hand from her coat.

"Miss Pritchard," he said, bowing as well as he could from the back of his horse.

"Lieutenant Redepenning." She did not sound at all pleased to see him.

Richard Redepenning. What on earth was he doing in a field in Surrey? As if her running away conjured him! She almost smiled. He had appeared out of nowhere to rescue her so many times when she was young.

Then she remembered—he had been in London for two months, and hadn't called on her once. Today, she was rescuing herself, thank you very much.

Good manners, however, prompted her to say, "I was sorry to hear about your wound. I trust you are recovering?"

He was dismounting, and she could see for herself that the wound left him lame. His boot hit the ground, and he lurched, catching his balance against the saddle. She almost dropped her bags and put out a hand to help him, but she could hear her father's voice saying, "Let the man keep his pride, child."

Instead, she surreptitiously eased her shoulders. The bags had not felt nearly as heavy when she strode away from the others at the coach, after a short argument with the coachman about the merits of following the road versus trusting her navigation skills.

The coachman insisted that sticking to the road was a much better idea, since who knew what barriers might appear on the path that cut down the hill. "I know what I'm doing, Miss," he insisted. If he thought she was going to trust a coachman who had finally landed them in the ditch after multiple near misses, he was soon disabused of the notion.

As soon as she struck out on her own, she questioned whether it had been wise. Even the silly coachman would have been protection from the three coach passengers who had been leering at her for most of the afternoon. She was, of course, duly grateful to Lieutenant Redepenning for happening along before they caught up with her. But she had a pistol. She would have managed perfectly well without him.

"I have some rope here," Lieutenant Redepenning was saying, as he looked through his saddle bags. "Ah. Here it is. Pass me the carpet bag, Miss Pritchard, and we'll let the horse carry it the rest of the way to the village."

She rather thought he needed the horse more than the carpet bag did, but arguing with Richard Redepenning had always been an exercise in futility. He was the only person she knew who could out-stubborn her, though that was at least in part because of the pointless *tendre* she had held for him since the first time he had rescued her.

She had been nine years of age, and cross with that year's nurse. She wanted apples for tea, and the nurse told her the country grew no apples. Silly woman. Mary had passed an apple seller in the market earlier that day. No point in taking an appeal to Papa. Papa would no more countenance insubordination within his family than within his crew.

So Mary waited until Nurse was asleep, then crept out of her cabin and set off to find the market.

Which was not at all where she expected it to be. She soon became lost in a maze of little streets, and her red hair and fair skin attracted a forest of locals, looming over her and making incomprehensible sounds, while she stood at bay against a wall and prepared to fight for her life.

Then the crowd melted, and Midshipman Redepenning was there, smiling at her and holding out a hand, all the time talking to the village people in their own language. At fourteen, he had been a beautiful boy, tall and slender, with a crop of golden blond hair and intensely blue eyes.

He didn't growl, or complain about the nuisance of girl children. He didn't suggest that her father beat her (not that Papa ever did).

He escorted her home to the ship, and helped her sneak back into her cabin. He even took a detour through the market and bought her an apple.

Mary had fallen in love that day, and she stayed in love as the boy grew to the handsomest, kindest man she knew. No other man ever measured up. Not that Lieutenant Redepenning cared. As far as she could see, he still thought of her as the child that continually needed rescue.

"Miss Pritchard?" There she was lost in memories of some far-off sunny shore, while Lieutenant Redepenning stood in front of her with his piece of rope at the ready.

"Thank you." She hoisted the bag up and balanced it on the saddle while he tied it, with quick efficient sailors' knots. The band box went up next, tied in front of the bag.

"If you would see to the gate, Miss Pritchard?" he suggested. "I can walk well enough, but I'm not as spry as I was."

They slowly sauntered down the hill path, Mary holding the proffered arm but attempting to put no weight on it.

Anxiety made her cross. He shouldn't be walking. Idiot man. He should have stuck to riding, and the road. If he were sore tonight, it would be his own fault. She didn't ask him to follow her.

They came to another gate, and, on the other side, to a bench seat that looked over the village, now almost close enough to touch. The church roof and the top floor of the inn were at eye level.

The last stretch of path, though short, was going to be a problem. It was steep and narrow. How would Mary get the lieutenant down it without injury? She frowned at it with disfavor.

"Let us sit for a minute," she suggested.

He was willing enough, tying the horse to a handy bush and lowering himself to the seat with a sigh.

Best to be frank. "Lieutenant Redepenning, the path is very steep and narrow. How are we to manage it?"

"You used to call me 'Rick,'" he observed.

Dear God, how blue his eyes were. That twinkle was just as devastating as ever. What had he said? Oh, yes. "You used to call me 'Mary,'" she retorted. "And how are we to get you down the path, Lieutenant?"

"Rick," he insisted.

"Rick, then." She gave way on that point, but continued to glare. She would not be distracted from her purpose.

"Mary." His voice was a caress, giving her plain name a music it never had. Good heavens, was Rick the Rogue flirting? With her? With Mary Pritchard, the bluestocking, forthright as a sailor and homely to boot? He was just trying to divert her.

Her frown deepened, and she raised one eyebrow.

Rick complied.

"I confess it is a problem. The doctor says the break is knitting well, and I just need to wait for the tissues to recover. It will repair entirely in time, but after a day's riding or much walking, the leg does not obey as it ought. I think if you will lead the horse, Mary, I can lean on the bank and make my way safely down. Shall we rest here a moment, then give it a try?"

Chapter Two

Usually, he hated admitting his weakness. In his own mind, he feared the doctor was wrong about his eventual recovery, and he sometimes wondered if the decision to keep the leg was doing him any favors. Somehow, he didn't mind Mary knowing about the pesky thing.

Perhaps because he knew she wouldn't make a fuss. In London, his male friends had looked away, embarrassed, and his sister and her friends had hovered over him and fussed around till he was ready to scream.

Mary just said, "Very well."

They sat in silence for a few minutes.

Rick broke the silence. "May I inquire about your intended direction, Mary?"

She frowned at him, then looked pointedly away. "Am I in another bumble-broth from which you must rescue me, you mean?"

He smiled back. "Are you? I would be happy to be of service, you know."

"I am no longer nine, thank you, Lieutenant Redepenning." Her voice dripped ice. "I would not at all wish to further inconvenience you."

Miss Mary was in a taking. What had he done to offend her? Rick hazarded a guess. "I called on you in London. Did you know?"

She turned startled eyes to him. "You did? When?" Then, brows drawing together, she asked, "Did my aunt send you to find me?"

So she had run away. "I called several times. Not recently. Not since your aunt told me that you had no wish to see me."

An angry huff of air escaped. "She... I... That..." Mary swallowed whatever words might have finished the interrupted sentences, taking to her feet to march up and down the small, flat ledge, with her lips tightly pressed together, as if to stop any further outburst.

Rick waited. Her angers were sudden, but quickly over. In a few more strides, she would be calm again. How pretty she was, with indignation coloring her cheeks under the light dusting of freckles.

She stopped in front of him, looking down. "Rick, I had no idea you had visited, and I certainly never gave such a message. I would never turn away..." She blushed a little more, and finished, "...someone who served with my father."

Rick wondered what she first thought to say.

"My aunt takes too much on herself." She fairly quivered with indignation.

He ventured another guess: "And is that why you're here, Mary? Your aunt taking too much on herself?"

Mary didn't answer; not directly. "I am going to Haslemere to live with my Aunt Dorothy and my Aunt Marjery. I find the frivolous life does not suit me" She frowned down at the rooftops. "It is not far, is it?"

He accepted the change of subject, levering himself back to his feet. "Shall we have a go at this path, Mary? I can hear the coachman and his ducklings up on the road above us, and I would like to secure rooms at the inn before they arrive."

Mary and the horse went down the path first. She waited at the bottom, trying not to let her anxiety show as Rick slowly and carefully worked his way from rocky step to rocky step. He was pale and pinched when he reached the bottom, but made a brave attempt at his usual jaunty grin.

"There. That is the worst of it. Lead us to the inn."

They took the last one hundred yards slowly, he leaning at least some of his weight on the horse, she matching her pace to his without comment.

The innkeeper took the news of a stranded coachload of passengers in his stride. "Some of the men will 'ave to double up, sir, but I've a good suite for you and your sister: two bedchambers and a private sitting room." He looked at the two of them suspiciously. "And will Miss Reid's maid be arriving with the others?" Reid was the surname Rick had written in the register.

"My maid, unfortunately, was taken ill and was not able to accompany me," Mary said.

"You should not have gone on without her, sister, dear," Rick scolded. "Fortunately, I was at home to receive your message and was able to follow after you before any harm was done."

My goodness, he sounded exactly like a patronizing older brother. She snapped back, "All would have been well, if the coachman had not landed us in a ditch."

He opened his mouth to say something more, but his leg suddenly gave way, and he lurched, catching her shoulder as she moved to support him, her irritation forgotten.

"Rick, you've overdone things. Oh, dear, I should never have let you walk. Innkeeper, you take his other side, and we'll get him to his room. Oh, dear, why did you not say?"

Together, she and the innkeeper supported Rick up the stairs to a small but comfortable suite, leaving a servant to bring her luggage and Rick's modest saddle bags.

"I just need to sit for a while," Rick insisted. The innkeeper helped him to the room's sofa, where he was able to stretch out the damaged leg.

Mary ordered water for washing, brandy for Rick, and a glass of negus for herself, to be delivered immediately. "And we shall want a hot meal, innkeeper, but that can wait until..." She looked at Rick uncertainly. A lifetime on shipboard had taught her that men needed to be fed regularly, but she also knew that pain suppressed the appetite.

"An hour, perhaps?" Rick suggested. He was lying back on the cushions, his eyes shut.

"An hour," Mary confirmed to the innkeeper. After she had settled on a selection of dishes from those the inn offered, she kept herself busy to avoid thinking about the fact that she was alone with the man they called Rick the Rogue. Not that he'd ever been anything but a gentleman with her. And she was pleased about that. She was.

In the bedchamber allocated to her, she removed her bonnet and turned down her sheets, slipping a hand between them to check for damp. She then set out clothes for the next day, arranged her hair brush and tooth powder on the night stand, rearranged the screen in the corner, and used some of the water a servant brought to wash her face and hands.

She didn't quite dare to enter Rick's room, but she instructed the servant who arrived with the hot water to turn down Rick's bed, and she stood in the doorway while the servant tested the sheets.

"Now put Lieutenant Rede... Lieutenant Reid's bags on the coverlet so he can easily reach them. There."

Rick was propped on the sofa cushions, his brandy cradled in both hands, his eyes still closed. Every few minutes, he would lift the glass and take another sip. She bustled around the small sitting room, moving the fire screen so he wouldn't get too hot, placing a small table conveniently close to Rick's elbow for his brandy and later his dinner plate, moving a light wing chair for herself, so he could easily see her without turning his head.

When she ran out of things to do, she sat and watched him. He really was devastatingly attractive. For a moment, she let herself dream she had a right to sit here opposite him, studying the planes of his face, the lock of hair that had escaped his ribbon and was teasing the side of his cheek, the broad shoulders in the uniform jacket he had loosened but not removed.

A knock on the door broke her reverie. Dinner. Yes. No more of this nonsense, Mary Pritchard. As if Lieutenant Richard Redepenning, Rick the Rogue, could ever be interested in someone like her!

Chapter Three

What a woman she had grown into! She made Rick comfortable with quiet competence, leaving him to rest until the pain died down to a quiet ache. No fussing. No questions about what she could do for him. She just set the suite to rights and sat peacefully until the meal arrived.

Over dinner, they fell back into the easy habit of conversation they'd enjoyed aboard her father's ship, before Rick had been promoted elsewhere in the fleet.

They disagreed about Russia's trustworthiness as an ally in the long war against France, and agreed that General Bonaparte was a dangerous man, and debated passionately about the wisdom of a reduction in the militia, Mary's color rising to tint her skin pink. Skin so fair as to be translucent, with a soft dusting of freckles across her tip-tilted nose. Her long pale eyelashes glinted in the candlelight as they swept down to brush her cheeks, and her copper curls, as averse to confinement as the rest of her, sprang free of her ribbon as she shook her head at whatever he had just said. What had he said? Lost in totaling her features, he had lost track of his argument.

"You are tired," she decided.

You are pretty, he thought. But she was correct, as well, so he let her chivvy him off to bed.

In the morning, he felt considerably more the thing, and after breakfast, they set off in a hired chaise for Haslemere, where her aunts lived.

"It is on my way, Mary," he told her, and she allowed him to escort her.

They arrived in Haslemere in mid-afternoon, and stopped across the street from the address Mary had been given.

She turned to smile at him, a full Mary Pritchard beam. The smiles of Admiral Pritchard's daughter had been known to melt the heart of the toughest bo'sun, and to turn the crews of an entire fleet into putty in her hands.

"Lieutenant Redepenning, Rick, I cannot thank you enough." She held out her little gloved hand expectantly.

"I will see you inside, of course," he said. And check the aunts were really there, and the place was a safe one for Mary to stay.

"I suppose you will insist." Mary frowned. "I'd hoped to save you from getting down out of the curricle."

He ignored her protests and lowered himself carefully, good leg first, then turned and offered her a gallant hand. Good sailor that she was, she made no fuss, but nor did she put any weight on him as she hopped down to the pavement.

"Let's leave the bags there while we check to see if we have the right place?" Rick suggested. He told the post boy to keep an eye on the bags as well as the horses, before he and Mary crossed the street.

The door was opened almost as soon as he banged the knocker, and they walked into chaos. A bewildering number of maids were running back and forth along the hall. Laden trays appeared from the back of the house, from which delicious smells of spice and baking wafted, then disappeared into the front room to the right. Empty trays were whisked back down the hall, the two processions of maids turning sideways to prevent collisions. A short, plump, elderly woman in an old-fashioned print gown and large, white pinafore stood at the door to the front room, watching all that went on with the eye of a ship's captain.

Rick would have known her in a crowd for the admiral's sister. She had the same light blue eyes, the same determined chin, the same bulbous nose (albeit in a more feminine cast), and the same air of command.

Mary was in no doubt either. "Aunt Dorothy?"

Next moment, she was enveloped in an enthusiastic hug. "Fletcher's little girl. It must be. Darling Mary, let me look at you." The woman held her at arms' length, then pulled her in for another hug. "Why, you are the image of my mama. Did your dear papa ever tell you that? He must have. Just look at you."

Ignoring Rick and the maids, Miss Pritchard proceeded to hug Mary, untie her bonnet, hug her again, help her off with her coat, clucking over her the whole while.

After a few minutes, she seemed to realize she had spectators. "But what am I thinking! Maudie, dear, look after the baking. Mary, come away into the house, and you—Mary's friend—you come too."

Rick excused himself after promising to send in Mary's bags and to visit again tomorrow.

He carried away an image of her looking a little lost. *If she isn't happy with her place when I return,* he vowed, *I'll carry her off and find her a safe berth somewhere else.*

Mary found herself swept along by a sort of a female tempest to the rear of the hall, avoiding the continuing procession of maids as they went. They came to harbor at the end of the hall in a small, cluttered, feminine parlor.

"Now then, Mary, my girl. Tell me what you are doing here, and who that gentleman was. Not that I am not pleased to see you, for that I am, and no mistake, but fetching up on my doorstep with no warning, and in the company of a gentleman, with not even a maid to give you countenance! It needs to be explained, my dear. That it does."

"Aunt Dorothy, that was Lieutenant Redepenning. He served with father, and he was kind enough to escort me from Merroham after the coach broke down."

Aunt Dorothy eyed her thoughtfully. "Hmm, that explains the young man, I suppose, but what were you doing on the coach in the first place?"

Mary blushed a little, and looked at the paintings on the wall rather than her aunt. "I found that London life did not suit me, Aunt. And in your letters, you said I would always be welcome."

"That you are, dear, that you are. Never doubt it. Though if I'd known you were coming... Well, here you are, and I am so pleased to see you, and so Marjery will be." She pursed her lips a little. "And your cousin, Enid, of course." The broad smile returned. "They are making afternoon calls, dear, but will be home soon."

A maid arrived with a large trolley containing a tea service and a plate tower with different types of cakes and tarts on each layer.

Aunt Dorothy busied herself with pouring the tea.

"You will wonder at the bustle here, my dear. We are known for our baking, you know." She puffed herself up, looking for all the world like a contented hen. "We are always called on to supply baking for church fairs, assemblies, and other such things. And, just think, dear, our baking is much in demand at the market!" She deflated a little. "It is not trade, dear, whatever Enid says. Your cousin is a little sensitive." She shook herself, as if to settle her feathers.

"Now, Mary, tell me the truth. What happened in London? I thought your mother's sister would have found you a husband. Aha! That is it, is it not? She picked someone, and you ran away!"

Chapter Four

After his visit to check on Mary, Rick reluctantly left Haslemere, because he couldn't find a reason to stay. He wasn't family, and Mary was an adult, able to make her own decisions. Rick had no right to interfere with her choices.

That's what this reluctance was; concern she was making the wrong choice. Rescuing Mary Pritchard was the habit of half a lifetime. She was a friend. Just a friend. He wasn't so foolish as to dangle after a girl who showed no awareness of him as a man.

When he called that morning, Miss Pritchard and her sister, Lady Rumbold, had been as protective of her as they should be. Rick couldn't doubt that Mary was welcome, and that she would be looked after.

Even so, all the way to his father's house in Portsmouth, where he planned to stay for a month, he felt a nagging sense of loss. He kept turning to Mary to tell her something, and she was never there.

The hollow ache didn't go away. It followed him around Portsmouth. He visited with friends. He travelled across to Haslar to see a doctor at the naval hospital who recommended leg-strengthening exercises, which he carried out faithfully several times a day. And all the time he missed Mary.

Papa couldn't get down from London, but he said Rick was to treat the house as his own. The staff had either been ship's crew with Papa or servants at Longford, his boyhood home, when Mama was chatelaine there. Rick had never been better looked after. Or more lonely.

He came home one day from dinner, with a friend who'd just

been raised to commander, and who was about to take his new ship to join the fleet in the West Indies. If it hadn't been for a freak gust of wind, it could have been Rick; he was due his own ship. Who knew how many of his friends and colleagues would jump ahead of him while this stupid leg healed?

"There is a letter for you, Lieutenant," said Markham, the butler. "From your sister, I believe."

He pounced on the letter and carried it into the study, where the brandy decanter was waiting on a small table next to his favorite chair. He took a letter opener to the wax seal and was soon settled with his leg up on a footstool, a glass of brandy at hand, and Susan's letter spread before him.

She must be on an economizing drive again. The feminine loops and swirls were tiny, and she'd used every inch of the sheet of paper, writing on both sides, and crossing the horizontal lines of text with vertical lines, and then writing more on the inside and edges of the enveloping sheet.

He deciphered the first page: Susan started with an outline of her social activities, interspersed with news of his baby niece, little Amelia, the only occupant of Susan's nursery. Captain Cunningham, Susan's husband, had been posted to the Far East shortly after Amy's birth, more than four years ago.

Here were a few sentences about their father, who was, Susan said, working long hours at the Horse Guard, but still found time to come and play with his granddaughter.

Ah. Here's what he'd been looking for.

You asked after Admiral Pritchard's daughter. Does this mean you know where she is? For I swear, her aunt does not, though she is putting a good face on it.

After I received your letter, I went to one of the Lady Bosville's afternoons at home. Such a bore, so you owe me the new bonnet you promised me. She does not offer refreshments or any entertainment, so one sits and talks to people one does not know about people one does not like.

Rick frowned as he read on. Susan said it was an open secret that Mary's aunt had been warning off suitors all season, meaning to keep Mary for her son—or Mary's money, more to the point. When Susan asked after Mary, Lady Bosville claimed she was in the country, recovering from a small cold, and would return soon.

At the Haverford Ball several nights later, Susan had danced with Bosville in order to interrogate him. Rick's frown deepened as he read.

I asked him if it was true that he was betrothed to my friend, Mary, and he said his mama had it all arranged, and he would have to comply because they were near rolled up. He really did. And I a near stranger to him, and like to be more so, I can assure you.

So, I said that she was a sweet thing, and very pretty. Well, he told me that he did not admire pasty skin and red hair, and I would not call her sweet if I had heard her in a temper! But, he said, he could always park her at his country estate, which he never visits, because it is so boring. I know what you are thinking, and I agree with you.

Susan finished with a few trenchant observations about the Bosvilles and a sisterly farewell. After reading her final admonition to follow the doctor's instructions, Rick refolded the letter. His mind was made up. It was time for him to return to London, anyway. And he would do it via Haslemere. He was sure Mary was in safe hands, but he would not rest easy till he saw for himself.

Mary smiled with satisfaction as she placed the last of the little gingerbread ladies into the box. In the four weeks she had been at Aunt Dorothy's, she had learned a number of recipes, and helped with all kinds of baking, but the gingerbread biscuits, which she had learned from the cook on the Olympus, became her specialty.

Making them took her back to the galley where Cook ruled with a rod of iron over various helpers, but always had time for a lonely little girl. She could still hear his deep, gravelly voice telling the story of the runaway gingerbread horse, or it might be a dog, or whatever cutter shape he had used at the time. She would be hovering over the tray of hot biscuits, waiting for them to cool enough to ice and eat.

"And he ran, and he ran," Cook would say, "with all the village behind him: the old lady, the fat squire, the pretty milkmaid, and the hungry sailor. But none of them could catch the gingerbread horse."

The story would continue, with the gingerbread horse escaping one would-be eater after another, and mocking them all, until Cook had iced the first biscuit. Mary would wait, patient and giggling, for the gingerbread horse to encounter the river, and the fox.

First, he'd put the horse over her back. Then, as the river water rose, on her head. And finally, she would tip her head back, and he would perch the biscuit on her nose, and say the words she had been waiting for: "And bite, crunch, swallow, that was the end of the gingerbread horse."

Aunt Dorothy had round and star cutters, and cutters in the shape of various animals. When the alderman's daughter asked for gingerbread ladies and gentlemen for her wedding breakfast, Mary had been delighted with the notion, and the cutters the tinker made to her pencil drawings worked very well.

The icing gave them clothes and features; a whole box of little gingerbread grooms, and a box of little gingerbread brides. The alderman's daughter would be very pleased with this trial run, Mary thought.

But as she folded tissue over the biscuits to keep them safe, she sighed. She should love it here with her aunts and her cousin. She enjoyed making delicious things to eat. Though Aunt Dorothy and Aunt Marjery thought it improper for her to help at the market, she did join them for meetings with people who were commissioning food for their entertainments, and they were encouraging her to take more and more of a lead in those meetings. For the first time since her father died, she felt she was doing something useful.

And she had company. Although she was currently alone in the small workroom off the kitchen, she could hear the kitchen staff busily working a few feet away. She and her aunts spent much of their time together, though her cousin Enid was often out visiting friends. Aunt Dorothy was as sweet as the confections she made, delighted to have Mary with her, and eager to teach her all about what was clearly a business, though Aunt Dorothy insisted it was merely a hobby.

Aunt Marjery was more reserved, but it was only natural for her to be more interested in her own daughter than a niece who was a stranger, except for a lifetime of letters. Mary got on well with the maids, and it was nice to spend time with women near her own age, though their consciousness of the class difference, and Mary's relationship with their employer, stood in the way of close friendship.

But four things conspired to spoil her enjoyment. First, she missed the sea. She had lived her entire life within the sight, smell, and sound of it, until she first came to London, and as each day passed, she yearned for it more and more. The sea was home, and this land-locked valley, however pretty, was not.

Second, no matter how sharply she spoke to herself, she could not stop thinking about Rick Redepenning. She couldn't possibly miss a man she had spent less than a day with in the past five years. She was merely worried about his injury, that was all, that he might not be taking care, might not be healing. No matter what excuses she made, she was well aware she was in danger of once again falling in love with Rick the Rogue—if, in fact, she'd ever fallen out of love.

Third, Cousin Enid did not want her here. At first, Mary had been sure she was just being over-sensitive, but Enid took every opportunity to find fault and to sow discord between Mary and Enid's mother. And all was done with a smile, with poisonous remarks in a voice that dripped treacle, until Mary doubted she'd heard correctly.

Mary tried to like Enid. They were cousins, after all. But she was impossible to like. She made it clear she did not want to live in this country town, and she resented the enterprise absorbing Aunt Dorothy and distracting Enid's mother, another dumpling of a woman, but a faded shadow of her sister.

Enid would be leaving, she told her mother bluntly, as soon as she had control of her inheritance. That happy day was still some six years in the future, when she turned twenty-five, unless she found a man of suitable rank and wealth to be worthy of her hand in the country backwater in which her mother insisted they remain. Meanwhile, she refused to have anything to do with the baking for fear the taint of 'trade' might follow her into a life better suited to her consequence as daughter of an esquire.

As Mary carefully tied the two boxes of gingerbread ready for delivery, the fourth cause of her discomfort came in.

"Well, hello, Miss Pritchard. All alone, are we? How pretty you look this morning."

The alderman, Mr. Owens, was a regular and popular visitor to the house, so much so, he wandered freely into the kitchen and its attached workrooms without announcement, as he had today. According to the maids, the widower had set his sights on Miss Dorothy Pritchard for his next wife, and she—Mary was convinced—was not averse to the idea. Recently, however, his heavy compliments had been addressed to Mary, and he seemed to go out of his way to find her alone.

She inclined her head, the barest minimum politeness required.

"Have you come to collect your daughter's baking, sir?"

"No, no. Ruthie will do that herself. She's just out there in the kitchen with your good aunts. What have you there, eh?" He came around the table to her side. As Mary moved backward to avoid him, her head struck the shelf behind her, upending a canister that struck her a glancing blow as it fell. Mary staggered, and was momentarily grateful for Mr. Owens' steadying hands.

Until she heard the gasp from behind him.

Until she opened her eyes to see both aunts, her cousin, and Ruth Owens standing in the doorway, their mouths identical O's of shock.

Chapter Five

She should visit her mother's sister, Aunt Theo. That's what Mary told Aunt Dorothy and Aunt Marjery. Like them, Aunt Theo had faithfully written every month of her life, and now that Mary was in England, the least she could do was visit her.

She didn't tell the aunts Enid had suggested she leave town, unless she wished to break Aunt Dorothy's heart.

The aunts had accepted Mary's explanation of what looked like an embrace. Even so, Aunt Dorothy had been looking askance at her suitor since the incident, and Mary didn't want to make more trouble.

Aunt Dorothy and Aunt Marjery raised all kinds of reasons why Mary should stay, but were no match for her determination. However, they put their foot down when it came to Mary's travel.

"Not in a public coach, Mary," Aunt Dorothy said, "and what the viscountess was thinking when she let you travel that way, I do not know. You'll take a post chaise, and Polly from the kitchen shall go with you."

Mary was pleased to be persuaded, and on a fine morning in early December, she and Polly climbed into the yellow bounder for the three-day journey to Oxford, where Aunt Theo lived.

"I wish you would stay for the wedding," Aunt Dorothy said, for the thousandth time.

Mary shook her head. The wedding was later that morning, but Enid and Ruth Owens had made it clear Mary would be unwelcome. "If I leave it much later, I will not be able to go until after Christmas. I will not be missed, Aunt Dorothy, but you have a wonderful time."

Soon, they were on their way. Polly was good company, full of stories about people and activities in the village, and endlessly curious about Mary's travels and adventures. The aunts had packed a huge basket of food, enough for the two women, the post rider, and (Polly joked) a small village of hungry orphans. They nibbled throughout the day, rather than stopping somewhere for a meal.

When Mary ventured a wish that Ruth Owens would have a good day for her wedding, Polly snorted. "Pity poor Thomas Wright, that's what I say. He'll be under the cat's paw, just like her poor father."

"Miss Owens seems very fond of Mr. Wright," Mary ventured.

Polly snorted again. "A cat may be fond of a mouse, I suppose, but that is not a benefit to the mouse, is it, Miss?"

"She will be going to live in Bristol, I understand."

"She wants her da to move to Bristol with them," Polly said. "She was wild as fire when her da started calling on Miss Pritchard. Wants to keep him for herself, and doesn't like Miss Enid above half. Can't be two queens in the same house, and that's a fact.

"Stop him, she will, if she can. But he is stubborn, is Mr. Owens. He will outlast her, I reckon. Just keep on sticking where he is, he will, until she goes off to Bristol, and then he will ask Miss Pritchard to walk out."

"He was very attentive to me," Mary said. What would Polly say to that?

Polly went off into a peal of laughter. "Oh, Miss, you didn't think...? Why, Miss, he told everyone you reminded him of his own Mary, Ruthie's older sister who died. She would be about your age if she lived, Miss. Mind you, Ruthie didn't like that. No, not one bit. Miss Enid used to rub it in ever-so. Not that Miss Enid is good at sharing, either. Now, Miss, how about another of your stories? Did you ever go to one of them islands with the palm trees? Is it true they don't wear hardly any clothes?"

The house was closed for a wedding, one of the elderly

gentlemen lounging outside the tavern told Rick. The daughter of one of the local notables was wedding a lawyer's clerk from Bristol, and most of the village was attending.

Rick arranged a room for the night, ordered a jug of the local beer, and found a seat in the sun to wait for the ladies to return home.

The sun was setting when Miss Pritchard's aunts and cousin came up the road, surrounded by a bevy of women brightening the evening in their pretty bonnets and hats. But none were Mary.

Miss Pritchard invited him into her comfortable parlor, where she told him Mary had decided to visit her Aunt Theo in Oxford.

"We sent her off in a post chaise, Lieutenant Redepenning," said Miss Rumbold, the cousin, "so you may be quite comfortable about her safety."

Rick wasn't comfortable, though. After he finished the tea Miss Rumbold insisted on serving him, and made his careful way back across the road to the inn, he sat on the edge of his bed, worrying about all the things that could go wrong when two young women travelled with just a post boy for protection.

He slept poorly, and by morning, he had made up his mind. He would follow Mary to Oxford, and see for himself that she was all right.

Mary was pleased to reach the end of the first day's travel. She climbed down at the posting inn, stretching the kinks out of her back and knees, as Polly clambered down to join her.

The inn allocated them a pair of rooms on the second floor, near the back, and they were climbing the stairs when they passed someone coming down. He was looking at the gloves he was putting on, rather than where he was going, and Mary had to step smartly to the right to avoid a collision.

He looked up impatiently, saying, "Watch where you are going, Ma—Cousin Mary? Good God, it is. What are you doing in this godforsaken place?"

Lord Bosville. Of all the people Mary imagined meeting, he was the last she'd expect to find this far from London. "Cousin," she replied, giving him a frosty nod. They had parted on unfriendly terms, after he had tried to kiss her and she had, as her father had taught her, punched him in a vulnerable part of his anatomy.

Bosville rearranged his face into a friendly smile that did not reach his eyes. "I do apologize for my language, Cousin Mary. I was startled. How nice to see you. Mother will be delighted to hear you are well. She has been so worried."

What nonsense. Mary suppressed a snort. Worried to have lost Mary's money, perhaps.

"If you will excuse me, Cousin, my maid and I are tired."

But Viscount Bosville turned and accompanied them up the stairs, insisting he would see them safely to their rooms. "And after you are refreshed, dear cousin, you will, of course, allow me the privilege of providing a small dinner? In a private parlor, so you need not hesitate for a moment."

"Thank you, Cousin, but we are very tired…"

Viscount Bosville kept arguing all the way to their rooms, and stood in the doorway, still insisting, until Mary agreed, just to be rid of him.

"Excellent, Cousin. I will do myself the honor of escorting you myself. Shall we say eight o'clock?"

Mary closed the door on him, and wondered how she could gracefully extricate herself from his fulsome and insincere compliments over dinner. Perhaps a sudden and unexpected dose of the plague?

Bosville kept to his side of the table. Mind you, that could be because Mary took Polly down to dinner with her, and showed the viscount the little pistol that Mary always carried for protection.

Even if he wasn't a danger, he was a bore. He couldn't seem to grasp she didn't find him, his friends, and his activities as engrossing as he did. And he seemed to have convinced himself her refusal of his advances was modesty, not repulsion. He said, several times, he realized he had rushed her. He apologized for his haste, but assured her it was her fault for being so beautiful.

Mary, who had heard him describe her to a friend as his homely cousin, was not fooled. Replying in monosyllables, changing the subject, looking all around the room instead of at him; all the little strategies she could try and still stay just this side of good manners, he ignored. He was delighted to carry the full burden of the conversation, ignored any topic she raised, and did not look at her often enough to notice her distraction. As soon as she could, she escaped to bed.

Mary and Polly left the inn before the sun was fully up, to avoid his escort. Mary felt silly. Surely she was overreacting. What could he do, after all? This wasn't medieval times.

Even so, as the post chaise left the inn, and turned onto the Oxford Road, she relaxed. She needn't think about Bosville again.

"Would you care for a game of cards, Polly?"

The morning passed quickly, and in the afternoon, both women fell asleep after finishing the picnic lunch packed by the inn.

Mary woke when the post boy shouted, and all of a sudden, the carriage leapt as it sped up. With difficulty, she pulled herself to the front window. The increased velocity set the carriage lurching and swaying worse than a ship in a storm. The windows were too dirty for easy viewing, but she could see no sign of the post boy, and on either side, the hedges rushed by. The horses must have bolted!

Could she get to the front luggage rack from the side door? If she didn't try, would she and Polly survive?

Balancing herself as best she could, she used her free hand to pull her skirt up from the back to tuck it into her sash, leaving her legs free. She wound one end of a long shawl around her wrist, and gave the other end to Polly.

"Polly, hold tight," she said. Polly, veteran oldest sister of a tribe of boys, wedged herself into the corner of the seat.

When Mary opened the door, it whipped back out of her hands. She caught both sides of the doorway, and then, grasping every handhold she could find, she pulled herself forward up onto the luggage rack. The horses were uncontrolled, galloping heedless and headlong with the post boy nowhere to be seen.

She sent up a quick prayer of thanks that this part of the country had long straight roads, sunk between hedges. In any other carriage, she might have had a chance of grabbing the reins, but this was a post chaise, controlled by the post boy who rode one of the horses. Back here on the carriage itself, there were no reins to grab.

The carriage bounded over a large rut or rock, and she was airborne for a moment, holding the front rail of the luggage rack with a white-knuckled grip. With a thump that jarred every bone in her body and expelled what little breath she had left, she crashed back onto her trunks. She would be safer inside the carriage.

As she edged her way cautiously back to the door, a flash of movement behind the hedge to her left caught her eye. A rider? The hedge thickened again, and she couldn't be sure. Another bounding lurch prompted her to move again, and she swung herself back inside to rejoin Polly—though not without a few extra bruises.

"The post boy is gone, and the horses are bolting," Mary told Polly. "Stay in your corner and hold on tight. And pray that they run themselves out before we reach a bend in the road."

Following her own advice meant she couldn't see whether the glimpse she'd caught was a rider. Someone riding to their aid would be wonderful, but unlikely. Might as well wish for Rick to save her once again.

Polly, to her credit, didn't panic, just held on grimly, her face white and her lips moving—whether in prayer or cursing, Mary couldn't tell. Mary was praying. This was no time to annoy God!

Were the horses slowing? Yes. They were no longer in a full-out panicked gallop. Quite quickly, the gallop became a canter, and the canter a walk. The horses would be tired, of course. Mary didn't know how long she and Polly had slept, but they must be close to the next posting inn.

She carefully made her way back to the door. Perhaps now that they had slowed, she might be able to do something to stop them?

But there was no need. At the head of the offside horse, shouldering into it with his own horse and pulling the pair to a slower walk and then a stop, was a rider—a rider she recognized.

Rick Redepenning had rescued her again.

Chapter Six

Rick had ridden hard that day, and his leg was complaining bitterly. He'd left Haslemere at first light, making haste along the road to Oxford, compelled by an impulse he didn't understand. He'd lunched at the inn where Mary spent the night, and been alarmed to hear about Viscount Bosville's presence—and Bosville's departure not long after Mary.

He had no cause for concern, surely? Mary was not alone, and this was the end of the eighteenth century, not the middle ages.

Nevertheless, he called for a fresh horse and pressed even harder on Mary's trail.

They were clearly in no hurry. Two more posts later, he was only an hour behind them. This was the last post of the day. He'd see them at the next inn, if he didn't catch up with them beforehand.

Half an hour later, he crested a slight rise, and they were in sight ahead of him on the long straight road, toy-sized in the distance. He narrowed his eyes. What were those men on the side of the road doing? Throwing something?

Several somethings, and the horses reacted, moving from an amble to a panicked gallop in a stride. Rick urged his own horse to a gallop. Pray God the post boy could pull them up! No. There was the post boy, sitting on the side of the road rubbing his head. The assailants had disappeared. Rick didn't have time for them, anyway, and the post boy would have to fend for himself.

Somewhere, off in a compartment of his brain, was the urge to beat the stone throwers, to wail to the sky his fear for Mary. He allowed the emotions to lend him strength and separate him from his pain, but he had no time to pay further attention. Mary needed him.

His best chance was to leave the road; something galloping from behind would panic the team even more. If he could come up beside them, he might have a chance.

He set the hired horse at the first gate he saw, and thanked all the powers of heaven that the beast had a jump in it. More than one, for it gamely soared over several stone walls and hedgerows as they slowly gained on the post chaise.

In glimpses, as the ground on his side of the hedge rose, or as the hedge thinned, he saw his quarry. What was Mary doing? Climbing onto the luggage compartment at the front of the carriage? Did she have any idea how dangerous that was? Of course she did, but he'd be a fool to expect her to wait patiently in an out-of-control chaise bounding towards disaster. It was like her to climb out to see what she could do. She must have concluded there was nothing, for she edged backwards and disappeared again, but not before his brain had recorded an image of her legs that he knew would keep him awake many a fevered night.

Idiot. This was no time for lust. He needed a gate or a low point to get back onto the road at the horses' heads.

There. His horse was tiring, but gathered itself for one more effort and cleared the gate, with a jarring stumble on the other side. He ignored the effect of the sudden lurch on his leg, as he had ignored it on previous jumps, and urged the horse forward. Moments later, he had the bridle of the offsider and was urging the team to a halt.

He looked back at the carriage in time to see Mary jump down from the door, and couldn't help noting she'd dropped her skirts back to where they belonged. He dismounted, taking care to keep hold of the carriage horses, as she hurried towards him.

"Rick, I'm so pleased to see you. What happened to the post boy, do you know? What spooked the horses? What are you doing here?"

Now that the immediate danger was over, his leg hurt like hell. He opened his mouth to reply, but the world spun around him, and he clutched his horse's neck to stay upright.

"Polly, take their heads." Through a haze of pain, he could hear Mary taking over, and suddenly she was under his arm on his better side, supporting him. "I have you, Rick. Just a step. Here, and another."

"A minute," he gasped. "It's jarred. The leg. Not ready for jumping. Good horse, though."

Mary lowered him onto the slope at the side of the road, and was gone. He missed her. She felt good tucked into his side, his arm around her shoulders.

Then she was there again, holding his head against her chest with one hand while she held something to his mouth with another. His mouth flooded with brandy from the flask he carried in his saddle bag.

"Just stay still, Rick. You will be fine in a minute." She sounded calm and confident, but for the edge of a question in the last few words. Brave girl. He had always been able to count on Mary in a crisis.

He took another sip of brandy. Not too much. He would have to ride the horses to the nearest inn, though how he would mount, he had no idea.

Mary would not allow it.

"You will ride in the chaise, Rick, and I will have no argument. You are in no fit state to ride, and I will not have you hurting yourself more on my account. Besides, a fine mess Polly and I would be in if you fell off and the horses spooked again."

"Someone has to ride the horses," he protested.

"I will do it. Just to the nearest farmhouse, so you need not worry for me, Rick."

"Aye, aye, Captain," he managed, which made her smile, but didn't banish the anxious wrinkle between her brows.

Chapter Seven

Mary entered the bedroom she had commandeered on Rick's behalf, her brow furrowed with concern.

"The doctor thinks the leg is just bruised," Rick told her, "and I have done no further damage."

Her face cleared, and she rewarded him with a beaming smile.

"Was the post boy hurt?" he asked. He had heard Mary marshalling the troops when they arrived at the farmhouse: bargaining with the farmer's wife for bedchambers, sending the farmer's son galloping for a doctor from the nearby town, and instructing others to go back along the road to hunt for the post boy.

"They did not find him. I cannot understand why he did not follow after the horses. Do you think he was confused?"

"Perhaps. Perhaps he went for the constables."

"Yes. You said that some people threw rocks, deliberately frightened the horses. Do you think they meant to kill us, Rick?"

Rick avoided a direct answer. "When you and Polly go on to the inn, make sure you take some of the farmer's men to protect you."

"Go?" Mary put a hand on each hip and frowned. "We are going nowhere until you are fit to travel. Did you think we would leave you? Besides, I have told the farmer's wife you are my brother. A fine sister I would be to leave while you are bedridden!"

"But, Mary..."

"No, Rick, I will not leave you." She gave a decisive nod, her lips firmly pressed together. He sank back against the pillows, too tired and sore to fight her. At least she had claimed to be his sister, which should be some sort of protection to her reputation.

Her stubborn glare dissolved into concern.

"Oh, Rick, here I am brangling with you when you have been injured on my account. No more. I will not leave, but nor will I bother you with arguments."

She made sure he could reach the glass on the bedside table, plumped his pillows, and straightened his blankets. "By the way, our name is Reid, as it was that night on the way to Haslemere. You are Lieutenant Rick Reid, and I am Mary Reid. I hope you do not mind?"

Good girl. She had thought of everything. With a false name, the fiction they were brother and sister, and her maid to keep her company, she should come out of this with an unscathed reputation. If ever she accepted his suit, he wanted it to be her choice, not something she was forced to do.

The thought startled him awake. Was he courting Mary Pritchard? It seemed he was, the decision made without him knowing it and firmly lodged in his mind. He settled himself more comfortably, his leg now just a dull ache, and fell asleep wearing a smile.

The following morning, Mary sent a message to the posting inn, telling them what had happened and asking for a postilion to present himself, so they could continue their journey.

Rick insisted he had slept and was well enough to travel, though his heavy-lidded eyes suggested an untruth. He insisted on dressing, the farmer's son acting valet, and came down to breakfast, white under his tan and moving stiffly, but refusing to acknowledge weakness.

The postilion was slow arriving, but by mid-morning, they were all in the post-chaise, Rick and Mary sharing the bench seat while Polly sat on a small seat that folded down from the front wall.

Polly was shy at first, but soon the three of them were chatting away, Mary just as enthralled by Polly's and Rick's tales of growing up in England as Polly was by Rick's and Mary's stories of their journeys and the places they'd seen.

By the time they stopped for a bite to eat in the early afternoon, Rick's pallor had increased alarmingly, and he'd been clenching the front of the bench for more than an hour, his knuckles white with the force of his grip.

He managed a slow, awkward descent from the carriage and twisted his mouth into a shadow of his usual jaunty grin when he caught Mary's concerned frown.

"I'm feeling a bit battered, Mary, but no harm done."

Mary felt a bit battered herself. The carriage was not called a bounder for nothing.

"Let us take our meal in the garden, so we can stroll a little," she suggested, "unless... should you be sitting down, Rick? Or lying even? We could enquire about a room."

"A walk would be just the thing," Rick assured her.

Mary sent Polly off to order sustenance. "We will eat in the garden, Polly. I can see tables under the trees. Order for three. You'll eat with us."

Rick opened the gate from the inn-yard to the garden, and Mary went through it on his arm, trying to support him as much as she could without being obvious.

Another guest was before them, sitting at one of the tables and staring disconsolately at the small, dirty pond that adorned one corner.

"What is the matter?" Rick asked. Mary realized she had halted and was clutching his arm in a death grip. She willed herself to relax.

"Nothing. It was a surprise to see him here, that was all." Before she could explain herself, the man at the table turned to the sound of their voices, then leapt to his feet and hurried towards them.

"Cousin Mary! You're safe! I'm so..." He stopped just short of them and started again. "Hello, Cousin Mary, what a surprise to see you here. I had thought you at your aunt's already."

He was not looking at Mary any more, but had fixed Rick with a hard stare, which Rick was returning full measure. Any moment, Mary fancied, they'd start snarling and circling.

"Viscount Bosville, may I make known to you Lieutenant

Redepenning? Lieutenant, my cousin, Viscount Bosville."

"I know your cousin, George," Bosville said.

"Of course you do," Rick replied.

Bosville, whose color was already high, flushed still more. "He is a good man, is George. Good *ton.*"

"No doubt you think so." Rick knew Cousin George to be a rakehell and a bounder.

Bosville, his nostrils flaring, decided on another point of challenge. "Cousin Mary, whatever are you doing alone at an inn with a gentleman? I know you have had... an unusual upbringing, but Lieutenant Redepenning is from a good family. He should know better. You will come with me, Cousin Mary, and we will see what we can salvage of this situation."

Did Bosville realize he had just insulted her family? Mary wondered whether to laugh or hit him, and decided to do neither. "Lieutenant Redepenning and I are about to eat, Cousin. You will excuse us, I am sure."

Bosville drew himself up to his full height, a full head shorter than Rick. "Cousin Mary, I demand you come with me. You have no idea of the damage..."

"No damage," Rick said, moving in so he was looming over Bosville. "Miss Pritchard has been accompanied by her maid at all times, since before she honored me by accepting my escort. Besides, she has been recognized only by her cousin, who will, I am sure, not speak a word of the encounter, nor even think a slur on the lady's reputation."

Bosville took a step back, but said, "Maid? I see no maid."

"Miss Pritchard?" Polly, as if summoned by Bosville's disbelief, appeared at Mary's elbow. "They do a good bread here, they do. And oxtail soup, I thought, if it pleases you. Thick, it is, like your aunt makes, Miss. And a lardy cake too, and cheese and fruit."

"That sounds excellent, Polly," Mary told her. "Cousin, if you will excuse us."

Rick held a chair for her, and then for Polly, eliciting a disgusted snort from Viscount Bosville.

"Really, Redepenning, you should know a maid doesn't sit with her mistress."

Polly, looking distressed, made to stand, but Mary put out a hand to stop her. "Stay where you are, Polly. Really, Cousin Bosville, I certainly cannot eat in public without a companion."

"As your nearest male relative..." Bosville began.

Mary interrupted, "No sermons before our meal, Bosville, I beg you. Ah, here it is now."

A procession of servants from the inn brought the dishes Polly had mentioned, plus fresh butter, dishes of pickled red cabbage and pickled onions, a plate of pork pies, and jugs of cider and beer.

Bosville watched, clearly trying to decide what to do next. Mary ignored him. Any hope he might just go away was dashed when he pulled out the remaining chair at the table.

"Dashed if I won't join you. You do not mind, do you, Cousin?" He sat without waiting for an answer, and helped himself to a wedge of bread and a mug of beer.

"So, Redepenning," he began. "How do you happen to be travelling with my cousin?"

"It is my privilege to escort Miss Pritchard," Rick said.

"Lieutenant Redepenning saved our lives, and so he did," Polly said, nodding to emphasize her words. "Broken to pieces, that's what would have happened, if he hadn't stopped them horses."

Mary prepared to defend Polly from Bosville's fire. He was outraged at a servant eating with them; surely, he would be furious she dared to speak? But Bosville just looked away, meeting no one's eyes and shifting uncomfortably. "Horses bolted, did they?"

Surely Bosville wouldn't have... She and Rick exchanged glances. He had the same thought, clearly.

"They were deliberately spooked," Rick said. "Know something about that, Bosville?"

His eyes darting everywhere, resting nowhere, Bosville protested. "What do you mean? I don't know anything. What could I know? Ridiculous accusation, Redepenning. Why, I wouldn't hurt a hair on Miss Pritchard's head. I was nowhere near. Word of a gentleman. And if the post boy says different, he lies."

Rick was on his feet, suddenly all hard edges, the cheerful companion submerged in the dangerous warrior. "You fool. Miss Pritchard and her maid could have been killed. What did you plan to do? Ride up and claim the hero's reward? What stopped you? Did your horse throw you?"

Bosville flushed bright red. "Nonsense. Absolute rubbish. You have no proof. None at all. Never meant the chit any harm. Word of a gentleman." As he spoke, he abandoned the table and started backing towards the gate to the inn's yard. "Goodness. Is that the time? Must take my leave, Cousin. You are in good hands with Redepenning. Earl of Chirbury's cousin. Your servant, Cousin. Word of a gentleman. Your servant, Lieutenant."

He reached the safety of the gate and disappeared from sight, obviously fearing that Rick was about to pursue and dismember him.

Mary, though, saw the gray edge of pain at the corner of Rick's lips. "He is gone, Rick. Sit down before you fall," she said.

"That swine. You heard him, Mary. I should strangle him with his own entrails, the stupid, lily-livered cockroach."

"Yes, I heard." Mary supported Rick from his good side, as he lowered himself into his chair, then sat back down next to him. "How did you know what he meant to do, Rick?"

"I was guessing," Rick admitted. "But I was right. You saw him, Mary. He as much as admitted he paid the post boy—and, I imagine, the rock-throwers—to frighten the horses so he could rescue you from a runaway carriage."

Rick's anger was gratifying. He must be a little fond of her, surely?

"I think he meant it when he said he did not mean for me to be hurt. He was genuinely pleased to see me when we first arrived."

How did a man so fair manage to look so dark? Rick's face was a thundercloud. "I daresay he was sorry he'd lost his chance at your fortune," he growled.

Chapter Eight

That might not be the most stupid remark Rick had made in his lifetime, but it was certainly in the top ten. Mary closed up like a tulip at night. He knew what she was thinking: that Rick, like Bosville, thought her fortune was her main attraction. He even knew how to convince her he thought nothing of the kind.

But his hands were tied. She was alone with him, with only the dubious protection of her maid. It would be unconscionable to begin to court her in such circumstances. In all honor, he had to hold her at a distance until he returned her to her family. No matter that he wanted to take her in his arms and kiss her until the fire sparking under her chilly surface flared up to consume them both.

In truth, he was not up to much kissing, and certainly not anything more than kissing. He'd strained the deuced leg again, and would be paying for it the next sennight, undoubtedly. Six months before he could return to the sea, the doctors had said. He hoped this latest strain would not delay his recovery.

Mary's aunt and her husband invited Rick to stay with them in their large rambling house in the countryside, just outside of Oxford.

"This place is much too big, now that all the children have flown," the aunt insisted. "It will be delightful to have young people under our roof again, will it not, Eustace?"

This proved to be an exaggeration: young people trooped in and out of the house all hours of the day. Rick soon found that Dr. Wren, though he had given up his fellowship when he married thirty years or more ago, was much in demand as a tutor. Mrs. Wren, Mary's Aunt Theodora, mothered a large and constantly changing horde of young men and their sisters, and their sisters' friends.

Everyone was full of plans for the Christmas party they would hold in just a few days, before most of them departed for family celebrations. Some, however, would stay on.

"We have eight children, dear," Mrs. Wren explained, "and some of them are too far away to come home for Christmas. I'm happy to give a little love to some other mother's child, and perhaps someone else is doing the same for mine."

They looked an ill-assorted pair: tall, thin, and elegant Mrs. Wren, and short and dumpy Dr. Wren. Her tidy afternoon gown was a triumph of understated elegance, but Dr. Wren might have been wrestling in the clothes he wore under the open academic gown. The gown, too, sat half on and half off his shoulders, and his Tudor cap tilted insecurely on his balding head.

But the connection between the two was palpable, she catching his eye and smiling at the end of every sentence, he watching her over the top of his spectacles, with a twinkle that seemed to approve of whatever she wished to say.

Rick was barely able to move the day after they arrived, but he lay on the couch in a sun room off the Wrens' parlor, where he could join in or rest, as he needed, simply by asking for the connecting doors to be opened or closed.

Mary organized the room for his comfort: a jug of iced tisane close to his elbow, a jar of biscuits, in the unlikely case he became hungry between the large meals Mrs. Wren produced at regular intervals, a rug for his knees, several books, the day's newspaper, and writing materials, so he could catch up on correspondence. Her attentions never bothered him the way his sister's had. Mary didn't fuss. She just got on with the job of making sure he had whatever he needed.

At first, apart from checking from time to time to see all was well, she left him to rest, but when he complained that he lacked company, she turned the room into a gathering place for the visitors, and he found himself discussing philosophy with an undergraduate, arguing naval strategy with another, and playing chess with a disconcertingly clever young woman who trounced him soundly but was magnanimous enough to suggest his leg might have been a distraction.

Chapter Nine

On the following day, he was up and about again, but still found it impossible to get Mary alone. Indeed, she seemed always to be leaving a room as he entered it, and when he tried to follow, good manners required him to stop and attend to whichever person she'd sent to ask his opinion, challenge his beliefs, invite him to a game, or otherwise distract him. He grew sick of hearing, from one person after another, "Lieutenant, Miss Pritchard says..."

So it continued, a cat-and-mouse game that Mary appeared not to notice, and the Wrens watched with benign amusement. He was well enough now to continue on to London, but somehow, he couldn't bring himself to leave.

On Friday night, several days after he arrived, and only a few days before Christmas, they sat fifteen for dinner. It was cheerful, loud, and not at all decorous. People talked across the table, and several were participating in more than one conversation. Dr. Wren was holding his own in a debate about whether Lancelot was a later addition to the Arthurian canon or an original round table member under another name, while simultaneously sharing recipes for mead and arguing about a point in mathematics that Rick nearly understood.

Farther down the table, a group of young ladies were proposing ideas for setting up a dance floor in the garden, since no room in the house could accommodate dancing, as well as the number of guests who would be at the Christmas party on the twenty-third. The chief problem, it seemed, was providing sufficient light so the dancers could see, without setting fire to the trees.

The house would be full on the night of the party, with those staying for Christmas arriving early, and those leaving for home waiting till the next morning. Rick had already told Mrs. Wren he'd move to one of the Oxford inns ahead of the festivities.

The butler, who was really a general factotum, came to stand between Dr. Wren and Rick, and bent over so he would be heard above the hubbub. "Doctor, your nephew, Viscount Bosville, has arrived."

Rick turned to look at the door. Sure enough, the blackguard was there, studying the noisy dinner table with a barely concealed sneer.

"Theo," Dr. Wren bellowed, silencing the guests. "Theo, young Bosville is here for a visit. What do you want to do with him?"

Mrs. Wren went to greet her nephew. The guests took up their conversations, so Rick couldn't hear what she said. In any case, he was watching Mary struggle to maintain an expression of benign indifference.

What the hell was Bosville after? As if Rick didn't know. He toyed with the idea of telling the Wrens what Bosville had done, but he had no proof, and, after all, the man was their nephew.

That settled that. He could not leave now. However she might feel about it, Rick was sticking to Mary. Limpets would be amateurs, compared to Rick, for as long as Bosville stayed in this house.

Chapter Ten

Mary spent the morning dodging Bosville; successfully, thanks to several timely interventions. She was in the dining room near the front door, helping to decorate for tomorrow's party when Cousin Enid arrived.

As if Cousin Bosville were not enough.

"I do beg your pardon for coming unannounced," she heard Enid say. "But my mama was so worried about our dear Mary, after we heard that the coach nearly crashed. And we are such dear friends, Mary and I..."

Mary's hands stilled on the ribbon she was tying around a kissing bough. The lying cow!

Aunt Theo answered, her voice too low for the words to be understood.

"Oh, thank you. I would love to stay, if you are sure it will be no trouble. Why! Lieutenant Redepenning! Are you still here? I had no idea... How delightful."

"Miss Rumbold." Rick sounded politely bland, the voice he used when he wished he were somewhere—anywhere—else. She'd often heard him use it, though, come to think of it, never with her.

They moved away from the door, Enid chattering gaily about how happy she was to see Oxford—"so beautiful, just as I'd heard"—and how pleased she was that Lieutenant Redepenning was back on his feet.

Mary tugged the ribbon with such unnecessary force, it knotted, and she could not unravel it. "Such dear friends," was it? Well, if Enid Rumbold thought to catch Rick Redepenning in her marital claws, she could think again.

Over the noon meal, without a word being said, Mary and Rick joined in a mutual defense pact. Bosville circled, but was deflected with by a sharp glare from Rick. Enid fluttered her eyelashes madly, but desisted when Mary asked, "Why, Enid, darling, do you have something in your eye? Come to the kitchen, and I'll help you wash it."

Bosville tried to enlist Aunt Theo. "Seems like the lieutenant is well enough to move on and stop taking advantage of you, Auntie."

"Lieutenant Redepenning is welcome to stay as long as he wishes, Bosville," Aunt Theo told him. "We enjoy his company."

"We like invited guests," Uncle Wren added, with a frown.

As at every other meal in the Wren household, an assorted group of people who happened to be in the house at the time sat to eat, but didn't stop the conversations about the projects or activities that brought them to visit.

Bosville had already repelled all attempts at familiarity, and was now being ignored, but the assembled young people were generously willing to include Enid in their conversation.

Their friendly overtures were unsuccessful. Enid had no opinion on water wheel systems for lock construction, or whether Merlin's real name was Myrddin, or the best translation for the Greek word paidiskê. When Mary suggested that women should be allowed to attend lectures at the university, Enid was invited to give her thoughts on the vigorous debate. She batted her eyelids at Uncle Wren, "How dreadful. As if any real woman would want to know about such unladylike things. Oh, but of course, Mary was raised on a navy ship. Very hard to be a lady in such circumstances. I do feel badly for you, Cousin."

Uncle Wren frowned at Enid, and then deliberately turned a shoulder to her. "May I pass you the soup, Mary, my dear?"

Despite the snubs, the two unwelcome guests persisted. Mary avoided them by retreating to the kitchen to make gingerbread shapes—stars, bells, holly leaves, hearts, and ladies and gentlemen, using the cutters the tinker had made for her. She would ice them in the morning.

Aunt Theo knocked on the door just before she hopped into

bed. "May I have a moment, my love?"

"Of course, Aunt Theo. Polly, off you go to bed. I won't need you again tonight. Is anything wrong, Aunt?"

"Just those two cousins, my dear. I am sorry that you are so bedeviled. Dr. Wren wishes to toss them both out, but we can hardly send Miss Rumbold out the door when she has travelled three days to be here, and if I cast Bosville into the night not a day before Christmas, my sister will be most offended."

"Oh, Aunt, I do not expect you to do that."

"Just be careful, my dear," Aunt Theo warned. "Do not be alone with my nephew, and do not leave your poor lieutenant alone with Miss Rumbold."

Mary blushed scarlet. "He is not my lieutenant, Aunt Theo."

Her aunt just smiled. "He will be if you want him, dear." With that, she left Mary to her dreams.

Chapter Eleven

When Mary came down to breakfast the following morning, Uncle Wren was there, deep in a conversation with Rick about the kinds of ships that might have been available to King Arthur in defense of his realm. Mary smiled.

Rick, who was looking her way, stumbled over his sentence.

"I am sorry, sir," he said to Uncle Wren, "I have forgotten what I was saying."

Uncle Wren gave him, and then Mary, a benevolent smile. "Well, it does not matter, young man. I have suddenly thought of some correspondence I must to attend to. Will you excuse me?"

As soon as they were alone, Rick crossed to Mary. She looked up into his vivid blue eyes. Could such a magnificent man possibly want her, plain Mary Pritchard?

"Mary." His smile was warm, and his voice, when he said her name, purred along all her nerve endings. A caress in a single word.

"Rick." She tried to match him, and, judging from his sharp intake of breath and the flare in his eyes, was not a total failure.

Then Enid arrived, followed closely by Bosville, and Mary could not help but believe they were up early just to annoy her.

As the morning wore on, she became convinced of it. Bosville was everywhere she turned, and Enid, too, though Mary blamed that on Rick's constant attendance. Enid had clearly decided Rick was to be the next victim of her charm, and was pouring it out with such a lavish hand that Rick looked decidedly ill.

All three even followed her to the kitchen and watched her decorate her gingerbread biscuits with boiled icing and bits of dried fruit.

Mary was grateful to escape on a brief shopping excursion with Polly, slipping out the kitchen door to avoid company, though if she'd been able to attract Rick's attention without alerting Enid's, the walk would have been even more pleasant.

She could not see Rick when she arrived back and delivered the reels of ribbon her aunt had needed. Bosville was there, instructing a bemused undergraduate on the correct tying of a cravat. Enid had finally found common ground with one of Aunt Theo's daughters, vigorously discussing how to attach the swags of evergreen, ribbons, and bells to the picture rail of the main parlor.

When Mary went upstairs to take off her bonnet and pelisse, though, Enid came too. "Mary," she said, "I found something I want to show you. Come this way."

Mary, curious, if a little cautious, followed behind, out the side door and into the garden. "What is it, Enid?" Enid said nothing, just lead Mary down a path until they came around a hedge, and there before them was a small tower, perhaps as tall as the house, but less than ten feet in diameter.

"How charming," Mary said. "What is it for?"

"I have no idea," Enid said, "but I found it yesterday when I walked this way, and I remembered it when you mentioned the dance floor. Wouldn't lanterns up there by the window light this part of the garden?"

It could work. Mary opened the door with some difficulty, because it was stiff, and stepped inside. The tower was hollow, and blank walled until just below the roof, where a series of window spaces let light in. They could easily also let light out, but getting a lantern up could be tricky. Though she could see some possible handholds and footholds...

At that moment, the door shut behind her with a tired groan and then a thud. Shut and—from the sound of it—bolted.

She called out, but Enid was gone, and Mary was well out of earshot of anyone else in the house. What was Enid up to? No good, that was certain. Mary frowned. She would not let her cousin get away with it.

She examined the inner wall of the tower again. Moments later, she'd stripped off her dress and petticoat and was climbing the wall in her stays and under-drawers. It was as tricky a climb as she expected, and Enid was out of sight by the time she reached the windows.

Now what? The outside of the tower was smooth, and besides, she could not climb in the open air in nothing but her undergarments.

Rick came into view, entering the garden through the gate from the road. She smiled. He must have found a way to elude the two cousins and followed her. What a pity she came back the other way.

The next moment, she frowned again. Bosville appeared from the direction of the house, and approached Rick. A few moments of conversation and Bosville handed Rick something—a note, it looked like—clapped Rick on the shoulder, and went off.

Rick stood there, reading the note. He frowned at the path that led down the garden, and then back at the house, clearly suspicious.

Whatever those two were up to, it was time to stop it. Mary, with some effort, managed to push out the ornamental trellis that blocked the window. As it crashed to the ground, Rick stopped in his tracks, looked up at the tower, then turned and went hurrying back towards the house.

Bother. Was she going to have to rescue herself? But as she thought that, the top legs of a ladder appeared. Looking over the side of the tower, she saw Rick holding the ladder steady.

"Your stair awaits, fair princess," he joked.

Dressed, or rather undressed, as she was? She looked back at the inside wall. Perhaps she could climb back down, and he could let her out. But she'd only just made the climb, and her arms were still trembling; she wasn't sure she could get back.

Rick was looking anxious. "Is there a problem?"

"Shut your eyes, please?"

His face cleared. "Of course." And he screwed his eyes shut, rather more dramatically than she thought necessary.

The ladder made the descent easy, and she breathed a sigh of relief as first one foot, then the other, reached the ground. She stopped breathing altogether when Rick's arms came round her waist.

"Do you have any idea what it does to me to see you clambering around a roof, Mary Pritchard?" he asked, holding her so tight she squeaked. He didn't release her, but, instead, bent his head to rub his cheek on her hair. "I'm confident you had an excellent reason, but I swear, I've aged ten years in the last five minutes."

She had had a reason, but for the moment, it escaped her. "Rick?" she asked.

He let her go, stepping backwards. "I beg your pardon. For a moment I... I take it you didn't send the note your nasty cousin gave me?"

He pulled it from his pocket and handed it to her.

"Dear Rick," she read, "please meet me in the summerhouse. With all my love, Mary."

Mary saw red. "That weevil," she hissed. "That sneaky, mean, two-faced little maggot!"

Rick caught her around the waist again before she could storm down the path. "Whoa, Mary. Who is a maggot? Not Bosville, I take it?"

"Him, too," she fumed. "They're both in on it. Enid locked me in the tower, and Bosville gave you the note."

"Ah," Rick nodded. "Husband-hunting. I thought that might be it. You want to tell them what you think of them, I take it? You might want to get dressed first."

Mary felt the heat of her blush, but Rick the Rogue barely looked her way. He opened the tower door and waited outside while Mary changed.

Chapter Twelve

Rick needed the time on his own to recover. Mary felt every bit as good in his arms as he had imagined, and her state of undress disclosed a shapely form, to which the high-waisted fashions did not do justice. Thinking about the blush that had covered every inch of skin he could see, and clearly carried on where he desperately wished to see, was not helping him calm himself.

Think of something else. Anything. Ah. Here was the perfect distraction—Bosville, rounding the corner and stopping to gape at Rick, the tower, the ladder, and again at Rick.

"What are you doing here?" he asked.

"Waiting for Miss Rumbold, Bosville. She is in the tower, but I'm expecting her to join me."

"But… but my cousin, Mary…"

Rick chose to take that as a question. "Miss Pritchard? She went that way." He pointed down the path.

Bosville opened, then shut, his mouth and hurried away down the path.

Moments later, several other people rounded the house: Dr. and Mrs. Wren and several of the students. "Come along, Theo," said Dr. Wren impatiently. "That young pup insisted on us seeing the surprise in the summerhouse."

Rick and a somewhat-rumpled Mary joined on the tail of the group, and arrived at the summerhouse to find Miss Rumbold in Bosville's arms, her dress drooping to display a naked shoulder and quite a lot of her chemise.

"What, young Bosville, is the meaning of this?" demanded Dr.

Wren.

"She just... I just..." Bosville glared at Miss Rumbold in a far from lover-like manner. Clearly, she had decided a viscount in the hand was worth more than a cautious sailor in the bush. "What Lord Bosville is trying to say, Dr. Wren, Mrs. Wren, is that he has asked for my hand in marriage, and I have accepted."

"That isn't... that is to say..." Bosville started, but Dr. Wren shook his hand, Mrs. Wren kissed them both and said she would write immediately to Bosville's mother, and the students declared tonight's Christmas celebration should also be a betrothal party.

"Bosville does not look happy," Rick whispered to Mary.

"How awful Enid is," Mary replied. "I don't like cousin Bosville, but to trap him!"

"They intended to trap us both," Rick pointed out. "They were in it together. She locked you in the tower, and he sent me to the summerhouse."

He had little sympathy for the viscount, and even less as the day wore on. Bosville, at least, had secured a bride, if not the one he intended, but Rick couldn't find even a moment alone with Mary.

She was everywhere, always busy, always in company. More of the Wren offspring arrived, with spouses and children, all delighted to meet Mary, the cousin whose letters from far-flung places had enlivened their lives for many years. She was in demand in the kitchen, where she was making and icing gingerbread shapes for the party supper. She was involved in the last of the decorating.

He gave up, and decided to move his baggage to the inn where he was booked for the night.

"Rick? Are you leaving?" Mary. She stopped in the parlor doorway.

"I'll be back for the party, Mary, but I'll leave from the inn in the morning. My father expects me in London tomorrow night. Mary? Will you walk into Oxford with me?"

Just then, Mrs. Wren and two of her daughters came down the stairs.

"Mary, dear, would you help with the kissing bough in the garden? Lieutenant Redepenning, you're off to the inn? What time do you expect to be back, dear?"

Rick gave some kind of an answer, watching Mary slip away from him again, carried off by her cousins.

Tonight. At some point tonight, he would find her alone, if he had to carry her off into a dark corner of the garden across the dead bodies of all her relatives.

Rick wanted to see her alone, and Mary had a fair idea why. He thought he'd compromised her when he helped her out of the tower, and he wanted to do the honorable thing. Mary wasn't having it. Enid might be satisfied to trap a husband, but Mary would rather stay single all her life than be married to someone reluctant to have her. Not that Bosville was reluctant anymore. Someone—Enid probably—had told him about Enid's trust fund, and he was as happy as a dog with two tails.

Mary wished them well. She did. But if Rick insisted on proposing, she would turn him down, even though it would break her heart. How she wished he wanted her. For a while, she had hoped... but he had said nothing.

She made her way back to the kitchen. Baking always made her feel better, and gingerbread brides would be a fine betrothal addition to tonight's Christmas party.

The kissing boughs had all been hung, making it perilous to traverse the house and garden. By the time the party started, Mary had been kissed at least twenty times, all polite salutes on the cheek.

The party spilled all over the house and beyond: carols around the pianoforte in one of the parlors, silly games in another, a continual feast in the dining room, and dancing outside in the crisp night air. Mary managed to avoid being alone with Rick until almost the end of the evening, when he cornered her in a temporarily deserted parlor, most of the party out on the dance lawn in the garden.

"Mary." There it was again. Her name, hummed in that beautiful voice of his, sounding like music. She turned her face upwards, tipping her cheek within easy reach, but he curved his neck as he bent, so that his lips touched hers.

They felt warm and soft and so gentle; as light as a feather, brushing along her mouth as if they would flutter past, then returning to settle. She stood frozen, all consciousness focused on the point of connection. Persuasive lips grazed against hers, until she responded, softening against him.

He moved closer then, sliding his hands around her waist. His mouth opened, and his tongue swept along her lower lip. Startled, she drew back, and he let her go, though his eyes clung to hers.

"Mary, dear Mary, may I...?"

"Don't, Rick, please?" After that kiss, her wits were scattered to the four corners of the garden. All she knew was that she didn't want to hear him propose. She couldn't bear to say no to him, and she had to.

"Rick, I know what you want to say, and you mustn't. There is no need. Really, Rick. We are friends, are we not? We have always been friends. You mustn't try to make it more."

"But, Mary..."

"No. I'm not Enid. I wouldn't do that to you. Please, Rick. Just leave me be." Her eyes were swimming with tears. She would not cry. She never cried.

One of the Wren cousins came in, thank Heaven above, stopping whatever Rick was going to say next. "Oh, excuse me, I was looking for Mama."

"In the garden, I think," Rick said. Mary took the opportunity to sidle to the door and make her escape, hurrying up the stairs to the safety of her bedroom, where she sat, holding in the tears, listening to the sounds of jollity from the garden, remembering Rick's kiss, and trying not to imagine what might have been.

It seemed like hours before the party slowly wound to a close, but the house was silent when the knock came on her door. It was Aunt Theo, who said, without preamble, "You seem to have successfully chased off your dear lieutenant, Mary. He left very subdued. You have been running from him all week, and what I do not understand, is why you do not let him catch you?"

"He is not my lieutenant. I have not been running. And I do not believe he wishes to catch me."

"I beg to differ, Mary. Young Redepenning is in love with you, or I know nothing about young men. And I have raised six of my own, not to mention all Dr. Wren's students and the strays that find their way here. And you, dear, are in love with him."

Mary picked at her nightgown, not meeting her aunt's eyes. "He... Did he tell you he loves me?"

"He does not need to, Mary. I have eyes in my head. His eyes follow you whenever you are in the room, and he follows after you whenever you leave. When he cannot be with you, he talks about you, and when anyone flirts with you—not that you ever seem to notice—he glares until they slink off."

Mary shook her head. "But, Aunt Theo, he has never said a word."

"Have you let him, Mary, dear?"

She hadn't. She'd seen the look Aunt Theo mentioned and had been afraid to believe it was true. So much so, she had gone out of her way not to be alone with him, had changed the subject whenever he seemed ready to say something serious, and the rare comments she'd been unable to deflect, she had dismissed as Rick the Rogue, flirting as usual. Even tonight, she had refused to let him speak.

But she had to admit he had flirted with no one else. He had been polite and friendly. But he had been attentive only to her. And that kiss...!

Aunt Theo bent over to give her a peck on the cheek. "Think about it, Mary, dear. And pleasant dreams."

Chapter Thirteen

There were no dreams for Mary that night. She lay awake, turning over in her mind all that Rick had said and done since she first met him two and a half months ago in a field in Sussex. In the early hours of the morning, she gave up on sleep and lit her candle to wash and dress, then crept down to the kitchen. Rick would probably leave the inn at first light for his trip to London, but perhaps, just perhaps, she could reach him first.

Rick spent the night awake. Mary's rejection hit him hard; he'd been so sure that she still cared for him, and not just as a friend. Had he been imagining the sideways looks when she thought he wasn't watching? Were the thousand small services she rendered him, the kindness she always showed him, just signs of affection? Did the blush he could provoke with a compliment mean nothing?

He'd been halfway back to Oxford before the remark about Enid started to bother him, and all the way to his room at the inn before he made sense of it. His foolish Mary thought she had been compromised, and that he had been trapped into proposing. Of course. She had a sense of honor equal to his own, and never a thought of taking advantage of circumstances beyond their control.

He almost turned back then and there, but she had gone to bed. He wouldn't be able to see her until the morning. By everything holy, he was not leaving for London until he got Miss Mary Pritchard on her own and made her listen to him.

In the half-light before dawn, he set out for the Wrens' house, walking his horse carefully on the icy surface of the road. He'd covered perhaps half the distance when he saw her trudging towards him. He knew her immediately, even from several hundred yards in uncertain light.

He dismounted, and waited for her, the anxious uncertainty in his chest easing a little further when her face lit up at the sight of him.

"Running away, Miss Pritchard?"

"Running towards, Lieutenant Redepenning." She blushed then, stopping several paces away, just out of reach. Some perverse imp, still smarting from last night's rejection, kept him silent.

"I brought you a present." She came close enough to hand him a box, tied shut with a ribbon. His heart sank, then. A present. One friend to another. He was reading the signals all wrong, it seemed. He mastered his disappointment enough to smile, to thank her, to hand her the reins, so he could open the box.

It was one of her gingerbread biscuits, cut in the shape of a lady, with an icing dress and bonnet and currant eyes. "A gingerbread lady?"

"A gingerbread bride, Rick," she corrected. "If..." She blushed and stumbled a little over her words, "If... you h-happen to be in n-need of a bride."

"As it happens, I am," he said. Could a man survive such a rebound? From despair to jubilation in a few short words. The birds were beginning their dawn chorus, but none of them sang as loudly as his heart. "I am in need of you, Mary, my love."

Who reached for whom remains forever a mystery, but the box dropped onto the path, unheeded, as their arms wrapped around each other. Their lips met for the second time in their lives, and for many minutes, nothing further was said.

Eventually, Rick found himself considering the logistics of icy roads and wet hedgerows, which recalled him to himself enough to impose discipline on his wayward impulses.

"Mary, I had better put this precious little gingerbread bride safely back in her box before I crush her, and take my own dear runaway bride home to her family. Do you think they will let you come to London with me? If we take Polly, for propriety's sake?"

"To London?"

He put the bride in her box and kissed Mary again. "To stay with my sister while I arrange the wedding. You will marry me straightaway, will you not, Mary? As soon as I can arrange it? So we can spend the rest of my leave together?" He kissed her again, before she could answer.

"Yes, as soon as we can," she affirmed when she was able.

"My dearest love," Rick said.

"Am I your love?"

He loosened his hold enough to lean back so he could see her face. "Surely you know you are."

She shook her head. "I thought I was just the nuisance you had to keep rescuing."

He bent to kiss the tip of her nose. Tall as she was, he was taller.

"Rescuing you is, and has always been, one of my favorite things to do, Mary. I am proud that you have promised me the right to rescue you always."

"Always, Rick, and whenever I run, it will be to you, not from." His beautiful bride giggled. "But right this minute, the gingerbread bride needs rescuing—from the horse!"

Their tender moment ended with Rick chasing the box-chewing horse down the icy lane, while his runaway bride, now truly caught, stood laughing.

THE END

Candle's Christmas Chair

When Viscount Avery comes to see the best invalid chair maker in the southwest of England he does not expect to find Minerva Bradshaw, the woman who rejected him three years earlier. Or did she? Older and wiser, he wonders if there is more to the story.

For three years, Min Bradshaw has remembered the handsome guardsman who courted her for her fortune. She didn't expect to see him in her workshop, and she certainly doesn't intend to let him fool her again. Even if he is handsomer and more charming than ever.

Chapter one: *An unexpected meeting*

"Tha' wants to talk to Min about they chairs," said the man in the office, and directed Candle Avery to the far corner of the carriage-maker's yard.

Candle strode through the light rain, dodging or leaping the worst of the mud and puddles. Min. Short for Benjamin, perhaps? Or Dominic?

No, he concluded, as his eyes adjusted to the light inside the shed. The delightful posterior presented to his eyes belonged to neither a Benjamin nor a Dominic. The overalls were masculine, but the curves they covered were not.

She was on a ladder, leaning so far into a bank of shelves that lined the wall opposite the door that her upper half was hidden, but he had no objection to the current view—said delightful posterior at his eye level and neatly outlined as she stretched, a pair of trim ankles showing between the tops of her sensible half boots and the hems of the overalls.

"Botheration." Whatever she was reaching for up there, it was not obliging her by coming to her hand. Perhaps his lofty height might be of service?

"May I help, Ma'am?" he asked.

There was a crash as she jerked upright at the sound of his voice, and hit her head on the shelf above. As she flinched backward from the collision, the ladder tipped sideways, spilling its occupant into Candle's hastily outstretched arms.

The curves were everything he thought, and the face lived up to them. A Venus in miniature, black curls spilling from the kerchief that held them away from the heart-shaped face, that quintessentially English complexion known as peaches and cream, grey eyes fringed with dark lashes.

Grey eyes that had haunted his dreams for three long years, ever since she'd led him on at a house party for the amusement of her friends, and then left without saying goodbye.

Grey eyes that turned stormy as he held her a moment too long. He hastily set her down.

"Miss Bradshaw."

"Captain Avery. No, it is Lord Avery, now, is it not? My condolences on the death of your father."

He bowed his acknowledgement, his mind racing. Bradshaw Carriages. He hadn't made the connection. Had he known when he was courting her that she was a carriage-maker's daughter? He didn't remember anyone mentioning it.

But he did remember that her friends called her Minnie. Miss Minerva Bradshaw. Min.

Lord Avery was broader than she remembered. He'd been little more than a boy at that horrid house party, but even then the tallest man she had ever met. Isolated and nervous in that crowd of scheming cats who had only invited her to humiliate her, she'd believed him when he claimed to care. She'd been thrilled when he called her a little goddess, and asked for leave to worship her.

With him at her side, she'd braved the crush at the ball. Short as she was, she usually found such occasions overwhelming. People looked over her, bumped into her, ignored her. But Lord Avery— Captain Avery he'd been then—kept her safe. She'd even, for the first time in her life, been enjoying herself at a ball. Right up until she overheard his best friend talking to him, and it became clear that Lord Avery despised her common origins and was only courting her for her money.

That had been Min's last venture into the aristocratic world her parents had educated her for. She'd come home to Bath, and told her mother that she would marry, if marry she ever did, within her own class. But none of her suitors had ever measured up to the tall red-headed guards officer who even now, standing here in her workshop, turned her knees to jelly.

What was he doing in her workshop? Why would he track her down?

"Can I help you, Lord Avery?" She couldn't do much about the colour that pinked her cheeks, or the way her heart pounded. But she could, and did, keep her voice level and her tone cool.

He was immediately all business. "I am after a chair, Miss Bradshaw. It is still Miss Bradshaw?"

She nodded, seething. How dare he comment on her marital status. She wanted to tell him that she'd refused five proposals in the last three years. But he was continuing: "The Master at the Pump Rooms told me that Bradshaw Carriages makes the best chairs in Bath, and the man in the office sent me here."

"I see. And what sort of a chair do you require?"

His brows drew together. "An invalid's chair. That is what you make, is it not? What your father makes, I mean?"

He might as well know the whole of it. She was not ashamed. And if his eyes turned cold and scornful, what was that to her? She was, no doubt, just imagining the warmth she saw. As she had imagined his admiration so long ago.

"You were right the first time, Lord Avery. I design the chairs. And I make each prototype for my assistants to copy."

"I say," he said, "good for you!" And he smiled at her. She remembered those smiles. And, though her mind knew he couldn't be trusted, her foolish heart didn't believe her.

Miss Bradshaw was as lovely as he remembered. Such a shame that she preferred other women! He'd refused to believe it at first, when her friend hinted it to him after she had run off. What a fool he had made of himself over her.

"So can you sell me an invalid's chair, then?" he asked.

She sighed, and in a patient voice explained, "I need to know more about how the chair will be used, Lord Avery. We have chairs suitable for street use, chairs that work well in a park, chairs that can be easily pushed inside a house, even chairs that can be propelled by the occupant. What sort of chair do you require?"

"I see." That made sense. What didn't make sense were the signals he was receiving. Three years ago he'd been as close to an innocent as a 19-year-old with a father like his could be. But his time in the Coldstream Guards had taught him a great deal, including what to think when a woman's pupils dilated, and she became breathless and flushed.

Perhaps it was wishful thinking. Certainly, his own anatomy had a strong opinion about what to do with the delectable Miss Bradshaw and his own reaction might be predisposing him to misread hers.

Inspiration struck.

"Can you show me each different type and explain what the different uses are, please, Miss Bradshaw?"

There. That should win Candle at least 15 minutes to observe her while she showed him around.

She stood her ground. "Who is the chair for, Lord Avery."

Good point. He needed to remember his key purpose in coming here, which had nothing to do with pursuing the elusive Miss Bradshaw.

"My mother was injured in the same accident that killed my father," he told her baldly. "She is paralysed from the waist down. I wish to buy her a chair so that she is not totally dependent on being carried to go where she wishes."

Miss Bradshaw's lovely grey eyes softened and warmed. He remembered how changeable those eyes were. They could go cold with disdain, hot and stormy with anger, and warm with compassion. Lying eyes. He had to keep reminding himself that she had made a fool of him.

"Ah, your poor mother. Yes, we will certainly find a chair for her. And what sort of places does she wish to go?"

Min showed Lord Avery the inside chairs first. He was very taken with the Merlin chairs, named after the inventor, a clockmaker who had built a self-propelled chair after he'd broken his leg. Lord Avery asked her to demonstrate how to turn the handles on the arms, and then insisted on trying the chair himself, folding his great length in order to fit.

"I think we should have one of those," he said, brushing past her as he circled the chair, examining it from all sides. He skimmed his hands down the chair's sides, gently caressing, and Min's mouth went unaccountably dry.

"Yes, well," she said. "Over here we have the outdoor chairs." She had designed them for different types of surface, changing the size and pitch of the large wheels on either side of the chair, and lengthening or shortening the undercarriage to change the distance between the chair and the small front wheel that the occupant could turn in order to steer.

Once again, Lord Avery insisted on trying the chairs, handing her into each one, parading her solemnly up and down the workshop, and then handing her out. Fortunately, he seemed focused on the chairs, and didn't notice her fingers trembling. His effect on her seemed stronger than ever.

"I like this one," he said, finally, pointing to the one chair they hadn't tried.

"I am sorry," she told him. "That one is not for sale."

"But it would be perfect," he said. "The wheels are broad, so Mother won't sink into the grass when she strolls in the garden, and they are slightly skewed to give her greater stability. The longer undercarriage also improves stability, but it isn't long enough to impair turning, so she will be able to manage even the paths in the maze. It's perfect."

He'd listened to her every word. More; he'd understood exactly what she was trying to do.

"It is a prototype," she explained. "I do not sell my prototypes, and I do not manufacture until the prototype has been thoroughly tested."

He was nodding before she'd finished. "That's even better. Let us test it for you. And once you are satisfied, you can sell us one of the new models."

He took both her hands as she opened her mouth to reply, speaking before she could. "Please, Miss Bradshaw. It would mean so much to her. She used to practically live in her garden, rain and shine. To be able to get there again without being carried; to be able to move around and decide where she wants to go—it would mean the world to her."

His big hands cupped hers; his thumbs stroked across her trapped fingers. For a moment, she was almost mesmerised, but then she tugged her hands, and he released her instantly.

"But you wanted it for Christmas." It was a weak protest, close to a capitulation, and he clearly knew it.

"But this is even better, don't you see? She'll get the use of a chair immediately, without waiting for Christmas, and at Christmas she'll have one made just for her. Oh. But will there be enough time?"

It was late October. Not quite two months to go. Yes, they could do it. Min would need to start building the model before she got the prototype back, but the final testing was unlikely to prompt major changes.

"I will need to upholster the chair and to run some final tests, then your mother could have it for perhaps a month? I will need to talk to her after that."

"Of course. I'm going to take that—did you call it a Merlin? I'll take the Merlin with the red cushions. She loves red. Could you cover the new chair in the same fabric?"

"I could possibly do the same colour," Min agreed. Did she have enough red leather? No; she'd cut the last skin a few days ago. Perhaps she could get some from the main carriage works. If not, she'd have to make a trip to the leather merchants.

He nodded, running a hand over the plush surface of the Merlin and immediately leaping to the right conclusion. "You use leather for the outdoor chairs, don't you? They might get wet, I suppose."

"Minnie, are you in here?" That was her cousin Daniel's inevitable greeting, as if her presence in her own workshop was a perpetual surprise to him. He followed his voice into the room, and drew himself up to his full height, still a good seven inches shorter than Lord Avery.

The man who called Miss Bradshaw 'Minnie' in that familiar way was built like a bull: broad in the shoulders and chest, with massive arms and a thick neck. Candle grudgingly admitted he was handsome enough, in a thick-set kind of way, his blond hair slightly overlong, square-cut even features, and fine hazel eyes currently fixed on Candle in challenge.

Miss Bradshaw kept her smooth calm. "Lord Avery, may I present my cousin, Daniel Whitlow? Daniel, Viscount Avery is here to purchase a chair for his mother."

The bull relaxed slightly, returning Candle's nod. "Minnie—Miss Bradshaw—designs the best chairs in Bath, Lord Avery." He rested a proprietary hand on Miss Bradshaw's shoulder. "You won't regret choosing one of her chairs."

"Two," Candle said. "Two chairs." How proprietary was this cousin? Not that Candle cared. Not after what she did three years ago. Or did she? If her friend was mistaken about her preferences, did she tell the truth about Miss Bradshaw's reasons for leaving? The bull was saying something else.

"One for indoors, and one for outdoors," Candle explained.

"Daniel, I need dark red leather for the outdoor chair. Can I purchase some from your stock?"

The bull nodded. "Yes, we bought a whole cart-load of skins dyed for the Mail order. We could spare you a skin or two."

"The one you're using is a bit more orange. I had in mind this colour." She ran her hand over the Merlin chair, as Candle had a few minutes ago. In precisely the same place. He wondered if she realised that. He shifted his hat, strategically.

The bull shook his head again. "No. Nothing that colour."

Candle was opening his mouth to say he'd choose another colour when the bull went on, "And I can't spare anyone today to take you down to buy some. We're going to be all hands working late as it is."

"I could escort you, Miss Bradshaw?" Candle offered.

The bull examined him with narrowed eyes.

"After all, the sooner the chair is covered, the sooner my mother can try it out," Candle went on, looking as innocent as he knew how.

It was enough. The bull nodded again. A beast of few words. "Take your maid, Minnie. Your servant, Lord Avery."

Min changed into an afternoon dress in the room her father kept for her in the main building, while Lord Avery waited for her in the office downstairs. He hadn't blinked at the price she asked for the two chairs, writing a bank draft for the first chair, and promising payment on delivery for the other. Rumour had it he'd inherited a fortune from a nabob uncle. Perhaps, for once, rumour spoke true.

As she buttoned her pelisse and tied her bonnet strings, she thought wistfully about the far more fashionable clothes that she had at home. How silly. Lord Avery was a client like any other, and she would no more dress up for him than she would for… she cast about for the person she least wanted to impress. Daniel. She would no more dress up for Lord Avery than for Daniel.

They walked down Cornwall Street into Walcot Street, Polly Stample keeping pace behind.

"How did you come to be making chairs, Miss Bradshaw?" Lord Avery asked. He couldn't really be interested, but she would tell him, since he asked.

"I began when my mother broke her hip, Lord Avery. She was not entirely happy with the chair made by one of my father's workmen, and I designed some improvements. It has grown from there."

"An unusual hobby for a woman," he commented.

A hobby, indeed. Every man Min knew, from her father down, insisted on seeing her work as a hobby. Never mind that invalid chairs were one of their most profitable lines. And she managed it all, from designing the chairs to keeping the accounts.

"It is a business, not a hobby," she told Lord Avery.

He opened his mouth to say something, then visibly thought better of it.

"Go on," she said.

He didn't pretend not to know what she meant. "I don't wish to make you cross," he told her. "I value my skin."

"I will try to resist tossing you into the Avon."

He laughed out loud. "You would need to trip me, Miss Bradshaw. I'm rather too large for you to lift."

"Are you changing the subject, Lord Avery?"

He spread his hands in surrender. "I was just going to say that business is rather an unusual hobby for a lady," he said. "I meant it as a joke, but I decided it wasn't very funny. Truly, Miss Bradshaw, after the last six months, I have nothing but admiration for anyone who can run a business."

He sounded and looked sincere, but it couldn't possibly be true. Min knew what the gentry thought of trade. She'd heard it often enough while she was at school. "Mini, darling, whatever is that smell? Have you not washed today? Oh, but I forgot. You cannot wash off the shop, can you darling?" 'Mini' was short for 'Minimus', a comment on her size, and she hated it.

But Lord Avery was continuing. "I was raised to run the family estate, of course. But I also inherited from my uncle six months ago. He ran a huge business, and now I'm trying to learn how to do it. So far, I've been lucky in my managers, but Mother says I need to know the impact of every decision made in my name, and how everything works, and that seems sound to me."

Min nodded. "That is what my father, says, too. My mother says the same applies to running a house. You have to know how to do everything in order to know everything is being done well. This is Pursell's."

Lord Avery opened the door to the showroom.

At first the sales assistant assumed Lord Avery was the customer, but Lord Avery said, "I am just here to escort Miss Bradshaw."

Min pulled out an off-cut of the velvet they were matching, and leafed through the sample book until she found a match. They didn't have that colour in stock, but she was assured they could have it dyed and ready for her within a week. Min reviewed her schedule. If Lady Avery was happy to trial the chair for three weeks instead of a month, they could still make the Christmas deadline.

"I wish to select the skins," she told the sales assistant.

In the storeroom, she inhaled a deep lungful of the smell of fresh leather, then laughed when she realised Lord Avery was doing the same.

"It reminds me of the saddle room at Avery Hall when I was little," he said. "What about you?"

"My father's harness shop. When I was little, my mother was in charge of it, and I spent a lot of time there. My mother was a Conti."

"Conti? Your mother is related to Gavriel Conti?" Lord Avery whistled. "I am sorry, Miss Bradshaw. That was most impolite of me. But Conti Saddlery is a legend. I have a Gavriel Conti saddle, and I wouldn't part with it for the world."

"Gavriel Conti was my grandfather." She had found the stack of skins she wanted and the sales assistant was pulling them out so that she could inspect them.

The sales assistant's superior attitude changed to reverence when he realised that he was serving the granddaughter of the great Conti. He must be new or he would have known. She seldom bought skins herself, usually picking what she wanted from the manufactory's stores, but she'd been coming here with her parents since she was a babe in arms.

The sales assistant and Lord Avery began exchanging stories about Conti harnesses and saddles that had come unscathed through trials that would have shredded lesser leatherwork.

Lord Avery was not what Min had expected. For a brief week, she had convinced herself that he was not like other offspring of the nobility—that he saw past her modest birth and liked her as a person. Then, for three years, she believed he was just like all the others; an idler who thought his noble birth entitled him to a life of ease and plenty, and who looked down on those whose labours made his leisure possible. Now, he confounded her.

If he wasn't after her money—and if the fortune he had inherited was a tenth of what people said, he didn't need her money—why had he come seeking her? She discounted the story he'd told; it was, after all, highly unlikely the Master of the Pump Rooms would send him to her, of all people.

She would have to watch him carefully, and guard her heart.

Chapter two: Truth in a tea shop

Miss Bradshaw chose the skins she wanted and arranged for them to be dyed and delivered. Out in the street, it was raining again. Candle unfurled his umbrella. He was so much taller than she that if he held it over both of them, she would be soaked in every gust of wind. When he tried to hold it just over her, though, she objected.

"My bonnet will keep me dry, Lord Avery. I must not take you out of your way."

"I promised to escort you, Miss Bradshaw. Surely you will allow me to keep my promise? Do you return to your workshop?"

"I am for home on Henrietta Street. Polly and I will be fine."

Candle turned, and handed the maid his umbrella. One of them might as well be dry.

"Then we will brave the weather together, Miss Bradshaw." He offered her his arm.

They hurried down Northgate Street and turned towards the bridge. Miss Bradshaw leant into him as she jumped over the puddles he strode past. The magic was still working; she still made him feel strong and capable.

Three years ago, fresh out of university and new to the Guard, he'd been nervous in company, expecting the teasing he'd endured at school to follow him into Society. And it did.

But Miss Bradshaw had talked to him about books, and gardens, and animals. She'd listened as he explained his plans for a military career. She'd taken his arm on walks and waved admiringly as he showed off his one skill, outriding all the other male guests.

Tiny though she was, she never made him feel over tall and clumsy. Indeed, she liked his height. She had confided that she was always nervous in crowds, but not when he was there to protect her. Was it all a tease?

On an impulse, he pulled her into the doorway of Crofts Tea House, at the entrance to the bridge.

"Miss Polly," he said to the maid. "Your mistress and I will take shelter here while you hurry home and fetch another couple of umbrellas."

The maid turned uncertain eyes to Miss Bradshaw. Would she agree? Candle held his breath.

"Run along, Polly. We will wait in the tea rooms."

He opened the door for Min as the maid hurried off, almost invisible under the big umbrella.

Following behind, he almost collided with Min's back when she stopped suddenly. He was close enough to feel the tension radiating from her, and the effort she made to relax and continue into the little tea shop.

A servant hurried up. Candle absently asked for a table for two and for tea to be served. Most of his attention was on the couple already seated at the far side of the shop. Guy Kitteridge was one of those who had made his life miserable at Eton and later at Oxford. Kitteridge was with his sister Genevieve, Lady Norton, a slender blonde with a waspish tongue.

They were absorbed in their conversation, and with luck wouldn't notice Candle and Miss Bradshaw. He waved Miss Bradshaw ahead and followed her to a small table near the window that looked out onto the street across the bridge.

Interesting that Miss Bradshaw reacted as she did. Lady Norton had been a great friend of hers three years ago. Although, come to think of it, he hadn't seen any signs of closeness between them during the house party. It was only after Miss Bradshaw left that Miss Kitteridge told him they'd been at school together.

Miss Bradshaw had seated herself so all the brother and sister would see was her back. Candle angled his chair so he, too, would be hard to recognise.

Lady Norton was the one who had told him why Miss Bradshaw left so precipitously. Wasn't that interesting? Candle beamed. Miss Bradshaw raised her eyebrows. No. He would not explain to her why he was suddenly happy. Not yet, anyway. Perhaps one day.

The servant brought a laden tray. Two cups, a teapot, milk and sugar, a three-tier cake plate filled with savoury tarts on the lowest tier, delicate iced cakes on the middle tier, and candied fruit and flowers on the top.

As Miss Bradshaw poured the tea, he tested his new theory. "Mr Kitteridge and Lady Norton are over there in the corner," he said. Yes. That was a slight grimace, quickly controlled. But it was definitely a grimace.

"No doubt you wish to greet your friend," was all she said. But the warmth that had begun to creep into her voice during their afternoon was markedly absent.

"He's no friend of mine," Candle assured her.

"You have had a falling out?" She handed him his cup, prepared just the way he had liked it three years earlier.

"We never had a falling in," Candle said. He was watching the pair from the corner of his eye. They'd seen him—it was hard to be inconspicuous when you were well over 6ft tall and had red hair.

"Don't look now," he told Miss Bradshaw, "but they're coming over."

"Lord Avery? It is Lord Avery. I told Guy it was you." Lady Norton was fluttering her eyelashes at him. She must have heard about his inheritance. Three years ago, she had barely acknowledged his existence, except to show her contempt.

The contempt was well veiled today, at least in his direction. She didn't acknowledge Miss Bradshaw's existence at all.

Well, he could fix that. "You remember Miss Bradshaw, of course," Candle said.

Genevieve Norton, known at school as Kitty Cat, rounded her blue, blue eyes into her innocent look. Min had seen her practicing that look and a dozen others in front of a mirror. "Why, if it isn't little Miss Bradshaw. Fancy seeing you here."

"I live in Bath," Min said.

"Oh, I know that." Lady Norton slid her eyes sideways to Lord Avery, inviting him to join in the fun. "I meant here in a tea shop. With a man. On your own. Oh but perhaps I am mistaken. Perhaps the rules are different for those who are not ladies." And she lowered her voice to not quite whisper to Lord Avery, "She is a tradeswoman you know. Carriages or some such."

He smiled warmly at Min. "As it happens, Lady Norton, you have interrupted a business meeting. Miss Bradshaw is designing an invalid chair for my mother. I know you will excuse us if we continue."

"I know what kind of business I'd like to discuss with Miss Bradshanks." Mr Kitteridge said, waggling his eyebrows at her.

Lord Avery's nostrils flared. She had heard the expression, but she'd never seen it happen. But his voice was quiet and controlled when he said, "Kitteridge, Perhaps you and your sister had better leave now."

Lady Norton fluttered her eyelashes at him again. Practiced expression number 8, or was it 9? "Lord Avery, you must call while you are in Bath. Perhaps tomorrow afternoon?"

"Thank you, Lady Norton. However, I expect to be leaving Bath in the morning."

Kitteridge, his eyes on Min, opened his mouth and then thought better of whatever inappropriate remark he was about to make. He said good day, instead. "Come on, Vivi. Better be on our way. Things to do tonight, you know."

Lady Norton laughed, a tinkling little sound of amusement, also practiced. "Such a busy place Bath is this month, Lord Avery. Tell me, are you staying at the Royal?"

"I am not," Lord Avery said.

"Come on, Vivi. Your servant, Avery. Miss Bradshanks."

Lord Avery took his seat again, and picked up the cup Min had poured for him.

"Do you suppose he gets your name wrong on purpose?" he asked? "Or is it general stupidity?"

The twinkle in his eyes put the nasty couple back into perspective. Now she was an adult, their petty insults had no power to hurt her. She didn't move in their circles, and they weren't respected in hers. Anxiety, indignation: both receded under Lord Avery's calm amusement.

"A little of both, I believe," she replied.

"What a poisonous pair," he said. "Did she make your school days as unpleasant as he made mine? You know, when you disappeared from the house party, she told me that you had just been playing at liking me for the amusement of your friends. Her exact words, if I remember, were 'after all, Captain Avery, you are not exactly the answer to a young girl's prayers, are you?' I shouldn't have believed her, should I?"

Good heavens. She shook her head, her mind racing. Those past few hours at the house party had been too painful to remember, but she was now reliving the conversation that had sent her running to her room, to wait, wide-awake, till morning dawned and she could leave.

"Why did you leave?" Lord Avery asked.

"I heard... I thought I heard you discussing me with Mr Kitteridge. But I have just this moment realised. I heard his voice, but the other voice. It was very low; I assumed it was yours, but... Kitty Cat—Lady Norton—had told me you were just after my money, but she always sees the worst in everyone... And then... Do you remember that I tore my hem and went to have it sewn up?"

"I remember. It was the last time I saw you." His eyes were sombre.

"I came back to the alcove where you were waiting, and I heard Mr Kitteridge say, 'Avery, old chap, you have to admit, if you must marry the shop, it comes in quite a tasty package.' I could not move. I just stood there. I heard someone reply, very low. I couldn't make out the voice or the words, but Mr Kitteridge said, 'That's right, Avery. No need to take her into Society once you've got your hands on her lovely money.'" She blushed, remembering the rest of his sentence, which she wasn't going to repeat. 'Keep her at home and enjoy all her other lovely assets where the smell of the shop won't bother the neighbours. I wouldn't mind getting an heir and a spare on that one, I can tell you.'

"Damn his lying, cheating eyes," Candle said, forgetting for a moment that he was in the presence of a lady. "I beg your pardon, Miss Bradshaw. Will you believe I wasn't there? When you left for the retiring room, I went to get us some punch. I stopped to talk to some people. I was watching the door, but someone..." he stopped, his eyes unfocused for a moment as he remembered. "Lady Norton bumped into me and spilled the punch. I had my eyes off the door for several minutes."

Miss Bradshaw nodded. "She was in the retiring room. She spent 10 minutes telling me how improvident you were, and how unworthy I was, and on, and on—all in that sweet 'I am only trying to help' voice of hers. She left just before I did."

"They planned it. They were in it together."

Miss Bradshaw had clearly come to the same conclusion. Slowly and deliberately, she repeated, "Damn their lying, cheating eyes."

Candle gave a bark of laughter, then turned suddenly serious. "We have wasted a bit of time, haven't we? May we start again, Miss Bradshaw? I was courting you, you know. I'd like to court you again, if I may."

Miss Bradshaw shook her head, sadly. "We come from different worlds, you and I. The Kitteridges were right about that."

"It didn't matter back then."

"I was 17 back then. I believed Cinderella could marry the prince. I did not think about what her life would be like the next morning, raised to scrub out the kitchen and surrounded by people who despised kitchen maids."

Candle would have argued, but the maid arrived with the umbrellas. Miss Bradshaw thanked him for the tea.

"Polly and I will be fine from here, Lord Avery. It is only just around the corner."

Candle insisted, though, on escorting them both to her father's fine terraced house on Henrietta Street.

She gave him her hand in parting, and one of those warm smiles that melted him from the centre. "I am so glad to know what really happened at the house party, Lord Avery. All these years, I have believed I was mistaken in you. I am happy to know that I was not."

He raised her hand, so tiny and delicate in his, but wiry and strong and capable. "Please know that my admiration was, and is, genuine, Miss Bradshaw." He kissed the air above the back of her hand, fighting the temptation to press his lips to her glove—or to strip the glove off and lay his kiss in her palm.

He doused the thought. All unbidden, it had left her sweet palm to travel up her arm and beyond, and he had to remain respectful if it killed him. Any sign that he regarded her as less than a lady would, he was sure, condemn him take her decision on his proposed courtship as final. And that, he had no intention of doing.

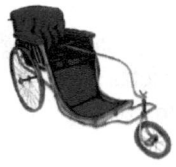

Chapter three: A choice of suitors

Mama was in a flap. One of tonight's guests had cancelled, and the table would be unbalanced. The cook had taken back the turbot, saying it was not fresh, had started a screaming match with the fishmonger, and was now sulking. Papa had sent a message saying he and Daniel would be late. And the roses for the dining room were yellow, not pink as Mama had ordered.

Min nodded, and agreed, and nodded again. Mama would work it out. Mama always worked it out, and the dinner would be magnificent, as it always was. But Mama seemed to need the drama of solving one crisis after another.

Min, though she took her colouring and size from her mother, was far more like her peaceful father in temperament. "If you can solve it, Min," he would say, "Then do so. If you can't solve it, it isn't your problem. But worrying never changes anything."

Sure enough, by the time the first guests were announced, the chaos had been resolved and all was in readiness. Mama, with Min at her elbow, presented Papa's apologies for his tardiness.

"A big order. He is upstairs changing for dinner. He and our nephew, Daniel, will be down shortly."

The guests were all from trade families. Several times a week, the Bradshaw dinner table became a location for what Papa called the great game of business. Mama was an even better strategist than Papa, choosing who to invite with an eye to advantage for Bradshaw Carriages, keeping the dinner table conversation light, but providing many alcoves and separate rooms for the private conversations that led to alliances for the benefit of each party.

Martin Billingham, who escorted Min into dinner once her father and cousin arrived, was the son of the man who was trialling them on a Royal Mail order. Mama had suggested the contract might be sealed with a marriage. Mr Billingham was, Min supposed, a nice enough young man. But—whatever the business advantage—Min was not going to marry him.

At dinner, most of the talk was about the French, and whether they would invade. Some of those present believed Napoleon was no longer a danger, now that he was committing troops to fight the Austrians.

Others thought it was only a matter of time until he beat the Austrians and returned to Boulogne.

Min pointed out that the French naval commander, Villeneuve, had combined his fleet with the Spanish fleet, at Cadiz.

"It is a worry," her father agreed.

"Trust Admiral Nelson to deal with them," Daniel insisted.

"And if they don't, we have the militia, do we not?" one of the other ladies said. This was a sore point. The volunteers and the militia were not paid, but they needed to be equipped, trained, and paid when they were mobilised.

Mr Billingham senior summed up the general view. "Mark you; it's us that pays when they raise taxes. It always comes back to us trade folk, whether it's windows or servants or sugar. One way or another, it comes back to us." Mr Billingham held the current Royal Mail contract; if Bradshaw Carriages met the deadline with the current order, they'd have a lucrative partnership for the next five years.

"You need not worry, Miss Bradshaw," the younger Mr Billingham assured her, when the men joined the ladies after dinner. "I am confident that Napoleon will not dare to invade. He knows the English will rise up to the last man to oppose the French should they land on our shores."

"Minnie doesn't worry, Martin," Daniel said, taking the seat on her other side. "If the French took over Bath, Minnie would sell them chairs for all the soldiers injured in the invasion, wouldn't you, Minnie? Did you manage to get the leather you wanted?"

"They're dyeing some for me," she said.

"A happy customer then. Although he's not your usual sort, Minnie."

Mr Billingham frowned. "I cannot like you dealing with customers, Miss Bradshaw. The risk! The scandal! I am surprised your father allows it."

Daniel laughed. "Oh Uncle thinks anything Minnie does is exceptional." Was that a sour note? Daniel had no right to be jealous. If anything, the shoe was on the other foot. Daniel was Papa's business heir, and was being trained to take over. Min's childhood dream of running the carriage works would never come true. She knew as much as Daniel, but she was a woman and he was a man.

"Indeed, if I were to have the privilege of taking a jewel such as Miss Bradshaw into my home," Mr Billingham was proclaiming, speaking to Daniel rather than Min, "she would never have to lift a hand in any kind of work."

Min and Daniel exchanged glances. Daniel changed the subject. "So who was the long streak? Avery, you said?"

"Viscount Avery. He has an estate a few hours from here," Min said. She knew exactly where it was, too.

"He was buying chairs for his mother." Daniel made a statement of it, a frown creasing his forehead. "I'm sorry, Minnie. I was distracted. I should have sent someone to escort you or asked you to wait till tomorrow."

Mr Billingham looked indignant, his chin jutted forward and his eyes protruding more than usual. "If you suffered insult, Miss Bradshaw, I will... I will seek this viscount out and demand an apology." He nodded as if satisfied with that solution, though the anxiety in his eyes hinted that he hoped such a move would not be necessary.

"Lord Avery was all things gentlemanly, Daniel. Thank you, Mr Billingham. I suffered no insult."

"You must know that I would do anything for you, Miss Bradshaw."

Best to put a stop to that conversational direction immediately. "How kind, but I am well able to depend on my father and my cousin," she said.

Daniel turned a laugh into a cough. "I think my Mama wants me," Min said, suppressing the urge to kick her cousin. "Excuse me, gentlemen."

For the remainder of the evening, she managed to avoid Mr Billingham. She could not keep him from coming to the point indefinitely, but in a few more weeks she would be able to refuse him without any damage to her father's business.

Mama came to tuck her in. "You may be 20, Minerva," she had replied, when Min suggested that she was too old for tucking in, "but you will be my baby girl till the day I die."

"Not Mr Billingham, my love?" she said, as she pulled the sheets up to Minerva's chin and smoothed them out.

"No, Mama. Not Mr Billingham."

"Don't leave it too late, Minerva. Invalid chairs won't keep you warm at night, and you cannot rock business ledgers in a cradle. I know what I'm talking about, baby. Papa and I—Papa was 41 and I was 38 when you were born. We had a happy marriage, but you made our lives complete."

"That is part of the problem, Mama. You and Papa show me that marriage can be a partnership, and I want that. Mr Billingham likes the way I look, but he doesn't like me. He doesn't know me, and he doesn't want to know me."

But Lord Avery does, a small voice whispered. She ignored it. Lord Avery was not for her.

Candle went to dinner with a couple of friends from army days, and they spent the evening fighting an invasion. Beckett was still in the Guard, but their host, Michaels, had sold out about the same time as Candle, and was fascinated to hear that Candle had set up and was training a local company of volunteers.

"If we can hold Napoleon off at sea, we'll be fine," Michaels said. "But we'd be fools to discount the possibility of him landing. And he'll be back when he's finished in Austria."

"It's not like regular army work," Candle explained. "Our farm boys and footmen won't be able to stand up to Napoleon's trained soldiers, and we won't try. But every Englishman and every Englishwoman will be able to strike a blow when the French aren't watching. A broken wheel here, a shot from the darkness over there, a purge in their soup somewhere else."

Beckett winced. "That's hitting below the belt," he joked.

"But you are teaching them to fight," Michaels said.

"Yes, but a different kind of fighting. A few people moving fast in and out of cover, and striking only at weak points."

They spent hours fighting skirmishes and sneak attacks with the salt cellars and the cutlery, taking advantage of every bit of cover provided by a dinner plate or a fold in the tablecloth.

When Candle and Beckett left Michaels' lodgings, the dawn was just lightening the sky. The shortest distance to the hotel district led through the south end of the town, where weary prostitutes returning home from work passed day-labourers heading to the better end of town to begin theirs.

One particularly pretty girl walked towards and then past them, and Beckett turned to watch. "We could pick up a couple of girls... no, you don't do you."

Candle shook his head. "You go ahead, Beckett." He hadn't been with a purchased woman since his 16th birthday, when his father took him to a brothel as a present. That virgin boy had been first embarrassed, then delighted, then—when he read the contrast between the smile on the painted lips and the hopelessness in the kohl-lined eyes—horrified.

Fortunately, his father had lost interest in him again, and he'd remained nearly an innocent until his disappointment over Miss Bradshaw had sent him seeking experience. He spared a smile for the bored lusty widow who had educated him in London. She was still a good friend; remarried now, and he was glad of it. She deserved happiness.

Her successors had likewise been widows who enjoyed a discrete liaison with someone who treated them with respect and was happy to squire them to social events. He had not had such a liaison in six months; not since he sold out when his father died and his mother was injured. Was that the reason for his lustful response to Miss Bradshaw? He didn't think so. He was all but certain he would respond to her if he'd just been intimate with an army of widows, end to end. And he was completely certain an army of naked widows wouldn't have half the effect on him of Miss Bradshaw's delectable posterior in a pair of workman's overalls.

He continued on, smiling at his own besotted imaginings. He could see glimpses of the Abbey. The buildings behind it blocked his view of the river across which Miss Bradshaw would be sleeping. He passed a flower shop that was just opening its doors to offload a cartload of flowers, still in buckets and fresh from the fields. Flowers. Why not?

He was whistling when he exited the flower shop. A wash, a quick nap, a shave, and he'd be as good as new. And in four more hours, when he called to collect the Merlin chair, he would see her again.

Lord Avery was precise to his time, arriving on the dot of 11 o'clock. Min and the worker Daniel had spared to her had the chair packed around with blankets and wrapped in a canvas against the weather.

"My mother asked me to thank you for the flowers." He must have bought every bloom in the shop. They were delivered to her mother; a polite fiction that she appreciated. Min was both appalled at his extravagance and flattered by his attention. "They are lovely, but I told you not to court me," she scolded, when the worker was out of earshot.

"To be precise," he said, "you told me that the Kitteridges were right. This being completely beyond the bounds of possibility, I decided you must be having a momentary lapse of reason, quite out of character, and it would be kindest to ignore you."

"Lord Avery!" She didn't know what else to say. She wanted to laugh, but that would just encourage him.

"You will note, however, that the flowers were not addressed to you, but to the lovely Mrs Bradshaw," he reminded her.

"You have not met my mother."

"True. But I'm sure I would conceive a hopeless passion for her if I did. If I had not already given my heart to her daughter."

"Lord Avery!"

"You could call me Candle if you like," he said.

"I could not."

"You're right," he admitted. "It's a silly name. They gave it to me at school. Because I'm tall and thin and have a flame on top. Call me Randall. That's my name, you know."

Min did know. She had looked him up in Debrett's at the circulating library. She wasn't going to tell him that.

"I will call you Lord Avery," she said, firmly.

"Really? Think about it. You're an efficient woman. Wouldn't Randall be quicker and easier to say?"

"Or Ran," she said, the words slipping out before she could stop them. Sometimes, in her daydreams, she had called him Ran.

Lord Avery was delighted. "Yes. Please call me Ran. That would be very efficient."

"And very inappropriate," she said.

She could tell he was going to argue some more, but the worker called out to say he'd secured the chair on the back of Lord Avery's high-perch phaeton, and Daniel arrived.

Daniel wasted no time. "You sent my aunt a lot of flowers, Lord Avery."

"I did, Mr Whitlow. I wished to show my appreciation for her daughter's help, and my delight that we have met again."

"Is that right? You didn't say you'd met Lord Avery before, Minnie."

"It was three years ago, Daniel."

Daniel turned his suspicious eyes back on Lord Avery.

The bull was very protective. Cousinly? But it wasn't unknown for cousins to marry. Surely Miss Bradshaw would have told him if she had an understanding with the pugnacious Mr Whitlow?

Certainly Candle wasn't going to have another chance for a private word with Miss Bradshaw. His teasing was having the desired effect before the bull butted in. Ran, indeed. He liked it. Ran and Min Avery. He liked it very much. And not least because the way it slipped out showed she'd been thinking about him.

"When should I return for the other chair," he asked. "In 12 days?"

"Yes. I'll have it ready by the 6th of November. Shall we say the 7th to be safe?"

As he prepared to climb into the phaeton, the bull crowded in on him, ostensibly to make a hand to give him a leg up. "Be very careful, Lord Avery," he muttered. "My cousin has relatives who will protect her honour."

"I promise you," he said, keeping his own voice low, "I will guard her honour with my life."

The bull looked at him long and hard, then nodded. "Fair enough." And he gave Candle a heave, propelling him up into the phaeton.

Candle leaned down to take the reins from the worker.

"Good day, Mr Whitlow. Your humble servant, Miss Bradshaw. I will see you in a fortnight."

Chapter four: Families have their say

It was a long fortnight. Candle was busy, but he still found time to dream when he wasn't attending to his business interests and the estate, and choosing presents to send to Miss Bradshaw. He wanted her and her family to be in no doubt about his intentions. That meant he couldn't send her anything that would be inappropriate between a gentleman and an unmarried lady, even if everything was addressed to her mother or her father. Clearly, the cousin was ready to believe that Candle was up to no good. If he sent Miss Bradshaw anything too personal, the cousin would be after him with one of those wheelwright's mallets Candle had seen at the workshop.

But flowers were very ordinary. He rather thought he was doing better than that.

Meanwhile, the news from Europe was bad. Napoleon had won a major battle, devastating the armies of the third coalition. From the reports in the newspaper, the allies had suffered devastating losses at a place called Ulm. Candle looked it up on the map in his study.

"Randall, dear." His mother's voice made him jump. Her new chair let her glide around the ground floor on her own. She loved the freedom it gave her, but he still wasn't used to her sudden appearances. Perhaps he should ask Miss Bradshaw if there was a way to make the wheels squeak.

"Mother," he said. He bent to kiss her check and examined her face as he did. She was too thin, too pale, and the pain lines around her eyes were highlighted by dark shadows from too many nights without sleep. "How are you, my dear?"

"Well, thank you, Randall," she said, as she always did.

"You haven't been sleeping. Won't you take the medicine the doctor gave you? Just for one night?"

"It gives me bad dreams, Randall, and makes my head feel as if it is stuffed with cotton wool. Now do not fuss, dear one. It is a mother's job to fret over her child, not the other way around. I came to ask if you would run some messages for me when you go into Bath."

"Willingly, of course. What do you need?"

"I have a list."

It came as no surprise that most of what Mother wanted was for her garden. She was so looking forward to the new outdoor chair so she could supervise the plantings of the new bulbs she wanted him to buy. Her favourite nursery company had sent her a catalogue with hand-tinted tulips and crocuses. "They will be so pretty next year, Randall."

"You'll be careful, won't you? You will stay indoors if the weather is unkind? You will wrap up warm?"

"You are fussing again, my son," she scolded.

"You're very precious to me, Mother. May I not look after you?"

"You need a wife of your own to fuss over, I think. What of this Miss Bradshaw who made the chairs?"

"Miss Bradshaw?" Sometimes, Candle thought, his mother lifted thoughts right out of people's heads. How else would she know to ask that question? Confined to a bed and now a chair, she didn't see him around the estate organising deliveries to Bath, and she didn't have access to his correspondence.

"Don't look surprised, dearest. I am your mother. I know you better than anyone on earth. Your eyes go soft and misty when you mention her, and you have mentioned her several times every day since you came home."

She frowned a little. "I do hope you have resolved whatever came between you last time."

"Last time." What did she know about last time?

"Lady Cresthover wrote to me when you began to show an interest in Miss Bradshaw at Lady Cresthover's house party. A charity case of her daughter's, she said, and perhaps not suitable for a peer's son. But Lady Cresthover is a silly woman, so I discounted that. And then she wrote again to say that you had broken the poor girl's heart by courting her for her money. Which is patently ridiculous, Randall, because you would never do such a thing."

"I hope you told her so, Mother."

"Oh no, Randall dearest. Such gossips are so useful when one does not go out in Society much. As long as one keeps in mind that 90% of what they say is exaggerated and the rest is invented. I would not discourage Lady Cresthover's letters for the world. So have you resolved your difficulties with Miss Bradshaw?"

"I am working on it, Mother. You wouldn't mind?"

"Mind you marrying into a trade family? Darling boy, I am from a merchant family, which the gentry consider to be the same thing. Except your father married me for my money, whereas you are in love, are you not?"

"I think so," Candle said. "I think I have loved her since I first met her."

Lord Avery must have left an order at the shop, because more flowers arrived the day after he left, and more the day after that. Then the first package arrived: an edition of Mother Goose Tales, Robert Sanders' translation of Charles Perrault's fairy tales. The story of the Little Glass Slipper was among them. It had clearly been much read.

"Who is it from," Mama asked.

"There is no note," Min told her, but she had no doubt who had sent the package.

The flowers kept arriving, different each day. The miscellaneous baskets of the first day gave way to blue salvia and tea roses the second, wrapped in ivy and ferns. The ivy and ferns reappeared on the third day with zinnia flowers, and on the fourth—the day the book arrived—irises.

The bouquet of white roses and daisies on the fifth day had the usual ivy and ferns, but sprigs of myrtle and rosemary had been added, and after that, the flowers changed every day but they always came with ivy, ferns, myrtle, and rosemary.

On the sixth day, two brace of pheasants, a basket of apples, and a large bag of walnuts were delivered to the kitchen, this time with a note to Min's mother. "Viscount Avery begs that Mrs Bradshaw will accept this small offering from his estate."

Mama raised her eyebrows, but said nothing. That day, the flowers were delicate orchids, and the following brought anemones.

On the next day, she was hovering in the hall when the yellow roses arrived.

"More flowers from your young man, Minerva?" It was Mama, watching her from the stairs.

Minerva, sure her smile was beyond fatuous, pretended to sniff the roses until she could school her face to calm again.

"He is not mine, Mama. He is just amusing himself, as the aristocracy do."

She hurried away before Mama could say more. The skins had arrived at the workshop the previous evening, and she had a chair to cover.

The ninth day brought hollyhocks and a jug of cider addressed to Papa, prompting Papa to ask what "young Avery is after, trying to turn me up sweet."

"Minnie, Uncle George," Daniel explained. "Lord Avery is after Minnie."

"I can see that," Papa growled, "but what does he mean by it, that's what I want to know."

"He means to court her, George," Mama said. "That's what the myrtle means. Myrtle for marriage, ivy for faithfulness, ferns for sincerity, and rosemary for remembrance."

Min had taken four days to realise that Lord Avery's choices were deliberate, and had been able to decipher only some of the messages. Mama might have said she knew what they meant!

"He sent blue salvia and tea roses first; that's 'you occupy my thoughts, always'. Then zinnias for absent friends; 'I miss you.' The day after that, he sent irises; 'your friendship means so much to me'. He sent white roses and daisies on the day he added the myrtle and rosemary. White roses and daisies are both for innocence. 'I remember you are an innocent, and I intend marriage.' He followed those with anemones, which mean fragile or forsaken. With the myrtle and the rest, he means, 'My heart is fragile; do not forsake me.' Orchids for beauty the next day; 'I find you beautiful'. Then yellow roses for friendship and caring; 'I care for you and wish to have your friendship.' Today's blossom is hollyhock. That means ambition; 'I strive to win you'."

Daniel and Papa stared at Mama, and then turned to contemplate Min.

"I had better put these in water," Min said, wanting time on her own to think about what Mama had said. Did Lord Avery really mean all of that?

But even if he did, he was still a peer, and the gap between them was still too large.

Now that Mother had opened the way, Candle found himself talking to her about Miss Bradshaw. He'd never told anyone about the ill-fated house party, but he could make a story of it without bitterness now that he knew that he and his beloved had been the victims of malicious scheming.

"Why would they do it, Mother?" he wondered.

"I can think of a number of reasons, Randall. Some people like to break anything pretty or pleasing. They cannot stand for other people to be happy. From what you say, the brother thought of you as his natural victim. And the sister probably felt the same about Miss Bradshaw. I daresay the pair of you ignored them, and they would hate that."

Candle nodded. "I wouldn't even remember them being there if Miss Kitteridge had not been the one to tell me Miss Bradshaw was gone."

"Another possibility is that Miss Kitteridge had hopes of her own. It was about that time my brother retired to England, and she may have thought you would inherit—which you did, of course, though not until this year."

"I don't think so, she wasn't even nice to me... although..." Candle stared into the past for a moment. "Actually, around six months later she tried to... warm the acquaintance, I suppose. All of a sudden, she seemed to be at all the events I went to, and she stopped making cutting remarks and—I got the impression she wanted me as part of her court."

"I expect she hadn't been in town till then."

Candle agreed. Kitteridge and his sister had come up to London for the Season.

"So what did you do," Mother asked.

Candle flushed a little. "Seeing her reminded me of losing Miss Bradshaw. So I stopped going into Society until she left London again."

"And then look what she did next."

"I don't know what she did next."

"She married Baron Norton, Randall dear. And gave birth to a very premature baby five months after the wedding. A son, after Lord Norton's previous four wives had failed to have any children at all."

"Good Heavens, Mother. Are you suggesting what I think you are suggesting?"

"I think you were Miss Kitteridge's first choice to father her cuckoo. On the whole, she did not do too badly in choosing Lord Norton."

"You shock me, Mother. You think him a preferable husband to me?"

"I think she would have found you far less malleable than she expected. And Lord Norton suffered a seizure at the christening party after over-imbibing in celebratory punch. He was dead before his heir was six months old. Yes, she didn't do too badly at all. Of course, the money is in trust for the little heir, and she is not a trustee. Or the boy's guardian. But Lord Norton left her a moderate income and a house in Bath as her widow's portion."

"How on earth do you know all this, Mother."

Mother smiled, gently. "I told you Lady Cresthover has her uses."

Sunday morning brought carnations, a mixed bunch of red and white. "'You are sweet and lovely, and my heart aches for you'," Mama translated.

After the Sunday service, Daniel found Min in the conservatory, sketching an improvement to the gearing that moved the wheels on a Merlin chair.

"What's that you've got? Something for one of your chairs?" he asked.

"A gearing," she said, shortly, but he didn't take the hint.

"I'm glad I found you alone. Are Uncle George and Aunt Gavriella..." he looked around as if he was expecting them to leap out from behind one of the potted ferns.

"Papa is resting, and Mama is sitting with him."

Daniel looked alarmed, and Min hastened to reassure him. "He is just tired. You have been working long hours, and he is not a young man."

"Yes. It has been hard on him, but you know how he is. He needs to watch over everything." Daniel shook his head. "I've told him he needs to slow down. But he won't."

"He will soon. He says he plans to retire once this contract is signed. When do you expect that?"

"We'll have the order done tomorrow, so that will be the worst of it. We won't be able to relax till the client has finished inspections, but by the end of the week we'll know for certain whether the contract is going ahead." Daniel grimaced. "I don't know, though. He has talked about retirement before, but it has never happened."

"Mama has never been in favour before," Min told him. "This time, she is saying it is time to let go. She knows you can handle it. I know you can handle it. Even Papa knows. You are an excellent manager, and of course it will all be yours one day."

She had resented that, when she was younger; being overlooked as an heir to the carriage works just because she was female. But building the chair business had taught her her father's decision to choose Daniel to inherit was a practical one. The buyers wanted to deal with a man. The suppliers wanted to deal with a man. The workers wanted to deal with a man. At every turn, she had to prove herself, struggle against their preconceptions, and—even then—often call her father or her cousin to back her up.

She was slowly building a reputation and a set of relationships that made those help calls less necessary, but her father's support meant she remained in business while she did so.

"Thank you, Minnie. That means a lot to me, to have you say that."

"So what did you want to say to me, Daniel?"

Uncharacteristically, Daniel looked at his feet. "Minnie, I was wondering, are you going to accept Lord Avery?"

No, she wasn't, but she choked on saying so. "He has not asked me, Daniel."

"Aunt Gavriella says he will. She is generally right, you know."

"It would not work, Daniel, you know that. They can put up with us if we stay in our place, the upper classes. But if we dare to think we are as good as they are..." She trailed off. Daniel had been to a school for gentlemen. He knew how the gentry treated their sort.

"Perhaps. Well, what about Billingham?"

"Are you trying to marry me off, Daniel?"

"Minnie, you have to see. If your father retires and moves away, you can't stay here. You can't go on working in the yard, and you can't go on living in the same house as me. There. That's what I came to say."

His back was stiff with embarrassment as he left.

Min sat by herself for a long time. Of course she couldn't stay. Cousins though they were, and raised as brother and sister, they could not live under the one roof without Mama and Papa in the house.

As soon as Daniel said so, she realised it. Mama and Papa planned to retire to a country village where Mama could have a garden and, Papa said, where Daniel wouldn't feel Papa breathing down his neck.

But she hadn't considered how that might affect her. How foolish.

When the last of the order was filled the next day, Papa took the rest of the afternoon off.

"Papa, may I walk with you?" Min asked.

"Leaving early, daughter?" Papa said. "Yes, walk with me." He offered her his arm, and they set off down the road together. "I want to ask you about Lord Avery," Papa said. "Roses, this morning, was it? What does Mama say about that?"

"Buds of moss roses with lily of the valley. 'Confessions of love to one who is sweet', Mama said." She mightn't want Lord Avery's pursuit, but she couldn't help be touched.

"Do you like him, daughter?"

"It does not matter, Papa. He is a viscount, and I am a carriage-maker's daughter. It would not work."

"Is he a good man, Little Owl?" Papa hadn't called her 'Little Owl' in years. It was his pet name for her, a reference to the familiar of the goddess she was named for.

"I think he is, Papa. But he is still a viscount. Papa, have you thought about where you and Mama will go when you retire?"

"I have promised Mama a garden. I have promised Daniel that I won't look over his shoulder. And I've promised myself I'll be close enough to Bath to come back if Daniel needs me." Papa laughed at his own reluctance to let go.

"Anywhere in particular, Papa?"

Papa shook his head. "We haven't started looking, yet. After Christmas. After Christmas we will decide a place and a date. Do you have a place you would like, daughter?"

"I do not mind, Papa. As long as it has a workshop big enough for me to make my chairs."

"You should be making babies, not chairs," Papa grumbled. "Marry your viscount or choose another man, and give me and Mama grand-babies."

"I would marry a man who would let me make my chairs," Min said.

"Ah Min. Your Mama was right. She told me that if I encouraged you I would end up breaking your heart. Min. Little Owl. Face facts. Women aren't meant to make carriages, even your little ones. I've let you make your chairs and sell them, and a very good job you have done of it too. I've been very proud of you. But a man doesn't want his wife to go out to work."

"You let Mama work in the harness shop," Min protested.

"Remember that, do you? I had no choice, Min. We didn't have the money, when we started out, to hire a good harness maker. Mama was the best. But as soon as I could, I replaced her so she could stay home. A man doesn't want his wife to go out to work. Looking after the home, visiting her friends. That's enough."

Not for me, Min wanted to say, but Papa kept talking.

"No, Min, give up this notion and look around for a husband. I don't blame you for not wanting Billingham. How a bright man like his father has such a foolish son is beyond me. But come out of your workshop sometimes. Go to a few dinners and parties. Meet people. Look around. What do you say, Min? It'll be fun."

Chapter five: News from abroad

Candle arrived in Bath on the evening of the 6th, and had to fight the urge to go immediately in search of Miss Bradshaw. He wandered down to the florist shop. Mrs Brown, the florist, greeted him with enthusiasm.

"Have the deliveries gone as planned?" he asked, and was assured that flowers had been delivered every morning. He and Mrs Brown had spent nearly two hours, the week before last, planning the flowers to send and the order to send them.

"My delivery boy tells me that the whole household waits each morning to see what's next," Mrs Brown said. "It's the Christmas Roses for tomorrow, sir?"

Candle nodded. 'I am all anxiety until I see you,' they meant. The large pot of honey from the estate's hives should have been delivered this morning. He had sent a note presenting his compliments to Mr Bradshaw, and asking leave to call on him tomorrow afternoon. Half his anxiety was for what Mr Bradshaw might say, and the rest for his beloved. Had his persistent assault by flower and food softened her towards him? He could only hope so.

He made his way back to the White Hart Inn, surprised at the number of people on the streets. His friend Michaels was in the crowd in front of the inn.

"There's been a great battle," he told Candle, not bothering with greetings. "Someone who's come in on the coach is going to read the Gazette. They're just setting him up in a window so everyone can hear."

"Where? A battle where?" Candle was torn between staying to listen and rushing across the river to assure himself of Miss Bradshaw's safety.

"A sea battle. A victory, they say, but Nelson is dead."

The great Nelson, dead. It was hard to believe.

"Is it true?" Candle turned at the new voice. Miss Bradshaw's cousin, with a much older man. "Is Nelson dead?"

"So I'm told, Mr Whitlow." Candle introduced Whitlow and Michaels, and was in turn introduced to the older man, Mr Bradshaw. He was built on the same powerful lines as his nephew, but had eyes as grey as his daughter's.

"So you're Lord Avery," he said.

"Quiet," Michaels interrupted. "He's starting."

From an open window on the second floor of the inn, a stout man in a florid waistcoat began, "Dispatches, of which the following are Copies, were received at the Admiralty this day, at one o'clock a.m., from Vice-Admiral Collingwood, Commander in Chief of his Majesty's ships and vessels of Cadiz."

At the words 'Commander in Chief', a murmur ran through the crowd, followed by whispered commands to hush.

"Euryalus, off Cape Trafalgar. October 22nd, 1805," the reader continued.

He paused, and looked out at the people, silent below him.

"Sir,— The ever-to-be-lamented death of Vice-Admiral, Lord Viscount Nelson, who in the late conflict with the enemy fell in the hour of victory, leaves to me the duty..."

The crowd listened for the most part in hushed silence, though they cheered when the reader reported, "...it pleased the Almighty Disposer of all events to grant His Majesty's arms a complete and glorious victory," and groaned at, "His Lordship received a musket ball in his left breast... and soon after expired."

It took nearly 40 minutes to read the two closely printed sides of the newsheet. Afterwards, the crowd dispersed in small clumps, all discussing the news.

"I don't know whether to cheer or weep," Candle said.

"I know, lad," Mr Bradshaw agreed. "Napoleon has suffered a heavy loss, that's certain. But Nelson is a heavy loss to our dear England."

Michaels muttered something about an appointment and left. Candle didn't fancy going into the inn. The noisy public bar or a lonely private room—neither appealed. For want of a better option, he walked with Mr Bradshaw and Whitlow around the Roman Baths and past the Abbey towards the bridge.

"So you're the young lord who has turned my house into a flower shop and who wants to come and see me tomorrow," Mr Bradshaw said.

No time like the present. "Yes, Sir. I wish to ask your permission to court your daughter, Sir."

"You're already courting my daughter, seemingly. Unless you are carrying on a clandestine affair with my dear wife." Mr Bradshaw looked stern, but one of Candle's colonels had displayed just such a twinkle when apparently chewing out a subordinate he was pleased with.

"After all, Uncle, he has sent Aunt Gavriella all those flowers and most of the notes," Whitlow offered, finding his own remark enormously amusing.

"You'd better come to dinner, then," Mr Bradshaw said, and led the way onto the bridge. "Do you think this victory will stop the Corsican?"

"It will at least stop him from invading England until he has built some more ships," Candle said.

"Yes," Whitlow agreed. "We don't know the details yet, but whatever ships we've lost will be replaced by the ships we've captured from the French and the Spanish."

"Nothing will make up for the loss of Nelson," Mr Bradshaw said.

Candle nodded, but was still thinking about stopping Napoleon. "We can hold Napoleon off by sea, but we'll need to meet him on land to end his ambitions."

They continued discussing the battle and its implications for the rest of the walk, until Mr Bradshaw opened his front door and ushered Candle inside.

Miss Bradshaw and a much older woman, clearly related, were just descending the stairs.

"My love," Mr Bradshaw told his wife, "I have brought Lord Avery for dinner, and we have sad but glorious news."

It was Lord Avery. Here. In her house. She had been steeling herself to be indifferent to him tomorrow, when he came for the chair. Now was too early. She wasn't ready.

He smiled at her, and her knees turned to jelly. Yesterday he'd sent asters ('I love you'), a watercolour of a country house, and a note that said his mother had asked him to send her mother a painting she'd made of their home, Avery Hall.

This morning, it had been damask roses and stephanotis, plus a large pot of honey. The flowers, Mama said, meant 'I send these flowers as an ambassador of my love, and I look to be happy in marriage'. The note that asked for an interview with Papa needed no interpreter.

And now he was here. In her house. Almost a whole day early.

Something they were saying caught her ear; something about Nelson?

"Dead?" Mama was asking.

"Just a moment," Papa said. He turned to the butler. "Heath, assemble the staff in the drawing room. They'll want to hear this."

Min took a seat with Mama in the drawing room, and—once the house's staff were gathered—listened to the report of the battle, the great victory, and the great loss.

Lord Avery stayed with the two women after the staff had dispersed and Papa and Daniel had gone upstairs to change for dinner.

"Will this loss of all his navy stop Napoleon, do you think?" Mama asked.

"It will stop him invading us, Ma'am," Candle answered, "at least for the moment. It won't stop him rampaging all over the continent."

Mama had more questions, and Min was content to sit and watch Mama and Lord Avery talk. The other two joined them and they all went in to a much delayed dinner.

Napoleon and Nelson continued to dominate the conversation. Lord Avery was knowledgeable and ready to defend his own opinion, but also willing to change his mind if someone else offered a persuasive argument. And he showed no signs of distinguishing between the arguments of the women and those of the men; none of the condescension Min was used to from every man she knew. Even Papa and Daniel were not quite exceptions, since she was sure they'd just learned to keep their condescension veiled from her and Mama.

By the second setting, Min had forgotten her wariness. Lord Avery behaved as if he came to dinner every day, and the family all treated him as if he belonged.

"Cook used your honey in this, lad," Papa told him, taking a spoonful of the syllabub.

"It is good, isn't it," Lord Avery replied. "My beekeeper tells me that this year's honey is particularly strong in orchard flavours. The fruit trees blossomed well, I'm told."

Mama's eyes crinkled at the corners, as she smiled at Lord Avery. "I have not thanked you, yet, for all the lovely flowers you sent me. Such charming messages."

He took her teasing in his stride. "A fitting tribute to your beauty, Mrs Bradshaw."

After dinner, Min reluctantly left the dining room with Mama. What would Papa and Daniel say to Lord Avery with the women out of the room? What would he say to them?

"I like your Lord Avery, child," Mama said, breaking into her thoughts. "But he is still an aristocrat, however nice he may be."

"He is not mine, Mama. I am not foolish enough to think I could marry a peer."

"I worry, my love. I do not want to see you hurt. And I cannot help but remember what happened when we sent you to school."

"So, Lord Avery," Mr Bradshaw began, as soon as the door shut behind the two women. "You want permission to court my daughter."

Candle hadn't thought to have this conversation in front of a witness, but if that was the way Mr Bradshaw wanted it, so be it.

Mr Bradshaw correctly interpreted his glance at Whitlow. "Daniel is Minerva's cousin and my heir. If anything happens to me, you'll be dealing with him."

Candle nodded in acknowledgement. "Yes, Sir. I want permission to court your daughter."

"Rumour has it that you're a warm man, thanks to your uncle. Think you can keep it?"

"Yes, Sir. I think I can. I'm not a man of profligate habits, and I'm working hard to learn the estate my father left me and the business my uncle left me. I mean to make a success of them both."

It was Mr Bradshaw's turn to nod. "So I'm told." To Candle's surprised look, he said, "I asked questions, lad. She's my one ewe lamb. Of course I asked questions."

"I understand." Little though Candle liked the idea of someone poking around and asking about him, he did understand Mr Bradshaw's need to protect his daughter. "And were you content with the answers, Sir?"

Mr Bradshaw didn't answer him directly. "She says she won't have you. She says that the middle sort and the peerage don't mix, and that a marriage between you won't work. What do you say to that?"

"I hope to change her mind," Candle said. "I think we can make it work. Yes, the Society cats will have their claws out, but we don't need to live in Society. And my mother and I will love her just as she is."

"Love, is it? You said so with your flowers. Do you say it straight, lad? To me, and to Daniel here?"

Candle met his eyes and said, firmly, "I love her. I love your daughter, Sir."

"Well, Daniel?" Mr Bradshaw asked.

"I'd say give him your blessing, Uncle, and wish him luck. She's stubborn, my cousin. You'll find you need all the luck you can get."

"My blessing? No. No offense, lad, but I'll save my blessing for my lass if she decides to accept you. She'll need it, and a powerful load of luck. Mixing your sort and mine; I've seen a lot of sorrow come that way. But I won't deny my Minerva if you're the one she wants. You can court her, Lord Avery. But as to where the luck lies..."

Mr Bradford shook his head and poured them all another glass of port.

Candle exerted himself to be agreeable, and by the time they joined the ladies, Candle and Daniel Whitlow were on first-name terms.

Miss Bradshaw was at a desk in the corner, and Mrs Bradshaw sat sewing by the fire. Her tambour was half filled with colourful flowers, bursting joyously across the canvas.

Candle stopped to admire the embroidery, then looked over Miss Bradshaw's shoulder. Engineering designs. He might have known.

"It's gearing of some kind," he said.

She went to put her work away. "No, don't let me stop you working," he said. "But would you explain it to me?"

An hour later when he took his leave, he was much more knowledgeable about the benefits of differential gearing. He'd found it strangely compelling—Miss Bradshaw was experimenting with progressive changes in size so that less strength was needed to work the mechanism, while still keeping the mechanism light enough and small enough not to weigh down the chair.

They'd agreed he would come to the works in the morning. Candle was keen to get home to Avery Hall with the news of the battle, and he'd leave the White Hart as soon as the morning mail coach arrived with the newspapers from London.

"I'll bring copies for you, Sir," he told Mr Bradshaw.

Crossing the foyer of the hotel, he was hailed by a peremptory, "Lord Avery!"

He turned to see a dumpling of a woman whose generous figure was amplified by a plethora of floating scarves, fringes and ruffles in shades of purple. Lady Cresthover. She was bearing down on him, her daughter and Lady Norton in her wake. For a fleeting moment he contemplated pretending not to hear and bolting for the stairs. He resisted the temptation. The old besom was his mother's friend. Sort of.

He pasted on his best social smile, and gave each lady a small bow. "Lady Cresthover. Miss Cresthover. Lady Norton."

"Lord Avery, what brings you to Bath? How is your dear mother? And what do you think of this terrible news about Nelson? Do you think Napoleon is finished, as they are saying? How long are you in Bath?"

The questions came in quick succession, while Lady Cresthover took him by the arm and herded him into a private parlour.

"The girls and I are just about to have supper. You will join us, Lord Avery." This was a royal command, not a question. When Candle protested that he had already eaten, he was bidden to sit and have a glass of wine, and to answer Lady Cresthover's questions.

An experienced officer of His Majesty's Coldstream Guard should show courage under fire. Besides, he was considerably taller than he'd been twelve years ago, last time Lady Cresthover had rapped him on the head with her formidable thimble. She would have trouble reaching his head now.

"Certainly, my Lady," he said. "Could you repeat them one at a time, please?"

It was an hour before he was finally able to make his excuses, citing the trip he needed to take the following morning. By then, he'd drawn several conclusions.

Lady Cresthover's incessant gossip, though often ill-informed, was not ill-intended, but Lady Norton was a cat of quite a different colour. Lady Norton had her knife out for Miss Bradshaw—she had made several derogatory comments, which Candle judged it best to ignore or deflect, since any defence would just encourage the lady to make trouble.

Lady Cresthover, on the other hand, proclaimed Miss Bradshaw, 'a sweet girl, quite the lady, and a very good friend to poor Nelly Maybury, when her husband died'.

And Miss Cresthover also came to Miss Bradshaw's defence, insisting that Miss Bradshaw was far more of a lady 'than some who lay claim to the term'.

Lady Cresthover and her daughter might be allies if the new Viscountess Avery wanted to go into Society.

Oh yes, and he'd learned one more thing. Lady Norton's schoolgirl nickname of Kitty Cat was an insult to felines everywhere.

Lord Avery collected the chair and was gone from Bath by 11 o'clock in the morning. Min found the rest of the day sadly flat. He hadn't said anything lover-like as the chair was tied to the back of his carriage, but the warmth in his eyes had set her tingling.

Perhaps she only imagined it. Perhaps, too, she imagined the press of his fingers when he said, as he took his farewell, "I very much look forward to seeing you and your mother in three weeks, Miss Bradshaw."

That morning's floral tribute spoke of anxiety. If he felt anxiety, he didn't show it. She was the one who was anxious, her heartbeat speeding up when she thought of him, the heat igniting in her belly at the mere thought of the warmth in his eyes.

She was the one who couldn't keep her mind on her work, who had lost interest in food, who lay awake at night remembering every gesture, every word, every look.

She would not fall in love with a peer. She could not. She was not so foolish. Was she?

Chapter six: A visit to the country

The flowers kept coming, the type repeated, but in different combinations each day. Each day, Mama interpreted the message for her, and Daniel took great delight in offering an alternative reading. According to Mama, Christmas roses and asters with sprays of mimosa meant 'My concealed love is now disclosed. How will it be received?' Daniel suggested, 'I wish to hide because the thought of love makes me anxious.' Blue salvia, irises and yellow roses meant 'I think of you, miss you, and long for your friendship' to Mama. But Daniel claimed it meant 'When I think of you, I miss having friends'.

The gifts of produce from the estate kept coming too, prompting Cook to tell Daniel (who passed it on to Min) that she hoped Miss wouldn't turn the young Lord down too soon, because his presents were so useful.

Walking home from the workshop one afternoon, Polly in attendance, Min had to stop suddenly to avoid a fashionably-dressed young woman who burst out of a shop door without looking, to stand frozen in the road, her hands clenched at her sides and her face stiff with the effort of holding back tears.

Min, who had been about to circle around her, took a second look. "Cara? What's wrong? May I help?"

Caroline Cresthover had been closer to a friend than any of the other girls at the select girl's seminary Min's parents had sent her to.

"Min? Min Bradshaw? Oh Min, if I had stayed in the shop I would have killed that woman." The tears had escaped, spilling down Cara's cheeks.

The shop door opened to let out a maid carrying a reticule that matched Cara's pelisse. Min could see past her to Lady Norton and a gaggle of her friends. Kitty Cat was clearly up to her usual tricks.

"Do not let her see that she upsets you," Min counselled Cara. "Come; let us move away where they cannot see us."

"I know I should be charitable, but..."

"Never mind being charitable. Just do not give her a stick to beat you with." Min turned to the maid. "Do you have a handkerchief for your mistress? Here, Cara, dry your tears and let's go and have tea and tear Kitty Cat's character to tiny little shreds."

Over tea, Cara confided that Vivi Norton loved to commiserate with her about being 'on the shelf', which Cara mostly ignored. But today's nasty remarks had included a series of snippets about the activities of one Captain Marsh who, according to Lady Norton, had cut a swathe through the widows of London and was about to announce his engagement to a debutante of 17.

"And Vivi says she is blonde and slender, and everyone knows that slender blondes are more fashionable." Cara, whose hair and eyes were brown, and who was generously curved, began to cry again.

"Captain Marsh is special to you?" Min ventured. It seemed a safe enough guess.

"He said we would announce our engagement as soon as he had the approval of his grandfather. His father is the third son of the Earl of Scuncester. He said we had to keep our courtship secret in case his grandfather did not approve."

"If it was a secret, Cara, how did Vivi find out?"

Cara blushed. "I might have hinted. Just a little. Only in the strictest confidence, and only because she teased me so about being twenty and unmarried."

Several cream cakes cheered Cara up. She was not, Min deduced, particularly attached to Captain Marsh. His status as the grandson of an Earl and his professed interest in marrying her seemed to be the sum total of his attractive features. Cara found his conversation boring, his lack of dancing skill annoying, and his repeated attempts to kiss her frightening.

"Mama said I should never be alone with a man because he would try to kiss me, and then I would be ruined," she told Min. "I wasn't even alone with Captain Marsh; well, not really alone. The first time was in the garden, and there were other people there, but it was dark and we couldn't see them. And Mama was right. He did try to kiss me. I did not let him, though." She nodded, pleased with herself.

"And then the next week he stopped me in the hall at a party. He said he was dying of love for me, which was very romantic, I thought. And he asked me to meet him outside and tried to kiss me again when I said no. I told him I did not want to be ruined. He said I would not be ruined for just one kiss. That was when he said he planned to marry me. He said it was alright to kiss the man you were going to marry. But Mama came and he went away."

"Then what happened?" Min was finding the whole saga morbidly fascinating.

"He kept trying to get me on my own so he could kiss me. And in the end, I let him. It was not very nice." Cara frowned. "It was wet. And I could not breathe properly. Has anyone kissed you, Min?"

Min shook her head, mostly to dislodge a sudden wish to know how nice Lord Avery's kiss might be. Certainly she had, on several occasions, seen Mama and Papa kiss, and Mama seemed to like it very well.

"I do not recommend it," Cara said.

"Perhaps Captain Marsh is not very good at it," Min suggested.

Cara shrugged. "Anyway, then he went off to London. He said that he could not write because we could not yet announce our betrothal, but that I should just wait and he would come back. He did not mean it, did he Min?"

"I do not think so, from what you have told me, Cara."

"Well, I do not care. But I would have liked to have one over that cat Vivi. You know that she had to marry? She would have been ruined if she did not, my Mama says. But now she is Baroness Norton and she takes precedence over me, and it is just not fair, Min."

Cara helped herself to another cream cake, which seemed to console her.

"Vivi is not very popular you know, Min. I only spend time with her because she is my cousin. Most of the girls we were at school with do not like her at all." This seemed to console Cara even more. "I know, come to my afternoon at home tomorrow. The girls would be so pleased to see you."

Min refused, but Cara was so enthusiastic about the idea that, in the end, she went. To her surprise, she enjoyed herself, and even accepted an invitation to walk in the Sydney Gardens with a group of the ladies later that week.

It seemed that most of them had suffered under the rule of Vivi Kitteridge's little group. Min, sunk in her own misery, had never realised that the school was split into two groups. On the one side, the vast majority, trying hard not to be noticed. On the other, Kitty Cat and her three disciples.

But outside of the enclosed environment of the school, the small group of bullies had lost their power. Even Cara, most of the time, ignored Lady Norton's spitefulness, though she couldn't completely cut herself off from her cousin.

"Randall, darling, do stop pacing. You have been to the window so many times the carpet is developing a groove." Mother was smiling. His nervousness amused her. How nice for Mother.

"I wish they had let me escort them," Candle said. Had he met them in Bath, they would be here by now, or—at the very least—he would know the delay was because they had left Bath late, and not because of any of the disasters along the way he could picture all too clearly.

"Do you think she'll like her room," he asked.

"Randall, you have asked me the same question three times in the last hour. And driven Mrs Howard nearly demented in changing Miss Bradshaw's room six times in as many days, moving furniture in and then out again, and I do not know what else. I know you want everything to be perfect, my love, but just relax. I'm sure your Miss Bradshaw will like her room."

"My Lord." It was the butler. "Young Jem has just arrived my Lord." Jem was the youngest groom, and had been posted on a hill overlooking the road from Bath, as an early warning system.

"They're coming?"

"Yes, my Lord. A chaise, my Lord, coming fast."

Not too fast, he hoped. That bend at the bottom of the hill could be tricky at speed. He should have had the curve reformed in the summer.

"Whatever you are worrying about now, Randall, don't," Mother said.

The chaise arrived safely at the foot of the stairs, and Candle was at the door with an umbrella almost before it had come to a stop. Daniel descended first, but stepped under the umbrella a footman offered him and waved to invite Candle to hand down first Mrs Bradshaw, then her daughter, and then the maid, Polly.

He handed Mrs Bradshaw over to Daniel and escorted Miss Bradshaw inside himself, leaving the footman with a third umbrella to bring the maid in.

Daniel wouldn't stay, saying that he needed to get back to Bath. After a cup of tea and a plate of sandwiches, he took leave of his aunt and cousin.

"I'll be back for you in four days," he told them, then met Candle's eyes over their heads. "You'll take care of my family, Candle," he said; a statement, not a question. Candle agreed, anyway.

Mrs Bradshaw went to rest to recover from the trip. Miss Bradshaw refused the suggestion, and instead closeted herself with Mother to ask questions about the chair. At a loose end, Candle took himself off to his study, but he couldn't settle to work. Not with her in the house at last.

He wanted to show her everything. He wanted to hold her and kiss her till she agreed to stay forever. No. That would frighten her off. But somehow he would find a way to convince her that she belonged with him. She was only here for a few days. He would have to make the most of them.

Lord Avery's mother was a darling. She never complained, though she was clearly often in pain. Instead, she would turn the conversation somewhere else. Min coaxed her into being clear about how the chairs worked for her.

"If anything hurts or is uncomfortable, I want to know so that I can fix it, my Lady."

Afterwards, Min went in search of Lord Avery. The butler directed her to the study, where he was working at a huge old desk, his back to the large window. The fitful rain of the past few days had cleared, and sunlight was pouring over Lord Avery's shoulder onto his work. The light glanced off his red hair, setting gleaming threads on fire.

He felt her gaze and looked up, meeting her eyes with a slowly warming smile that set light to a slow burn in her.

"Miss Bradshaw, please come in."

"I am sorry to disturb your work, Lord Avery."

He rounded the desk and set a chair for her, hovering over her as if he wanted to guide her physically into the seat. Her skin seemed to yearn towards him. She held herself stiffly in check.

"It is about your mother."

Lord Avery's eyes grew concerned, the heat that disturbed her banked for the moment.

"Is there something wrong?"

She hastened to reassure him. "Nothing we cannot fix. She is developing sore patches. Because she is unable to move herself, and because she has no feeling in her lower torso," Min blushed at mentioning such a word to a man. But it needed to be said.

Lord Avery frowned. "I will have a word with her maid. She must be more vigilant. Could we find an unguent or something to soothe...? But you said you could fix it. What is your plan, Miss Bradshaw?"

"What you suggest is good, and I have discussed it with your mother and the maid. But I would like to try something that one of my customers told me about. Would you be able to procure a sheepskin with the wool still on?"

"We keep sheep on the home farm, as well as up on the wolds. I should think I already own any number of sheepskins."

"Sitting on sheepskin may help. And lying on it, as well, in bed."

They talked a little more about the possible benefits, and Lord Avery sent a servant down to the home farm to order at least three skins of various depths and sizes.

"May I show you through the house, Miss Bradshaw?" he asked.

Min panicked. The thought of being alone with him, even in a house full of servants, suddenly seemed overwhelming. She muttered something about resting, and made her escape.

By dinner time, she was ashamed of herself. Lady Avery and Mama had discovered a mutual love of embroidery, and of the language of flowers. When Mama mentioned her hope of soon having a garden, this spread into a deep conversation about methods of cultivation, and what did best in their local climate. Lord Avery suggested a stroll in the picture gallery. Mama waved her compliance without halting what she was saying to Lady Avery. Min took Lord Avery's arm and let him conduct her down the hall.

The gallery stretched across the back of the house. He left her in the doorway while he lit candles in sconces all along the walls, then came back with a candelabra to escort her to the first picture.

The Averys had been at Avery Hall since the dawn of time, it seemed. And all had been recorded in paint for this moment; to look down in scorn and judgement on an interloper of the middle sort who had begun to dream of stepping out of her class.

Lord Avery took them in his stride, telling stories about the people in each portrait, describing them with affection and familiarity. He could, of course. He belonged here.

She nodded, and smiled, going through the motions from behind the wall she'd long since learned to erect. Never before with Lord Avery, though.

Suddenly, two thirds of the way down the long room, he stopped and turned her towards him, his hands on her shoulders.

"This was a stupid idea, wasn't it?" he said. "Look, Miss Bradshaw. Min." He released one shoulder to raise her chin with his finger, so that her eyes looked straight into his. "Min," he repeated, his voice pleading, "they don't matter. You have as many ancestors as I do, you know. All human beings do. But none of them matter, on either side. You matter. We matter. Don't let them come between us."

Lost in his eyes, she couldn't remember why they should. There was only him. Randall. Ran.

He stooped, curling his head down to her height and brushing her lips gently with his. A soft caress of the lips, over too quickly.

She gave a small sound of distress, quickly stifled. He was right to stop. They were alone, unchaperoned. Mama trusted her to behave.

As if he could read her mind, he said, "We had better go back, Min. Your Mama trusts me, and I'm afraid I cannot be trusted too far. I should not be alone with you. Will you...?" He didn't finish his sentence, but just gestured to the door at the far end of the gallery.

She led the way, silently. Her knees did not quite belong to her; she felt as if she needed to carefully plan each step in advance or she would find herself in another room, another house.

As she approached the door, a painting on the other side caught her eye—a man on a horse with the look of Ran. He was older though, and the artist had caught a mood, an expression that she'd never seen on Ran's face. This man's face, Min thought, would fall easily into a sneer or a leer, but never into the kindness that was natural to his son. She didn't need Ran's muttered: "My father, the previous Viscount Avery," to tell the relationship.

Somehow, her earlier discomfort with the array of ancestors had gone, but Ran was tense and miserable beside her. "He was not a good man," she said, afraid when she heard her voice that she'd gone too far.

But Ran nodded. "You're right. He was an indifferent landlord, a neglectful father, and a bad husband. He wasn't a bad man, exactly. He just never grew up."

"A lot of Society men are like that," Min said.

"Yes. When we are children, we think our parents are unique. But he was very ordinary, really."

"He made you unhappy."

"He ignored me, mostly. He spent all of his time in London, and I stayed here at Avery Hall with Mother. I had a wonderful childhood. Then Father took it into his head that he should send me away to school."

She was holding his hand. She wasn't sure how that happened, but she squeezed it. She didn't need to be told that he hated school. Min had been miserable enough as a day pupil. Ran went to Eton, far away from home.

Again, his thoughts had tracked hers. "I lived for the holidays when I could come home."

"Your mother must have missed you."

From his surprised look, he hadn't consider that. "Yes. She was always so calm, I had not thought... But, yes. Poor Mother. I never really came back. Just holidays. I went from school to Oxford, to the Guard."

He looked so sad. She put her arms around him to give him a hug, and his came around her. With her head on his chest, she could hear his heart thumping. He shifted, so his body moved back from hers, and she blushed. How forward he must think her.

One moment Candle had been lost in a sad past, and the next he could think of nothing but the woman in his arms. He'd had to move her away from his groin. He wasn't sure how much Min knew about male anatomy. He'd like nothing better than to teach her, preferably right this minute, what the hardness he was hiding from her was for. No. He had enough sense left to know that he shouldn't take the power of choice away from her.

"Min? We need to go back to our mothers."

She had turned the most delightful pink. He wondered how far it spread then shut that thought off. It was not helping.

"I apologise, Lord..."

"Ssshh." He put a finger on her lips to stop her. "No apologies. I won't apologise to you for desiring you, and you won't apologise for being kind when I needed kindness. And it certainly isn't my fault or yours that you are still my goddess."

She smiled against his finger and he couldn't resist tracing the smile. One day; one day soon, he would feast on those generous lips.

Min asked questions, took measurements, made adjustments, and asked more questions. But by the end of the second day of her visit, she had run out of things she could do unless the rain let up for long enough to take the chair out of doors.

Everywhere she looked, Avery Hall showed signs of coming back from a long period of neglect. Ran said he was spending most of his efforts on improvements to the broader estate, investing so he and his tenants would benefit in future years. But he was clearly also bringing the house back to its former glory. The legacy from the uncle must have been every bit as large as rumour painted it.

After dinner that night, Lady Avery asked Min for some music. "I am not an accomplished pianist, my Lady," Min said.

"She sings very nicely," Mama said.

"Randall, play for Miss Bradshaw," Lady Avery commanded.

So they put their heads together to choose music, then Ran's long fingers coaxed the keys. Min remembered how they felt on her lips. And his eyes held hers as she sang:

> "Ten thousand mile it is a long way
> To leave me here alone,
> To leave me here to sigh and complain
> Where you never will hear my moans, my dear,
> Where you never will hear my moans."

And he replied, in a warm tenor:
"Your moans, my dear, I shall never hear,
No likewise none of your crying.
If I go away, I'll come back again
When from your friends you're free, my dear,
When from your friends you're free."

They finished to applause from the mothers, whom they had quite forgotten.

"The tea tray, I think," said Lady Avery. "Ring the bell, please, Randall."

The rain had cleared the next morning, and Lady Avery insisted on riding the invalid chair to Sunday service, the rest of the party walking alongside.

Min tried to ignore the curious looks of the villagers, and focus on the performance of the chair. It handled the solid ground well, though the footman pushing it struggled when they hit soft ground.

Lady Avery was having a fine time, surrounded by people who flocked to talk to her.

"This is the first time she has taken the chair down to the village," Ran said from behind her. She felt herself warm in his direction, as if he was the sun and she a flower.

"It's a fine thing you do," Ran went on, "this chair building."

She waited. Now he would tell her that it wasn't proper for a viscountess; that she wouldn't need to continue when she was married.

Instead, he introduced her to the Vicar, and then to other people, a sea of strangers who all shook her hand, and smiled, and told her how welcome she was, and how good it was to see Lady Avery out and about.

Lady Avery took the lead on the way home, while Ran gave his right arm to Min and his left to Mama. It was good to see Lady

Avery with colour in her cheeks, laughing up at Wilson the footman who was grinning back as he swerved the chair around the puddles.

"There will be no stopping her now," Ran joked. "Every fine day, she'll be running poor Wilson ragged, all over the garden and in and out of the village."

"She should be enjoying life," Mama commented. "She is a young woman, still."

"On her next birthday she'll be 41," Ran confirmed.

Min hadn't realised how young she was. She must have been little more than a child when Ran was born.

Ran was frowning a little as he watched his mother. Mama patted his arm with her free hand. "Let her enjoy herself, Lord Avery," she told him. "And you enjoy her, too, for the time you have her."

Min tried to peer around Ran. What could Mama mean?

"Did she tell you?" Ran asked.

"Yes, dear. She has had two seizures since the accident, and she has lost a little bit with each one."

"The doctor thinks..." Ran didn't finish.

"I know. She told me," Mama said. "Enjoy the time you have, dear. You are making her happy, with the work on the estate and the way you care for her."

"Randall!" Lady Avery called. "Take Mrs Bradshaw down to the gardener's cottage, my dearest, and ask them for the bulbs I promised her. Miss Bradshaw and I will wait at the lookout."

Ahead, the driveway took a curve to give a view out over the estate, Avery Hall foursquare below. Ran obeyed his instructions, and Wilson took himself a short distance away.

"I wished to speak with you, Miss Bradshaw," Lady Avery said.

Here it comes, Min thought. Now she will tell me I am not good enough for him.

"You will think me an interfering old woman, but please remember that I love my son, and I want what is best for him."

"I know that, Lady Avery."

"He wants to marry you. You know that of course."

Min nodded. She was afraid to speak in case she cried. She liked Lady Avery, and she couldn't blame her for being concerned about the same distance in status that concerned Min. But still, she could feel the tears gathering.

"I wish you would consider it, my dear. I can understand you being worried about the gossip, and I cannot promise you it will be easy, but I wanted to tell you there are two things you need never worry about."

Lady Avery paused as if to let Min comment, but Min still couldn't speak. This was so far from what she expected that she had no words. Lady Avery continued.

"You do not have to worry that Randall is like his father. He looks like his father, but he takes his nature from my family. We give our hearts once, and for a lifetime. He has given his heart to you, Miss Bradshaw. It will be yours forever.

"And, if you are concerned about living with me, do not be. I will not make old bones, though I would love to live long enough to see my grandchildren."

Min found her voice. "Lady Avery, I hope you live to be 100, and no woman in her right mind would be concerned about living with you."

"Then you will consider marrying Randall?"

Min looked down at the frail hands she'd taken in her eagerness to show Lady Avery how she esteemed her. "I am trade. He is a peer. You and I both know what Society will say."

"I do not give a fig for Society, and neither does Randall. But I understand that you must make up your own mind, my dear Minerva. I may call you Minerva, may I not?"

Chapter seven: A proposal and a proposition

Whatever Mother said to Min, she was quiet and thoughtful for the rest of the walk home. Both mothers went for a rest as soon as they'd eaten a nuncheon.

"Would you like to see the succession houses?" Candle asked Min.

He took her the long way around, through the gardens she'd not yet had a chance to see because of the rain. As he'd hoped, they were deserted. All the gardeners were with their families enjoying a Sunday rest.

Avery Hall had three succession houses. One was given over to grape vines that snaked along the walls and looped overhead, and strawberries in pots. One was growing late autumn and early spring vegetables. And in the last one, they saw the first person they'd seen since they left the house. Mugridge, the head gardener, was checking the fire that was used to keep the succession house warm.

He nodded to Candle, and smiled warmly at Min, giving her a somewhat deeper bow. The servants, who adored Mother, had taken Min to their hearts—at first for what her chairs meant to Mother, but then because she was sweet, unassuming, and genuinely interested in them.

"I be just checking this fire, my Lord, Miss. Won't be long."

Candle showed Min along the lines of seedlings—trees, shrubs, and flowers being propagated to fill the garden in spring. True to his word, Mugridge very soon said, "I be off now, then. No-one be coming this way till night time, now, my Lord. Close up when tha leaves, will 'ee?"

Candle promised, and turned back to Min. She looked both apprehensive and amused, with amusement winning.

"He thinks we want to be alone," Candle explained.

"I gathered that," she replied.

"Come. Take the chair near the stove."

It was somewhat battered, but sturdy. She sat in it and he settled himself at her feet.

It was an odd setting for a proposal, but safe. Any place he could be sure of being alone with Min in the house was a place he'd already imagined making love to her in. He wasn't confident that he could control himself if she accepted his proposal. Or even that he would get to the proposal before...

He had to stop that train of thought. The succession house was becoming less safe by the minute. He was already thinking of the logistics of lovemaking here in the dirt among the seedlings. His coat spread to protect her dress... No. Not here. Quite apart from the respect he owed to an innocent and his future viscountess, he had no intention of consummating his desire in front of a hundred glass panes.

"Min, you know what I want to ask you."

"I think I do."

"Will you, Min? Will you make me the happiest of men? Will you marry me?"

"Ran, I am not from your world."

"I know you are too good for me," he joked, "but I'm hoping you're prepared to make the sacrifice."

"Ran, I am serious. I am the daughter of a carriage maker. You are a peer. Society..."

"Min, I love you. If you love me, then Society can go hang itself."

"I want to continue making chairs."

"I hope you will."

"Really? You would not mind?"

"Min, you have a gift. I want you to use it. Say you will marry me, and I'll have the bans read. We can be wed before Christmas."

She withdrew. She didn't move a muscle, but he felt her pulling into herself, away from him.

"Don't, Randall."

His first name in full. That couldn't be good. But he wasn't Lord Avery again, which was a hopeful sign.

"Is that a no, Min?"

She shook her head.

"Is it a yes?"

Another head shake.

"Min?" He came up onto his knees in a single motion, and captured her face between both of his hands, looking into her grey eyes.

She collected herself then, his brave little goddess. "When I come back with the chair, I will give you your answer."

And then she pressed her sweet lips to his and he was lost. With a groan he enfolded her in his arms, slid his hands up behind her head, and deepened the kiss.

It could have been a minute; it could have been months. Time ceased to exist as he explored her mouth and she followed his lead. Her tentative movements, bold and shy at the same time, intoxicated him and he was conscious of nothing but the burning need to sink into her softness. Until a piece of gravel on the path turned as he shifted his knee, and dug into his skin.

He drew away from her with a groan.

Had he done that? Her lips were swollen and red, a sleeve was pulled down baring her shoulder, and one glorious breast was nearly tipped out of her dress. Another nudge, and he'd see...

He blinked, and shook the idea out of his head. "Min, my own dearest love." He had to be calm. She looked as dazed as he felt. Probably more so, given her innocence. If his world was shaken, hers must be reeling.

"I would help you put yourself to rights, beloved. But I don't dare touch you."

She straightened her dress, repinned the lace cap she wore in her hair, rewrapped her shawl around her, all the while sneaking peeks at him and colouring each time their eyes met.

Before they left the succession house, he put a finger on her now clothed arm.

"Min, will you accept my apology, beloved? I meant no disrespect, I promise you. I should never have kissed you. I know how powerfully I react when we touch."

To his surprise, she suddenly grinned. "Ah but Ran, you forget. I kissed you first."

Daniel must have left Bath before dawn. He was at the door by mid-morning, and wouldn't accept Ran's invitation to stop for lunch. Rain was coming, he said, and he wanted to be safely back in Bath before the deluge.

Min, her valise packed with all the notes and drawings she needed to finish the chair, kissed Lady Avery on the cheek, and gave Ran her hand. He lifted it and deliberately placed a kiss in the palm.

"Bring it back to me, Min," he said.

She almost told him, then and there, that she would marry him, but—no. She had to get back to Bath. She would make her decision without his disturbing presence tugging her to fall into his arms.

Neither Daniel nor Mama commented on the kiss. Mama asked after Papa, and then she and Daniel discussed the dispatches about the Navy's victory. They were calling it the Battle of Trafalgar, and nearly 450 British sailors had died. Almost ten times as many died on the other side.

Min didn't contribute. Mostly, she didn't listen. She sat and thought about chair design, and what she needed to do to finish Candle's chair for his mother in time for Christmas.

And all the while her thoughts kept going back to Candle's kiss, and to the answer she would need to give him.

Min strode across the yard, her patens sending sprays of water flying from puddles she ignored in her indignation. Daniel was in the outer office. She didn't trust herself to speak in front of the clerk; she jerked her head towards the inner office, and went through to wait for him.

He was quick to join her, his face wary. "Now, Minnie, what's got your back up?"

"Did you tell..." She caught herself. Took a deep breath. Best to check the facts first.

"Richards has ignored the instructions I left, redrawn my designs, and reworked the chairs for the Barfoot sale. He claims he had your authorisation."

Her cousin's eyes gave him away, sliding evasively to one side. "Now, Minnie. Richards is a good foreman."

"You gave him authorisation to change my work," she said flatly.

"He's highly experienced, Minnie. He said a few changes would save materials and increase our profit."

"A few changes that mean we do not meet the client's specifications and will not make the sale."

"You are exaggerating. He showed me his drawings. Sound carriage design."

"Unsound chair design," she snapped back.

Papa entered the room, saw the two of them, and closed the door behind him.

"What's going on?"

"I want Richards out of my workshop," Min told Papa, not taking her eyes off Daniel.

"She is upset about a few economies that I approved." Daniel put on his 'I am reasonable and you are a female' voice. "Look, Minnie, you have to let go and let us take over. After all, you will leave all this behind you when you marry your Viscount."

"Point one," Min thought she did well to keep her voice calm and level, "I have not accepted Lord Avery's proposal. Point two, if I do accept, he has promised that I can continue making chairs.

Point three, the chair workshop is mine, and you had no right to allow Richards to disobey a direct instruction."

"Well, Minerva. Strictly speaking Daniel is general manager of the whole works," Papa said. The traitor.

She looked at the two of them in silence for a moment. First things first. She needed to deal with the chair disaster.

"Let me explain the problem, gentlemen. Richards has scaled down standard carriage parts." Blank looks. "Scaled them precisely. Without any consideration of the structural integrity of the new thicknesses."

The two men exchanged glances again. Consternation had replaced smug commiseration. Just so, she thought with a grim satisfaction.

"All three chairs will need to be remade if we are not to forego 90 guineas and the chance of future orders. And I am fully committed on Lady Avery's chair." Fortunately, Richards had left that chair alone. She had made every inch of it herself, investing hours. She didn't just want efficient engineering; she wanted a superb piece of furniture. Carved, turned, and polished woodwork for the handle; upholstery in the finest leather with a buttoned back and seat, sewn detail, and cording on the edges.

"I'll see to it, Minnie." Daniel sounded humble, but she couldn't expect that to last. She was so used to his persistent belief in his male superiority that she noticed it only because of the contrast with Ran's respect.

"Very well then. And Richards goes."

"I'll reassign him."

"Thank you." She could be gracious in victory.

She left her menfolk in the office they shared. She wanted to cut the leather for the arms and leave it to relax, and add another coat of polish to the handle. It could be drying while she went out to tea with Cara and her friends. She was cautiously venturing into Society, and finding it less threatening than she expected.

Bother. She had forgotten to tell her father that she wouldn't be walking home with him.

Turning back through the outer office, she started to push the inner door open, and paused.

"Do you think Lord Avery means to let Minnie make her chairs?" That was Daniel.

"Don't be daft. Whoever heard of a viscountess doing that sort of stuff? No he's just saying it. Or he means it now, but will come to his senses soon enough." That was Papa.

"Yes. You should have put a stop to it long ago, Uncle."

"It made her happy. And she's done some good work, you can't deny it."

"It isn't right, though. A woman shouldn't be doing carriage work, Uncle. I'm sorry to hear that Lord Avery is encouraging her."

"You know what they say, lad: 'When a man grows hard between the thighs, he grows soft between the ears.' He's soft on my girl, right enough."

Min had heard enough. Her ears burning, she retreated to her workshop.

Were they right? Ran had sounded so convincing when he spoke of his hope that she would continue her work. But she had always known that marriage would make her dependent on the goodwill of a husband, and the face a man showed before marriage was not always the one his wife saw after.

Could Ran be trusted?

The flowers continued to arrive, and so did presents of produce from Avery Hall. Min didn't need the constant reminders. Ran was a phantom presence wherever she went. Everything she saw or heard, she wanted to share with him. Ran would like this. Ran would find that funny. Ran would be interested.

The nights were worse. Ran had woken something in her. She didn't know how to ease whatever he had aroused, but she knew who could ease it.

And all the time, Ran's view of her chair making, and her father's opinion of that view, warred in her head.

One morning, the note with the day's present went beyond the usual compliments, adding:

"I beg Mrs Bradshaw and Miss Bradshaw to do me the honour of accepting my escort to the Lower Assembly Rooms this evening."

Min had been planning to go—the next step in her experiment in social climbing. But going with Ran would be wonderful. Mama sent a note back with the Avery servant, inviting Ran to dinner, and Min hurried to the workshop to make an early start on the day's work.

Ran was in Bath! Min half expected to see him on her walk to work. She almost stayed in her walking dress, in case he came to her workshop, but common sense prevailed and she donned her overalls.

She would see him tonight. Tonight, she could tell him all the things she had been saving up to say, and she could hear about his week at Avery Hall, and about Lady Avery, and the planned gardens, and the performance of the chair, and the progress of the renovations...

Min caught herself. When had her life begun to revolve around this man and his concerns?

Suddenly, he was there. "Min."

She dropped her tools and walked into his open arms for a kiss that satisfied and, at the same time, left her longing for more. All too soon, he put her gently from him.

"Min, I won't stay. But I couldn't wait to see you. Have you been well? You look well."

"Yes. And you?"

"I'm well now," Ran said, and the warmth in his eyes said much more. "I must go. I have appointments today... I will see you tonight, Min."

One more kiss, and he was gone. So much for keeping her head until she had made her decision.

After daydreaming for an hour, Min packed up and went home. She was accomplishing nothing today.

Candle was humming to himself as he walked into the White Hart after seeing the Bradshaw ladies home. The evening had been wonderful. The dancing, the conversation, the food, everything had conspired to provide a perfect evening. And, at the centre of it all, his Minerva.

She was his, he was almost sure of it. He hadn't asked her again, but tonight she'd had her armour down. She'd been happy to be with him; she'd let her hand linger on his in the dance, and she'd leant into him when he'd offered his arm to go in to supper. Two dances had not been nearly enough; Candle would have taken every dance, given a choice.

But he'd played at being civilised, even danced with other females, although there was only one in the room worth thinking about.

Surely she was planning to say yes? Her father thought so, but her mother warned him not to be too certain. And in the light of what her cousin had let slip, Candle was more and more sure that it might take his secret plan to convince his Min she could trust her future to him.

Candle stopped at the desk to see if there had been any messages, and waited while the clerk checked.

"Candle, old man."

"Michaels; good to see you."

His friend grinned. "I saw you at the assembly, but you didn't have eyes for anyone but that black-haired beauty you were escorting. Gorgeous female. Lovely..." He cupped both hands in front of his chest and jiggled them up and down.

"The future Lady Avery," Candle warned. The clerk was shaking his head. No messages.

Michaels said a cheerful, "Sorry," but was not at all abashed. "When's the happy day?"

"She hasn't accepted me yet. But she will." If he said it often enough, perhaps it would be true.

"I imagine she will," his friend agreed. "Candle Avery, the man who never gives up. Look, Candle, I thought you might have those volunteer training plans you promised me."

"They're up in my room; come on up and I'll give them to you."

They were discussing the most recent news from the Fleet as Candle opened the door to his room and led the way in.

"Will you have a drink?" Candle asked, crossing to the decanter on the sideboard.

"Uh, Candle." Michaels was stock still in the middle of the room, his face suddenly neutral. He was staring at the bed.

"Candle, darling, come back to bed." Lady Norton, her hair hanging down across her shoulders, sat up in his bed. A sheet preserved some shreds of decency, but she was clearly naked. Very naked.

Candle was suddenly coldly furious. "You mistake, madam. I would sooner bed a snake."

"But Candle! After the afternoon we had?"

The door opened again, and Kitteridge burst in. "What are you doing with my sister, you villain?" he declaimed, then frowned at Michaels. "He isn't meant to be here."

Lady Norton struck her forehead with the back of one hand. "Guy! Candle, we are discovered! My brother knows all!"

Candle suppressed a laugh. High melodrama indeed! Though it would be quite unfunny if he had come up to bed on his own, or if he didn't have witnesses to how he'd spent his afternoon and evening.

"Michaels, shut the door, will you? We'll keep this to ourselves if we can."

"You have compromised my sister! I demand satisfaction." Clearly Kitteridge intended to follow the script despite the unexpected addition to the cast.

"Very well," Candle said. "Michaels, will you stand my second?"

"Not a duel. Marriage. You're meant to marry her," Kitteridge explained.

"No," Candle said.

"But she's in your bed. You have to marry her." Kitteridge was pleading now.

"Kitteridge, I have been in company every minute of the day since I arrived in Bath. I have witnesses who will swear to that. The only one to suffer if you and Lady Norton insist on making a scandal is Lady Norton."

He turned, then, and locked eyes with Lady Norton, but continued to address Kitteridge. "I don't know whether your sister is after my money or if she is with child again, but I will not be her dupe."

Lady Norton shrieked at the suggestion she might be pregnant. "Guy! He has insulted me! Call him out!"

"But Vivi, he has been a soldier. He's probably a good shot."

"Regimental champion three years running," Michaels offered. He was bouncing forward on his feet, like a boy on outskirts of a fistfight: close enough to see the blood but preserved from any pain and having a wonderful time. "And he's none too bad with a sword."

Kitteridge nodded vigorously, and said, "He's good with his fists, too. You should have seen him at school. He'd go into this sort of calm rage, and nothing would stop him."

"I've seen it," Michaels agreed. "A sort of cold, logical berserker. Very scary. I wouldn't duel with him if I were you."

Candle was keeping an eye on Lady Norton. She was assessing every object within reach. He recognised the signs. He'd had a mistress who threw things when she was upset. Yes. There went the jug, water and all. He'd been ready to duck, but obviously she was angrier with her brother.

The jug struck a glancing blow, and what water hadn't already soaked the bed and sprayed across the floor finished up on Kitteridge's jacket.

"Vivi!" he complained, "I hope that doesn't stain."

"Mr Michaels and I are going downstairs," Candle told them. "We will return in 30 minutes, bringing the manager with us. I suggest the two of you leave before that time. And Lady Norton, Michaels and I will keep this to ourselves. But only if you do not try anything like it again."

They didn't speak as they descended the stairs. Candle ordered a brandy each, and they took it to a corner of the public room.

"Well," Michaels said. "You do know how to make an evening entertaining, old chap."

Chapter eight: A Christmas present

The chair was done. It was, perhaps, the best Min had ever made. It was wrapped in protective blankets and secured to the top of the carriage that would take her and Mama to Avery Hall the following day.

As she sat with Cara in the tea rooms at the Roman Baths, waiting for Lady Cresthover to return from the retiring room, Min was thinking about the answer she would give Ran. She had done a great deal of thinking in the last two weeks.

She was no longer afraid of going into Society. Oh, the high sticklers and the bullies might never accept her. But enough of her old schoolmates had become friends that she need not fear isolation. She would never be a darling of the ton, but neither did she wish to be.

And she had learned that she could ignore any nasty remarks made to her. They no longer had the power to crush her, even without Ran's support. If he stood at her side, she could face anything.

Ran at her side. That was the biggest lesson of all. Whether he meant what he said about her chairs or not, she was going to accept Ran. If she had to make a choice between her work or her love, she chose love. With him, she felt complete. His absence felt like a gaping hole in her personal universe. She could, if she must, do something other than build chairs. She could not contemplate facing the rest of her life without Ran.

"You are thinking about Lord Avery again, are you not?" Cara said.

"Is it so obvious?"

"You are just like Henrietta Millworthy. She loved the man she married, too. And before the wedding she used to drift off into nowhere, just like you." Cara reached across the table and grasped Min's hands. "Marry him, Min. Do not let cats like my cousin stop you."

Min laughed a little. "I plan to, Cara."

"And you will still be my friend, will you not?" Cara looked a little lost. "I will miss you when you move away from Bath."

"I will write, and I will not be far away. I imagine we will be able to visit, you and I."

"Well, is this not sweet? My cousin and her little shop-girl friend." Lady Norton, her voice pitched to carry across the room, sneered down at them.

"I suppose you think you are so smart, Mini Bradshaw, trapping a peer. But you will never fit in. Do you hear me? Never."

"Lady Norton, this is a private conversation," Min said.

"He will not be faithful to you, you know. His father was notorious for his affairs. Ask her mother." Lady Norton pointed a gloved finger at Cara. "Everyone knows her mother was one of his amours, when she was just plain Sally Hemple. He had a taste for a bit of the common, just like his son."

Min met Lady Cresthover's shocked eyes over Lady Norton's shoulder and attempted to stem the flow. "Lady Norton, that is quite enough."

Lady Norton took no notice. "Sally Hemple. My mother told me that she trapped my uncle. Just like you are trapping poor Lord Avery, Miss Bradshaw." She gave her cousin a poke with one finger. "You should try it, Carrie darling. Before you crumble to dust on the shelf, you poor old thing." She swayed a little. "Ooops." She caught herself by grabbing the back of a chair, and laughed her tinkling laugh.

Lady Cresthover was whispering to a footman, who nodded and hurried away.

"He is not very good in bed, Miss Bradshaw. You should not hope for much. Perhaps you could get my Auntie to give him a few pointers?"

The footman was back, with a colleague. Lady Norton yelped as they took an elbow each.

"How dare you! Unhand me. Do you know who I am?"

She was continuing to protest as they half carried her out of the room. "A very sad case," Lady Cresthover said in a carrying voice. "A sad unsteadiness in her mother's family, you know." She dropped into a piercing whisper that could be heard in every corner of the room. "It is said that her grandfather thought he was an elephant."

"Come, Cara, Miss Bradshaw." Ignoring the embarrassed titters, she sailed out of the room, Min and Cara in her wake, and Polly the maid scurrying behind.

In the foyer, Lady Cresthover ordered Lady Norton into a sedan chair. "It will keep her out of the public eye," she said, her voice back at its normal volume. "Miss Bradshaw, do not be concerned about my niece. She will retiring to a quiet place in the country." She turned away to follow her daughter and the chair, then turned back again. "And I can assure you that young Lord Avery is nothing like his father."

The men worked all night by lantern light to finish Candle's surprise. He was tempted to wait until she had given him her answer and then show her. He would love her to choose him without his gift. But no. He wouldn't play games, and wouldn't take the risk she'd turn him down and then refuse to change her mind.

He would show her first, and then propose to her again.

He checked the surprise for the third time that morning, ran inside again to see if a message had arrived from the gate yet, stopped to ask his mother how she was, and went back out to the steps to see if he could see their carriage.

The weather was cold, with gusty showers that hinted at sleet in their future. He hoped Bradshaw's carriage was warm. What was he thinking! The man was the king of carriages. He would send his womenfolk in the best he had.

Returning inside, Candle looked around the entry hall. Yes. It looked splendid. Mother loved Christmas, and took no notice of the tradition that decorations must wait until Christmas Eve. As soon as the Christmas Octave started on the 17th of December, she mobilised the entire household to transform the house into a Christmas paradise. The servants had outdone themselves this year. Every surface sported ivy, holly, and greenery. More greenery was tied to the stair balustrade with bright ribbons, and ribbons festooned the kissing balls of holly, ivy, rosemary, and mistletoe. Mother had made enough kissing boughs to put one in every room, upstairs and down.

"My Lord, she be here! Her carriage be coming down the hill."

Candle waited impatiently at the bottom of the steps, and was at the carriage door as soon as it rolled to a stop. The door swung open before he could grasp the handle, and Min tumbled out into his arms.

"Yes," she said. "Yes, Ran, yes. I will marry you."

Later, after he had kissed her, been kissed on the cheek by Mrs Bradshaw, and escorted them inside to his mother for congratulations and more kisses, he managed to detach Min from the admiring group around the new chair.

"I have something for you, beloved. A surprise present for Christmas. Mother, Mrs Bradshaw, I am taking Min to show her her present."

The mothers waved them away.

Ran refused to tell her what the surprise was, but he took her outside, and to a building behind the stable. "Stop." he commanded. He rushed ahead and opened the door, then returned and covered her eyes with his hands. "I'll guide you. Take three paces forward. Now turn slightly and take one more pace. Now feel forward with your foot for the step. There are three steps. One; two; three. Two more paces. Stop."

He removed his hands.

Min stared. Then turned her head. Then turned in a complete circle.

"Ran? Ran, it's my workshop." She ran forward and brushed her hand over the drafting table, picked up and put down the pens and pencils waiting for her, straightened the blotter. Next, the workbench, where racks waited for her tools, still back in Bath in the racks he'd duplicated. The shelves of supplies were mostly empty, too, but she could imagine them filled.

"Ran." She smiled at him and his dear features wavered as her eyes swam with tears.

He looked concerned. "Min? Is it alright?"

"It is the most wonderful thing anyone has every done for me. My workshop."

"How else are you going to keep inventing your wonderful chairs, my love?"

"Ran." That seemed to be the only word she could say, but she invested it with a wealth of meaning. Then she melted into his arms, and neither of them spoke for some time.

Candle Avery was climbing the hill track in the rain. He was cold, wet, and thoroughly happy.

He and his companions had refused a lift on the cart taking the freshly cut yule log back to Avery Hall. The hill track was the quicker way. And at the Hall Min waited for him. Min Avery. His wife of three days.

He'd be hard put to pick the happiest moment of his life. When she tumbled out of the coach and accepted his proposal? When she agreed to using the special licence he'd obtained, and to marrying him as soon as her family could come from Bath? When he'd turned from his place before the altar and seen her walking towards him in a cloud of lace, or a few minutes later when she'd given him her hand and her trust with her vows? When she welcomed him into her embrace and her body later that night? When he woke up the next morning to her shy suggestion that they should make love again?

Each day, he fell in love a little more.

They crested the top and Daniel said something Candle didn't catch. Michaels gave Candle a friendly punch on the arm. "No point in talking to him," he told Daniel. "The man walks around in a daze."

"To be fair, we are intruding on his honeymoon," Daniel noted.

To be fair, they were mostly being careful not to intrude. But it was Christmas Eve, and it was his job as master of the house to collect the yule log. "My wife and I want you to enjoy your Christmas in our home," he said. As well as Min's family, Michaels and Miss Cresthover had come for the wedding, and were staying for Christmas.

"Preferably without disturbing you and your wife. Yes, we understand," said the irrepressible Daniel.

Michaels gestured ahead. "Who, if I do not mistake, is coming to meet us."

Below, two women waited in the shelter of the summerhouse.

Sure enough, as the men drew level with the structure, Miss Cresthover and the new Lady Avery dashed down the steps under their umbrellas.

"So do we have a good yule log," Min asked.

"An excellent one," Daniel said, "but I'm sorry to say we failed in one mission." He let his eyes, lips and shoulders droop.

"What was that?" Cara could be depended on to ask the questions that set Daniel up for whatever punchline he intended to deliver.

Candle held Min back, letting the others go on ahead, but they could still hear Daniel's reply as the three in the lead turned the corner of the path.

"We couldn't find any mistletoe to replace all the berries Min and Candle have used, so nobody else in the Hall can be kissed, Miss Cresthover."

"But Mr Whitlow, you kissed me this morning!" replied Cara.

"I kissed you this morning," Candle told Min.

"Really? I am not sure that I remember. Perhaps if you do it again?"

After several minutes, he drew his head back. "Min, the yule log won't be here for another hour. Shall we go up to bed?"

"Up the stairs in front of our friends and family? Ran, I could not."

He thought for a moment of suggesting the back stairs, but through the kitchen full of servants wouldn't appeal to her, either.

"However," said Min, "your study has a sofa and a warm fire, and I unlatched the window before I came out."

"Ah, Min," Candle told her, "how lucky I am to have a clever wife."

THE END

Lord Calne's Christmas Ruby

Fashionable London holds nothing for wealthy merchant's niece, Lalamani Finchurch. Except perhaps for an earl with a twisted hand and a charming smile. Why, for all the fortune hunters she has fended off since returning from India, is the one man who seems to like her so against marrying for money?

Philip has inherited an earldom that his only two choices are to marry for money or to abandon Society altogether and return to his work as an engineer. Which is no choice at all, until a tiny woman with beautiful eyes and a fine mind dances with him on his last night in London.

When they meet again in a small country village, they join forces to uncover larceny and deceit, to rescue Lalamani's aunt from poverty, and to discover that pride is a poor reason to refuse a love for a lifetime.

Chapter One

Philip Daventry escorted yet another vapid debutante back to her Mama, who coyly remarked that dear Amanda had never been so pleased with a dance, and another would not be beyond the bounds of propriety. "Dear Amanda" giggled and nodded, but not without an anxious look at Philip's twisted hand, the scarring hidden by the glove but the deformity in no way concealed.

Philip made the excuse he was promised for the rest of the evening, and must, even now, find his next partner. Before he could extract himself, the mother declared both ladies would be at home to the newly minted Earl of Calne whenever he cared to call. "Amanda so enjoys a drive in the park, Lord Calne," she hinted, broadly.

Philip, who lacked a carriage, horses, and the inclination to give Miss Amanda any encouragement, pretended he had not understood, merely bowing and taking his leave.

Now he would need to either seek an introduction to another partner, or hide so he was not caught in his untruth.

The evening's hostess, the Duchess of Haverford, was nowhere to be seen among the crush she called, "just a gathering of friends with perhaps a little impromptu dancing or a game of cards; nothing so formal as a ball."

Or so his uncle reported, when he insisted Philip attend. "Your man of business is right, Philip. You need to marry money if you're to save what remains of the estate. No need for it to be a cold business affair. Men have fallen in love with heiresses before now.

At least come with me this evening, and see if there is anyone you might be able to warm to."

Philip had allowed himself to be persuaded, but without much hope. He had been right. Every one to whom the duchess presented him simpered and tittered, and openly displayed their willingness to accept the position of Countess of Calne, while unsuccessfully hiding their distaste for his deformity. Their mothers or aunts or older sisters ignored the hand entirely, which was somehow worse, since their only interest in him was to show off the paces of their particular maiden with the enthusiasm of a fairground horse dealer and, he rather thought, with as much veracity.

The evening was an off-season event. By far the largest part of the *ton* was already off on some country estate, enjoying the peace of early winter or the bustle and drama of a house party. Thank goodness. At least the experience had taught him the folly of breaking cover in the height of the Season, to be hunted by an even larger pack of matchmaking mothers.

If he couldn't find the duchess, perhaps Uncle Henry would introduce him to a suitable partner. His uncle had made himself scarce as soon as he had handed Philip over to the duchess. No doubt he had found some friends with whom to play cards or talk about politics and the war. Philip should have turned back when Uncle Henry admitted, in the carriage, that without his daughter to run interference, he would avoid the main dancing rooms and thus the snares and pitfalls of those who felt his widower status made him fair game. And Uncle Henry was thirty-five years Philip's senior and not an earl, but merely the fourth son of one; a career officer with the Horse Guard.

Mind you, Uncle Henry was neither crippled nor all but destitute, conditions which must count against Philip. He'd ordered everything marketable in his inheritance to be sold, but the earldom would still be in debt when the accounting was complete.

While he had been pondering his sorrows, Philip had skirted the dancing floor, still without seeing the duchess or Uncle Henry, and the sets had formed for the next dance. Perhaps he would find the card room, and stay with Uncle Henry until it was time for the appointed dance. After which, he was leaving. This whole evening had been a mistake.

A long hall with doors on either side led from the ballroom. He strode along, having learned earlier in the evening that strolling was an invitation to acquire a twittering female on either arm. Nodding politely as he passed those he recognised, he glanced in each room with an open door. A retiring room with chaperones drinking tea or ratafia, a group listening to a singer, two closed doors in a row and then a room set up with tables, and intent groups of two or four or six playing cards.

Philip stood for a moment just inside the door, until the nearest group asked if he would like to join them. But Uncle Henry wasn't in the room, so he declined politely and went back to his search.

The next room was dark. The one after was lit, the door partly open, though not enough to see into the room. Women's voices indicated the room was in use, and he paused to listen. He would not intrude on a private conversation.

"Really, Miss Finchurch, I cannot imagine what Lady Carngrove is thinking, bringing you here to mingle with your betters."

Another voice; a vicious purr somehow familiar to Philip. "Perhaps she imagines the perfume of Miss Finchurch's wealth will overcome the stench of her origins?"

Definitely not the card room. Harpies of this stamp would not attack so openly in front of an audience, and Uncle Henry would not stand by while they did. Philip should do something. While he hesitated, those inside continued to talk.

"I do not believe so, girls. Lady Carngrove intends all that lovely money for her darling Ceddie. As if he would even consider such a thing! Why, Miss Finchurch is quite old!"

The next voice was crisp, but with a bubble of a laugh running through it. "My goodness, I must really worry you, for you to descend to such a puerile level of nursery bullying."

Philip grinned. The victim was not entirely helpless then.

Before the babble of rejoinders sorted themselves out, he pushed the door open. "Miss Finchurch? Ah, there you are." It was a small reading room, lined with bookshelves and with comfortable chairs grouped around low tables, just the right height for a drink and a book.

The target of the others' spite was clearly the one at bay, seated by the fire with an open book on her lap. She turned her face to him an instant before the others. Old? True, she was not a girl fresh from the schoolroom, but rather a lady in her mid-twenties, unlined face a perfect oval, with large brown eyes under arched brows, a tilt-tipped nose, and a quantity of light brown hair pulled up into a confection of hair atop her head, a few strands pulled loose to frame the delightful whole.

She met his smile with a quizzical tip of the head, and he ignored the five ladies standing over her. "Our dance is in a few minutes, Miss Finchurch, so I came to find you. Would you care to take a short stroll while we wait?"

Would she take the rescue, he wondered, glancing from her to the others? Three were strangers. One, he vaguely recognised. But the remaining woman... He nodded a polite but cold acknowledgement to Lady Markhurst, who had pretended to accept his courtship when he was last in Society four years ago, after recovering from the injuries that ended his army career and brought him home to England.

Lady Markhurst had soon made it clear his only attraction was his unwed cousins, one an earl and one the heir to an earl. Philip wasn't close to either, and had not seen her since she discovered that fact. He assumed her pursuit was unsuccessful; certainly, she had wed before the end of that season, to a lowly and rather elderly baron who proved to be not as wealthy as rumour had painted.

Clearly, Philip's attractiveness had increased with his accession to the title, since Lady Markhurst fluttered her fan and her eyelashes, and fingered the diamond drop dangling from her ornate necklace into the valley between her breasts. "Why, Lord Calne. Surely you cannot intend to dance with a merchant's daughter. Your inheritance cannot be in such a dire state as that. Let me save you from such a fate by offering myself as a partner instead." The throaty note in her last sentence made it a naughty innuendo.

He ignored Lady Markhurst and her outstretched hand, offering Miss Finchurch his bad arm, which functioned well enough as a prop for a lady. Lady Markhurst's face flushed and then whitened. She had not learned to control her temper, then.

Miss Finchurch made up her mind, set her book to one side, and stood to slip her hand into his elbow, and he turned to the door. Lady Markhurst launched another attack before they reached it.

"Do be warned, Miss Finchurch. The Calne title comes with a bankrupt estate and a crippled earl."

Miss Finchurch gripped his arm, making him wince, and she sensed it, too, the fires she was about to turn on Lady Markhurst doused by her concern for him. He took another step towards the door.

"Ignore Lady Markhurst, Miss Finchurch. I would say her disappointment in her ambitions has made her bitter, but she was always a scold."

His mother would have punished such rudeness, but he was well compensated by the gasps from behind him as he whisked Miss Finchurch into the hall and pulled the door closed. She was tiny; perhaps no more than five feet tall, the top of her head barely on a level with his shoulder, and he shortened his steps when he realised she was near running to keep up with him. She was, however, by no means quelled. "You and Lady Markhurst are old friends, it seems, Lord Calne."

"Not since I discovered her heart was made of the same substance as the stones in her necklace."

Miss Finchurch laughed, an amused gurgle. "Paste, you mean? Very appropriate! Cold, hard and false."

"Paste? Really?"

"I am the daughter and niece of diamond merchants, Lord Calne. I would need to examine the smaller stones more closely, but the drop is decidedly not a diamond. Perhaps it is ill bred of me to disclose the lady's secrets, so I shall compound the error by making it clear I am not looking for a husband, and if I were, I would not accept a fortune hunter under any circumstances."

A game of truths, was it? "Nor am I looking for a wife, Miss Finchurch. Especially one prepared to take a destitute cripple for the sake of his useless title. But a dance might be safe enough? I have managed several tonight and am as yet unwed."

That earned him the gurgle again, and they took the positions for a long dance, Philip apologising in advance for being unable to grasp with his withered left hand.

Miss Finchurch assured him she would grasp well enough for them both. "What happened, Lord Calne? Or were you born with it? Or should I not ask?"

How refreshing to meet someone who said outright what everyone else speculated about in whispers behind his back. Philip answered as simply. "I was in the wrong place at the wrong time. We were crossing a newly repaired bridge in Sicily. But the French had set dynamite, and it blew up, with half the baggage train. I lost the use of one hand." His writing hand, but he could manage well enough with his right, after years of tutors who had punished the use of the other. "Many lost more." His brother-in-law for one, which directly led to the deaths of his sister and her baby. She had gone into labour shortly after the news reached her in Malta, and when the child was born dead, she had turned her face to the wall and died. Or so Philip had been told when he recovered from the fever, by which time he was in England, in his uncle's care.

"You were in the army?"

"With the Engineers." And in charge of the repair of the bridge. He should have detected the sabotage. The deaths—all the deaths, not just those of his family—were his fault.

Their turn came in the figures of the dance, giving him time to bludgeon his mind into accepting that the room was not caving in on him; that the glittering crowd were not about to turn on him to demand his immediate conviction for dereliction of duty.

Either something in his face caused Miss Finchurch to take pity on him, or she was bored with the subject, because when they stood out next, she reopened the conversation by asking whether he enjoyed this kind of entertainment in a voice so doubtful he laughed.

"No more than you, I suspect, Miss Finchurch, though more so since fate handed me a partner who does not send me to sleep with talk of fashion and gossip. Tell me, what is a diamond assessor doing in a Haverford House entertainment? You came with Lady Carngrove, those vixens said?"

"My aunt." The mournful tone suggested this was not a circumstance for congratulation. "I live with her. At the moment."

He sensed tragedy and, come to think of it, she had referred to her father and uncle in the past tense. But she did not wear black, which hinted her bereavement was not recent. He was uncertain whether to express his commiserations.

"I lived in India until eighteen months ago. My parents died there when I was a child, and my uncle raised me. When he died, I returned to England, and to my mother's sister. And thus, you have my whole history, my lord."

"I grew up in various ports around the globe," he offered in return. "My father was a naval officer, and my mother took me and my sister in his wake. I was intended for the navy myself, but I..." He had been about to tell her about his terrible *mal de mer*, which was not something he disclosed to anyone if he could help it. "I discovered I loved designing and making things: useful things like roads and canals and bridges. So, I trained as an engineer at the Royal Military Academy, and there you have my history."

"Ah," Miss Finchurch reminded him, "but I brought mine up to date. You neglected the small matter of your title. Did you always know you were to be an earl?"

"Not at all. My father was a younger son, and I barely knew my uncle and cousins. The earldom was safe in their line, with an heir and his younger brother, and the heir betrothed. It would be yet if the two cousins had had the sense not to travel together in a racing carriage through a forest in a storm, several weeks after their father died. The lawyers had the dev-- a difficult job finding me, because the last address my uncle had for my father was before he died, and that was eight years ago, and in South Africa." They'd been surprised to find their lost heir in the north-west England, working on an aqueduct for a canal. But not as surprised as Philip had been to find he was now the Earl of Calne.

Miss Finchurch raised her brows, and her eyes smiled if her lips didn't. "I feel you would prefer commiserations on your new title rather than congratulations."

He did not bother to suppress his bark of laughter. "You are correct," he told her, "and the sooner I can get back to my real work the better." Winter had put a stop to canal building, or he'd be there now. Still, meeting Miss Finchurch had made the evening bearable, and would be one of the pleasanter memories of his expedition into the foreign landscape of high Society.

"What is your real work, my lord?"

Philip needed no more encouragement to give her a quick overview of the canal, and especially the aqueduct that would take it across a valley to join with the Bridgewater. At least, he had intended a quick overview. But her intelligent questions lured him into a far deeper discussion, which they continued when the music ended, strolling through the rooms to avoid being caught up in any other group. When a lady who must be her aunt retrieved Miss Finchurch, shooting Philip a resentful glare, he let her go with real reluctance.

What a lovely woman Miss Finchurch was, and what a pity he was too poor to think of pursuing the acquaintance.

Chapter Two

"You need not think of Calne, Margaret," Aunt Cecilia told Lalamani Finchurch in the carriage on the way home. "The whole *ton* knows he has not a feather to fly with. But your uncle will not consider him for you, even though you are an heiress, and the best such a poor specimen of a man might hope for. You are to wed Cecil as soon as he is of age."

Lalamani didn't comment. No point in reminding Aunt Cecilia that she used her second name, not her first. Nor would she say Lord Calne had offered no flattery nor promised to visit, but had instead discussed aqueducts and canals, those he had built and those he planned to build. She would certainly not argue that Calne was a fine, fit, elegant man whose withered hand did not disable him, his enthusiasm and intelligence far more to her taste than the lazy and effete gentlemen who flattered her out of one side of their mouths while sneering from the other. Above all, she would not point out she was twenty-three, nearly twenty-four, and neither her marriage nor her fortune were under her uncle's control.

Aunt Cecilia would have ignored any remark she made as irrelevant, since Aunt Cecilia believed the world would march to her order if she only charged on in her chosen direction. She ignored any facts that did not fit her preconceptions, including her own son's opposition to marriage with his older cousin, the five years between his age and hers seeming an insuperable barrier to an eighteen-year-old.

Cecil's guardian, his father's uncle, had forbidden the match while Cecil was so young but, despite this, in Aunt Cecilia's mind the matter was certain. She nonetheless kept a careful watch for possible poachers in her son's preserves.

It didn't matter. This was the last *ton* party Lalamani would attend, if all went as planned in the morning. She and Cecil had decided. Or, rather, Lalamani had made up her mind, and Cecil had cooperated, since it fitted with his own desires.

Tomorrow, they would leave together, and disappear. Cecil was heading north to a hunting lodge with friends. Lalamani had received a friendly letter from her father's sister, the widow of a country rector who still lived in the village she and her husband had served for forty years. Lalamani had grown up with letters from Aunt Hannah, and couldn't believe she hadn't thought of going there before now.

This morning, Cecil had escorted her to her man of business, who was also her trustee, to collect this quarter's pin money. Tomorrow, he would see her to the coaching inn, and onto the coach for her aunt's village. She would visit, and if all went well, she would take refuge with Aunt Hannah until her twenty-fifth birthday, when she had control of her own fortune.

With luck, Aunt Cecilia would assume she and Cecil had eloped and would keep their absence a secret so her brother-in-law did not come running to stop his ward's marriage.

With even more luck, her first inkling Cecil and Lalamani had gone in different directions would be when Cecil returned from his hunting trip in the new year. Time enough for Lalamani to find out whether she wanted to stay with Aunt Hannah, and whether Aunt Hannah would want her to stay. She could deal with Aunt Cecilia easily enough if only she had a safe place to wait out the next year.

Chapter Three

Lalamani, waking in the little room she had been assigned when she arrived in Feldon Roding late the previous evening, looked around it without pleasure. The walls were covered in a faded print that must have been a dull puce when it was first put up and was now an indeterminate beige, almost the same colour as the painted ceiling. Its trim had once, perhaps, been gold but was now a rather dirty brown. The walls were panelled to chair-rail height in a dark wood made dull by unknown years of poorly applied polish. The drab curtains added to the overall impression of being in a muddy hole underground.

"What colour would you call those curtains, Milly?" she asked when her maid arrived with a jug of hot water and a warning her Aunt, Mrs Thorpe, always rose to break her fast in the downstairs dining room, and Miss Lalamani had better look sharp if she wanted to join her.

Milly looked doubtfully at the curtains. "Chocolate?"

"I was thinking mud," Lalamani said. "The yellow sprigged, Milly. I feel the need of something cheerful."

Milly put the pink gingham back on the hooks and lifted down the dress Lalamani selected. The muted pink, which Lalamani had always rather liked, today looked almost the same shade as the wall it hung on.

Dressed, Lalamani went down through a stairwell and hall of the same faded, depressing hues to a dining room that might have been rather fine fifteen years ago, had it been decorated in more appealing colours and had the black crepe swags draped along every available surface been folded away, or at least shaken out and dusted.

Aunt Hannah was helping herself to a heaping plate of food. Lalamani noted the food, at least, was not depressing. Aunt Hannah clearly believed in starting the day with variety and quality.

"Lalamani, my dear, how lovely you look, and how you brighten up this sad old house." Aunt Hannah dabbed at the tears that overflowed from her pale blue eyes.

The house was, Lalamani had to agree, rather sad, with its drab colours and mourning swags. Aunt Hannah, too, was swathed in deep black though her husband the rector had been gone for nearly nine years.

"Have some bacon, Lalamani, dear. And eggs? How do you like your eggs?" Aunt Hannah fussed over making sure Lalamani had a loaded plate, clucking anxiously that Lalamani must say if anything was lacking and Aunt Hannah would order it for the morrow.

"I am very pleased to see you, Lalamani, of course. Dear Hadley's little girl." Aunt Hannah leaned over the table to pat Lalamani's hand, her eyes watering slightly. "I do not know when I last had company. And is your aunt, Lady Carngrove, well? And little Lord Carngrove?"

"Yes, very well," Lalamani said. "They are both well." How Cedric would frown to be referred to as little Lord Carngrove, as if he was still in leading strings.

Aunt Hannah's face glowed with the warmth of her smile. "They will miss you, I am certain. But how kind of them to spare you to me for Christmas."

"I am very happy to be here, Aunt Hannah."

"It is lovely to have you here. I could not be more pleased, Lalamani, but…" The anxious expression that seemed habitual deepened to a frown. "I do not know, my dear, how I shall keep you entertained. I live very quietly, you know."

"I am here to visit you, Aunt Hannah. I am happy to keep you company, and perhaps I can help with your visiting and your parish work?" Lalamani had long been fascinated by the many activities Aunt Hannah had written about over the years.

"Oh, my dear, I do not do much anymore." The faded cheeks turned pink, and the ready tears brimmed over again. "I know I said in my letters… It was wrong of me. One should never tell falsehoods, but truly I did do all those things. Just not since the new rector… His sister, you know. She is quite right, quite right. It is her place to… And I would not want to… I truly would not, my dear. I feel so old and useless, and when I wrote to you, I could pretend, for just a while…"

Her voice faded away as tears sleeted down her cheeks. Lalamani patted her on the arm, wondering somewhat desperately what to do next. This was completely outside of Lalamani's experience. Her life had not provided a plethora of weeping elderly widows.

"Dear Aunt Hannah, of course you pretended. Anyone would have done the same. There was no harm in it. Oh, Aunt Hannah, please do not cry."

After several minutes of patting and reassurances, Aunt Hannah visibly pulled herself together and gave Lalamani a watery smile. "There, you will be running away when you have barely arrived. I am so sorry to be such a watering pot, my dear. Come, try some of this lovely bacon. I must say the parish people are so good to me. I never want for food for my plate. I really do not. Why Mrs Wright brought me this lovely cut of bacon just yesterday morning…"

She carried on while Lalamani ate, enumerating all the givers of the food they enjoyed. The tea, brought by the servant who had opened the door to Lalamani and Milly the night before, was not up to the same standard; it was weak and of an indeterminate flavour between milky water and, Lalamani thought, dishwater.

Aunt Hannah, after taking a sip, looked with consternation at the servant, a small bent elderly lady in the same faded black as she herself wore. "Oh dear, Addy. It is worse than I remembered."

"I told you, madam. Gave you the floor sweepings, I shouldn't wonder."

"Addy! No uncharitable remarks, if you please. As if they would. It is very kind of Dr Wagley and his sister. Lalamani, the rector and his sister give us a canister of tea every Christmas. A whole canister! Is that not generous?" She looked doubtfully at the cup.

Lalamani exchanged glances with the servant and resolved to have a private conversation with her very soon.

Something was wrong here. Uncle Herbert had bought Aunt Hannah a house when her husband died, and set up a trust to provide her with an income. She should not be dependent for her very food on the generosity of her departed husband's former parishioners.

Everything Lalamani had seen in the house was faded, dismal, and much mended, from the furnishings to the clothes Aunt Hannah and her servant Addy wore. Yes, and not too clean. Surely a house of this size needed more than one servant? But Addy, bustling out and then back again with a pot of peppermint tisane to replace the undrinkable China tea, was the only one Lalamani had seen, and far too old to manage all the work on her own.

Lalamani and Milly would have to help. Ladies' maids generally held themselves above housework, but Milly was an agreeable girl, and would probably consent to work alongside Lalamani to make the place more comfortable for Aunt Hannah and her woman, especially if Lalamani paid Milly extra to assuage the loss of dignity.

Yes. Dealing with the dirty corners would be simple enough. Finding out the cause of Aunt Hannah's unexpected poverty was unlikely to be as easy.

Chapter Four

Philip had been warned. But he found Highwood Hall in an even worse state than he expected. "The house in Feldon Roding has been the main seat of the Calnes for hundreds of years," the lawyer had said, "but your uncle hasn't lived there for fifteen years, or kept it staffed for ten. And he refused to allow money to be spent on repairs. I understand the roof has failed in places, in the main house and in the outbuildings."

The entire west wing had failed, the roof collapsed into the crumbling walls that were all that remained. The centre block was still largely intact, but the east wing was going the way of its counterpart, with gaping holes instead of tiles and the rafters showing through.

The stables were in no better case. Philip tethered his borrowed horse where it could reach water and grass, and poked around as best he could without risking life and limb. He'd hoped to be able to do some repairs in order to increase the possible sale price, but razing the place to the ground might be the best use of his meagre savings.

One thing was certain. He would not be staying in his own house tonight. He'd better get settled at the local inn and walk back later, to make a start on a proper assessment.

A day with her aunt only deepened Lalamani's concerns.

Adidiah—Addy—was happy to express an opinion, as she and Lalamani scrubbed the kitchen floor. "It's a crying shame, Miss

Lalamani. Mrs Thorpe don't have but a pittance for herself. If not for the people roundabouts, why, she'd starve."

"But, Addy, she has an income. She could even sell this house and move into a smaller place if she needed to."

"Is that a fact, Miss Lalamani? Rector, he gives her a bit of money now and then. Don't know about no income, though. I never heard of such."

Lalamani wasn't sure of the details of the trust; it had been set up before she began acting as her uncle's secretary. But her uncle loved his sister, and he was a wealthy man. Why, the house itself attested to his generosity; shabby though it was, it was large, well built, and had lovely proportions.

An interview with her aunt was in order, and afterwards, perhaps a letter to Lalamani's lawyer who had served her uncle well over many years.

"Aunt Hannah," Lalamani began as they took a break from housework that afternoon to walk the two miles to the village, "it is impertinent of me, I know, but I am concerned about you."

"You do not need to be, dear Lalamani." Aunt Hannah's eyes watered again. "I have all I need. Everyone is so generous to me." A shadow crossed over her face. "I do wish, though, I was able to pay my dear Addy. I worry about her, dear, I do indeed. If anything should happen to me… Well, I must just pray about it and trust God would look after her."

"Aunt Hannah," she tried again, "what happened to the money Uncle Herbert left you?"

She stopped in her tracks and peered at Lalamani, her pale blue eyes bewildered. "Money, dear? He paid for the house; the man from London came and found it for me. That was so lovely of Herbert, sweetheart. Though I could wish it was closer to the village, but Miss Wagley—she's the rector's sister, dear—she told me it was better I put a bit of distance between myself and the village. The people needed to get used to calling on her, she said. And she was quite right, no doubt, but I do find it hard sometimes, my dear." She began walking again, shaking her head.

"But the money, Aunt Hannah," Lalamani reminded her.

"No one told me anything about any money, my dear. I was not very well, of course. Such a terrible ague. So many people died. My poor dear husband. The inn keeper. Twelve babies they told me, so sad, I always think, when a baby dies." Her eyes filled again.

Lalamani was becoming inured to the easy tears and carried on regardless. "I'm so sorry to make you think about that sad time, Aunt Hannah, but it is important. When did you hear about the house?" It must have taken some time for word of Uncle Thorpe's death to get to India and for Uncle Herbert to send back his instructions to his lawyer.

"Let me see, dear. Mr Thorpe took the ague in January. He was one of the first in the village. I nursed him, of course, and we thought he was rallying, but he died in early February. Too much strain on his heart, dear, the doctor said.

"So many sick people in the village and out on the farms. So sad, my dear, especially when it started in the foundlings' home. I did what I could, but I was so tired, and then I fell sick myself. If not for Addy, I would have died too, I expect.

"How mysterious are the ways of God, for me to be spared and not those little children. A useless old woman like me, living past her time." Paradoxically, Aunt Hannah seemed cheered rather than depressed by this and blew her nose enthusiastically on the handkerchief with which she had been dabbing her eyes.

"So, when did Uncle Herbert's lawyer come to see you about the house?" Lalamani asked.

"Oh, I never met him. He visited while I was sick. I had the ague again twice more that year, and he came the second time, in the summer it was. Indeed, by the time I was well enough to go about a bit again, they had already moved me into the house. I was so grateful, for I cannot deny the cottage they found for me when they moved me from the rectory was draughty, and the roof leaked. But there. I must not complain, and it was good of the people to find me a place.

"The new rector—he was the new rector then—came to see me and explained my brother had rented the house for me, though what I will do when the lease runs out I do not know, my dear.

"And he said the parish would look after me, since I had no income. And they have, Lalamani. Why, Dr Wagley even gives me money from time to time. One does need money, unfortunately. At last quarter day, he gave me a whole ten pounds! Think of that. Ten pounds."

The lease? The house was Aunt Hannah's free and clear. And ten pounds? Lalamani had spent much more on a walking dress.

They'd arrived in the village, and Lalamani dropped the topic for the moment, but she would be seeking an introduction to this Dr Wagley without delay!

Miss Finchurch was the first person Philip saw as he rode into the village. At first, he did not believe it, since he had been seeing her in every short comely woman he passed for days. But there she was, her face turned his way as she talked to the elderly woman beside her.

She wasn't aware of him, her focus all on her companion. He noted the shop she entered, a village general store. Should he follow immediately, or take a room at the inn first and look her up after? The hired horse was tired. He should hand it over to the care of the grooms. He nudged it on into the inn-yard and dismounted with his usual care, pleased the damned hand managed to maintain hold on the reins. It ached a bit, but his exercises had helped him to gain and keep some measure of function.

A walk would do him good. He gave his saddle bags to the innkeeper with instructions to prepare a room, and headed out to find Miss Finchurch.

She was still in the shop. He knew her by her lack of height, and by some indefinable knowledge of her shape and the way she moved, though her face was hidden by her bonnet and she was half hidden on the other side of a stack of shelves.

"Oh dear," the elderly woman was saying, "Lalamani, my love, are you sure? Can you afford it? I should not wish you to spend your money on me."

Lalamani. What an unusual name. Beautiful and exotic, and somehow precisely right for the lady whose memory had haunted him for days.

"And why not, may I ask?" Lalamani replied firmly. "Who else should I spend it on than the aunt who was like a mother to my papa? Why, it is my Christian duty, Aunt Hannah."

Philip rounded the shelves and was gratified by Miss Finchurch's expression of surprised delight before she schooled her face to gracious welcome.

"My lord! What a surprise to see you here! Aunt Hannah, may I make known to you Lord…?"

Philip interrupted, holding out a hand to the lady. "Lord Calne's engineer, Philip Daventry, madam, at your service."

Miss Finchurch's eyes narrowed, but she did not betray his prevarication. "My aunt, Mrs Thorpe."

Mrs Thorpe held out a wrinkled hand for him to salute. "Mr Daventry? Oh my goodness. I suppose you have come to see to the Hall. Daventry is the earl's family name, of course, so you must be some kind of cousin. Does the earl wish the Hall repaired? But I cannot think it is fit for anyone to stay in. Certainly, no one has stayed there this past thirty years. More! You will stay with us, of course. Only, Lalamani," and here she dropped her voice to what she clearly imagined was a whisper, "I'm not perfectly sure we have another whole set of sheets!"

"I have a room at the inn, Mrs Thorpe, but thank you for the offer."

Mrs Thorpe looked relieved, but insisted, "But you will visit. You must. You have come all this way. And you are a friend of my niece's."

"I expect Mr Daventry is as surprised to see me as I am to see him," Miss Finchurch said.

Philip hazarded his luck. "Yes, but I am always happy to see a friend, Miss Finchurch, and feel very fortunate my duties brought me to the same village you were visiting. I had not hoped to see you again so soon." Or at all, though he had thought about her more often than he should, given his lack of a decent future to offer her.

Her slight frown was doubtful, but she refrained from commenting, and Mrs Thorpe filled the awkwardness of her silence by declaring she would ask the shop assistant to cut off twenty yards, if dear Lalamani was absolutely certain it would not be too expensive.

Receiving Miss Finchurch's assurance, she bustled off to make her purchases, leaving Philip to make his explanations. He took the high ground by speaking first. "Thank you for not exposing my title, Miss Finchurch. I hope to avoid the village either toadying to me because I'm the earl, or pursuing me with duns because my predecessors owed them money. And I really am here as an engineer."

Her face cleared and she laughed. "I cannot blame you, and will support your deception, Mr Daventry. Do you make a long stay? I thought you would be back to your aqueduct."

"I hope to be able to return once the weather is settled enough for the work to start again, but meanwhile I can use the time to find out what repairs the Hall needs. And you? I did not know you planned a visit to Feldon Roding."

Miss Finchurch's eyes sparkled and her lips curved beguilingly, but she did not speak whatever mischief had amused her, saying only, "My Aunt Hannah has lived here for fifty years, and has often written to me about the village. I expect to enjoy my stay, although…" She trailed off, her smile turning to a frown.

"Although?" he prompted, when it became clear she was not going to continue that sentence, but she just sent him another bright smile.

"Aunt Hannah is ready," she said. "It has been lovely meeting you again, Mr Daventry."

He followed her to the counter, and swooped on the large parcel before she could add it to her own load, tucking it under his less functional arm so he could reach for her basket with the useful one. "Please allow me to carry your parcels to your carriage," he begged, to the amusement of both ladies.

"We are walking, Mr Daventry, and would not wish to take you out of your way."

"On the contrary," he rallied, "a walk is just what I need."

Once he knew which direction they were walking, Lord Calne assured Lalamani and her aunt the house was barely out of his way at all, being a mere five minutes beyond the turnoff to the Hall.

Lalamani suggested he could surrender his load when they reached the half-collapsed tangle of wrought-iron that had once controlled access to the Hall's main carriage way, but now merely wilted against the brick pillars on either side. Lord Calne insisted on escorting the ladies all the way home, and then accepted Aunt Hannah's offer of a cup of tea.

The arrival of a representative of an earl sent Addy into a brief panic. The parlour, she told Lalamani, was the proper place for such an august personage, but she and Milly had been clearing the other rooms to give them a thorough clean, and the parlour was now full of furniture, drapery, paintings, and ornaments.

But Lord Calne assured Addy he would prefer to have his tea in the kitchen, if she would be so kind, for then he would feel at home, and he had not had a home since his mother died. Which set both Addy and Aunt Hannah fussing over him to make him comfortable, and Lalamani was torn between gratitude at his swift intervention and exasperation at his skilful management of the two older women. Yes, and Milly was a victim of his charm, too, sneaking peeks at him from the stool she reluctantly occupied after he insisted they all sit down, and blushing whenever he smiled in her direction.

The sooner he finished his cup of tea and his large helping of pound cake, the sooner he could take his leave and they could settle to their work, for Lalamani and Milly—with the enthusiastic support of Addy—were determined the whole house would be clean from the cellars to the attics before Christmas Eve.

Lord Calne accepted the second cup of tea Aunt Hannah offered, sipping it as he listened with every evidence of enjoyment to her stories of village life back when she was the rector's wife. She had a storyteller's gift for drama and pacing, and Lalamani was soon hanging on her words as much as she had when those stories arrived in letters. Gone was the anxious and diffident Aunt Hannah of today. As she talked about her life so long ago, her voice gained certainty and humour, her posture became confident, and Lalamani caught a glimpse of the warm, calm, loving rector's wife who had mothered the whole parish side-by-side with her beloved husband.

Lalamani was astounded when Milly began lighting candles and Lord Calne suddenly looked up at the window and said, "It is getting dark!"

"Oh dear," Aunt Hannah said, "I have kept you from your work."

"You are too kind to say I have been an importunate guest, far outstaying my welcome," Lord Calne replied. "But I beg you hold me excused, Mrs Thorpe. I was so absorbed in your stories I quite forgot myself."

"You must not neglect your work for the earl, Mr Daventry," Aunt Hannah scolded, and then cast a doubtful look outside.

"I will make an early start in the morning," Lord Calne promised, "but for now I had best make my way back to the inn while it is still light enough to see my way."

With a further exchange of mutual compliments, he disengaged himself from the kitchen and allowed Lalamani to usher him to the front of the house and out the door.

She locked the door behind him and slid the bolts, then rested her back against it, closing her eyes for a moment. For seven years, first in India and more recently in England, she had been courted and flattered by one man after another. She was not beautiful, and she was far too short, but she was passably pretty and, though merchant-born, she had the manners and training of a lady and her wealth covered a mountain of deficiencies. But none of her suitors tempted her to forgo her independence; none of them seemed to be aware of her mind or to care about engaging her in interesting conversation; not one could make her whole body tingle with just a smile.

Until now, she would have said, but Lord Calne was not a suitor. *He could be*, a treacherous voice whispered in the back of her mind. *He needs your money*. With a bit of encouragement... She shook her head but the thought would not be dislodged. What nonsense. As if she would want a husband she could purchase. As if Lord Calne would marry out of his class, even to save his estate. After all, heiresses were not unknown among the gentry, especially for a man as charming and kind as Lord Calne.

She pushed off from the door. *A lot of fuss about nothing.* Lord Calne would inspect his property tomorrow and then go back to London, and she would stay here and help her aunt. And the first step was to finish the cleaning.

Chapter Five

Three days of hard work saw a transformation of the main floor and the two occupied bed chambers. There was no disguising the shabbiness of the wall coverings and furnishings, but the ugly black swags were gone, bowls of holly leaves with their cheerful red berries brightened dust-free tables, and the woodwork gleamed.

Several times a day, their work was interrupted by visitors, locals who called to deliver gifts of food, examine the niece of their beloved 'Old Rector's wife', and gossip about the earl's man, who was spending every day at the broken-down old Hall.

"And not to hunt for treasure, like the last fellow," they agreed, for periodically the previous earl had sent outsiders to dig in the gardens or haul down walls, seeking something, and what could it be but a treasure. This man, though had hired several of the local men to work on the Hall with him, and he was focusing on salvage, not destruction.

"And right grateful for the work they are, Miss," one garrulous farm wife explained, "for with the enclosures and the taxes, it's hard enough to feed a family, especially at this time of year. Always some as starve afore the spring sowing. Not like when Old Rector was alive." She slid her eyes to Aunt Hannah and said no more.

Lalamani mentally measured what remained of her quarterly allowance against the cost of employing one or more of the locals. It had seemed a vast sum when she expected to pay only her own expenses and Milly's wages, and would certainly stretch to firewood for every room they had in use and other necessities for Aunt Hannah and Addy. But the two old ladies must have new garments, and her list of necessary repairs was growing room by room. Let alone refurbishment, though that might have to wait until after her twenty-fifth birthday. The house could be a very pleasant and comfortable place with a little work.

Aunt Hannah really needed a cook to take over the kitchen, a maid to assist with the housework, and someone to manage the garden and do necessary small repairs around the property. And a woman her age should not have to walk the two miles to the village, particularly on rainy days. But that would mean not just the cost of purchasing a gig and pony, and hiring someone to care for them, but also demolishing what had once been the stable and was now a pile of dangerous scrap, and building a new stable. Plus feed costs for both the animal and the stable hand.

Lalamani sighed, and started another list on a new page of her notebook.

Philip was also counting pennies. Most of his savings were invested up north with the consortium for whom he was building the aqueduct. Once he'd spent the absolute minimum needed to put what was left of the Calne holdings into marketable condition, he'd be left with a pittance until the canal started operating and earning.

He had hired local labour to help shore up sagging walls and make the roofs watertight over those parts of the buildings worth repairing. They were sullen to start with, and it didn't take him long to discover they were suspicious of anyone connected with the earl. "Old 'un never did anything good fer us'n," one of them said, as they began to relax around him. New 'un hasn't been next nor nigh the place since the old 'un died near a year ago. Stands to reason we don't expect much. Savin' your presence, sir."

Philip asked a few cautious questions, hoping to find out what had happened to the steward who vanished several years ago and the rents that hadn't been paid since. He got more than he bargained for.

As he worked alongside them on shoring up a wall or building a temporary shelter over a pile of recycled lumber, one man after another told him about the poverty resulting from the local enclosure act, pushed through several years earlier by large landowners such as the earl and rector. Smallholders had been left with too little land to farm, and most had left the area, abandoning properties that had been in their families for hundreds of years.

Two of his workmen proved to be his own tenants, barely able to farm the land they held from him because his absent predecessor had refused to make needed repairs and improvements for the past thirty years. The absconded steward had been a local man worn down from years of acting as a buffer between the local people and the earl, who drained resources and income from his unwanted property but never answered the steward's increasingly desperate appeals to put some money back in.

The men he had hired introduced him to others in the public room of the inn, and he spent his evening getting to know the local menfolk. Philip soon realised their expectations of the new earl might be low, but their hopes were high and had soared still higher on learning the earl had sent a man to repair the broken-down Hall.

"Stands to reason he plans to live here," one of the men argued, "And then he'll see for himself how things are, and will help us."

Philip soothed his increasing guilt with a silent promise to find a buyer who would want to spend most of the year in the village, and would look after his people. Those who were left.

Opinions on the rector were divided on class lines. The prosperous local farmers, crafters, and shopkeepers praised him as a man of faith, whose rousing sermons and firm management of the parish finances were a stark contrast to his predecessor. "Good man, the Reverend Thorpe, I'm not saying other," the innkeeper said. "But too soft on the poor. He'd give away the shirt on his back to a beggar would Old Rector Thorpe."

Under their breath and behind the backs of their betters, the poorer men painted a different picture: of a harsh zealot who showed one face to those who supported him and another to those he considered beneath his notice. Philip's disquiet increased at a casual reference to the quarterly rental owed to the earl and collected, since the steward left, by the local rector.

Chapter Six

On Sunday, Philip stood in the rear of the village church with other men he'd met during the week. "You could sit up there," one of them said, pointing to a box pew on the other side of the tall pulpit. "That's the Daventry pew, that is. And you're a Daventry, aren't you?"

Philip shook his head. "I'm more comfortable back here with you," he answered, though he promised himself a closer look later. Already, he'd noticed Daventry tombstones in the cemetery he'd passed on his way in, and Daventry memorials on the walls. Once, long ago, the Daventrys had valued this village and sent down deep roots. He could feel them tugging at a part of him he hadn't known existed. He had never belonged anywhere; had spent a lifetime roaming, first following his father from port to port, and later with the army.

"Home is not a place; it's people," his mother used to say. And with that his eye fell on Miss Finchurch, who was just entering the church with Mrs Thorpe, their maids behind them. The ladies made their way to the front of the nave, nodding and smiling at the gathered villagers as they passed.

Not long after they took their seats just under the pulpit, a man strode down the aisle, the academic robe he wore over his cassock billowing behind him. His identity was confirmed when he began to declaim the opening prayer, his congregation dutifully responding.

The service engaged only a fraction of Philip's attention. He watched the rest of the assembled villagers, and one bonneted head in particular, and let his mind drift to the conundrum of how to secure the future of the people of Feldon Roding while still meeting the debts he had inherited from his reckless uncle. Or, more properly, from his cousin, who had outlived his father and brother for four weeks before dying of his injuries.

The shouted word "Harlot!" jerked Philip's attention back to the rector, whose homily had begun while Philip was distracted. The rector, it transpired, had a low view of women, and was able to support his case with multiple passages from the Bible. Not just Proverbs chapter thirty-one, his ostensible text, where a mother warns her son against giving his strength to women, and against drunkenness. It was all one, the rector explained.

"For when a man allows himself to be blinded by lust, it is the woman who rules, and so it has been since the first woman sinned with the serpent and dragged all creation down into perdition."

He shot out a finger, and a woman in the gallery above him blanched as her neighbours pulled away. Another woman illustrated the story of Jezebel; a third, Delilah. David, whose lust for his general's wife led him to commit murder by enemy army, had his sins glossed over by the rector, who laid all the blame on Bathsheba. At least he had no candidate for Bathsheba in the congregation.

But the relief was short lived, because he found a Gomer, and a Potiphar's wife. Yes, and a Lot's wife, too. All, Philip noted, among the poorer members of the conversation, though at one point his gaze lingered on Miss Finchurch. Philip tensed, ready to leap to her defence, but the rector moved on to another victim. Which was probably just as well, since Philip could hardly challenge a man of the rector's age, and in a church, at that.

The rector was waiting in the doorway when they left the church, Aunt Hannah congratulated him on his homily, her voice doubtful. He narrowed his eyes at Lalamani. "My niece, Lalamani Finchurch, my brother Hadley's child. So lovely of her to visit. Lalamani, you have heard me speak of dear Reverend Wagley."

"A heathen name," the rector observed, sourly.

He was interrupted by the local squire and his wife, eager to meet Lalamani. Before she and her aunt had made their way to the gate, Lalamani had been introduced to most of the local gentry and the more prosperous farmers and tradespeople of the town, all of whom expressed their delight she'd come to keep her aunt company.

The squire's wife, Lady Picknell, was only the first to express her intention of making an afternoon call. "My son Arthur shall escort me this very afternoon," she said.

"My son would be delighted to meet you, Miss Finchurch, when he is home for Christmas," said another.

Lalamani suppressed a sigh. Perhaps Feldon Roding would not be the sanctuary from match-making mothers she'd longed for.

A few spots of rain, harbinger of a steadier downpour, sent those lingering in the churchyard scurrying for their homes or their carriages, and Lalamani put up the umbrella for their walk home. But when she and Aunt Hannah reached the gate, a voice called, "Mrs Thorpe!"

Lord Calne was holding the door open to the carriage from the inn, looking far more handsome than any man had a right to. "Quickly, ladies, come in out of the rain."

"But Milly and Addy–" Lalamani objected, planning to accept for her aunt and walk home with the maids herself. Anything to avoid being at close quarters with the pesky man, who had been invading her dreams, awake and asleep, since their waltz. Even more since his visit to the house days ago. Four days ago, and not a word since, which should be enough to prove he was not interested in furthering their acquaintance. And yet here he was.

"Your maids are already in the carriage," Lord Calne assured her. "Hop in, and I'll have you all home in the dry in no time."

"How thoughtful of you," Aunt Hannah said, as he propped the door open with his shoulder and offered her his good hand to help her up the carriage steps. With no alternative, Lalamani took his hand next. Even glove to glove, his touch sent a shiver through her, and she motioned to the maids to make room for her on the bench, leaving Lord Calne to sit next to Aunt Hannah.

"I feel sure," he said to Aunt Hannah, "that I remember my mother reading to me about some virtuous women in the Bible. Do you think we should inform the Reverend Wagley?"

Aunt Hannah suggested charitably the rector perhaps ran out of time to discuss the many heroines of Bible stories. Why, even Chapter 31 of Proverbs was primarily about the characteristics of a virtuous woman: the wife who was worth more than rubies, who managed a household, a family, a vineyard, and a textiles business.

"And Lalamani is a very pretty name, I think," she added, and then had to repeat what the Reverend had said at the gate. Philip agreed, and Lalamani found herself explaining it meant 'Ruby', in celebration of a spectacular trading deal her father and uncle had signed just before her birth, which set their enterprise on the road to success.

At the house, Aunt Hannah invited Philip to join them for lunch, and he sent the carriage back to the hall without him. Aunt Hannah was telling him all about the work they had been doing, "which is just as well, for we are to have visitors! Why, I believe half the village intends to call. They wish to meet Lalamani, of course. We shall be quite merry, and I am so grateful to my dear niece and her maid, for I do not mind telling you the heavy cleaning has been too much for me and poor Addy for some time."

Let him make what he would of Lalamani doing the cleaning. She was not ashamed of working with her hands to help her aunt. The smile he gave her seemed admiring, but she knew aristocrats demanded idleness from their wives and daughters. They could direct servants, but never sully their own fair hands. Well. She was no aristocrat, and she wouldn't pretend to a gentility she lacked. And as to the gentry of the village who had so neglected a woman who had served them for forty years, she would be polite for Aunt Hannah's sake, but she would certainly not pretend to them, either.

However, Lord Calne showed no signs of scorn, nor of objecting to once more eating in the kitchen with the maids. And when, as they were finishing their meal, Aunt Hannah and Addy began a low-voiced debate about what time to light the fire in the parlour for the expected guests, and which other rooms in the house could be left fireless until they could find someone willing to chop some of the wood in the woodshed into fire-sized pieces, he demanded to know the location of the axe.

"I will be back for visiting hour," he said, and set off to chop wood.

After an hour and a half, Lalamani went looking for him. The woodshed allowed for large pieces to be stored—drying—along one side and stacked chopped pieces on the other. The stack was at least triple its former size. Lord Calne, stripped to the waist, was at the chopping block in the centre of the shed, and she stood for a long moment admiring the width of his shoulders and the ripple of his muscles as he lifted a heavy mallet with his good arm and brought it down on a metal wedge inserted into the slice of trunk on the block.

The other arm was well muscled to the elbow, but the scarred forearm was markedly less robust than its counterpart, and his ungloved hand was twisted and deformed.

He brought the mallet down again, a mighty blow with all his weight behind it, and the trunk split, a chunk falling to the ground. He bent to pick it up, and his pantaloons tightened over his buttocks, riveting her eyes.

As Philip bent to pick up the bit of wood he'd knocked loose, he sensed Lalamani's presence and turned in time to see her admiring his anatomy. A moment too late to disguise her interest, she dragged her eyes up to meet his, flushing to her hairline. He was in time to squelch his smirk, which—he was certain—would not find favour with her.

"My aunt sent me to let you know there is warm water in the scullery, for you to refresh yourself," she said, her gaze now fixed on the rafters of the shed and her voice higher pitched than usual.

"Thank you." Philip reached for his shirt, then changed his mind and bundled it in his jacket, pulling on his great coat instead. He'd been perspiring freely while chopping, and would like to wash before dressing again, but even in the shelter of the shed he could feel the chill now he'd stopped.

The rain had cleared for now, and the afternoon was fair but cold, with a biting wind that hissed across the small kitchen courtyard and infiltrated beneath the skirts of his coat.

Lalamani was halfway to the house before he caught up with her. "I have a stack of wood we've cleared from the buildings at the Hall, Miss Finchurch. I'll have a cart load chopped into manageable pieces and send it over."

"That would be very kind of you," she said.

He cleaned himself as best he could in the scullery, grateful for the warm water and a handful of soap jelly. Beyond the door to the kitchen, he heard her telling Mrs Thorpe of his offer. He dried himself off and dressed again, resigned to being thanked, and sure enough, though he assured Mrs Thorpe the scraps he planned to give her were destined to burn and might as well provide someone with warmth while doing so, he had to bear the burden of her gratitude until the first of the afternoon callers arrived.

He had intended to leave in proper form after the civil thirty minutes. But Arthur Picknell annoyed him, with his sullen and reluctant attentions to Lalamani, and the other puppies accompanying their mothers were no better. And so Philip appropriated for himself the duties and privileges of a nephew of the house, even to addressing Mrs Thorpe as Aunt Hannah, and advising one over-enthusiastic youth to mind his manners.

Aunt Hannah failed to notice. Lalamani's glare promised retribution, but she went along with his masquerade until the last of the afternoon visitors was escorted to the door, and even then, allowed him to make his own farewells and escape into the evening.

Chapter Seven

It was a reprieve only, and when he stopped work the following day to let the men go home for their nooning and saw Lalamani waiting for him, he knew he would need to account for his sudden desire to slay dragons for her, or—failing a good fire breather—to protect her from nuisance. Though he doubted he could explain. He had spent the past evening and all day so far today trying to understand it himself.

"I am sent with food, Lord Calne," his damsel told him. "Our Aunt Hannah is anxious her new nephew should not starve."

"About that." He trailed her to where she had set a blanket in a patch of weak sunlight against the one stone wall still standing from the carriage house. "I can explain."

"What did you think you were doing?" She sounded more bemused than annoyed. "If you sought to convince those silly women and their sons you are courting me, I cannot fathom the purpose. And it won't serve, since you will be gone soon. Besides. It is ridiculous."

He had been intending to apologise, but that distracted him. "How is it ridiculous? That a poverty-stricken engineer like me might look so far above him?"

"That is not what I mean, and you know it. You are an earl, even if none of them realise it. And only an idiot would mistake you for anything but a gentleman. While I am daughter and niece to a merchant, without a drop of blue blood in my veins. Which at least means no one will be surprised when you disappear. They will simply decide you could not stomach the smell of the shop."

That sounded like a quote. From those women he'd interrupted at the Haverfords' dance, no doubt, or others just like them. Philip swallowed the urge to tell her what he really thought of her. For one thing, she wouldn't believe him. For another, he couldn't act on his feelings. Yes, she had more than enough money for both of them, but if he found the idea of marrying an heiress undesirable in the abstract, he discovered it was even more distasteful now he had found an heiress he could fall in love with. He could never consent to touching the money her uncle left her. And without it, he could not afford to marry.

"I do have to leave," he said. "But I am torn to pieces about it. For one thing, working here brings back all my father's stories. He grew up here, and used often to tell us stories about him and his younger brother, and the games they played in the grounds and in the dower house where they lived. I thought it would be no hardship to sell a place I had never seen, and didn't want to inherit. But it is wound around my bones, thanks to my father."

Lalamani's eyes widened. "You plan to sell? But what of the entail?"

"There is none. An entail must be renewed from time to time, and my cousin outlived my uncle long enough to inherit. The earl had sold everything that was his to sell, even the lands around here he acquired through enclosure, but under the entail he held the Hall in trust for his son, and his son held it in trust for the next heir."

"You."

It was not a question, but he confirmed it anyway. "Me. Because my cousin didn't renew the entail, I inherited free and clear. Apart from mountainous debts, which I have no way of paying except for selling what is left." Whether he wanted to or not.

Lalamani passed him a cup of something from a flask, and he took a sip. A lemon drink, still warm and rich with honey.

"You said that was one of the reasons you feel torn."

"I feel guilty about leaving the local people to the non-existent mercies of the local gentry. I have heard a few stories this week, and they're suffering. You'd think the rector would champion them, but... Well. You heard him yesterday. And according to those I've spoken with, he was the power behind the enclosure act, and is ruthless in collecting his tithes."

"But what can you do about it," Lalamani asked.

"I am the earl. I hold his living. I could show by example how to act. If I could stay."

He was going to tell her his third reason, which was his attraction to her, but he suddenly realised that, in connection to the first two, it would sound as if he was trying to persuade her to put her fortune at his disposal. And it was the rest of her assets he wanted. Her charm, her intelligence, her sense of humour, her delectable body.

"Come on," he said, scrambling to his feet. "Let me show you around and tell you what I'm doing."

He found himself sharing the stories he'd had from his father, who had known every inch of these lands where he and his twin had roamed until Gerard died and Hugo was sent to school, seldom to return.

Lalamani took Lord Carne a midday meal the next day, too. And the day after.

When she slipped up and called him 'my lord' in front of the workmen, he brushed it off with a laugh, but after they had left, asked her to call him Philip. "For if I have adopted Mrs Thorpe as my aunt, you must be my cousin," he suggested.

"Or your sister?"

He froze, every muscle alert, his eyes suddenly intent. "Definitely not my sister."

She couldn't look away. The conversation of the departing workmen faded and the corner they had chosen as their own picnic spot dimmed. Philip was suddenly more real than all of it; the only solid thing in a ghostly world. She swayed towards him and he gripped her shoulders, his eyes fixed on her lips, his face moving towards her... Until he straightened and turned away.

"I beg your pardon, Miss Finchurch." He kept his back to her, as if the ruin of his Hall was far more appealing than one slightly over-aged spinster.

He must have heard her sigh, because he spun round to face her. "You must know that, if circumstances were different…"

Was she supposed to believe she had swept him off his feet and he was only resisting with difficulty? What he took from her expression she didn't know, but he suddenly swore, and reached again for her shoulders, crushed her to him, then cursed again and lifted her bodily onto the log they had been using for a seat.

Now her head was a little higher than his, so she had to curve her neck to reach his lips when he lifted his face. She had been kissed before, a few times. Some of the ambitious young men who thought to win her uncle's favour had been almost convincing in their courtship. Besides, she was as susceptible as anyone to curiosity and the temptation of a private spot in a warm lush garden after a night of music and dancing. On the whole, the experiences had been unremarkable.

She could, were she not so distracted by his firm but gentle lips, catalogue the many differences between those disappointing kisses of long ago and this one, from the setting to the sensations. But he was running his tongue gently along her lips, and she opened, wondering what he intended, then forgetting everything. The oak, the chill wind, the possibility a workman might return early. Philip was all that existed in the world. Philip, and her body coming alive where he touched her, still only with his lips, and a hand lightly kneading each hip.

Until he groaned and wrapped his arms around her, pulling her from the log to mould her against him, his mouth hardening over hers, his tongue stroking even deeper over hers as she clasped him back and lifted her legs to curve them around his hips, heedless of anything except the urge to be closer still.

For one long endless moment, she was lost in sensation, and then he drew his head back, to drop a flurry of kisses along her jaw bone, so she tipped her head back to give him access, and blinked as a large rain drop fell in her eye.

It was followed by others, first a spattering, then a deluge, and Philip stumbled a couple of steps to set her down against the trunk, out of the rain.

 His laugh was rueful, and his voice shook as he said, "They said in the inn last night that the rain would set in this afternoon."

He still held her, and she leant against him, uncertain her legs would hold her up. "That was…" She didn't have the words. "Philip," she said, instead. A statement, because she was afraid to make it a question.

"Lalamani," he breathed back, and rested his chin on her head, which had somehow lost its bonnet in the past fifteen minutes. One hand rested on her waist while the other stroked her back. "Lalamani," he said again, then, just as quietly, murmuring into her hair. "I owe you an apology, but I am not sorry. To have missed that kiss would have been a crime. But I had no right."

His obtuse male attitude steadied her, and her own voice was calm as she reminded him, "If any apology is required, it is for me to offer it. I started our kiss. And I am not sorry, either."

He chuckled. "I am glad. But I still… Were circumstances different, I could court you in proper form and hope one day for the privilege of taking our kiss to its proper conclusion, but I have nothing to offer a wife, Lalamani. It could be five years before the canal pays enough to provide more than bachelor accommodations. Even were you not used to the best of everything, I could not…" He trailed off.

"I do not need someone to provide for me," Lalamani reminded him. "I have more than enough money for me and anyone I truly loved." That was as close to a declaration as she dared, but it did not have the desired effect.

"Ah, Lalamani." He sighed, then kissed her again, a light touch on the forehead, and pulled away. "I cannot live off my wife. Can I?" He shook his head as if to clear it, then held out his undamaged hand. "Come. I should see you home to your aunt's house."

Ridiculous man. In their conversations, and in that kiss, she had glimpsed a hope for which she had thought herself too old. If he didn't see it too, or if he would let his male pride stand in its way, then she was too proud to pursue it. "I will show you a quicker way," she said. "There is a path and a gate straight to the house."

They ran through the rain hand in hand, and arrived at the house's side door, wet and laughing, the awkwardness left behind at the tumbledown Hall.

"Was this once part of the estate?" Philip asked, as he sat in the parlour rubbing his hair dry with a towel.

"It was the dower house," Aunt Hannah told him. "The earl sold it after his mother died, though by rights it should have gone to his youngest son. But, of course, young Hugo had been gone for many years by then."

"The dower house?" Philip was looking around, wide eyed.

Aunt Hannah lowered her voice so it did not carry beyond the room. "Yes, my lord. This was the home of your great grandmother, for whom you are named. Your father and uncle grew up here."

Lalamani looked from her aunt to the earl. His eyes were round with shock. He pulled himself together enough to close his gaping mouth. "You knew?"

"I was rector's wife here for forty years, Lord Calne. I knew all the Daventrys, especially the Dowager Lady Calne, who raised your father and uncle after their mother died. I daresay you think if the villagers knew you were the earl they would expect you to solve all their problems overnight. I do not blame you for keeping your identity hidden until you work out how you can do your best for your people. Do not worry. I will keep your secret. And so will Addy, of course."

Milly came in just then carrying a tray of tea makings, and Aunt Hannah changed the subject.

"It is so delightful to have plenty of tea, dear Lalamani. I do enjoy it, though one should not be attached to worldly things."

Philip was reeling. His father had loved the house in which he and his twin had grown, exiled from the Hall when his mother died shortly after their birth. Loved it, at least, until the incident that had cost him his brother. It must have been before Mrs Thorpe arrived in the parish, but perhaps she could answer some of the questions Philip had always had about his father's family. Surely people had talked, and if they talked to anyone, it would have been to the rector or his wife.

And she took it for granted he planned to stay. He wished he could. Not just so he could court Lalamani, but so he could do his duty by the people who had served the earldom for many generations.

There was one possibility, and to follow it through he would have to disclose his identity. The villagers would not be impressed with his deception, but perhaps they'd be grateful at the unmasking of a villain.

When a break in the rain came, he said his farewells. "I will be sure to bring an umbrella next time I come," he said.

"Will you come to dinner this evening," Mrs Thorpe suggested. "We always have the rector and his sister on the third Thursday of the month, so you would have fine company."

Philip accepted. Meeting the rector on a social occasion would suit his purposes nicely.

Mrs Thorpe smiled. "Excellent. And Lalamani shall enjoy having a young person to talk to; for we have been deserted by our usual visitors, Lord Calne. Mr Daventry, I mean."

"Please call me 'Philip'," he suggested. "After all, you knew my father and my great grandmother, so I am practically family."

Mrs Thorpe's eyes twinkled. "If you call me 'Aunt Hannah'."

Lalamani scrambled to her feet. "I shall walk you to the Hall gates," she said.

Within minutes, she had fetched her pelisse and bonnet and they were strolling up the lane, dodging the worst of the puddles.

Lalamani tucked her hand confidingly into his elbow. "Philip, I cannot be sure, but I suspect the Reverend Wagley of wickedness. Will you help me find out?"

Philip nodded. He would do more than help. After all, this was his business, and he said so. "I intend to unmask him, Lalamani. If he has been stealing the earldom's rents, perhaps for years, then he has to be stopped. And if I can recover any of the moneys, they should go back into the estate. Perhaps there will be enough…"

But he trailed off. She had stopped and was staring at him in surprise. "He has been stealing the rents?"

"He has been collecting the rents, according to the tenants to whom I've spoken, and my lawyer denies ever seeing them. One of them is lying."

"The rector, certainly, for I am sure he has been stealing from Aunt Hannah. You will help me, will you not? You don't have to leave the village yet?"

If Lalamani was heading into danger, the whole of Napoleon's army wouldn't be able to shift him from her side.

"Tell me," he suggested, and when she told him the whole story, he agreed it sounded suspicious.

"Write to your uncle's man of business and ask him for the details of the inheritance and the trust," he advised. "I'll find out how to get the letter to the mail collection point." He corrected himself. "Your man of business, now, of course."

"I wish he thought so." Lalamani sighed. "In his mind, Mr Wiggens still works for Uncle Hadley. 'A young lady like yourself, Miss Finchurch, need not worry her pretty little head about figures and other such fusty stuff.' I look forward to the day I turn twenty-five and can find a man of business who does not think a woman incapable of thinking."

"Does he know you were your uncle's secretary and managed all of his affairs from the time you were seventeen?"

"He is convinced I wrote to my uncle's dictation. He disapproves. He tells me Uncle should have sent me home when I was seventeen 'so you could make your curtesy to the Queen, Miss Finchurch.' So I could catch a husband before I become so elderly, he means."

They had reached the gates to the Hall's coach road, and before they parted, Philip enjoined Lalamani not to let the rector know of her suspicions. "We do not want to give him time to cover his tracks," he said. "If he has been stealing from your aunt, we'd do better to surprise him with the evidence."

Lalamani turned back. Philip walked the rest of the way into the village, turning what he'd learned over in his mind.

Perhaps he should take Lalamani's letter up to London himself. Interviewing Mr Wiggens could be useful. But first he wanted to meet this villainous rector.

Chapter Eight

Lalamani joined Aunt Hannah and Addy in the kitchen to help cook dinner, overriding her aunt's objections.

Lalamani took the opportunity to try to persuade Aunt Hannah someone had been stealing from her. The suggestion fell on deaf ears. Aunt Hannah could not believe it. Certainly, it could not be Dr Wagley. The mind revolted! He might be a little strict, Aunt Hannah conceded, but no one could doubt his faith. His sermons were thirty minutes long! He always knew the right passage from Scripture to show others the errors of their ways. No, Dr Wagley was a fine Christian man, though not, perhaps, as generous to the poor as her own dear Mr Thorpe.

Perhaps Dr Wagley's way was better. He said helping the poor only made them lazy. But Aunt Hannah sounded doubtful. "My dear Mr Thorpe said all of us faced trouble in our lives, and the good Lord wanted us to help others when they were in need."

Lalamani carefully studied the gingerbread stars she was icing to decide whether she should add more lines. "I like that, Aunt Hannah. He sounds lovely."

"He was, dear. Such a kind man. It did cause trouble sometimes, because he hated upsetting people. I remember one Easter when he gave three different women the lead solo, and the time he wanted to add five more grand prizes at the Whitsunweek fete, because he didn't want any of the entrants to be disappointed. The people loved him, dear, and they were all very helpful when I explained."

Lalamani managed to keep her face and her voice neutral. "Dr Wagley does not experience the same difficulty, I take it."

"Oh no, dear. Dr Wagley is very decisive. Of course, we do not have the fete any more. Dr Wagley felt it was a pagan festival and promoted licentious and debauched behaviour. And we do not have women in the psalm singers anymore." Aunt Hannah sighed. "I am sure it is all for the best."

Addy, who had been returning the chicken to its pot after turning it, slammed the lid back onto the dutch oven with quite unnecessary force. "Handsome is as handsome does," she muttered.

"He is very good about visiting the sick, Addy," Aunt Hannah said, but Addy just snorted.

With the three of them working, an expansive if simple dinner was ready for Addy and Milly to put on the table when Philip and the Wagleys arrived.

From behind the curtain in the parlour, Lalamani saw Philip arrive at the gate just as the Wagley's gig pulled up. The two who descended, as Lalamani had noticed at church, were male and female counterparts: tall, gaunt, and elderly; spry, but a little bent. They put Lalamani in mind of herons—sharp features and an alert forward-leaning stance.

Lalamani flicked the curtain back into place and hurried into the front hall in time to introduce Philip.

"Allow me to present Philip Daventry, who works for the Earl of Calne."

Two pair of pale eyes fixed first on Lalamani and then on Philip. Brother and sister both, Lalamani noted, jutted their chins forward and lengthened their necks, increasing the resemblance to herons. Dr Wagley, dressed top to toe in black, relieved only by a white stock, clearly stinted nothing on the cut and quality of his cloth, and Miss Wagley's grey silk gown was trimmed with, if Lalamani was not mistaken, real French lace. The contrast between their finery and Aunt Hannah's worn and much-mended widow's wear could scarcely be greater.

Dr Wagley surveyed Philip from top to toe, and asked, coldly, "And what do you do here, sirrah? The people of this village think highly of Mrs Thorpe, and will not see her put upon."

"I'm glad to hear it, Dr Wagley," Philip answered mildly. "I am here to survey the Hall, to decide what repairs are necessary."

Miss Wagley furrowed her brow. "You are a Daventry? How closely related are you to the earl, Mr Daventry?"

"The late earl was a connection of my father's," Philip prevaricated.

"Did you hear that, Jeremiah?" Miss Wagley tugged on her brother's arm, but Wagley's harrumph suggested he was not impressed.

The conversation in the parlour limped from one pronouncement by Dr Wagley after another. He frowned upon the evangelical fervour gripping a nearby parish, was suspicious about the proposed Act of Union, despised the call by radicals to widen the vote, and was scathing about the Speenhamland system of poor relief.

Addy's invitation to the dining room interrupted a homily on the place of women—silent and obedient.

Over dinner, Lalamani made an effort to turn the conversation. "Mr Daventry was formerly in the army. Before you arrived, he was telling us a little about the markets in Egypt."

Dr Wagley looked dourer than before. "Nothing unsuitable for a lady, I trust."

"Oh, Jeremiah," his sister chirped, "Mr Daventry is a gentleman; a relative of Calne, you know."

Philip, catching Lalamani's desperate eye-roll, picked up the conversational ball with a story about a carpet he and his friends had bargained for and how language difficulties had almost left them with a camel instead. He made an amusing tale of it, but only Lalamani laughed.

Dr Wagley spoke into the pause. "Another excellent meal, Mrs Thorpe. Mrs Thorpe sets a fine table, Daventry."

Lalamani did not try to resist the impulse. "My aunt is very grateful for the charity of the people of the parish, Dr Wagley, without which she would undoubtedly starve. Though…"

She felt a blow on her ankle. Philip, who had clearly guessed she was about to mention her uncle's provision for his sister. She shot him an accusing glance, but pressed her lips tightly together.

"The care of widows," Dr Wagley opined, "is, of course, enjoined on us in Scripture. 'But if any provide not for his own, and especially for those of his own house, he hath denied the faith, and is worse than an infidel.' Charity begins at home." He nodded seriously and took another mouthful of the donated chicken.

"And," his sister added, "it is the duty of every Christian to support the men of the cloth." She poked suspiciously at the chicken. "I would not like to think our parishioners were stinting their duty."

"Now, now, Euphrania," Dr Wagley said. "We do not begrudge Mrs Thorpe a chicken or two, especially when she has visitors. Do you make a long stay, Miss Finchurch? It would not do for you to be a charge on your aunt." He cast her an admonishing stare over the top of his glasses, which had slipped almost to the tip of his nose.

"My plans are not fixed, Dr Wagley." Lalamani was going to ask how it was his affair, but Philip spoke first, once again preventing her from antagonising the sour old man.

"How nice that you are able to support your brother in his parish work, Miss Wagley."

Miss Wagley needed no encouragement to dominate the conversation for the rest of that remove and all of the next. According to her, the parish had been neglected before the Wagleys arrived, and the people sunk in idleness and dissolute living. She seemed completely oblivious to any distress she might be causing Aunt Hannah, and—indeed—Aunt Hannah seemed barely to be listening.

Dr Wagley, when his sister asked his opinion—which was often—declared his agreement, often backing it up with a biblical verse, mostly, Lalamani noted, from the old Testament.

For the rest, he applied himself to his dinner, trying all the dishes on the table, and eating his way through every serving. He only took over the discussion once, when Lalamani pointed out Christmas was less than two weeks away.

"Christmas? Christmas? We do not celebrate that pagan festival in this parish, Miss Finchurch." The rhetorical bit within his teeth, he declaimed for several minutes on the pagan origins of traditional Christmas activities and the likely eternal destination of those who succumbed to the lure of evergreen decorations and other more licentious activities he would scorn to describe in the hearing of a lady. He graced his sister with a bow of his head.

By the time he pushed back a little from the table, the other four had long finished. Aunt Hannah had been looking uncertainly from him to Lalamani for some time, clearly wondering if she should signal the ladies' departure from the table. Before she could make up her mind, though, Miss Wagley stood.

"Ladies," she announced, and led the way to the parlour next door.

The men didn't stay at the table above ten minutes, and shortly after they joined the ladies, the Wagleys' gig arrived, and they said their farewells.

Lalamani waited for them to offer Philip a lift back to the inn, which they would pass on the way to the rectory. He was moving his arm cautiously after all his work at the Hall, and would surely be better to ride rather than walk. The Wagleys, though, collected their coats and shawls, and moved towards the front door without any such offer.

"Dr Wagley," Lalamani said. "Would you have room in your gig for Mr Daventry? I believe his arm is paining him."

Philip's glare suggested a total lack of appropriate gratitude, but he recovered himself to thank Dr Wagley politely, and the three left together.

Much though Philip wanted to stay behind for another word with Lalamani, he was glad not to face that walk, especially since it was raining again. The ride was short, only a few minutes of Dr Wagley's chilly disapproval and Miss Wagley's clumsy sycophancy.

As he prepared for bed, he turned over what they'd found out in the course of the day. Dr Wagley was an unlikely villain, however disagreeable he might be. But unlikely was not impossible. Lalamani was adamant her man of business was honest: an income had been left and income there was none. And Uncle Henry swore by Philip's own man.

By the morning, he had a plan. He walked the distance to the house once more, this time through driving rain. Lalamani scolded him for coming out and set his coat to dripping in front of the kitchen fire.

He admired the voluminous apron protecting her day dress. It had been made for Aunt Hannah, clearly, and wrapped Lalamani's slender body completely.

"We are turning out the rest of the bed chambers," Lalamani explained.

"We need to talk, Lalamani." He broke off to greet the smiling Mrs Thorpe.

"So lovely to have company, Philip. Come and sit down. You find us at sixes and sevens, but we can find you a place to sit and a nice cup of tea."

"No, Aunt Hannah, I'm here to help. Many a time I've cleaned up after myself. Lead me to a broom or a dust cloth, and I'm your man."

"We'll talk when she has her rest," Lalamani murmured as she passed him a bucket and a rag.

They stopped for a bite to eat at noon, and then Aunt Hannah went off to her bed, "For I am not as young as I used to be, my dears," and Addy to her room off the kitchen.

"Milly, Mr Daventry and I have some paperwork to take care of." Lalamani sent her maid to doze by the kitchen fire.

In the parlour, Philip explained what he had in mind. He would write to Brigadier General Lord Henry Redepenning, his uncle, explain their concerns, and ask him to visit both men of business and investigate.

"And you're sure your uncle would not mind?"

"Not at all," Philip reassured her. His uncle would assume Philip's interest in the matter was personal and would do all he could for a potential Countess of Calne. And his uncle would not be wrong, if Philip could find a way to provide for a wife without depending on her own wealth.

Together, they composed a letter, with many starts, stops, and insertions.

"There," Philip said after a while. "I think we have it."

"Give it here, Philip, and I'll write it out again."

Philip went off to put the kettle on the fire for another pot of tea, and Lalamani took their much-crossed draft to write it in a fair hand.

Chapter Nine

The rain set in for several days. Each morning, Philip made the trek to the house, declaring he could do no work at the Hall until the weather cleared. Aunt Hannah cheerfully accepted his presence without any comment beyond declaring they would eat their main meal in the middle of the day, "as the country people do, Philip," so he had only the one trip each day, and would not be walking in the rain and the dark.

Lalamani didn't comment either. She held herself at a slight distance, and Philip—conscious of his new feelings for her, but unclear about how she felt—did not try to bridge the gap. These days of domesticity were peaceful and pleasant.

Philip joined Lalamani in the kitchen, where she made gingerbread shapes and other Christmas treats, and he brought a huge box of ribbons down from the attic so she could concoct Christmas decorations to put up on Christmas Eve. He helped clean, mend, and even paint until the whole house was gleaming.

One day he ventured down into the cellars, which had loomed in his childhood as the gateway to hell. His father had spoken briefly of that watershed moment in his own childhood. Philip told Lalamani the story, holding her hand against the chill that had leaked into his soul from his father's memories.

Hugo Daventry's older brother, Walter, had locked Hugo and Gerard in their grandmother's cellar, then gone home and told no one they were there. Perhaps the older boy had not known Lady Calne was assisting at a birth and the servants were on their Sunday half-day. Or perhaps he intended the twins not to be found for twelve hours. Both boys had been chilled, and Gerard, already sick with a winter ague, had never recovered, dying several days later.

"My grandfather blamed my father," Philip told Lalamani. "His heir told him it was my father's idea, and my uncle tried to dissuade them. The earl believed Walter."

It was the beginning of the split in the family that became permanent when Hugo married a commoner, the younger sister of Lord Henry Redepenning's wife.

The cellar lost its terror after he told Lalamani its history, and it desperately needed sorting, so he spent an afternoon down there putting items on shelves and hauling the obvious rubbish outside for disposal.

One room on the lower side of the house, with a row of high windows letting in the light, had obviously been a play place for the twins, and perhaps previous generations of grandchildren, for Philip found the detritus of their games, and smiled as he recognised signifiers of some of his father's stories: a chest full of glass and gilt jewellery and costume crowns that had featured as a pirate's treasure, a pair of wooden swords and lozenge shaped shields on which the painted crosses still shone after he wiped off the dirt, a box filled with a carved army—no, two armies—their colours still discernible, though chipped and scratched after years of playing. Philip put those treasures on a shelf. He'd ask Aunt Hannah, later, if he might have them.

In the evenings, he mixed with the local patrons of the inn and found the village sharply divided in their opinions. Miss Wagley was roundly condemned by one and all as an interfering old besom, but Dr Wagley was regarded as a saint in some quarters and a tyrant in others. As the chairman of the workhouse committee and wielder of influence with the squire and therefore the constable, even those who didn't like him feared to cross him.

On the evening of the fifth day, Philip arrived back at the inn just as a travelling coach pulled in. He'd passed it and was climbing the stairs when a familiar voice said, "Good day, my boy."

Brigadier General Lord Henry Redepenning had just entered the main doors, a small, thin bespectacled man at his shoulder.

Philip turned, retracing his steps with his hand extended. "Uncle! What on earth are you doing here?"

"It's good to see you, too, Philip." His uncle grinned.

"I'm delighted, of course. I just didn't expect you to post all the way out here."

"Thought I'd bring Wiggens." He waved to his travelling companion. "Wiggens, my nephew."

The little man was clutching a briefcase with one hand and a file folder with the other. He managed to bow with a degree of dignity. "A bad business, my l—Mr Daventry. A bad business."

"Which we will not discuss in the public entrance of the inn," Uncle Henry said. "What are the rooms like here, my boy?"

Philip escorted them in, saw them settled with rooms, and ordered a nice dinner to be served in a private parlour, where he met with his uncle a short while later.

Mr Wiggens was anxious to talk to Dr Wagley that very evening, but Philip insisted they wait to consult with Mrs Thorpe and her niece, and Uncle Henry supported him.

Over a dinner served by Uncle Henry's own manservant, Philip questioned the two older men. Beyond a doubt, the rector had been sent funds intended for Aunt Hannah. And Uncle Henry also confirmed Philip's estate had received no rentals since the steward disappeared five years ago. "It is a substantial sum, my boy," Uncle Henry said. "Let's hope we can recover some."

The following morning, Philip escorted his uncle and the man of business on the two-mile walk to Aunt Hannah's. Uncle Henry, country born and still a fit active man in his early sixties, thoroughly enjoyed the trek. The rain had cleared, and the mud had dried between the ruts so that, by stepping carefully, one could avoid the worst of the puddles.

Mr Wiggens regarded the hedgerows with suspicion, the sheep with distaste, and the cows with alarm.

"You are not accustomed to the country, Mr Wiggens," Philip observed.

"I am a London man, sir. This place... the noises, the smells, the animals... How do people stand it?"

"Country people say the same when they come to London," Uncle Henry said. "But you were here once before, Wiggens?"

"Yes, my lord, when I came down to—as I thought—put in place measures for Mrs Thorpe's welfare. I blame myself, my lord. I blame myself very much. Had I not been so anxious to return to London… But a gentleman of the cloth, my lord, and so concerned for her, seemingly!"

"Yes, well, what's done is done, Wiggens. Is this the place, Philip? But I have been here before! Visiting your great grandmother with your father, Philip. It is surely the estate's dower house."

In the thin winter sunshine, it looked better than it had on Philip's first visit. The windows sparkled, cleaned inside and out, Lalamani had holystoned the front door slab and Philip had painted the front door a fresh green.

Philip had sent the pot boy ahead of them to warn the ladies of the visit, and morning tea was laid out in the parlour, where Aunt Hannah waited to preside over the tea pot, still in her faded black, but with a clean white fichu Lalamani had brought for her and a white lace cap decorated with pretty pink ribbons Philip had watched Lalamani making one afternoon while Mrs Thorpe slept.

"Lord Henry, this is such an honour. I do not know if you remember me, my lord, but I had the privilege of meeting you when you came here with the earl's father. Back when you were at school, that would have been."

"Indeed I remember," Uncle Henry agreed, bowing over her hand. "You gave us a great slab of gingerbread each. I still remember how delicious it was."

Aunt Hannah beamed. "Won't you take a seat, my lord? And, Mr Wiggens, how very kind of you to come all this way. Please sit down, sir. How very delightful this is, to be sure. Why, I do not remember when I last had such visitors."

Philip waited for her to get over her first fluster and to pour tea for Lalamani to carry to each of the guests. Once everyone was settled, he turned to Mr Wiggens. "Mr Wiggens, will you explain to Mrs Thorpe why we are here today?"

"Oh dear," Mr Wiggens said. He put down his cup, pulled some papers out of his omnipresent briefcase, and pushed his glasses back up his nose. "Mrs Thorpe, may I first say how very, very sorry I am."

Aunt Hannah was bewildered. "Why, whatever can you mean, Mr Wiggens?"

Slowly, the story came out, with many interruptions and exclamations from Aunt Hannah. Wiggens had come to the village to make sure his client's sister had a house to live in and an income to keep her comfortable for the rest of her life, as instructed by his client. "Your brother's instructions were very clear, Mrs Thorpe."

He'd found the village in some disarray even months after the epidemic that had carried off many, though mostly the elderly and the very young. The new rector had been in place a mere few weeks, and was working heroically. He much impressed Mr Wiggens with his commitment to returning order to the parish. Mrs Thorpe was sick, and—while past the crisis—in no fit state to hear business arrangements.

This, Mr Wiggens had from Dr Wagley and his sister, who assured Mr Wiggens that Mrs Thorpe had asked the Wagleys to take care of the matter for her.

"I never did! Oh, I never did." Aunt Hannah held out her hand, and Lalamani clasped it. "Lalamani, dear, how could they have said such a thing?"

Mr Wiggens, anxious to escape the uncertain countryside for the safety of his beloved London, had accepted Dr Wagley's offer to manage everything for Mrs Thorpe: the purchase of a house and the payment of a quarterly income sufficient to keep the admiral's sister in comfort and to assure her of some of life's elegancies. Here, Mr Wiggens cast a scornful glance around the room.

He had insisted on seeing Mrs Thorpe's signature giving Dr Wagley power to act as her agent in all things. "This, ma'am, is the document Dr Wagley brought me. See, witnessed by Miss Wagley, and signed by you."

Aunt Hannah shook her head. "No, Mr Wiggens. No, I did not sign that document. Why, that does not even look like my signature." The ready tears were rolling down her cheeks again.

Lalamani perched on the arm of her aunt's chair, all the better to hold the poor lady and pat her comfortingly.

"Oh, Lalamani, I cannot bear to believe it," she wailed. After a few moments, she lifted her head and straightened her back. "I need to know, Mr Wiggens. Have you been paying money to Dr Wagley?"

"I have, ma'am. I have paid him the sum of three thousand four hundred pounds, at the rate of one hundred pounds per quarter. This does not include the money disbursed for the repairs and furnishing of this house." Again, Mr Wiggens frowned at the shabby sofa and chairs. "A further sum, ma'am, of one hundred and seventy-two pounds when the house was first purchased, and sixty-five pounds three years ago."

Aunt Hannah's mouth opened and shut a few times as she clearly considered and rejected several words. Philip was a bit taken aback himself. Clearly, very little of the money had made its way to its rightful owner.

Finally, Aunt Hannah spoke. "Why, that fiend. He has not given me a tenth of that, Mr Wiggens, Lord Henry, and every penny has come with a sermon about how one should not be extravagant when living on the generosity of others. Why, Lalamani, he made me feel so guilty, and so grateful, and all the time it was my money."

The tears were gone. The colour high in her cheeks, Aunt Hannah was fast working herself into a temper. "Why the evil, evil, lying thief. Evil to them who evil thinks, Lalamani, and so I trusted him and look what he had done. Stealing from me! When I think of all the people I could have helped. Why, Mrs Bascombe's baby might be alive this very day had I money for the doctor, and I begged Dr Wagley, but he just shook his head and said how sad it was."

She could sit no longer, but was marching up and down the little parlour, her skirts swishing as she flicked them round at each end of the room. "As for that sister of his. Oh, if he is in it, she is too, you can be sure. 'I would like to wear colours again,' I said to her. 'Do you forget your husband so easily?' said she. 'Those of us who were not blessed with the holy state of matrimony find that hard to understand. Many a widow would be grateful to have such good cloth to their back and many years of wear in it yet.' All the time, it is my money that puts the clothes on her back, and so I'll be bound."

She came to a stop in front of Lord Henry. "You will put a stop to it, Lord Henry, will you not? Why, I should like to… I do not know what, indeed I do not, but it would be violent, beyond a doubt."

Philip met Lalamani's eyes, brimming with amusement at the sight of her plump little hen of an aunt ready for war. "This is the most animated I've seen her," he murmured.

"Just think," she whispered back, "I will never again have to listen to 'But Dr Wagley says…'"

Lord Henry broke away from the conversation he and Mr Wiggens were having with Aunt Hannah to say, "Philip, we will head to the rectory immediately to confront the gentleman. You will come?"

"Of course, sir," Philip agreed readily.

"I will not come," Aunt Hannah said, decidedly, "for I would not be responsible for my actions, Lord Henry. But, Lalamani, you shall go in my stead. I trust you to remain calm, my dear, and to come back and tell me all about it. Now send in Addy, so I might tell her. Why, my dear, next quarter day, I will be able to pay Addy her wages and buy her a new dress! Just think!"

"I am authorised to pay you a sum immediately, ma'am," Mr Wiggens assured her. "Even if my firm cannot recover the amount already disbursed, we cannot but feel responsible for your loss. I am authorised to pay you two hundred pounds pending further investigations."

Lalamani left Addy ensconced in the other comfortable chair by the fire, holding her mistress's hands, the two excitedly planning what they would do with the unbelievable wealth of two hundred pounds while Milly prepared them a fresh pot of tea.

Bless them. They had already, in their minds, outfitted the children of several local families with shoes against the cold and had cut back their own plans for a whole new wardrobe to accommodate a new dress for the eldest daughter of the Mrs Bascombe mentioned earlier. "For she has grown so much this last season, her skirts are up to her knees, and she cannot easily pin her bodice closed.

"I fear the boys have noticed already, and it may be a matter of shutting the stable door after the horse has bolted, but there's no use that villain preaching from the altar about girls being improperly dressed when the family does not have any way of buying cloth for a new dress. Oh, it makes me so wild, Addy, when I think of it. Why the she-fiend could have long since given the child one of the dresses that *I paid for.*"

Lalamani closed the door on the rest of the conversation and joined the three men where they waited for her in the porch.

At the rectory, they surprised Dr Wagley crossing from the house to the church. He stopped to let them catch up, his eyes wary behind his spectacles.

"Dr Wagley? I am Brigadier General Lord Henry Redepenning. Mr Wiggens I think you know. And, of course, my nephew and Miss Finchurch. We wish to have a word with you."

Dr Wagley started walking again, saying over his shoulder, "It will have to wait, sir. I am on my way to God's house for my daily devotions."

Philip moved to block him, while Lord Henry stopped him with, "Halt!" After that parade-ground bark, the Brigadier General dropped his voice to a low growl. "You, Dr Wagley, have some explanations to make, and we will hear them now."

Dr Wagley, his gaze darting from person to person, hesitated on the path. Suddenly, he rounded on Lalamani. "What are you doing here? You're not part of this. You shouldn't be here."

Lalamani took a step back in alarm. The man was almost foaming at the mouth, his pale eyes protruding from his head in the force of his anger.

Philip stepped beside her, placing his shoulder before her as if he feared a physical attack. Indeed, the rector seemed ready to explode, until Lord Henry said sharply, "That will be quite enough, sirrah. Miss Finchurch is here to represent her uncle's wishes and her aunt's interests."

Dr Wagley turned his wrathful eyes on the older man. "She is a woman, sir. She should be silent and obedient. At her age, she should be married and have several children, not traipsing all over the countryside with an…" he nearly spat the next word, "engineer."

"Enough!" Lord Henry's battle-field roar silenced the fulminating rector mid-rant.

With several resentful glances at Lalamani, and defiantly proud glares at the men, he led the way to his study. He denied nothing, but insisted he was on the Lord's work and was therefore above mere human rules. "Mrs Thorpe would only have frittered the money away. What was her brother thinking, leaving such a legacy to a woman? Ridiculous. I have made much better use of it. Why, I reroofed the church. I put up a new wall to stop cows grazing in the church yard. I paid for building the extension to the workhouse."

"Correction," Lord Henry said, in a deceptively mild tone. "Mrs Thorpe paid for those things. And you gave her no choice in the matter."

Lalamani, who had been examining the rich furnishings in the rector's study, asked, "How much of Mrs Thorpe's income did you spend on furnishing the rectory, Dr Wagley? And on clothing for you and Miss Wagley?"

The rector glared at her, but made no reply.

"Mr Wiggens will examine your financial records," Lord Henry declared.

"He will also be looking for the rents collected from Lord Calne's tenants," Philip added.

"Those rents are nothing to do with you," Wagley hissed. "I collected them on behalf of the Earl of Calne."

"Yet the earl's man of business has no record of their receipt," Lord Henry said. "I examined the books myself."

"How dare you!" Wagley was dancing in his rage. "You are interfering without right or justice. I shall complain to the Bishop. I shall complain to the earl."

Philip, who had remained seating while the rector stood to better express his fury, was forming a peak with the fingers of both hands, his gaze intent on pushing his deformed fingers into place. "I asked my uncle to investigate, and he did so on my authority." He shot a piercing glance at Wagley over his steepled hands. "As is my right and duty, as Earl of Calne."

Wagley froze, then broke into a frenzied diatribe about deceit and his duty to rescue the earldom's funds from a profligate who would only waste them on riotous living.

Eventually, Lord Henry shouted him into silence, and Wagley sullenly produced a tidy set of ledgers in which every expenditure had been meticulously recorded. "Scripture says, 'Thou shalt not muzzle the ox that treadeth the corn,'" he declared, "and again, 'A workman is worthy of his hire.'"

Despite his quotations of Scripture, the records in his own handwriting were damning, every receipt and expenditure meticulously detailed. Even the sceptical squire, sent for to officiate in his role as local magistrate, could not deny the evidence. Wagley and his sister were taken into custody, pending further examination.

Aunt Hannah was pleased to know the rector had salted away much of what he had stolen from her in savings and investments. It would take time, but Mr Wiggens thought he should be able to recover at least half of the purloined funds. "Your rentals, too, my lord," he assured Philip.

Chapter Ten

The Wagley's larceny was the wonder of the village, but it was overshadowed by the discovery that Mr Philip Daventry, the quiet-spoken engineer with the ready smile, was really the new Earl of Calne.

Lalamani informed Philip that the poorer villagers were happy to overlook the deception. Aunt Hannah's supporters deduced he had disguised himself at the service of catching out "that there Dr Wagley and his sister, and a good thing, too." Lord Calne was their hero, not least once the rectory maid spread the news his tenants' rentals had been stolen by the unloved pair.

She left unexpressed their expectation that Lord Calne would now stay and resolve all their ills, but Philip could read between the lines.

And he could. With the rents he would start to receive next quarter day, even if he reduced them to a level more in keeping with his tenant's ability to pay, and with the money from the earldom's other properties he had already ordered sold, he would be able to arrange part payments to the hovering creditors with the promise of the rest in quarterly payments over time. Better yet, Wagley's accounting book recorded investments and savings, some of which should come back to Philip once the courts had finished their slow work.

Meanwhile, the weight of villagers' hopes was in every look he received in the lanes, every curtsy or bow, or hand offered for him to shake.

The gentry, particularly those who had ignored the lowly engineer, were more inclined to take offence at his impersonation. Even those fathers and brothers of would-be countesses, sent to the inn to make Lord Calne's acquaintance, usually managed to work in an assurance they alone, of all the locals, would have kept Lord Calne's secret and assisted him in unmasking the villain.

The day after the confrontation, he and Lord Henry saw the Wagleys off to Horsham to await the assizes, escorted by a brace of constables, and Mr Wiggens onto the mail coach that would return him to the safety of London.

Lord Henry would leave the next day, going directly to his nephew's house in West Gloucestershire, where his family was gathering for Christmas. "You are welcome to join us, Philip, of course," he offered, as they strolled back to the inn after an afternoon visit to Aunt Hannah's house, "but I will not press you if you prefer to spend Christmas with your lady."

"Not mine, uncle, more's the pity. Even if we can recover some of the stolen rent money, I'll be in no position to take a wife for a long time, perhaps years. Especially if I choose to keep this estate, which I suppose I must. How can I ask her to wait?"

"Why should you wait? Miss Finchurch is a considerable heiress, and can well afford any level of comfortable living she requires."

"That makes it worse. The first time we met, she told me she would not marry a fortune hunter under any circumstances."

Lord Henry stopped, and regarded Philip solemnly. "Are you a fortune hunter, then?"

"Of course not! I wish she were of modest means, or even without a penny. She might consider me then."

Lord Henry strolled on, his hands clasped behind his back, his attention seemingly on the hedgerow on his side of the lane. "So, is it her pride that stands in the way of your marriage, or yours?"

It was Philip's turn to stop. "Pride?"

His uncle kept walking, looking back over his shoulder. "Of course, pride. You love each other, as is plain for all the world to see. You are not after her fortune, any more than she is after your title, which she is not, if that thought crossed your mind."

Philip denied it with a hasty gesture. "Of course, she is not after my title. If anything, she regards it as a hindrance."

"Just as you do her fortune. Think about it, Philip. You are both young, healthy, single, and in love. Between you, you have the means and social position to do and be whatever you want, as a couple and as a family. What can be keeping you apart, if not pride?" He carried on down the lane, clearly having said all he meant to say, for he turned the subject to the grandchildren who would be waiting to see him when he arrived for Christmas.

Philip was not required to do more than listen, which was just as well, for his mind was elsewhere, occupied in taking apart his set plans for his future and shuffling them into a more pleasing pattern. Uncle Henry was right. Or, at least, he was right about Philip. Lalamani was worth humbling himself for, and if he could not be as certain of her response as Uncle Henry seemed, he would at least put it to the test.

He would have returned to the house that very night, but he and Uncle Henry were promised to dinner at the squire's. Tomorrow would be soon enough, even if every minute between now and when he saw Lalamani again would be a lifetime.

Philip did not have, had never had, a valet. Except for his one excursion into London Society with his uncle, Philip happily dressed himself without assistance. He had done so, he told those who felt the dignity of an earl required a manservant, since he first went to school, and intended to do so ever more. But fashionable ball attire required a helper. And so, Philip found, did courting wear.

As they had on the night of the ball, Uncle Henry and his manservant hovered, advised, corrected, and occasionally took a direct hand in fitting him into his finest shirt, an intricately tied cravat, his best pair of moleskin pantaloons in a soft faun he could never wear on a building site, and an embroidered waistcoat he had regretted buying at the moment of purchase since he would never have a day occasion formal enough to require it. But today he was glad of it.

Next came boots polished to the highest shine they'd had since he brought them home from the bootmaker, and the jacket his friends had talked him into the day he bought the waistcoat. It took Uncle Henry and the manservant, working together, to coax his shoulders into the jacket.

The two of them exchanged a whisper, and the manservant left the room, to return a few minutes later with Uncle Henry's trinket box. Despite his protests, Philip found himself fitted with a gold cravat pin set with a small emerald and three dangling belt fobs.

Uncle Henry handed him his beaver top hat, and put on his own. Philip stood a moment more at the mirror, hoping he looked calmer than he felt. Turning to the door where the manservant waited with his great coat, he felt a momentary pang that it was such a workaday garment, which was silly, since he'd be removing it as soon as he arrived. Still, what would it have hurt to have allowed the tailor to add the extra capes he had suggested?

Uncle Henry's coach was already loaded; the horses harnessed and waiting. They were dropping Philip at the house on the way out of town, both Uncle Henry and his servant having forbidden Philip to walk in his finery. In moments, the trinket box had been restowed, and they were on their way.

For the few minutes of the trip, Philip kept his mind off the coming interview by sending messages to his cousins, but as the coach pulled up at the gate, Uncle Henry reached out to clasp his hand. "I will not get down, my boy, but will be on my way. You know I wish you every success. I like your young lady very much, and I am confident your father and mother would have approved. Write me a letter and tell me what she says, and I will expect an invitation to the wedding."

Lalamani was dusting the window ledge in the front room, watching the road because she hoped Philip would call in before he went to the work site. She stilled the duster as Lord Henry's coach pull up outside. After a moment, Philip descended. A transformed Philip, dressed as finely as a town buck. Where could he be going?

In here? Really? He opened the gate, and his face, looking up at the house, was anxious. Behind him, the carriage continued down the lane, so this must be his destination, all spruced up as if he was going courting.

At the thought, she dropped the duster and flew into the hall. "Milly," she called. "I need you."

How could he arrive in all his splendour and her in an old gown with a handkerchief to protect her hair and an apron tied around her twice because it was one of Aunt Hannah's.

Aunt Hannah and Addy had appeared at her call, as well as her own maid.

"Tell Lord Calne I will be down shortly," Lalamani instructed Addy, and hurried up the stairs, with Milly on her heels. "The rose morning gown. No. What if he wants to take a walk? The light green, and put out the forest green pelisse and the matching bonnet. My hair! You must do something with my hair. Oh hurry, Milly."

What if he wasn't planning to propose? What if he had come to say goodbye, and Lord Henry was merely walking the horses until he had said his farewells? But the horses had been at a trot when they left, and in a direction that led out to the main road west.

What if he was all dressed up to visit one of the many gently-born maidens who had been trailed before him since he arrived? No. He had shown no signs of interest. But he wouldn't, would he? He was far too polite to make a show of courting one woman in from of another he had kissed.

While she fretted, Milly helped her out of her simple wool gown and into the fashionable silk, its vertical stripes alternating a soft green and a cream figured with embroidered sprigs of blossom in shades of lemon, with darker green leaves and stems.

How embarrassing if he guessed why she had changed. She almost told Milly to reverse the fastening she had just completed, and get her back into her working dress. But Milly was now brushing her hair, then combing it and pinning it into an elegant but simple twist at the back of her head. In the small mirror, she looked—not elegant, she was too short and curved for elegance—but at least armoured for an early call from the man who haunted her every waking thought.

A knock at the door heralded Aunt Hannah, broadly smiling. "Lalamani, you look lovely. Here. I would like you to wear this." She fumbled at her neck, undoing the cross that was one of the three pieces of jewellery she always wore. A locket with a picture of each of her brothers. A mourning brooch with locks of hair from her departed husband. And the cross Uncle Thorpe had given her as a wedding present.

"For luck, dearest." She dropped her voice. "He wants to see you alone. Oh, isn't it exciting? I could not be more pleased."

"Do you think he means to…" Lalamani let Milly fasten the chain around her neck, and stood to slip her feet into the slippers that matched the dress. "He said he could not court me; he could not live off his wife."

Aunt Hannah snorted. "What nonsense. Well, if he is not here to propose, I much mistake the matter. He loves you. That has been plain as the nose on my face since he first came running to the shop to see you before he had even washed away the dust of his journey."

Strengthened by her best morning dress, and Aunt Hannah's reassurance and warm hug, Lalamani made her way down the stairs, turning Aunt Hannah's parting advice over in her mind. "If he does not ask you to wed him, dear, you just ask him." She couldn't. Could she? Why not?

Philip was waiting in the parlour, standing by the mantelpiece looking into the fire. But he turned and straightened as she entered, and the devouring heat of his look made her suddenly shy, so that she retreated to formality. "Good morning, Lord Calne."

His smile faded. "Not Philip?"

Her own anxiety sank at the need to smooth the worried crease between his brows. "Of course, Philip. Let me start again. Hello, Philip. How nice to see you. I thought you would be at the Hall this morning."

"I have given my work crew a few days off. Until after St Stephen's Day. You look very lovely in that gown."

"You are rather smartly turned out yourself, today."

Philip looked down at himself, and chuckled. "I gave my uncle and his man their heads. You have guessed why, perhaps?"

Lalamani could feel herself blush, but Philip did not expect an answer, rushing on to say, "I prepared a speech. I spent the whole night rehearsing, I think. I may have slept a little, but only in snatches. And now I cannot remember a single word."

"I am sure it was excellent, but I do not need a speech," Lalamani told him.

He sank to one knee and took her hand. "I love you, Margaret Lalamani Finchurch. Would you do me the enormous honour of consenting to be my wife?"

It was speech enough, saying everything needed, and Lalamani's response needed only one word, but for a moment she could only stand looking down at his dear face, smiling. He beamed in return, but his smile slipped as the moment dragged on. "Lalamani?" he prompted.

"Yes. Oh yes, Philip. Oh Philip, I love you, too."

Chapter Eleven

Sunday was Christmas Eve. Philip was at the house early enough to escort his ladies to church, having once again hired the inn's gig. The curate from the next parish undoubtedly did an adequate job of the service, but Philip sailed through the morning in a dream, conscious of little but his betrothed.

He did notice the stir when he escorted Lalamani to take her rightful place beside him in the Calne box at the front of the church. Aunt Hannah, too, resplendent in the new gown Lalamani had made from the material they had been buying the day he came across them in the village shop.

Yes, and the even greater rustle and murmur when the curate read the banns for the first time.

After church, they ran the gauntlet of well-wishers, some sincerely delighted and others wanting the favour of their future countess. Philip hovered, but he need not have worried. Lalamani managed them with grace, and Aunt Hannah, who had known most of them since they were in swaddling, was at her elbow to support her.

A welcome flurry of rain, cold enough to hint at snow, sent everyone on their way. Yes, and would discourage afternoon visits, so he would have Lalamani to himself, but for her aunt and the two maids.

Still, as they decorated the house that afternoon, he found plenty of opportunity for tender moments under the bunches of mistletoe he helped to hang, and less holiday-sanctioned kisses whenever he could get Lalamani alone and unobserved for a moment.

The shabby house quickly took on a Christmas gaiety, with evergreen swags and wreaths, kissing boughs, and hanging bunches of ribbons. Lalamani fetched some strings of glass beads to twine around the swags on the mantelpiece in the parlour, where they would sparkle in the candle-light.

"Pretty," Aunt Hannah declared. "Do you have any more?"

"Wait here," Philip commanded, and went to fetch his father's pirate chest from the cellar.

"Bring a sheet to put down on the parlour carpet," he suggested to Milly, as he passed her in the kitchen, and a few minutes later he deposited the chest in the middle of the sheet.

"These should clean up to be very pretty," he said. "Even the metal things." He rubbed a crown, and the metal under the dust gleamed in the trail of his finger. Aunt Hannah and Lalamani were silent, and he looked around to see them gaping at the chest.

"It cannot be. The Calne Treasure?" Aunt Hannah asked.

"A jackdaw's treasure most of it," Lalamani said, "but some of it…" She knelt beside him and pulled a necklace of red beads from the tangle, to rub them on her apron and hold them up to the light. "Philip, these are rubies. Very fine."

"Lady Calne's rubies!" Aunt Hannah touched them lightly, her face awed. "They went missing long before we came here to live. And all this time they have been in the cellar."

It took them the rest of the afternoon to pull everything out, cleaning them under Lalamani's direction and spreading them around the room. It was, as Lalamani said, the eclectic collection of a jackdaw, or an imaginative pair of boys, borrowing here and there, and interrupted before they could return what they'd taken. Some of the jewellery was genuine, and would bring a good price. A few items were antiquities in need of an expert appraisal. Most of the hoard was worthless, Lalamani said, but Philip disagreed. "Christmas decorations and children's toys have their own value," he said, draping a bright string of green glass beads across the mantelpiece.

Philip insisted the house belonged to Aunt Hannah, so the valuables were hers, but Aunt Hannah said it was the Calne Treasure, undoubtedly deposited in her cellar by his own father, so it was his. And, besides, she had everything she needed for the remainder of her life. And Lalamani and Philip were her only family, so they would just take the treasure and put it towards the cost of restoring the Hall, and say no more about it.

"So, Lord Calne," Lalamani said, when they had packed all the real treasures away except the ruby necklace and its matching earrings, which she had agreed to wear to the Christmas morning service, "you are now wealthy enough to give away rubies for Christmas when all I have for you is those embroidered slippers." She pointed to the comfortable knitted slippers she'd made with her own hands.

Philip heard the slight undercurrent of tension, and bent to kiss it out of her. "I have been a wealthy man since the day you looked on me with favour, Miss Finchurch. 'For your price is far above rubies.' You are my love, and with you by my side, all of this is trumpery. You, Lalamani Finchurch-soon-to-be-Daventry are my Christmas Ruby."

Magnus and the Christmas Angel

Scarred by years in captivity, Magnus has fought English Society to be accepted as the true Earl of Halwick. Now he faces the hardest battle of all: to win the love of his wife. A night trapped in the snow with an orphaned kitten, gives Callie a Christmas gift: the chance to rediscover first love with the tattooed stranger she married. (short story)

Chapter One

Imperatrix was not in Magnus's chambers. She had not been accidentally shut in the cellars or the attic or any of the dozen unused bedrooms, frozen in a state of readiness for guests who never came. She was not anywhere in the house.

She was not in the stables, or the dairy, or any of the sheds or other outbuildings. The children of the Fenchurch Abbey estate had searched high and low, and brought a score of cats for Callie to inspect, hoping to win the reward.

None of them were Imp.

Callie had questioned all the servants who had cottages near the main house, and none of them had somehow acquired an elegant, imperious, elderly, and very pregnant black cat.

Or not so pregnant now. Imp had gone missing three weeks ago. Somewhere, she had nested and produced her litter. Somewhere—and half an hour ago, Callie had suddenly had an idea about where. They had moved from Blessings more than a year ago, and Imp had birthed two litters since then, her latest at Fenchurch Abbey (in Magnus' dressing room on his cravats). But perhaps she had returned to the place that had been home for most of her life?

Callie shivered, and pulled her shawl further forward over her head. She had run impetuously from the house without first checking the weather, and without telling her maid where she was going, thinking she would not be long.

The clouds looked ominous, but her childhood home was only a brisk walk away; she could be there, retrieve her cat, and be back well before dark. She was not a fool. She wore a rain cape, and it never snowed this far south as early as Christmas Eve. Except, it seemed, this year.

Perhaps it would remain a few stray flakes, melting before they reached the ground, but the sky was black and heavy. She might not make it back to Fenchurch Abbey before the snow began in earnest.

The servants would fret if she stayed at Blessings overnight. Magnus would neither know nor care. He had spent more time in London than at the Abbey since their wedding. Proving his identity so he could take up his title, he said. This was true, but avoiding his unwanted wife was doubtless also on his list of reasons.

His brief impersonal note had said he hoped to be home before Christmas, and she had ordered his rooms prepared: his bed made with fresh sheets, and a fire burned each day to drive the chill and damp from the air. But he had not come. She imagined that London held attractions far greater than the country girl his sense of honour had forced him to marry.

She turned another corner in the path. Here among the trees, the hill between her and Blessings was hidden, but the path was rising and she would soon be at the crest overlooking her destination.

No. She could no longer claim to be a girl. In the years it took him to come home and honour their childhood betrothal, she had left girlhood behind.

Her old nurse would say she was being unfair. Nanny was the only servant to stay with her when she had no money to pay wages after her brother died a year ago and his creditors seized everything moveable.

"His lordship were castaway then seized by savages, Miss Callie, as you well know. He came home as soon as he could escape, and just in time, too."

Yes, and even if she found him much changed—a dour and silent man had replaced the merry boy she had loved her whole life—she was grateful to him for saving her from marriage to his dissolute cousin, who was claiming Magnus's title, his estate and his bride. Wedding Lewis Colbrooke, the putative Earl of Halwick, was a horrifying prospect, but the only path she could see to save her and Nanny from starvation or worse.

Undoubtedly, the gossip about Magnus's reappearance from the dead was still thrilling the *ton*. It was certainly dramatic. He strode into the church and voiced a loud objection to the ceremony currently in progress. "…for she is betrothed to the Earl of Halwick, and I am he!" She had turned, and recognised him immediately, for all that she had not seen him since he was 15, and he was now a man grown, hard, scarred, and grim. In her relief, she had fainted for the first time in her life.

Her thoughts had carried her up the path and out of the woods. From the crest, Blessings should be visible, but the snow was falling more heavily and the path ahead disappeared into gloom. She narrowed her eyes. Was that not a horse? It stood patiently in the swirling snow, while its rider had dismounted and was bending over something on the ground.

Perhaps she could ask for help. She hurried down towards the horse, but her feet slowed as she approached. Surely that was Magnus' horse? And, yes, it was Magnus himself, standing and turning towards her.

In his large hands, something hung limp and lifeless. Something black—an animal. "Imp! You brute, Magnus! What have you done?"

Chapter Two

Magnus Colbrooke pressed on through the gathering snow, determined to reach home before Christmas. Callie would be expecting him, though whether she wanted him there was another question.

His pulse quickened and his heart sank at the thought of her. Now he had been confirmed as Earl of Halwick, sorted out the mess his affairs had become in his long absence, and made certain his pestilential cousin could no longer trouble him or Callie, he needed to deal with the far less tractable problem of his reluctant wife.

The snow was getting heavier, but taking the short cut through the grounds of Blessings had cut three quarters of an hour from the journey. Even now, he was still closer to Blessings than to Fenchurch Abbey. He would need to push the horse faster if they were to be home before the worst of the storm.

Part of him wanted to turn back to Blessings. Abandoned for more than a year, it would be cold and lifeless, but not as cold and lifeless as his likely welcome from Callie. From the moment she had taken one look at his tattooed face and fainted, he had tried to impose on her as little as possible, keeping his distance. The scars on his face were nothing to the scars on his soul from all he had done to survive during the years of his captivity. He could not bear for her to despise him more than she did already.

A black shape in the snow jerked him from his reverie. Perhaps a rabbit, crawled off to die after being shot by one of the tinkers from the camp close by Blessings. But it was not the right shape for a rabbit.

He could not have articulated why he stopped and dismounted to look more closely. Some vague thought of helping the poor thing, if it still lived. Perhaps he already knew—even from his lofty seat on the horse—what he had found, but his mind chattered on about feral cats and tinkers' cats even as his hands picked up the cold dead body of Callie's beloved Imperatrix.

She was curled around a kitten, as dead as its mother, poor little scrap. What had Imp been thinking, bringing the little one out in this weather?

A gasp behind Magnus told him he was no longer alone; a voice he knew, a scent he would recognise till the day he died even if he never smelled it again, composed of the herbs she strewed among her clothes, the flower oils she used to scent her soap, and something that was indefinably Callie.

He turned to meet blazing blue-green eyes in a white face. "Imp! You brute, Magnus! What have you done?"

"I found her, Callie. She must have been trying to bring the kitten home."

The name slipped out. She had told him that first day, after he interrupted her wedding and proposed himself as replacement groom, that no-one had called her Callie since she was a girl. So he honoured her wish, and called her Caroline. But in his heart, she would always be Callie.

Magnus hurriedly wrapped the cat in his muffler, hoping she hadn't seen the rat bites that scarred her beloved pet. He let her take the cat from him and hug it to her, fighting the urge to put his arms around her as the tears streamed down her cheeks. She would not welcome his comfort, had shrugged it off before. He stood helplessly watching, the little kitten cradled in one hand.

"I am sorry, Caroline," he said, after a while. "I know what she meant to you."

She looked up from weeping into the cat's fur, her eyes still swimming with tears but her face calm. The Callie he had left behind him thirteen years ago showed every emotion on her face. What had happened while he was gone to teach her such control?

"I apologise, Magnus. I know you would not hurt her. Is that her kitten?" She moved Imp to one arm and held out the other hand.

Her use of his name set his heart rioting. She did that occasionally; forgot his title and called him by the name she'd used when they were children, and each time his whole being vibrated with the hope that perhaps they could bridge the gap of years to find their old friendship.

"Ah, poor little scrap," she said, echoing his own reaction. Small as her hand was, the kitten filled it.

"Are there more, Halwick?" And just like that, she doused his hope in a bucket of cold titles. He had to wade through his disappointment to comprehend her question.

"More kittens? I have not had time to look, and if there were tracks, the snow has covered them."

"Let us hope they are still safe at Blessings."

She started to walk away, and he turned the horse to follow her. "Why would they be at Blessings? Caroline, we need to get to the Abbey. The storm is getting wilder."

Callie waved a dismissive hand. "You go, if you wish. I am going to Blessings."

Magnus pulled the horse across in front of her, making a barrier. "There is nothing at Blessings. It has been empty for more than a year. Come home, Caroline."

She faced him, white-faced and furious, ready to take on him, his horse, and the whole confounded snow storm. "I am going to Blessings, Magnus. I believe Imp had her babies there, and she died trying to bring them to me. I am not going to let her down."

"It is not safe. There are tinkers camping near. There are no fires, no food. I cannot let you do it." As if he had a hope of stopping her, and so she immediately told him.

"You are bigger than me, Magnus. You can lift me up and carry me to the Abbey, screaming all the way. But as soon as you put me down, I will go to Blessings. If you are so concerned about me, then come and protect me. But I will go to Blessings."

Chapter Three

Magnus followed her, of course. Callie had known he would. Sometimes she thought the boy she loved was still inside the man who had returned six years late and changed almost beyond recognition. She had always been able to persuade that boy to support her.

"We will go to Blessings, then," he said, "but let me put you up on the horse, Caroline. We need to be under cover before this gets much worse."

He sounded tired, and for a moment she almost turned back. He must have been riding these two days, and she was keeping him from journey's end. But the kittens would not survive if she did not find them, and they were all she had of Imp; a gift from Magnus many years ago, just before his father sent him off to the other side of the world.

But before he lifted her onto the horse, she heard a faint sound. "Magnus, wait. Do you hear that?"

He lifted his chin, his face intent. The tattoos that covered his chin and cheek made his expression hard to read, but after a moment he said, "Yes. Up there."

She looked where he pointed. A large oak tree. A small white kitten clung to a broad branch just above head height, making an occasional attempt to stretch to a hole in the trunk just out of its reach. It had clearly clambered or fallen from the nest, and was too weak to return.

Magnus handed her the reins, and quickly scaled the trunk, returning with the small animal. Callie put its littermate and mother down, and took the living kitten, tucking it inside her bodice, where its tiny cold body could be quickly warmed. It was full-furred, and its eyes were open, but still very young; perhaps the same age as Imp when Magnus rescued her from their tormenting older relatives. And it had not been alone for long, its belly still rounded from its last meal.

Magnus was already back up in the tree, sitting on the kitten's branch and checking in the nest. He met her eyes and shook his head, his own eyes sombre. No more kittens? Or no more living kittens?

"She was taking them home," Callie told him. "She brought them this far, but then the snow came. There is no point in going on to Blessings, now."

"We have no choice, Caroline. We cannot cross the hill in this." Magnus bent to pick up Imp and her baby, and put them inside his coat. He was right. In the brief time it had taken to collect the kitten and check the tree for more, the volume of snow had doubled.

She let him lift her on to the horse, and swing up behind her. The wind was colder this high, less filtered by the low shrubs that bordered the path. He urged the horse into a fast walk, and soon the grey shape of Blessings loomed before them out of the gathering dark.

"I will see to the horse, Caroline," Magnus told her, "while you take the kitten out of the snow."

"Will you leave Imp out here?" she asked. If Imp had been driven from Blessings to save her kittens from rats, as the wounds suggested, Callie did not now want to leave her to them.

"I will bury her and the little one. I don't want..." he trailed off.

"I saw the bites, Magnus." She tried to keep any tartness from her voice. It was kind of him to want to spare her, though she was not the protected child he clearly still thought her.

"Do you wish to... say anything?"

"Prayers, you mean? No, Magnus. I..." she swallowed, as tears thickened her throat, "I will remember her in life, and will not scandalise the rector by demanding a funeral." Her forced laugh sounded more like a sob even to her own ears. "I will see if I can make a fire inside," she said, and fled before she collapsed to cry on Magnus's shoulder.

The house was freezing cold, and empty. Her brother's creditors had stripped it of anything saleable, and broken much else out of sheer spite.

She went straight to the room that had once been the library, the shelves now bare and forlorn. Thank goodness! The marauders had not found the secret room she and Magnus had discovered when they were children. It fitted into an odd corner between a round tower on the original house and the New Wing (built when Charles II was restored to the throne), and no-one but them seemed to know of it. It had become her refuge from her brother and his friends after her father died, and was still stocked for a stay of several days at need.

She bustled about, keeping busy, wondering what was taking Magnus so long. The room was provided with wood to make a fire, and she soon had it started. Next task was a pot of tea—a kettle full of snow melting over the fire and fragrant leaves from the tin of tea she kept on the mantle. The tea was still useable, but unfortunately the food she always kept in her hideaway had long since turned to dust and mould. She tipped it out of the window, container and all.

She collected more snow, using every container she could find, and set it near the fire to melt and warm. Magnus would need a wash when he returned, and they at least had plenty of tea, if nothing more substantial.

If not for her concern about the kitten, she could be pleased to be here again, in the hidden room. Here, the girl she had been and the boy she had loved had talked for hours, studied together, shared hopes and dreams for the future. Perhaps here she could summon the courage to try to find common ground with the man that boy had become, to try to make something real of their marriage.

The kitten revived in the warmth next to her skin, and when Magnus arrived it was in her lap, playing with a ribbon she dangled and occasionally stopping to declare, with a peremptory meow, that a meal might be pleasant at some point in the near future. Poor little thing.

Chapter Four

It was full dark by the time Magnus had stabled and rubbed down the horse, buried the cat and kitten, and negotiated with the tinkers for food and milk. He had also taken time, in the last of the light, to check the loft over the stable, where evidence of the battle Imp had escaped lay in the scattered bodies of rats. She had made a good account of herself before she set off through the woods in a desperate attempt to bring her babies home.

The snow was sheeting down now, thick and fast. They would be here for the night, and possibly for a day or two. The servants would worry, but he had promised the tinkers a bonus if they delivered the message he had left with them as soon as they could make the trip safely.

He traversed the pitch-black house, heading for the library, in no doubt about where Callie would go to ground.

Tonight, he had seen glimpses of the girl he loved in the still, dignified woman she had become. He had returned from London determined to talk to her, to find out what she wanted for the future. If it were in his power, she would have it, whether to lead her own life apart from him or build the kind of marriage of which they had once dreamed.

He fumbled for the hidden catch that released the bookshelf concealing the door, which opened to light, and heat, and the appealing sight of a pretty woman seated on the floor, her gown pooled about her, playing with a kitten. Her boots were steaming on the hearth next to several jugs and bowls of water, and one stocking foot poked from beneath her skirt, riveting his eyes.

She looked up and smiled, and his heart stuttered. He would give the world to have her look at him like that every time he entered a room.

"Halwick, I have made tea. You will have to have it without milk, I am afraid."

Magnus grinned. "Not so. I have treasures, Caroline. Let me just put these things down and shut the door, and I will show you."

He left the saddlebags in the corner; they would come in handy later. But the basket from the tinkers' camp he put on the floor by Callie, and sat down next to her.

"I have treasures," he repeated. "Goats' milk, enough for the kitten and for our tea too, bread, cheese, and some apples." He handed her each item as he named it: the jug with the milk, the round of bread and wedge of cheese, each wrapped in muslin, and four large apples, undoubtedly filched by the tinkers from Blessings' neglected orchard.

Wide-eyed, she admired his riches. "But how?"

"I saw tinkers in the woods when I rode past earlier. I thought they might be willing to spare a little for us. They offered us a corner of a caravan. The storm will be bad, they said, and the house is inhospitable." The contrast between the tinkers' expectations and the cosy room made him smile. "They have clearly never found our little room, Callie."

Bother. He had called her Callie again, and she was frowning, but not about that apparently, for she said, "I should have stopped to put on my gloves."

"Are you cold, I will..."

"Not for my hands, Magnus. To feed the kitten."

"Ah. Well, as to that..." He stripped off his riding gloves. Stout leather, they would hold milk in as well as they held water out. Callie made short work of turning the thumb and three of the fingers to the inside. He retrieved his belt knife to cut a tiny slit in the tip of the remaining finger, and then folded the tip over to stop leaks while Callie poured some of the milk into the makeshift feeder.

Bent over his hand, she was so close he could have brushed his lips over her hair. Bad idea, Magnus. Or perhaps the best he had

had in six months. After all, he had not made much of a job of pretending he did not desire her with every heartbeat, that he wasn't more in love with the dignified woman than he had ever been with the young girl when he was a green lad.

"There. That should be enough to start." Callie sat back and lifted the kitten, cradling it against her breast with one hand while she guided the milk-laden glove to its mouth with the other.

He was a fool. All she cared about was the kitten. But the little mite suddenly realised that milk was trickling into its mouth and began to knead, and purr, and suck, and Callie smiled up at him, her face glowing. "Look at the little angel. Oh Magnus, that is the perfect name for her. Angel. Our Christmas Angel"

"Angel out of Imp, Callie?"

"Well, yes, and why not?" The glove slipped and the kitten complained bitterly. Callie turned her lovely eyes back to her little patient, and coaxed the finger back into its mouth again. To hide his yearning, Magnus got up to wash his hands and slice the bread.

"She must be around three weeks old, Caroline," he said. "Imp has been missing for that long?"

"Yes," Callie confirmed. "We have searched high and low. I her kittens were due, so at first I was not worried."

"She always hides when she has her litter. Not nestled in my cravats, this time." He grinned, to show that he was joking, and after a moment she smiled back.

"I checked there first, Halwick. And then throughout the house, and the stables, and the neighbouring farm." She ran a gentle finger over the kitten's head. It was more than half asleep, its belly round and full. She went on with what sounded like a change of subject. "This morning, Mrs Mallock climbed all the way up to the top floor. One of the new maids found her asleep in the maid's bed. Apparently it was Mrs Mallock's bed when she was a new maid."

"Ah. You thought Imp might have gone back to the days of her first litter."

"She was getting old, Magnus."

"So you came to check the loft over the stable's south wing."

Callie's finger stilled and she looked up from the kitten. "How did you know?"

"You told me in your letters," Magnus said. "Imp always chose that spot to deliver her litters, at the least-used end of the stable, far away from your brother's hunters and their grooms."

Chapter Five

The hunters on which Callie's brother lavished his attention until he could no longer afford them.

And Magnus remembered her letters? From the day he left, she had written to him. A few lines a day, a letter a week, a bundle of letters posted every month. Trivial stories of a country girl on her ordinary daily round. And he had written back, letters from all down the coast of Africa, then up the other side and into Asia, and across the Pacific. Letters full of exotic stories and drawings of strange and wonderful places.

How boring he must have found her dull and commonplace ramblings.

"I kept writing," she blurted. Letter after letter, at first sent in the hopes the missing ship would finally appear, and later put into the chest where she kept the much read, much cried over letters he had written in return.

"After my ship went down?" Magnus asked, his eyes warm.

Until the evening before her date at the altar to marry Magnus's cousin. That letter, much smudged where she wept on it, and creased where she crushed it in her hands, lay with the others in her chest at the Abbey.

Callie nodded.

"I would like to read them," Magnus said.

Callie shook her head, helplessly. Her domestic ramblings, her outpouring of grief after her father died, her increasing desperation as her brother spiralled down into ruin, stripping the estate to spend his wealth and eventually her dowry on horses, gambling, drink, loose women, and ever more extravagant schemes to rescue their fortunes. Abetted and egged on by his dear friend Lewis

Colbrooke, who somehow always seemed to be the winner in any game of chance, and to come unscathed out of any risky venture. Until the swine won even the deeds to Blessings, and Callie took refuge with Squire Ambrose and his wife.

Magnus took her shake as refusal. "Not if you do not wish me to," he said, the warm eagerness in his eyes turning to disappointment.

"I am afraid you will find them dull," she explained. And far too revealing. She had censored nothing, thinking no-one would ever see them.

"Never dull." The warmth had returned to Magnus's eyes, and his voice slowed to the meditative tones, like rich brandied honey, that always sent a shiver through her. "They were home to me, Callie. I read them over and over again, until they were thin with touching, and they brought me here, to Blessings and to the Abbey; to my own land, and to you. When the ship went down, I had your latest package of letters with me, inside my shirt, and as they hauled me out of the water, all I could think of was that I had a little part of you still with me."

He shook off the mood. "Let us organise a bed for little Angel, and get some sleep."

Callie watched as he quickly and efficiently used an old discarded shirt to line one of the three chamber pots that had found their way here. He placed it on the hearth where it would be warm, but not too hot. Callie wondered if he recognised the shirt. He had been wearing it the day he fought the older boys for two wild kittens, and brought them to her, bloodied but triumphant. Magnus's father had sent him overseas after that, and Callie had washed and kept the shirt.

His next words showed he was traversing the same memories as her. "We did this for Imp and Glad. Do you remember?"

"Yes. We fed them through one of your riding gloves and put them to bed in a... bowl." She blushed a little at discussing such indelicate pottery, and he quirked a grin at her, the tattoos making it seem fierce.

Callie had named the black kitten Imperatrix, Empress, for her regal bearing and clear sense that the world would revolve to her command. The tabby became Gladiator for his combative nature. She had given him to the eldest daughter of a tenant farmer, and Glad lived up to his name, growing to become winner of a thousand barnyard battles and ruler of all the toms for a wide radius around the home farm where he was champion rat catcher and mouser.

"Does Glad still live," Magnus asked, as she settled Angel into the hollow Magnus had warmed by settling the still warm teapot in it for a few moments.

All of a sudden, memories of what she had lost collapsed onto Callie in an avalanche of sorrow. "No. He died last year," she choked out, "and now Imp has gone, and nothing will ever be as it was." Somehow, here in their past refuge, it seemed natural to be in his arms, crying on his shoulder as she had during childhood crises so long ago.

He wrapped his arms around her, rubbed his cheek against her hair, patted her shoulder, and repeated over and over again, "That is right, Callie. Let it out. All will be well. We will make it right, Callie. Let it all out."

It was a long time before she could collect herself, gathering the last shreds of her dignity and pulling away. Except for the night her father died, and the long, long night before the day she was to marry Lewis, she had not cried since she was a girl of twelve, grieving because her dearest friend had been sent to the other side of the earth.

Chapter Six

Callie cried no more tidily now than she had when they were
children. Her eyes were red and swollen, and her nose was running.
Another tear gathered in the corner of her eyes as Magnus watched,
and spilled down her cheek. He was far gone indeed if he found her
desirable even blotched and tear-stained.

"I never cry," she told Magnus, as she took the handkerchief he
handed her and blew into it, noisily.

"Then it was clearly time," he said, with a last pat, and took
heart when she did not twist away. He dared a little more, and gave
her a quick one-armed hug, before saying briskly, "You may have
the sofa, and I shall make a pallet on the floor." He handed her one
of the other chamber pots. "Here, Caroline. Take it out into the
library and leave it there when you are finished."

She blushed, then did as he said, blushing again when she
returned to find him in shirt and pantaloons, washing his face and
hands. He resisted the urge to put on his coat. She was his wife,
after all, and in any other circumstances would, after six months of
marriage, have seen him in an even greater state of undress. Except
that her reserve, her formality, her obvious fear of his tattooed face
(and, did she know it, shoulders and buttocks), had made him keep
his distance.

When he returned from the library, she was on the sofa,
wrapped in the blanket he had spread for her.

He banked the fire, and blew out the candle, and tucked himself
into his own blanket. He had slept on harder floors than this one.

"Sleep well, Magnus." The benediction she had given him years
ago, on stolen nights in this room.

"Sleep well, Callie," he returned.

He'd forgotten again, but she did not correct his use of her pet name, just closed her eyes and soon her even breathing said she slept.

He slept too, but woke when the kitten did. Twice, he cradled it inside his shirt while he warmed milk, then whispered nonsense to it as he fed it. Callie must have been even more tired than he was; she did not stir but remained tucked down in her cocoon of blankets.

After the second feed, with little Angel curled in a ball in her chamber pot on the hearth, he checked his timepiece. It was well after eight of the clock, but little light filtered through the window. Even with his nose nearly on the tiny panes of chilly distorted glass, all he could see outside was swirling snow. They would not be going home today.

He fed wood to the fire. He would need to replenish the wood pile, but they could burn some of the broken furniture that littered the outer rooms. Fetching water was of more importance, and best to do that before the tinkers were about. Not that he thought them likely leave their camp in this weather. Nor did he have reason to believe them dishonest, but just in case they decided to take advantage of being cut off from the world to lighten him of the rest of the purse from which he'd paid for the food and milk, he and Callie should stay in their hidden retreat today.

Once he had checked on the wellbeing of the horse, filled every convenient container he could find with snow and set it to melt, used and emptied the chamber pot, and carefully closed the hidden door, he set the kettle to boil. They would break their fast on bread and cheese, and dine on it too, but he had some treats in his saddle bags for a little Christmas cheer.

The toasting forks were where he remembered. He was threading a slice of bread on one when Callie spoke. "I will just attend to… things, and then I will do the toast, Halwick."

"The chamber pot is in the other room, Caroline, where we left it. Come straight back, please. There are tinkers about."

A few minutes later, she returned.

"We used to keep jam…" She fossicked around in the deep cupboard to one side of the little window. "Here! I have it, Halwick. And look," she had the lid off and was exploring the contents with a spoon, "… sugary, but still good. Try some," and she held the spoon in front of his mouth, and he obediently opened and sucked the sweetness.

Having her so close, her face alive and amused, in the hidden sanctuary he'd held in his heart for so long, broke down his defences. He blurted, "You used to call me Magnus. I wish you would again." He waited for her to freeze him with the glare she had perfected, but she simply looked surprised.

"I do call you Magnus."

"Sometimes. You mostly call me Halwick. I keep looking around for my father." He almost accused her of doing it to keep him at a distance, and was glad he had not when she explained, "I have got into the habit, I suppose. At first, I thought to show everyone that I accepted you as the Earl of Halwick, when Lewis kept insisting you were an imposter. You are changed, Magnus. But anyone who knew you would know who you are."

Really? All this time he had thought she was using his title to reject him and she was doing it to support him? "Thank you, Caroline. I appreciate your support."

"You used to call me Callie," she said, her voice sad.

What? But she… "You told me to call you Caroline."

"I did not! When?" Now she glared, but the crease between her brows said hurt rather than anger.

"At St Georges. I said your name and you said you were not called Callie anymore."

Her face cleared. "I did! I said no one called me Callie now. I meant no one knew me well enough to call me Callie, Magnus. And when you started to call me Caroline, I thought you meant to keep me at arms' length." She laughed, the amused gurgle that had lightened his dreams during his years in captivity. "Oh Magnus, how silly. You thought I was calling you by your title to reject you, and I thought the same about you."

A plaintive meow drew her attention to the kitten, which was awake and climbing out of its pot. She scooped it up with one hand

and tucked it under her chin. "Good morning, Angel. Are you hungry? Are you hungry, my sweet?"

In the same sing-song tone, so that it took Magnus a moment to realise she was addressing him, and not the kitten, she went on, "But then you stayed away. Even when you were at the Abbey, you saw me only at meals and you were cold and formal. You did not…" she didn't look up from the milk she was pouring into a pot to warm, and even the back of her neck turned bright red, but she did not falter. "You did not claim me as your wife, Magnus. I know you felt obligated to marry me, but I could not help but believe you regretted it."

"No!" Magnus's emphatic rejection startled the kitten and Callie alike, and he moderated his tone. "No, Callie. Never that. If you only knew… But Callie, how could I force myself on you when I am so awfully scarred that you fainted at the mere sight of me?"

Again, her eyes opened wider with surprise.

"I fainted from sheer relief, Magnus. For weeks, months even, I had been trying to find a way to survive without marrying Lewis. He enjoyed it, you know, closing off my options one by one. Lying, bribery, threats; whatever worked to stop anyone from offering me employment or a place to live.

"He told me he could do anything he liked with me, for my only other option was a brothel. He said he could demand that I became his mistress, and I should be grateful he was willing to take me to wife. But I knew he was doing me no favours. As his mistress I would have met other men, and I could, perhaps, have found a way out, even if it were another protector. As his wife, I would belong to him and never be able to escape."

The toast was burning, the bitter smell jerking Marcus from his red rage. "I should have killed him," he said. "I should have let the mob have him, as they wished."

He stripped the toast from the fork, and hurled it into the back of the fire, and was startled when Callie put the replete kitten down and leant forward to put a hand on his shaking arm.

"You saved me, Magnus. I was in despair, and you came."

"Callie, I should have come straight away, as soon as I arrived in England."

"Yes," she said, "You should have."

"I am not the boy who left here, Callie. I am not even the boy who was coming home to you, six years ago. I have seen things, done things to survive that I do not want to ever think about again. You deserve so much better than me. But even I was better than Lewis. When I heard... It was the morning of the wedding, Callie. The trustees for the earldom told me that Lewis was claiming everything. When one of them told me he was even marrying my betrothed—and within the hour—I came immediately. I was so afraid I would be too late."

"You came. You were in time." She had moved even closer, and he yielded at last to the driving urge to take her in his arms. Ah. She fitted as he had always known she would, resting against his chest, her head tucked under his chin, her arms as far around him as she could reach.

"I was in time. And that is why Lewis still lives."

He moved his chin backwards so he could see her. "I thought you were afraid of me, of the tattoos."

She put up a hand and traced the pattern that covered the whole of one side of his face, from jawbone to hairline.

"They are strange, but rather beautiful. Why did they do that to you, Magnus? It seems a strange way to punish someone."

He laughed. "Not a punishment. They mark the face and the body to reward a person, as we hand out medals. Only slaves and children bear no marks."

She traced the marks again. "You must tell me all that happened to you."

Perhaps not all. But more than the bare bones of the story he had given the Committee of Inquiry charged with testing his identity. The shipwreck, the nine months as a castaway, the capture by islanders and the slow steps to win his way free of slavery and into a war band, which he eventually led. And finally, the day an English ship put in for water.

He worked his passage home on HMS Swallow where he occupied a strange position between tattooed savage and Englishman, sailor and civilian, crew member and possible earl. He hid his fierce grin in her hair. Before the shipwreck, his status as an earl's son had protected him from the worst elements on board. As a castaway, he had been the youngest, weakest, and prettiest, at the mercy of the rest. The Swallow crew soon learned that he was a man grown, and a seasoned warrior at that, accustomed to holding his own in a world where promotion was largely on merit.

"The tattoos are not just on my face, Callie." His pulse quickened at the thought of showing her the others, and his smile softened.

A rattle drew their attention to the kitten. It had found the saddle bags, and was batting a loose strap so that it swung and knocked two buckles together.

"Ah, Angel, thank you for the reminder," Magnus said. "Callie, I have a Christmas present for you."

He didn't have to let her go—just lean across and pull the bags towards him, the kitten scampering behind, enjoying the new game. It pounced on the flap he wanted, and he picked it up and handed it to Callie while he pulled out the oilskin wrapped package he wanted.

"Here, Callie. I was going to give this to you for Twelfth Night, but I cannot wait. Merry Christmas."

She turned slightly so she could lean against him and use both hands to unwrap the package, and he kept one arm around her while with his other hand he turned the kitten on its back and tickled its belly with the end of a saddlebag strap.

"Marcus? These are the deeds to Blessings."

"I had them from Lewis just before I put him on a ship for South America. He will not be back, Callie. His schemes and lies and cheating are all public knowledge, and the men he has wronged are baying for his blood."

"And now you own Blessings?"

"You own Blessings. We didn't have time for a proper marriage settlement, and with my identity in doubt... Well, now that I am confirmed as earl, I have corrected that oversight. It is in the package. It just needs your signature. Unless you want changes. I will make any changes you wish, Callie. All I want is for you to be happy."

Callie was crying again, but smiling as well. "You are turning me into a watering pot, Magnus."

He bent to kiss away the tears, and when she turned further towards him to ease that gentle service, he drifted his lips across hers, at first just touching then settling to press and caress. He urged her mouth open with his own, and brushed her tongue with his. Her tentative return thrilled through his body and he sank into the kiss, feeling at last at home, after all these years.

Sharp pinpricks and an anguished yeowl recalled him to himself, and he eased slightly away from Callie to lift an offended Angel from between them.

"Even Christmas Angels should not come between a man and his wife," he told the kitten, sternly. Callie giggled, a happy bubble of a sound that he had heard many times long ago and missed like a lost limb. He bent to kiss her again, holding the kitten out of the way, this time.

"I don't deserve you, Callie," he said again.

"You will just have to make the best of it, Magnus," said his wife. "I waited twelve years for you to come home and another six months for you to come to claim me. I do not intend to ever let anything come between us again. Not distance, not misunderstandings, not even a Christmas Angel."

A Suitable Husband

As the Duchess of Haverford's companion, Cedrica Grenford is not treated as a poor relation and is encouraged to mingle with Her Grace's guests. Perhaps among the gentlemen gathered for the duchess's house party, she will find a suitable husband? Marcel Fournier has only one ambition: to save enough from his fees serving as chef in the houses of the ton to become the proprietor of his own fine restaurant. An affair with the duchess's dependent would be dangerous. Anything else is impossible. Isn't it?

This story was first published in *Holly and Hopeful Hearts*, a Bluestocking Belles collection.

Prologue

London
September 1812

Cedrica Grenford set her portable writing desk on the table. She
had freshly prepared quills, a full bottle of ink, and neatly cut
sheets of paper, each with the Haverford crest watermarked in the
background. She took a deep breath and pushed her glasses farther
up her nose. She was ready for this, her first test as confidential
secretary and companion to Her Grace, the Duchess of Haverford.

That is to say, to Aunt Eleanor. Who would have thought that
little Ceddie Grenford would grow up to one day call a duchess
'aunt'? Even if that illustrious personage was remotely connected by
marriage.

She had not imagined such a result when she had written to the
duke to beg a refuge for her father, his distant cousin, who was
failing in health and confused in mind. Papa was an ill-paid country
vicar with a lifetime habit of giving away whatever came into his
hands. Now the church he had served so devotedly proposed to
put him into a poorhouse. Or an asylum.

Two weeks ago, the duchess, escorted by her son, the Marquis
of Aldridge, descended upon their house and carried Papa off to be
cared for in a lovely pensioner cottage near Haverford Castle in
Kent, taking Cedrica to London to serve the duchess as a

companion. Of course, Cedrica had breathed a grateful sigh of relief… until this afternoon. She might be a little nervous, but she was determined to do well in her new role.

"Cedrica, my dear," said Her Grace, "come here and meet some of the ladies who form our committee."

Cedrica managed to acquit herself without disgrace as she was presented to some of the duchess's legion of goddaughters and their friends. Lady Emily Pembroke stopped her conversation with Lady de Courtenay to smile at Cedrica. Lady de Courtenay gave a friendly wave. Miss Sedgely offered a straightforward handshake, and Lady Elinor Lacey introduced the two bored schoolgirls with them as Miss Louise Durand and Miss Blanche Lacey.

The Belvoir sisters, Lady Sophia and Lady Felicity, also greeted Cedrica warmly. "I am to act as chairman, and Lady de Courtenay will make a third with you and I," Lady Sophia said. "This committee has much work to do, Miss Grenford, and the three of us most of all."

Lady Sophia introduced Miss Lockhart, who in turn made Miss Kate Woodville known to the company. Miss Woodville, it seemed, was a teacher at a young ladies' academy. Perhaps teaching might be a future for Cedrica. She would make a point of talking to the young woman.

"Aunt Eleanor, I brought my friend, Miss Baumann," Lady Felicity said, "Esther has a great interest in education for girls, and that is why we are here, is it not?"

The duchess smiled. "You must be Mr. Nathaniel Baumann's daughter, Miss Baumann. You are most welcome to our number. Shall we be seated, ladies?"

This is no different to taking notes for the meetings of the Ladies' Altar Society, or the Mothers' Union, or the Vestry. So Cedrica had been telling herself for days, but these were not farmers' wives and shopkeepers; these were fine ladies in fashionable silks with upper-class vowels and curious eyes.

And if the ladies were terrifying, the gentlemen would be worse. Lord Aldridge had suggested that she regard the proposed house party as an opportunity to meet a suitable husband and had promised to pay a dowry if such a gentlemen could be brought to propose. His money was safe enough. She preferred not even to speak to gentlemen of the ton if she could avoid it.

Cedrica sat in front of her desk, at the left hand of the duchess and the right of Lady Sophia, who took the head of the table and opened the meeting.

"Ladies, you know why we are here. Several of us were talking about the dearth of opportunities for women in all classes, should they want more of an education than the skills that our world deems 'appropriate for a woman.' We do not think ourselves less capable of great learning than our brothers, nor do we consider ourselves extreme examples of our kind. We believe that women who wish to study the arts or the sciences should be able to do so, as have some of us ourselves."

Goodness. Had such ideas been suggested at a Vestry meeting, the speaker would have been laughed out of the room, with her father leading the mirth. Even the Ladies' Altar Society would have been shocked. But these grand ladies were all nodding, even Her Grace.

"But talk butters no parsnips," Lady Sophia continued. "We agreed that we needed a fund to support schemes for assisting girls to be educated beyond the sphere to which their sex, class, or both assign them. Her Grace has kindly agreed to be patroness of this fund and has an idea for announcing it to the world and, at the same time, raising money to support it. Ladies, you, your family and friends, and anyone who is in the least likely to support us are invited to Hollystone Hall in Buckinghamshire this December for a holiday house party and a New Year's Eve Charity Ball."

The explosion of delighted comments that filled the room flowed over Cedrica. A ball. How on earth would she ever manage that, much less the house party that would precede it?

Chapter One

Hollystone Hall, Buckinghamshire
November 1812

Marcel Fournier sat on the bed assigned to him in the wing set aside for upper servants at Hollystone Hall and brooded on his wrongs.

The house was grand enough, the house party would serve the highest in Society, and Marcel could certainly not complain about the wages he would receive for a mere month of employment. The Duchess of Haverford was also compensating him richly for the few days needed to visit the house this month so he could advise on the construction of the kitchen he would use for the three-week event.

And that was the sticking point.

Not the kitchen itself. They were building—had almost finished building—a whole new kitchen out of some unused storage rooms. He was thrilled and flattered to have final say on the selection and placement of equipment, from the modern iron range to the last pot and spoon. No. He had no complaints about the kitchen he already regarded as his own.

Even the need for a second kitchen; he could concede the sense of that. To him would fall the important task of preparing the banquets that would thrill and impress the guests each and every night, culminating in the dinner on the night of the grand ball that would end the house party. He and the servants set to assist him would have their hands full with dish after dish after dish, each one different and each magnificent.

Let the English cook have her own kitchen to make little scones and heavy cakes, to fry eggs, bacon, and sausages, for the lesser meals of the day.

But she should answer to him. He, Marcel Fournier, was the master chef. He was a former apprentice to the great Carême himself. He should be in charge of all menus, ruler of both kitchens, deciding what would be made and how the kitchen staff were to be allocated. What was this Cissie Pearce but a country cook?

"Good English cooking," Mademoiselle Grenford had said. "Mrs. Pearce is known for her good English cooking."

Marcel could do good English cooking! Had he not grown up here in England after his family escaped from the Terror?

In Spitalfields, until he was apprenticed to a cook in an inn on Tottenham Court Road, then in Soho where he took charge in an earl's kitchen, and finally, after having himself smuggled into France and attracting the man's attention by the bold trick of sneaking into his office with a box of his own *pâtisseries* and menus for a year's worth of banquets, in the kitchen and under the direct supervision of the great Marie-Antoine Carême, chef to Talleyrand and through him to the diplomats of Europe.

For the past two years, Marcel had been one of the most sought-after chefs in the whole South of England. Good English cooking, indeed.

She was a little dab of a thing, Mademoiselle Grenford, with her light brown hair pulled back into one of the unloveliest coiffures he had ever seen and her thick glasses concealing rather fine eyes. He had thought her a mouse and had tried to overwhelm her with his masculine authority, honed by years as undisputed master of a kitchen. "I shall be in charge, of course, Mademoiselle," he told her. "I am a trained chef and a man. Madame Pearce shall lead in her own kitchen, but both kitchens shall answer to me."

"The two kitchens shall operate independently, Monsieur Fournier," the little mouse replied calmly. "Each of you shall be responsible for your own kitchen, its staff, and the food it produces."

Whatever arguments he raised, however loudly, she just repeated the same thing. When Marcel Fournier was displeased, sous-chefs made themselves inconspicuous, apprentices cried, and kitchen maids fainted, but Mademoiselle Grenford just repeated, "The two kitchens shall operate independently," until he ran out of ire, and came to bed.

So what now? Did he continue to agitate to be master below stairs? Or should he tell the duchess that he would not take the commission? Cede the field and with it the lucrative rewards of the handsome fee he was being paid and the opportunity to impress potential clients for the restaurant he would one day open when his savings grew sufficiently?

Put like that, there was little choice. The English had a saying about cutting off one's nose to spite one's face. He preferred his nose to continue in its current position. Well then. In the morning, he would concede, and he would do so with flair. Madame Pearce would be grateful for his magnanimity. Mademoiselle Grenford would be impressed at his generosity.

Since he was staying, he would inspect his kitchen again. He had some ideas for improving the layout. He would note them tonight and instruct the little mademoiselle in the morning.

Marcel found his slate and some chalk and threaded through the dark halls. His candle threw insufficient light in the cavernous space that would, in less than a month, be a bustling center for gastronomic excellence. He retraced his steps to Mrs. Pearce's deserted domain and retrieved a whole box of candles.

Two hours later, his slate covered with notes and his head full of plans, he went to return the box. In the morning, he would astound the little mouse with his brilliance! But he stopped at the kitchen door. There, enveloped in a shawl over her nightrail, with her hair cascading over her shoulders, was Mademoiselle Grenford herself, her elbows on the table, a cup clasped between two hands.

Hot milk, perhaps? He could have made her hot milk, with a touch of nutmeg and perhaps a hint of honey to sweeten. Perhaps he should offer.

No. He would not disturb her.

Marcel took the image of her back to his room. She was a sweet little mouse, was Mademoiselle. Out of his orbit, of course. He hinted to clients of his elevated family, brought low by the revolution. The claims were fantasy. He had been born in a noble household, as he claimed, but his father was a valet, and his mother a dairy maid. La Grenford really was a lady of the nobility, and from a ducal family at that.

But he could ease her way in this coming house party, and he would.

As he prepared for bed, he imagined her expressions of delight as guest after guest complimented her on the fine cuisine and the smooth running of the dinner service. The large, comfortable bed would do very well for the month he would be in residence. Yes. The decision to stay was an excellent one.

He reached over to douse the candle but stopped. What was that noise? There it was again. A squeak? Had he conjured mice with his thoughts of the little mouse lady? But no, it was not a mouse squeak. More of a...

In seconds, he was out of bed and zeroing in on his travelling trunk, from which the sounds came, and what he saw there sent him running to the kitchen.

"Mademoiselle, you must come. You must come immediately. It is an outrage."

She looked up and blushed scarlet. "Monsieur! Your..." She turned her head away.

He looked down. He wore his shirt to bed, and nothing more, except a night cap against the cold. Coloring himself, he backed out the door. "I will dress, Mademoiselle. But quickly, and then you must come. A minute. No more."

Soon, with the cap shoved under a pillow and his shirt tucked into hastily donned pantaloons and covered by a banyan, he stood beside the lady looking down into the trunk, where a scrawny white cat fed a litter of newborn kittens. Inside his luggage. On his chef's caps and aprons.

"It is an outrage," he repeated a little helplessly. The cat was watching them through eyes slitted with the joys of motherhood and purring loudly enough to wake the household.

"This is Cristal, the housekeeper's cat," the mademoiselle said. "Mrs. Stanley will be pleased that you found her, Monsieur Fournier. She was worried."

"Found her? Worried? But she…" Running out of words, he scratched the cat behind one ear, and she purred more loudly.

"You keep an eye on her," the mouse commanded, "and I shall find a box in which to move her. Do not worry, Monsieur. I will see to it that your garments are laundered in the morning, and they shall be good as new."

And she whisked out of the room, leaving him guardian of the feline and her young and in possession of the memory of an exceedingly trim pair of ankles.

Chapter Two

Hollystone Hall, Buckinghamshire
18th December 1812

"Excuse me, miss."

Cedrica did not have to look up from her writing desk to recognize the person who had interrupted their meeting. It was Mrs. Pearce's assistant cook this time.

Two hours ago, she had been taken away from her inconspicuous supervision of the house party's first breakfast service by Monsieur Fournier's senior kitchen maid. Yesterday, amidst the hustle of arrivals, no fewer than five inter-kitchen battles had broken out and needed mediation. And four the day before. And six the day before that.

Since Monsieur Fournier and his coach-loads of ingredients and equipment had taken up residence five days ago, the troubles between the two kitchens had been Cedrica's biggest headache, dwarfing her concerns about bedchamber allocation, seating plans, and spreading the services of the team of maids and valets among those who had arrived without servants.

"Oh dear," commiserated Grace, Lady de Courtenay. "Another shot fired in the kitchen war?"

"I am sorry, miss. It's the large soup tureen, miss. Mrs. Pearce says she needs it, and that Frenchie, he has it in his kitchen and won't give it up, never so." Aggie Wilkins nodded firmly, her message delivered.

"We are almost done." Lady Sophia Belvoir blotted the paper on which she had been neatly writing notes about the day's activities. "I shall report to Aunt Eleanor, ladies. Shall we check with one another here at," she consulted her notes, "two of the clock?"

Sophia had been right that the three of them would have the most work of all. Each led a team of volunteers to manage some part of the party: Sophia in charge of all the casual activities that would be available for guests to enjoy, Grace the many more formal events, and Cedrica the domestic matters such as food and bed linen. They had all arrived early to have the house in readiness, and every day, they would meet several times to make sure the organization was, as Her Grace insisted, both invisible and seamless.

Grace patted Cedrica's hand. "Cedrica, do you need help?"

Cedrica smiled, grateful for the offer. "I can do it."

In truth, Cedrica would rather be managing the kitchen staff than the grand ladies and gentlemen who fell into Grace's and Sophia's purview. She could talk easily with those below stairs and resolve their arguments, too. Cedrica was a veteran of the 1809 war between Widow Siddons and Miss Martha Ridley over the flower arrangements for the Easter ceremonies. Monsieur Fournier and Mrs. Pearce were child's play compared to those two ladies.

"One wonders whether the man's talent is worth his temperament," Sophia observed.

"After last night's dinner?" Grace asked.

Sophia acknowledged the point. "It was exceptional, was it not?"

"To be fair," Cedrica told them, "Mrs. Pearce is as bad. She has originated at least half the quarrels. Come, Wilkins, you shall tell me all about this soup tureen on the way below stairs."

The tureen lived, apparently, in one of the service pantries that the two kitchens reluctantly shared. Mrs. Pearce decided that the massive piece, which sat on its own warming burner, would be ideal for the potato and leek soup, served with crusty fresh bread, that would be one of the dishes offered in the less formal of the two dining rooms during the afternoon.

But the maid sent to fetch it returned empty handed, and further investigation disclosed that Monsieur Fournier had chosen it for the crème de champignons soup that was on the menu for dinner. He found it first, he said, and Mrs. Pearce would have to choose another tureen.

"But it's the spirit lamp, miss, see?" Mrs. Pearce explained. "Could be two hours that soup will be out, 'cause they don't all come in together, do they? Many of the ladies will sleep in and come down around noon, and some have broken their fast already, and won't want to eat till later. Most of the gentlemen have gone out for birds, and they'll want summat hot when they come in. Could be any time."

"Are there not other tureens with their own warmers? Or stands with spirit lamps you could put other tureens on?"

Mrs. Pearce reluctantly agreed there might be, but then rejected those they found. These were too small, and would lose heat too quickly. Those did not fit properly together. And that lot were not what she'd like to see in a duchess's dining room, and that was a fact.

"The big tureen is perfect, miss. And he don't need it, not really."

Cedrica sighed. "I shall go and see this wonderful tureen for myself, Mrs. Pearce. No, you do not need to come with me. I shall return and let you know what I have decided."

When she entered Monsieur Fournier's kitchen, he pretended to ignore her, though his gaze slid sideways and met hers for a second. Very well, let him carry on instructing some hapless undercook in the correct way to bone a swan. She was not waiting on his attention like a supplicant.

The disputed tureen was on a table on the far side of the room. He would notice her soon enough if she picked it up and started to carry it off! Not that she could even if she wished to. It was nearly large enough to bathe in and would need two people at least to lift it. She pushed at one handle, put her strength behind her hand, and managed to hoist the monstrous piece an inch or so.

It was a fine piece, she had to admit—fluted and curved, edged with scrolls and plaits of silver, polished to a mirror finish, and rearing majestically from the tiled warmer platform with not one but three burners to keep the soup hot.

But her eyes began to twinkle as she considered actually using it as part of a dinner service.

"Something is amusing, Mademoiselle?"

Monsieur Fournier had moved up beside her, the soft slippers he wore making no sound on the slate floor.

Cedrica blinked rapidly, determined not to show she was startled. "I came to solve your problem, Monsieur."

He gave a theatrical shrug, his hands widespread. "I have no problem, Mademoiselle. La Pearce has a problem. Not I."

"You are in the right, Monsieur. You were first to the tureen. It will look magnificent full of your wonderful mushroom soup. Only…" She allowed her voice to trail off and bent over to examine the platform more closely. Were the feet lion's paws? She rather thought they were.

Monsieur Fournier's hand appeared in her view, tapping on the table. He had long, rather elegant fingers, with neatly trimmed nails. He said nothing, but Cedrica could wait him out. And he proved no more immune to silence than a naughty choir boy caught with a broken window, an angelic smile, and a sling in his back pocket.

"You say, 'only', Mademoiselle? You will not judge in my favor despite your grand words?"

"Oh no, Monsieur. I cede you the tureen. If you wish to use it. Only…"

"'Only' again? Bah! What is this 'only'?"

She turned to lean against the table and smiled at him, trying to keep from laughing aloud. "Monsieur, it is very heavy, and we have fifty-six to dinner tonight. More, perhaps, if all those who are promised for the next two days arrive. How will you convey to them their soup? It is heavy even empty. Once it is full of soup…"

Monsieur Fournier's mouth dropped open, and he looked aghast at the magnificent tureen.

"I know," Cedrica said wickedly. "We could put it in a wheelbarrow, and the footmen could take it from guest to guest so that—"

She got no further. The chef's face darkened, and he roared, "A wheelbarrow? A wheelbarrow? You mock me, Mademoiselle!" He glared at the tureen. "A wheelbarrow, indeed!" He blinked, and his lips twitched. "The footmen could take it from guest to guest…" He began to chuckle and could barely get the last word out, "…in a wheelbarrow!"

The kitchen servants stopped what they were doing to stare as Monsieur Fournier roared with laughter, and Cedrica could not hold in her own amusement, until both of them were clutching the table with tears rolling down their cheeks.

At last, Monsieur Fournier collected himself, using the corner of his apron to wipe his eyes. As Cedrica used a kerchief for the same purpose, he asked, "And will you propose a wheelbarrow to Mrs. Pearce, Mademoiselle?"

"It is a different case, Monsieur. The monster here can be set up on the serving board ahead of time and filled with hot soup from buckets. Then the guests will go to the tureen themselves as they come to find sustenance a few at a time. For the dinner, though, we want something altogether grander, do we not? Four matching tureens, perhaps, each carried by a footman to a different part of the table, and the soup served from there. Or eight, marching in procession. Can I find you eight matching tureens, I wonder?"

Monsieur Fournier bowed elegantly. "Mademoiselle, you are as wise as you are beautiful. Let Madame Pearce have this monster. I, Marcel Fournier, will present the most delicious crème de champignons that England has ever tasted in a procession of eight tureens."

As Cedrica left to search the storerooms for matching tureens that would be worthy of the finest mushroom soup ever made in England, she heard the chef chuckling to himself in between barking orders at the undercooks. "Wheelbarrows! Was there ever such a woman?"

Chapter Three

It began with a set of ice molds.

Marcel planned a spectacular centerpiece for the second remove at tomorrow night's dinner—Italian creams made with eggs, rich cream, and a variety of fruits and other flavors molded into flower shapes, frozen, and then presented on a mountainous tower of ice, itself with pillars and platforms molded into fantasy shapes.

The Italian creams were made and stored in the estate's ice house. He sent an assistant to fetch the box containing the carved wooden mold for the tower. "Open it," he commanded. "Check that you have the correct box. The one I require has dolphin shapes to support the first tier."

But the assistant returned empty handed. "Monsieur, I cannot find the box with the dolphins."

He knew straight away of course, and a visit to Madame Pearce's kitchen soon confirmed it. The encroaching woman had taken the mold and intended to use the larger shapes for a salmon aspic!

Marcel tried to be reasonable. He really did. He could fill the molds with water this evening, and they would be set hard when the time came for setting up the display tomorrow. But Madame Pearce refused to consider it. Her salmon aspic was also for tomorrow and must remain in the molds until just before serving, or it would lose sharpness and definition.

"Then choose another set of molds, Madame," he suggested. "A set that is not a foundation piece of an entire tower."

The woman smirked. "You find something else. I got these ones first. That is what you said yesterday, Moosewer, when you refused to give up the waffle iron."

They had both wanted the waffle iron with the flower impression, but the mansion's shelves held three others equally pretty. He had found only one tower mold, and Madame Pearce did not even plan to make a tower! She could use any one of dozens of molds and make as lovely an aspic.

Marcel explained this to her, slowly, using simple words.

"You don't need to look down your long French nose at me, Moosewer," Madame Pearce told him. "I know I could use else, just like you could of yesterday. And I don't want to. Just like you yesterday."

He had promised Mademoiselle Grenford not to shout at Madame Pearce and not to swear at her in French. Or English. He had promised. He turned on his heel and marched away before he strangled the stubborn woman.

"Good riddance," Madame yelled after him.

Marcel went straight upstairs to the mademoiselle. At this time of day, she would be in the little sitting room where she and the other ladies of her committee had their meetings.

Once he left the service stairs for the main hallway, he set a bland look on his face and walked with determination. He passed several guests who ignored his existence, as he had expected. Servants should not be seen unless wanted, and therefore they would not see him.

Now. Around this corner and the fourth door on the right. Or was it the third?

He slowed, uncertainly. The third door was slightly ajar, and he could hear women's voices. Not the little mouse's, but those of the two ladies who were also helping to manage the house party.

"Lady Stanton is a difficult woman." That was the pretty young widow, Lady de Courtenay.

"Lady Stanton is a cold-hearted bitch." Lady Sophia Belvoir, the goddaughter of the duchess.

Marcel smiled a little. Who knew a lady would use such words? Deserved, undoubtedly. Even he, keeping though he did to his own domain, had heard stories of maids reduced to tears and footmen to helpless rage by the lady they named.

But the next words sobered him instantly.

"Do not cry, Cedrica. You are doing wonderfully well, and the duchess knows it. Lady Stanton will receive no support there."

Cedrica? That cold-hearted bitch had upset his mademoiselle?

"I agree with Grace, Cedrica. Aunt Eleanor shall give one of her deadly little set-downs, and I should dearly like to see it. Here. Dry your eyes, darling. It shall all be well, you will see."

Then the mademoiselle's voice sounded, trembling with unshed tears. "You are right. I know you are. I do not know why I allowed her to upset me so. Only I am so tired of stupid conflict. This gentleman does not want to share a room with his wife. That one has kept every guest in his wing awake with his snoring. This lady cannot have the same breakfast as that one, and another must be served the identical tray, right down to the color of the inlay. And as for the war between the kitchens! I swear, if I have to referee one more battle over who has first use of the lemon zester, I shall scream."

Really? She was not enjoying their little dramas as much as the two combatants? Marcel frowned and shot a glance both ways down the hallway to make sure he was not observed as he leaned closer. The two other ladies were making soothing noises and offering to take up the mademoiselle's duties while she rested.

"No, no. Aunt Eleanor would be so disappointed in me. Besides, you have your own tangles to straighten. Making sure that Lady Stanton and her cronies are not in a position to bully Miss Baumann, that Lord Trevor is dissuaded from taking out a gun, since he cannot see beyond the end of his arm and refuses to wear glasses, and that Lady Marchand can only cheat at cards with those who know her little ways."

The three ladies laughed together, Mademoiselle's chuckle still a little watery.

Her voice was forlorn when she added, "It was the other that hurt most, you know, because it is true."

More soothing noises, which she rejected.

"No. I am not a fool. I know that I have dwindled into an old maid. Well, look at me. Plain ordinary Cedrica Grenford. A useful person to have on a committee, but not one man has ever looked at me twice nor is likely to. I know Aunt Eleanor thinks dressing me up like a fashion doll and sending me in to talk to all these lords will turn me into a… a swan. But I am just a plain barnyard hen when you come down to it."

Lady de Courtenay disagreed. "Oh, but surely Lord Hythe—"

Another heart-wrenching chuckle. "See, his sister is shaking her head. And you are right, Sophia. Hythe is polite to everyone, and kind to me because I was at school with Felicity. He treats me as a lady, which is nice of him when I am, as Lady Stanton so kindly pointed out, merely hanging onto gentility by the charity of Her Grace."

"Oh, Cedrica…" That was both ladies.

Marcel's response to Lady Stanton's cruel words would have been much more forceful.

"He does not look at me and see a woman. No one does."

Lady Sophia spoke decisively. "You are blue-devilled, my dear. Who knows whether any of us will meet a man who can see past our elderly exteriors to the treasures we all are? If we do not, you and I shall be old maids together."

"Yes," Lady de Courtenay agreed. "Perhaps we should set up house together. Certainly Sophia and I have no more wish to live forever on the sufferance of our brothers than you do on the Haverfords'. Who needs men, after all? Selfish, conceited creatures, always jumping to conclusions."

This time, Mademoiselle Grenford's laugh was more genuine.

Lady Sophia said, "Rest for an hour. Read a book. I will order a pot of tea and some cakes, and Grace and I shall deal with anything that arises." Her voice was coming closer.

Swiftly, before she could open the door and find him listening, Marcel retreated down the hall and around the corner, all the way back downstairs, thinking furiously.

First, he must order a tray set with the most delicate of cups, the finest tea, and some of the little cakes from the test batch he had made that morning, in preparation for the real challenge of Christmas Day's dinner. Each was a work of art with its own sugar flower, and it had not escaped his notice that his mademoiselle liked them.

Then, while his assistants made the tray, he must make peace. This war must end. If that meant giving Madame Pearce her way on the tower, then so be it. He could not be part of causing pain to his mademoiselle.

His! How foolish he was. He was a chef. She was an aristo, of a family with a duke, despite her humble words. Yet *un chien regarde bien un évêque.* A dog can take a good look at a bishop. The English proverb was similar. A cat may look at a king. What would Mademoiselle Grenford think if she knew Marcel saw her as a woman, as she put it?

Perhaps bread to go with the cakes? Bread sliced thinly and buttered by his own hand and topped by some of Madame's conserve. A peace offering from them both.

Determined, he gave his orders to his kitchen and braved the kitchen of Madame Pearce. An odd quest, but would not a knight dare anything, brave any danger, undergo any humiliation, for the lady he must adore from afar?

Chapter Four

Christmas Day, 1812

If one more person arrived, they would need to sleep in the stables. Every room in the house was full, and the under servants were sleeping several to a bed.

Cedrica could not help a guilty thank you to whatever impulse set Mr. Arbuthwick climbing a tree to retrieve Miss Ellison's parasol, blown there by a stray gust of wind. He insisted that ice on the branches led to his fall, but Cedrica suspected a contribution from the warming punch he and his friends had been passing around.

Perhaps his relaxed state was for the best, as he suffered nothing worse than a sprained ankle. He was conveyed to the nearby town where his parents lived, to convalesce in the care of his fond mama, Miss Ellison's offer of nursing services having been vetoed by her own mother.

But Mr. Arbuthwick's room had not been empty above seventeen hours before Viscount Elfingham turned up at the door begging shelter. Yesterday, it was. Christmas Eve. He claimed his horse was lame, but Sophia confided that he was pursuing Felicity and that Hythe said it would not do.

Before the day was over, the sons of the duchess had also arrived. Lord Aldridge had been expected, but Lord Jonathan Grenford was thought to be somewhere in Russia. His mama was delighted, of course, but if Lord Jonathan had not cheerfully pronounced himself willing to sleep on a trundle in the room set aside for his brother, Cedrica did not know where she would have put him.

And now, on Christmas Day, another late arrival. Thank goodness Lord Elfingham did not object to sharing his room with Mr. Halevy! Mr. Halevy seemed a very nice gentleman, polite, not fussy, and with a charming French accent that reminded her of Monsieur Fournier. Although hearing him speak disproved one of the theories she had developed to explain her inconvenient fascination with the chef. The accent was clearly not the cause. She felt no such attraction to Mr. Halevy.

She left the new guest to the care of his room host and the servant allocated to valet far too many gentlemen for efficient service. What had seemed a large staff of servants was stretched almost to breaking point now the house was at capacity. To make things worse, Her Grace had declared that the servants were to work shortened hours today and a half day tomorrow, but her guests still wanted their breakfasts served, their clothing brushed, their chins shaved, their bath water carried, their corsets tightened, their forgotten gloves fetched, and on and on and on. So all day yesterday and today, Cedrica and Mrs. Stanley the housekeeper had been trying to juggle hours and people to perform the impossible.

The kitchens, her greatest trial in the early days of the house party, had become a haven, and she headed there now. She would just check that all was running smoothly for the second most important dinner of the whole event. And she would do so by way of the servants' stairs, thus avoiding the kissing boughs that Sophia and her decorating crew had hung everywhere. Cedrica had already been saluted by Hythe, Weasel Winderfield, and Lord Jonathan, and could not quite see the attraction of the pastime.

Since the kitchens had stopped sending for her several times a day, she had evolved the habit of visiting in the morning after the breakfast service and her meeting with Grace and Sophia. She took a cup of tea in one kitchen or the other, consulted with Mrs. Stanley, and admired whatever plans Mrs. Pearce and Monsieur Fournier had for the house party's meals. Frequently, she was called upon to sample some delicacy while its originator watched anxiously. She had no idea what had happened to the war, but the two kitchen heads were now firm friends, each bending over backward to help the other succeed.

Mrs. Pearce was alone when Cedrica arrived. Cedrica was not disappointed. Not at all. She was here to work, not to ogle Monsieur Fournier, however ogle-worthy he might be.

"No monsieur today?" she found herself asking.

"A busy day for Mark today, miss."

The words Monsieur, Fournier, and Marcel all being too difficult for Mrs. Pearce's tongue, she had taken to calling her colleague Mark.

"He gave permission for those who wished to go to the Christmas service, but of course that has put him behind and not many hours now until Christmas dinner."

Cedrica felt guilty. "Did Monsieur Fournier not wish to go to the Christmas service himself, Mrs. Pearce?"

"No church for his kind here, miss. He's a papist, see? French, of course. Lots of them are papists, so I hear. He's a nice boy for all that, and a good chef. He'll get his ordinary, right enough."

"'His ordinary?'" Was that a kind of award for chefs? Or something to do with being French? Or Catholic? It was not clear from Mrs. Pearce's speech which of the two made his niceness a surprise.

"You know, miss. A French ordinary in London. A place for the gentlemen to have their dinners. It's what Mark wants, why he is taking jobs like this instead of a proper position in a house, like me. Good experience, good contacts, and good money, Mark says."

Cedrica's spurt of resentment was most unreasonable. Monsieur Fournier was free to confide in his fellow cook if he wished. And Cedrica's life was calmer now the two were friends.

"Go and say hello, miss," the cook urged. "He'd appreciate the interest, I'm sure."

"I would not want to disturb him when he's busy."

"We're all busy today, miss, you as much as the rest of us, I'll be bound." Mrs. Pearce and her staff would be serving Christmas dinner in the servants' hall. Three times: once for her own kitchen staff and the outdoor servants, once for the upstairs servants when their masters and mistresses went down to dinner, and once and finally for Monsieur Fournier's kitchen.

And Cedrica, as soon as she put her nose above stairs, would be pounced on by a guest with a problem only she could solve. Indeed, even here, the housekeeper or the under butler might track her down. They would not trespass in Monsieur Fournier's kitchen, especially when the temperamental chef was under such pressure. He would not have time to make her a cup of the coffee she had come to enjoy since being taken up by the duchess, but perhaps she could just sit for a minute or two and watch other people work.

The kitchen was as chaotic as she had expected. She took a chair at the end of the kitchen table farthest from all of the activity, and a few minutes of careful observation disclosed the order and patterns of frantic movement centered on Monsieur who stood, the calm center of a purposeful storm: barking orders, giving advice, tasting from spoons and plates that anxious disciples brought to him.

A hand appeared over her shoulder, a cup of coffee, followed by another with a plate of the small cakes Monsieur decorated with such artistry. She smiled at the maidservant who was placing it for her, but the girl nodded toward Monsieur, who caught Cedrica's gaze for a moment, smiled, then turned back to the next in his line of supplicants.

She took a sip. Hot, creamy, and sweet. Just as she liked it.

Moments later, Monsieur Fournier joined her, hooking a chair with one foot and sitting on it back to front so he could rest one arm along the top rail while he sipped his own black, bitter brew. "Is there something I can do for you, Mademoiselle Grenford?"

"No, no. I had no wish to disturb you, Monsieur Fournier. I just wished to sit for a minute and not be interrupted. I can go."

He put a hand on her arm to stop her rising and snatched it back as if he, too, felt the shock of that connection." My kitchen is your refuge. I am honored, and only sorry it is so…" He shrugged helplessly, an expressive lift of his shoulders and a wave of his free hand.

"It is nice," Cedrica confided, "to see everyone working and not to be responsible for any of it."

He smiled. She had noticed before how the smile transformed his lean dark face, making it seem much younger. "I am responsible for them, and to you, Mademoiselle."

"To the duchess, surely."

"Oh no." He stared at the coffee cup as if it held the secrets of the universe. "To you, Mademoiselle, make no mistake." His dark lashes swept up, and his eyes, dark as his coffee, looked deep into hers. "My kitchen, my craft, my service. All are devoted to you, Mademoiselle Grenford." He pushed himself to his feet, flushing slightly. "I should not have spoken. I am tired, I think. Forgive me, Mademoiselle. You need not fear that I will embarrass or importune you. I know my place."

A loud crash startled Cedrica and drew Monsieur Fournier from her side to berate the boy who had darted through the door without looking just as a maid crossed the room with a stacked pile of serving bowls.

Cedrica sat and sipped until her cup was empty, hoping he would come back, but he did not look at her again, returning instead to conducting the work of the kitchen, and in the end she went back upstairs, where she did not belong any more than she belonged down here.

What good did it do knowing he was attracted to her as she was to him? He was right, of course. The duchess would never countenance such a connection. It was impossible.

Wasn't it?

Chapter Five

I *should not be doing this.*

Marcel flicked a non-existent speck of dust from the pristine folds of his extravagantly lacy cravat and frowned at his reflection in the small mirror that was all his room afforded.

I should definitely not be doing this.

On the other hand, who was to know? He wore a mask and would assume an English accent. If his French intonations seeped through, his costume would provide an excuse—he sounded French, because he was Louise XIV, the great French king. In any case, who would expect to see the duchess's chef dressed as *le Roi-Soleil* and dancing with her guests?

One guest. Or not a guest. A member of the family, rather.

For just one dance with her, I will risk all.

He doffed his tricorne hat as he bowed, the red-dyed ostrich plumes tossing gently.

Cissie Pearce had found the costume and had encouraged him to dare the masquerade. "What harm can it do? And don't you worry none about the supper, Mark. You have it all ready, and I can watch your people."

Was it a costume? Or something a former duke had worn? A white silk shirt with hugely puffed sleeves gathered to lacy cuffs, gold breeches tied below the knee over red stockings, a richly embroidered knee-length waistcoat, open from the waist, and, over it all, an ornately brocaded robe that just missed sweeping the ground as he stood. The cravat, buckled shoes, and a carved walking stick with a gold tip made up the rest of the costume. The wig had been in a different part of the attic but worked well enough: black, curly, and long enough to drape across his shoulders.

He answered the tap on the door cautiously, removing his hat and opening just wide enough that the visitor would see nothing but his head. It was Cissie, and he opened wider to let her in.

"Well, look at you." Cissie was all admiration, clucking over the fine lace and the perfect fit of the shoes. "Let's see you with your mask on. There. You're that fine, Mark. Now be off with you, and don't worry about a thing. Ain't nobody up here but us, and if you go out down the main stairs, no one will know any different, but you're a guest of the house."

Swept along on her confidence, he found himself approaching the rooms where a bare three hours earlier he had been one of the servants setting up for the duchess's costume party.

The rooms were full of kings and queens, gods and goddesses, Roman soldiers and cavaliers. Ah. There she was. One solitary shepherdess hovering in the supper room, keeping watch over the comings and goings of the servants.

The fates favored him. In the next room, the musicians began to play a waltz. Did he dare dance it as the current mode was in Paris? Yes. Ladies were taking the floor in the arms of their partners. Within minutes, he could be embracing his dear mademoiselle, albeit only on the dance floor. His breath caught at the mere thought.

Mademoiselle Grenford looked up as he approached, tipping her head a little to one side as she waited for him to speak.

"May I have the honor of this dance, fair shepherdess?" he asked.

She furrowed her brows for the briefest of seconds. "I do not dance, sir, but I will find you a partner—"

"Not dance? When your costume is made to swirl on the dance floor, and the music begs—nay, demand—for you to pay homage?" A slip there. He had pronounced homage in the French way.

Her eyes widened, but she said nothing, merely—oh joy—placed her gloved hand in his and allowed herself to be conducted through the doors to join the waltz.

They began slowly, his hands resting tentatively just above her waist, and hers placed lightly on his shoulders. He honored the respectable distance due to a maiden, but as they began to circle one another in the dance, his legs shifted past hers and could not avoid repeated touching.

Turn, turn, and turn again. The candles of the chandeliers seemed to whirl above them, the other dancers disappeared, and he and Mademoiselle Grenford were alone in the ballroom. She swayed and dipped and twirled with him, light as a feather but far more substantial, a delight to his hands, his arms, and his legs.

Her eyes fixed on his, her face flushed, she murmured, "Monsieur Fournier, what are you doing here?"

It was a dose of cold water, jerking him back to reality. Would she rebuke him? Tell the duchess?

"One dance," he managed, almost begged. "I promised not to importune you, Mademoiselle, but I thought… In costume, no one would know if I stole one dance."

Somehow, his feet kept moving, they kept dancing, round and round and round, their legs shifting past each other's again and again, their eyes still locked.

She smiled, a benison beyond his deserving. "This dance is not a theft, Monsieur, when I give it willingly."

"Give?"

He was in heaven. He was no longer dancing; he was floating several inches about the ballroom floor. *She knows me even in my disguise. She dances with me willingly.*

His heart was too full for speech, and she said nothing more as they continued around the floor, oblivious to everything except the music and one another.

Marcel stepped back when the music ended, dropping his hands from her waist to her hands, unable to resist touching her for a moment more. "Thank you, Mademoiselle. Thank you more than I can say. I will leave now, but you have given me food for many happy dreams."

"No." Mademoiselle Grenford folded her fingers around his and tugged him to follow her. By chance, they had stopped at the most poorly lit end of the ballroom, close to the corner where a door let on to a servant's passage, and it was to this she marched determinedly, with Marcel bobbing after in her wake.

No. Not that door. She was opening a door onto the terrace, and in moments, they were outside.

"I do not want it to end," she said. "Will you not consent to sit and talk with me for a little?"

Consent? Did she not know he would consent to the guillotine for her sake?

"But you will be cold! Here." He struggled out of his heavy robe and wrapped it around her, but she protested when she saw his arms unprotected by no more than the silk of his shirtsleeves.

"We shall share it," she proposed as she guided him through an arch into one of the hedged gardens and then to a hidden stone seat tucked into an arbor that in summer would be fragrant with roses.

It is a dream. I am asleep in my bed and dreaming of sitting here in the duchess' garden, sharing a robe with my mademoiselle. It is a dream, and I hope I never awaken.

She had commanded talk. What could he talk about? "Did the tenants like their gifts, Mademoiselle?"

They were wasteful, the aristos, with much food left after every meal. Mademoiselle had agreed it should go to those in need, and she and the duchess had asked for some of the finer dishes to be saved for the gifts traditionally given to the poor on St. Stephen's Day. Marcel had taken great care with the selection and the presentation in baskets.

For a time, he listened, commenting just enough to keep her talking as she told him about the trip she had made yesterday with the duchess and some of the other ladies.

"You have a generous heart, Monsieur," she finished. "That is what my father used to say. Some give reluctantly out of duty. You can tell those with generous hearts because they take pleasure in the happiness of those who receive."

He shrugged. "I have been hungry, Mademoiselle. When I was a little boy, after my family fled France, we had very little. I do not forget."

"Will you feed the poor of London with the leftovers from your Ordinary once you have it?"

"Did the excellent Cissie tell you of my plans? But she is wrong, you know. I do not plan a French *Ordinaire*, Mademoiselle. Say, rather, *Extraordinaire*. As they have in France. *Un restaurant*, Mademoiselle, with the finest cuisine listed on a menu from which patrons can choose, an excellent cellar, a quiet setting—perhaps with music playing, prompt and efficient service. A place where gentlemen would be proud to bring their guests or could dine alone without the expense of keeping a kitchen and a chef."

Now it was his turn to spin out the words, while she asked quiet questions, her eyes turned up to his in the light of the quarter moon.

"And so I take work wherever I can find it, Mademoiselle, and one day, I will have sufficient money, and *Fournier's of London* will open for business," he finished.

Marcel fell silent. The moon would set soon. They would need to go in while it still gave enough light to find their way without falling into one of the moats or ponds. He did not want the dream to end.

Mademoiselle echoed his thoughts. "We need to go. It will be full dark when the moon goes down."

Marcel stood reluctantly, and she stood with him, still in the warmth of his coat.

"It is cold, Monsieur," she said. "Keep the robe around us both until we are inside."

So he put his arm around her to help them walk in harmony, and—oh, magical night—she put her arm around him. Marcel said nothing as they walked slowly back to the house. He was soaking up the warmth of her, the curves of her, the way she fitted neatly under his arm.

He could not resist. Even one of God's saints would have done it, and Heaven knew, Marcel was no saint. As they rounded the corner that concealed the door, he stopped and used his other hand to turn her toward him. Naturally, she looked up.

Her lips were as sweet as he had imagined, and she did not draw back and slap his impertinent face. Far from it. She pressed herself into the kiss, and though she was untutored in the art, she learned quickly. Marcel was left reeling when at last a burst of noise from inside the ballroom intruded, and they parted.

"Mademoiselle—" he began.

"Don't." Mademoiselle put up a hand to stop his mouth, and he kissed her fingers. "Don't spoil it by apologizing." She stood within his arms, but he could feel she was poised to flee, and he had no idea what to say or do.

A moment, and it was too late. She stretched up, gave him a swift peck on the lips, and slipped away from under his robe. Marcel watched, his hand touching the lips she had so favored as she opened the door and returned to the party.

It is over, then, but more, so much more than I ever imagined.

He would not go back inside. He would find his way to his kitchen and become a chef once more. And this night would be forever a jewel to carry in his heart.

Chapter Six
New Year's Eve

That was it?
One magical dance? One enchanted hour in the moonlight? One kiss that thrilled her to the soles of her feet and left her tingling even days later?

And then nothing?

Perhaps not quite nothing, for his eyes followed her whenever she entered his realm, intent and sad. But whatever else she had expected, it had not happened. No declaration. No stolen moments. No whispered avowals of regard.

He behaved as if their time together had not happened and not changed the complexion of the entire world, destroying even her haven in his kitchen. No longer did she relax when she sat at the table watching the kitchen servants scurrying to his command. Far from it.

Being in the same room with him was painful. Her heart ached, and not just her heart. She had but to look at him to remember the touch of his lips, his hands, his body pressed against hers. Memories were pale ghostly substitutes for the real thing but enough to have her stirring restlessly and cutting her visits short.

Not that she had much time to brood. With most of the ladies' committee succumbing to Cupid's assault and absorbed in their suitors, Cedrica was busier than ever. Even her co-hosts had fallen victim. Sophia had left yesterday to join Lord Elfingham in London and, Cedrica hoped, would marry him there, and Grace had made up her quarrel with her Lord Nicholas and spent every moment she could with him.

Cedrica co-opted Esther Baumann to help. Esther's courtship had prospered, but her suitor had returned to London so giving her work to do was a kindness.

Esther was in the small sitting room that Sophia had dubbed the Command Tent, writing letters to every house with pretensions to gentility within a two-hour ride of Hollystone Hall. She looked up as Cedrica joined her. "Almost done," she said. "If all these people agree, we shall be able to billet half of Society on the neighbors."

"Which is to the good, Esther, for I swear Her Grace has invited the better part of Society, and if they all come, we shall be inviting dukes and earls to share their horses' beds!"

"It will not be as bad as that," the duchess soothed, startling Cedrica who had not heard her enter the room. "Most of them are too far away to travel for a single night's entertainment, but if they send a bank note for our Fund, I shall be pleased enough."

The size to which the fund had grown was astounding, far outstripping the colossal amount the duchess had spent on the house party, but the New Year's Eve Ball would bring in as much again, with each guest paying for their ticket and further opportunities to donate in the course of the evening.

"There." Esther blotted the letter she had been writing. "That is the last. I shall see to these being delivered." She gathered up the bundle of sealed letters and went to find the senior footman whose job it was to send grooms to the neighbors with Her Grace's missives.

The duchess took a seat by the window and gestured for Cedrica to join her. Her Grace had not been in this room since before the house party, contenting herself with daily reports and quick consultations wherever she happened to be during the day. Whoever did the bulk of the work, Cedrica was in no doubt that Her Grace was firmly in charge of the entire event, knew exactly what went on under her roof, and would step in if the ladies made a decision that was not to her liking.

Had that happened? Had she done something the duchess disapproved of?

"Did you need me for something, Aunt Eleanor?"

The duchess' reply was cryptic. "I think perhaps you need me for something, my dear."

Cedrica sat, her mind racing as she reviewed all the ways she might have fallen short of Her Grace's high standards.

"When I saw you slip away with your Sun King, I thought you had found the path to your future, Cedrica, but since then, nothing. Or am I mistaken? Are you and your suitor keeping your agreement secret for some reason? You do not seem happy, dear child, and that simply will not do."

Cedrica opened her mouth to protest and then closed it again. Her Grace could not possibly know…

The duchess was silent, too, her face alive with interest, her head on one side as if she would listen forever, if that was how long it took for Cedrica to think of something to say.

"You do not understand, Your Gr—Aunt Eleanor."

"I would like to. I am an interfering old woman, my dear, but I wish you well, you know. And Monsieur Fournier, too. Yes, Cedrica, I did recognize him in my husband's Louis XIV costume and that ancient wig."

Suddenly, Cedrica found herself pouring the whole story into the duchess's sympathetic ears. Everything: the first unfortunate clashes, the growing attraction, the quiet times in the kitchen, the chef's surprising appearance at the costume party, and what came of it.

At length, the duchess gave her a hug and handed her a handkerchief. "So, he thinks you are far above him and is being noble about it."

Cedrica, who had somehow arrived on the rug at Her Grace's feet and was weeping into the noble lady's gown, looked up in surprise. "Is that what he is doing?"

"Yes, of course. Silly romantic boy."

Cedrica blotted her eyes and blew her nose. The duchess did not sound disapproving. Quite the contrary. "You do not mind? You do not think I would be marrying beneath me?"

"Does it matter what I think, my dear? Unless you are thinking of the dowry Aldridge promised?"

"I do not care about the dowry. Monsieur Fournier has plans… But, Aunt Eleanor, I care about your good opinion."

The duchess said nothing, smiling gently, one brow slightly arched.

Cedrica felt as she had in the village schoolroom when suddenly she knew the answer to a question that had eluded her for days. "But not as much as I care about Monsieur Fournier. I am sorry if you disapprove, Aunt Eleanor, but I will marry him if he will have me."

The duchess beamed with all the delight of a dedicated teacher. "Excellent. You do realize that you will have to ask him, Cedrica? Men can be so foolish." She shook her head fondly. "Off you go. This is a quiet time in the kitchen, is it not? Take your Monsieur Fournier for a walk. If any problems arise while you and Esther are occupied, I am sure I shall manage."

Cedrica hesitated a moment more and then startled them both with an impulsive hug. "Thank you, Aunt Eleanor."

In the kitchen, she went straight to his side before she lost her nerve.

"Monsieur Fournier," she said, "I need a word with you. Will you spare me a moment, please?"

Monsieur Fournier said nothing but nodded and gave the ladle he was holding to his assistant. Cedrica looked back as she led him out of the kitchen and along the passage that led to the outside door. He was frowning, but he still followed.

She stopped just inside the door and helped herself to one of the warm serviceable coats. His frown had given way to puzzlement, but he shrugged into one of the other coats and continued to follow her around the house and across the short bridge to the sleeping rose garden in which they had kissed.

He held back when she made straight for the arbor and sat down, and he shook his head, his eyes wary and alarmed, when she patted the bench beside her. Oh, dear. Was she about to make an enormous fool of herself?

Cedrica swallowed against the sudden constriction in her throat. "Monsieur Fournier…" What did one say? The etiquette guides for young ladies gave no instructions for such an occasion. "You cannot be unaware that I have come to hold you in the highest esteem…"

But he was shaking his head. "Non. No. *Cherie*, you must not. You pay me a great compliment, but I cannot." Through a film of tears, she saw him backing away. "I will not. Ah, *cherie*, do not cry." Two steps and he was kneeling at her feet, attempting to dry her eyes with the corner of his apron. "You would grow to hate yourself and me if I dishonored you so."

Suddenly, she was angry. "How dare you decide what dishonors me? To marry out of my class is a dishonor? You are very wrong! Even if I belonged in this frivolous world, you would be wrong. Condemn me to a cold and lonely life if you do not love me as I have come to love you," she caught a long shuddering breath, "but do not dare pretend you do it for my sake."

He was staring at her as if she had grown a second head. "Marry?" he asked.

"Of course 'marry.' What did you think I was…? Marcel! I am a vicar's daughter."

"Marry." He was grinning broadly. "I never imagined… Are you sure, Mademoiselle?" He had both her hands now and was smothering them with kisses. "I cannot give you the life you have here. I could perhaps manage a small apartment. I have money saved, but it would not be what you are used to."

"Marcel, this is not the life I am used to. I am the daughter of a vicar, who was himself the son of a clerk in a counting house. My ducal connections are so far back that I cannot even tell you how distant a cousin Lord Aldridge is. I am used to a life of counting pennies, and I am good at making do, I promise."

"You deserve to be dressed in silks and have maids to tend you."

"And be cold and lonely?" she asked again.

His response was a kiss, which was very satisfactory, and little was said in the arbor for some time.

Eventually, though, Cedrica returned to the topic of their future. "We must not dip into your savings for the restaurant, Marcel.

When we have enough saved, we can open *Fournier's of London* and live above it in a little apartment."

"It could be three years, my own, and I do not wish to wait."

"I shall work, too," she assured him. "The duchess will let me stay, I think, and she pays me a salary and my keep."

"The duchess may turn you off if she knows you plan to marry a chef, Rica."

She smiled at her new nickname, the 'r' rolled over Marcel's tongue. "She knows. She sent me to you. I'll forfeit the dowry Lord Aldridge promised if I married a 'suitable' gentleman, but I told her I did not care about that, and she smiled. She will be happy for us, Marcel."

"Is it so?" he marveled.

"Yes. And I should return and tell her that we are betrothed. We are betrothed, are we not?"

"Yes, my Rica. I, Marcel Fournier, accept your proposal with a thankful heart." Marcel kissed her again to prove it, and it was some time later that Cedrica finally floated upstairs to tell her patroness her news.

Epilogue
London, August 1813

Fournier's of London had been open for three weeks, three weeks in which the numbers of diners had grown nightly until they needed to take bookings and began to turn people away at the door.

Tonight, though, no bookings had been accepted and nor would casual diners be able to penetrate into the elegant interior, where polished wood, crisp white linen, shining silver, and sparkling crystal waited for the few privileged guests.

And tonight, welcoming the diners would not be the task of the *maître d'hôtel* who usually managed the dining room while the proprietor controlled the kitchen.

Tonight, Marcel had left his chief assistant in charge of the final preparations. Tonight, Monsieur Fournier himself would greet his patrons, and not alone. For tonight, the restaurant, normally a sanctuary for gentlemen, would be entertaining women, and not only women, but ladies. Including Cedrica, who was waiting at the door.

Had it been less than a year since she had written to her father's noble relative in a last desperate bid to keep the bishop from locking the poor man up? How things had changed!

Here was the biggest change of all: her husband, looking splendid in a black dress coat and knee breeches. He slipped an arm around her waist and kissed the top of her head. "Are you nervous, cherie?"

"Proud, Marcel. I am looking forward to showing our investors what we have done."

He turned with her, surveying the largest of five dining rooms with satisfaction. Here, they could host up to one hundred diners at a time, with tables that could be divided or put together to suit the convenience of the patrons, from single diners to large banquets. The smallest of the rooms accommodated eight with comfort and could be configured for smaller groups.

Tonight, they would be using one of the medium-sized rooms, for tonight, they welcomed the friends who had taken shares in the restaurant.

It had been Lord Aldridge's idea. When Cedrica first realized that he planned to pay the dowry he had promised, she voiced her decision to split it between buying care for her father and helping Marcel pay for the restaurant, but Aldridge advised her to think again.

"The Grenfords owe your father a duty of care," he assured her. "Invest in the restaurant by all means, but not only in the restaurant. You also need a separate income. I suggest money in the Funds for security and then some other ventures that will give a greater return. You must think of your long-term security, cousin."

Cedrica had quizzed Marcel on his plans and then spent hours collecting figures and doing sums. "But we will need all that money if we are to open this year."

"We could work another year," Marcel suggested, "or open a lesser establishment."

"Or accept investors," Aldridge suggested. "You and Cedrica to hold the majority share, and no one else with more than…" He pursed his lips as he considered, "five percent. You would have my support. I am confident you will make me money."

Her Grace agreed, and so did the Laceys and the Suttons and others. In no time at all, it seemed, they had the funds to make over a building to Marcel's high standards, the rental on a comfortable home nearby, and investments in the Funds, Aldridge's cousin's trading company, a woolen mill in Manchester, and a canal building enterprise.

Less than two months after the end of the house party where it all started, Monsieur Marcel Fournier and Mademoiselle Cedrica Grenford were married. Twice. Once according to English practice and law and again in a small comfortable parlor off the side of the local Roman Catholic chapel.

And now Monsieur and Madame Fournier would say thank you to those who made it possible.

"It looks well," Marcel decided. "And the dinner, the dinner, my Rica, will be the most magnificent they have ever tasted."

Cedrica smiled. He said that every night, and every night, his guests assured him it was true.

Out in the hall, the restaurant door opened, and they could hear the *portier* greeting the first arrivals. In moments, it seemed, they were surrounded by cheerful friends, the men slapping Marcel on the back and congratulating him on making them all rich, the women kissing Cedrica on the cheek and gently scolding her for being too busy to meet friends for tea.

"Mama and I brought you a present," Aldridge said. "I left it in the hall. Just one moment." He left the room and returned a moment later with a long, flat, oblong shape wrapped in silk and tied with ribbon, which he handed to the duchess.

"We wanted to give you something useful but unusual, something that would always remind you of Hollystone Hall," she said.

Marcel, seated beside Cedrica, lifted her hand and kissed it. "I have a wonderful *souvenir* of that house party, Your Grace," he said.

The duchess smiled. "Indeed you do. To remind you of us, then, Monsieur. We consulted with Mrs. Pearce, and she suggested that this might be suitable."

What on earth could it be? Cedrica and Marcel took one end of the parcel each and began to untie ribbons. When Marcel cleared his end of the silk and saw the box within, he began to laugh. Cedrica was still mystified until she finished unwrapping and was able to open the box and see the pearwood mold within, the one with the dolphin shapes that had caused such contention.

"Look, Marcel, at last you will be able to make your ice tower!"

Leave it to Aldridge to have the last word, as he raised his glass of wine. "Ladies and gentlemen, I give you Fournier's of London. May it, and its proprietors, be a towering success."

THE END

All That Glisters

In 1860s New Zealand, gold miners poured into the fledgling settlement of Dunedin. Rose is unhappy in the household of her fanatical uncle. Thomas, a young merchant from Canada, offers a glimpse of another possible life. If she is brave enough to reach for it. (Short story: 13,000 words)

Chapter One

Rose was late. She'd been shocked, when she emerged from the Athenaeum, at how dark the sky was—her aunt would soon be looking for her to serve dinner. Rose had set a pot roast of beef on the back of the stove this morning, with the vegetables tucked around the meat, and she'd shelled the peas, too, before running Aunt Agnes' messages and stealing a little time for herself.

The Athenaeum was paradise. A subscription library and reading room at the Mechanics Institute, it provided warmth, books, and a peaceful place to read as much as she liked. And even books to take home, if she kept them hidden.

Scraping together the subscription to the Athenaeum each quarter meant sitting late over the sewing with which she earned a few extra shillings, most of which Aunt Agnes took 'to help pay for your keep, child'. As if her constant work, saving them the cost of at least one servant, were not sufficient to earn her food and a roof over her head.

She skirted around the Octagon, where the would-be millionaires flooding into the New Zealand gold fields had set up a squatters' camp with the blessing of the Dunedin Town Board. Down George Street next, thinking of her aunt, struggling to control her unchristian resentment, ignoring the drizzle and the sharp wind that wrapped her long cloak around her legs and billowed her petticoats out in front of her. As she turned the corner into Frederick St., a particularly sharp gust skittered a broken branch across her path, tangling it into her skirts.

She stumbled and would have landed in the mud, if firm hands had not suddenly caught her. As it was, in putting her hands out to break the expected fall, she had dropped her burdens. The shopping basket fell sideways, tumbling fruit, vegetables, and the wrapped parcel of meat into a waiting puddle. The bundle from the haberdashers that she carried on her other arm, thankfully, stayed intact and landed on a relatively dry spot.

She took all this in at a glance, most of her attention on her rescuer. A craggy face bronzed by the sun, amused brown eyes under thick, level brows, a mouth that looked made for laughter. He was bundled against the cold wind in a greatcoat, muffler, and cloth cap.

"Are you all right, Miss?" the man asked, as he set her back on her feet.

My. He was strong.

"Thank you. The branch... Oh, dear, my parcels!" He crouched with her to rescue tomorrow's roast, now peeping through tears in the soggy brown paper. He looked doubtfully at a particularly dirty carrot and wiped it off on a handkerchief he pulled from his pocket.

"Oh, no," Rose said, as he started to put her damp groceries back in the basket. She retrieved the book she had hidden there, tucking it inside her coat so it would stay dry. Her rescuer made no comment, just continued helping her fill the basket.

"That seems to be the lot," he said, bringing back an apple that had rolled a good distance along the path, and picking up the basket. "Which way now?"

Rose ignored the proffered elbow. "I can manage, thank you, Sir. If you would just give me my basket..."

He grinned, showing white, even teeth. "I must insist. Damsels in distress do not land in a knight errant's hands every day, you know. I shall, at least, escort you safely to your front door, fair maiden."

"You may not, Sir." He really couldn't. If a man escorted her to the front door, or even to her uncle's front gate, it would be fasting and prayer for her, and perhaps even the switch. She set her mouth firmly to stop it from trembling, but he must have sensed her alarm, because he handed over the basket without further argument.

"There, now. No need to be concerned. I mean no harm, Miss."

She was blushing again; she could feel the heat. The kindness in his eyes was as appealing as his strength and his cheeky smile.

"I cannot," she found herself explaining. "My uncle… he would be angry…"

He nodded as if he understood. "I will bid you good evening then, Miss. But before I go, can you help a poor, lost traveller and point me in the direction of Knox Lane?"

"Knox Lane?" she repeated, stupidly.

"Yes. Do you know it?"

"I live there," Rose said. It was a short cul-de-sac, with only three houses besides her uncle's. She looked at the man more closely, wondering which of her neighbours he intended to visit.

"Then, Miss, will you not reconsider your decision and allow me to escort you? I can leave you at the corner of this elusive lane, so you need have no fear, and it would be a charitable act to a poor traveller." He made a woebegone face, turning the corners of his mouth down with his lips poked out, wrinkling his brow, so his brows sank at the side and rose in the centre.

Rose smiled despite herself, and surrendered the basket to his waiting hand. "Just to the corner then, Sir."

"Allow me to introduce myself," he said, as they turned the next corner and walked briskly along Great King Street, pushed by the wind. "I am Thomas O'Bryan, from America."

Ah. She had been wondering about his accent. Beyond a doubt, he was another of the great army of men passing through Dunedin on their way to the gold fields at Tuapeka or Dunstan. Fools. Yes, a few of them would find a rich deposit, but most would abandon their families and their responsibilities and return, if return they ever did, with nothing. Rose knew only too well what became of those left behind.

"Rose Campbell." Her thoughts tinged her voice with ice, and he raised one of those mobile brows. "Campbell?" he repeated. "Do not be telling me, of all the women in New Zealand, I've collided with Agnes Campbell's daughter."

"Her niece," Rose corrected. "You know my aunt?"

O'Bryan grinned, a joyous beam that invited her to find life as delightful as he clearly did. "Not to say know, but isn't she my own mother's sister?" He bowed, an extravagant flourish. "How do you do, Cousin Rose."

"Not exactly a cousin, Mr O'Bryan," Rose demurred. "Your aunt is married to my uncle."

"Thomas, surely? For cousins so closely related by marriage?"

"Laura!" Rose could not help the guilty flinch at the accusing roar from her uncle. Thomas stepped in front of her, and held out his hand with another of his broad grins. "Do I have the honour of addressing my Uncle Campbell?" he asked.

The sour, old man ignored Thomas' hand, but turned his glower away from the cowering girl, which Thomas counted as a win. "Who are you, and what are you doing with my niece?"

"Thomas O'Bryan, sir, and I believe I am your nephew-by-marriage. I was asking the young lady for directions."

"Agnes' nephew." The thought clearly did not find favour. "I suppose you're here after the gold, like all those other godless sinners. Well, you had better come in." The old coot turned to lead the way down the street, saying over his shoulder, "Laura, I'll speak with you later, girl."

Thomas gave his new cousin a reassuring wink, but she dipped her head and hurried after the domestic tyrant.

Thomas' aunt proved to be cut from the same cloth as her husband, and as far from Thomas' cheerful mother as could be imagined. She reluctantly allowed that Thomas could stay to dinner, and swept off towards the back of the house, chivvying the niece ahead of her.

"No time to waste mooning in your room, Laura. We'll need to put on more potatoes to stretch the stew. Put those bundles away…" A closing door shut off the detail of Aunt Agnes' tirade, but not the sound of her scold, pitched at a droning whine that set Thomas' teeth on edge.

"Where do you stay this night?" the old man demanded.

Thomas had assumed he would be resisting an invitation to stay here. In Canada, where he was raised, his parents found room for any traveller, let alone a hitherto unknown nephew. In San Francisco, where his business partner lived, the same habits prevailed. Thomas had already taken rooms at the Empire Hotel, but he was surprised not to be offered a bed here.

Campbell made the wrong assumption from his silence. "There's a camp. In the middle of town. Those heading for the gold fields can find tent space."

So he'd be given dinner then turned out into the night. And leave without any regrets, except that he'd like to know a little more about his cousin-by-marriage.

"So they told me when I arrived, Sir," he said, perversely not wishing to let this poor excuse for an uncle know he had already arranged his own accommodation

He continued to make attempts at conversation, each one squashed by Campbell, until they were called to dinner. The table, in the second front room, sharing space with a pair of fireside chairs, a large roll-top desk, and a treadle sewing machine, had been moved far enough from the wall to allow the use of four of the six wooden chairs. Aunt Agnes brought a platter of fresh sliced bread, while Miss Campbell carried in a large pot and returned for another.

After a long prayer of thanksgiving that sounded more like a diatribe against persons unnamed, Campbell gestured them to sit. So began one of the most uncomfortable meals of Thomas' life.

The stew was delicious, if somewhat sparse. Thomas dug into the bread with enthusiasm to fill the gaps.

"My mother sends her love," Thomas said, a little mendaciously. Mama had actually told him, *I suppose you had better visit Agnes, though I don't suppose you'll be welcomed.*

This conversational opener fetched a contemptuous harrumph from Campbell, and a nod of acknowledgement from Aunt Agnes.

Thomas tried again. "The stew is delicious. My compliments." He nodded to his aunt, but it was Miss Campbell who murmured thanks, sliding frightened eyes sideways to her uncle.

What now? The weather? Ladies' fashions? Greek history? Stargazing or birdwatching? Did nobody at this benighted table talk over dinner?

Before he could make a comment on the beauty of the long Otago Harbour inlet, Aunt Agnes surprised him by asking, "How is my sister?"

"Well, Ma'am, she was well when I left San Francisco. She is staying with my sister, Catherine, to help with the older children, while my sister is lying in with the new baby."

"Three children is it, now?" Aunt Agnes asked, her tone softening, and something like longing in her eyes.

"Yes. Two boys, and now a little girl. Cath and Patrick are delighted."

"More half-breed, Papist idolaters bound for Hell," Mr Campbell grumbled, seemingly to his plate. Thomas controlled the urge to retaliate in kind. Campbell had clearly not softened since the days when his mother and her sister, two good, Presbyterian girls in Edinburgh, were being courted. Both married and emigrated. Mother had gone with her merry husband to Canada, where she was welcomed by his Irish father and his mother's large Métis clan, descendants of a French trapper and his Cree wife. Aunt Agnes and her dour non-conformist chose to move far from all they knew to New Zealand, where they moved from one congregation to another until he invented one strict enough for his tastes.

Aunt Agnes, who had been about to say something more, subsided. Another conversational sally cut off at the pass.

"I thought your harbour very beautiful," Thomas offered. "The hills either side... it is very like parts of the west coast of Canada, where I grew up."

Miss Campbell looked as if she might reply, but clearly thought better of it, and neither of the others said a word.

In the end, Thomas gave up and simply ate his meal. Another interminable Grace in place of dessert was clearly a signal that dinner was over, and Aunt Agnes and Miss Campbell began to clear.

Thomas stood when they rose. "May I pay my guest gift by helping with the dishes?" he asked.

Campbell answered for the women. "The girls will do it. My niece and the maid. Women's work."

Thomas, who had fended for himself in a long succession of miner's towns, where women were few and far between, once again swallowed his opinion. The evening would soon be over, and he could escape.

Sooner than he thought, it appeared. "Agnes, fetch the boy's coat," the old man commanded, and Aunt Agnes scurried to obey.

"Thank you for dinner, Ma'am," Thomas said. "Mama will be pleased to know I found you well."

Aunt Agnes handed him his coat with one hand, and waved Miss Campbell's book with the other. "Look what I found under the coats, Mr Campbell. That girl has been reading again!"

Miss Campbell had returned to the room to finish clearing the table, and stood behind her uncle, transfixed, her face white.

"My book!" Thomas exclaimed. "It must have fallen out of my pocket."

Aunt Agnes looked at him, doubtfully, but handed him the book, and Campbell shut the mouth that had been open to roar. "And what is that you're reading?" he grumbled, frowning.

Thomas, who had no idea of the answer, held the book up so Campbell could see the embossed title for himself.

"*Dombey and Son.* That Charles Dickens fellow. Rubbish."

Thomas tucked the book into his pocket, shook Campbell's hand, thanked him for his hospitality (may his lips not shrivel—two lies in as many minutes!), and gave his aunt a dutiful salute on a cold, papery cheek.

Miss Campbell had faded from the room again, silent as a ghost. No matter. As the front door closed behind him, Thomas ducked along in front of the parlour window and down the narrow path at the side of the house to the lean-to scullery at the rear.

Miss Campbell was bent over the sink, while another girl dried each dish as it was handed to her. He waited, watching through the window, as they completed the dishes, and then continued to wait some more.

He doubted that Campbell, the nasty old miser, let them burn candles sitting up late. Before long, each of them would make the journey down the path to the outhouse at the foot of the garden. With luck, he could return Miss Campbell her book with no one else the wiser.

Within half an hour, his expectation was fulfilled, as first the maid, then Campbell himself, then Aunt Agnes made the trip. When it was Miss Campbell's turn with the lantern, he waited until she returned and spoke from the shadows, keeping his voice soft, so as not to alarm her.

"Miss Campbell, I waited to return your book."

Clever girl. She kept her eyes on the back door, but slowed her steps, saying quietly, "Aunt Agnes is watching. I will be back shortly to collect wood. The wood pile is beyond that shed." She indicated with her head, still not looking at him.

"I will be there," Thomas told her. He kept to the shadows, but was in place to meet her when she carried out a basket to fill with wood for the morning fire.

"Maisie will be here in a moment, Mr O'Bryan, to help me carry the basket back inside. Thank you for telling Uncle Campbell it was your book."

"Here you are, Miss Campbell." He handed her the book, and she slipped it inside the waistband of her skirt, loosening, then retying, the shawl that insulated her against the chill night air.

A clatter of wooden pattens heralded the arrival of the maid, and Thomas faded into the darkness, leaving the two of them to their task.

He sauntered back along George Street to his hotel. He could write to his Mama and let her know her sister was well. He had done his duty and need not visit again. But he would not at all mind seeing Miss Campbell once more.

Chapter Two

Mr O'Bryan was a bright spot in an otherwise dismal week. Rose's lateness returning home that night had been overshadowed by the American nephew's crimes of being a Papist, a gold miner, and an uninvited dinner guest. She escaped with no more than an extra fifteen minutes on her knees, and the linen closet to turn out. She managed to read the book Mr O'Bryan had saved for her in the week before it was due for return, keeping it in her apron pocket, stealing moments at the clothesline or in the kitchen when Aunt Agnes was occupied with the ladies' church committee.

On Thursday, Mr Hackerton came to dinner. A widower and an elder at the Congregation of the Elect meetinghouse, he was looking Rose over for her potential as a wife and housekeeper. Rose shuddered. Imagine: a lifetime of being called 'Laura', and being touched by those cold, pudgy hands.

On Saturday, the entire house had to be cleaned from top to bottom, and the next day's food cooked, so the day could be spent in prayer and meditation, when not at one of two long church services conducted by Uncle Campbell and the other elders.

And on Monday, she saw Thomas O'Bryan again. She was coming back from shopping, nervously skirting the noisy camp in the Octagon, when he materialised beside her, tipped his cap, and held out a hand for her basket.

"Let me carry that for you, Miss Campbell. It looks heavy." He fell into step, saying cheerfully, "As I thought. Far too heavy for a little bit of a thing like yourself."

"I thought you would have gone to the fields by now, Mr O'Bryan," she said.

"There now, you have been thinking of me!" Something in his grin made her insides feel peculiar, and she looked away, feeling the heat rise in her face.

"I have business to attend to in Dunedin, but I've passage booked on the coach tomorrow," he explained. "And what are we shopping for, this fine, crisp, spring morning?" He lifted the corner of a package, and shifted another sideways, ignoring her anxious fluttering. "Is there another book concealed beneath the potatoes, Miss Campbell?"

"Don't say that," she darted her eyes about, hoping no one who knew her uncle had overheard. They were all strangers, intent on their own affairs, and Mr O'Bryan was regarding her with chagrin.

"I was only teasing, Miss Campbell. No one heard, and your secrets are safe with me. The old crow and his wife object to you reading?"

She flushed to hear her secret description for her nearest living relations on the lips of this irreverent man, but something about his clear interest tugged a murmured admission from her. "Uncle says the Bible is the only proper reading for a pious woman."

"Which bits?" Mr O'Bryan enquired with interest. "The Song of Songs? The story about Lot's daughters? Or Tamar?"

"Mr O'Bryan!" He could not possibly know of her minor rebellion, seeking out the most shocking stories she could find in the Bible, whenever her uncle set her reading.

"What?" He tried to keep his face bland, but one corner of his mouth twitched, and his eyes twinkled.

By now, they were out of the shopping area and approaching the turn into Frederick Street. "Thank you for your escort, sir," Rose told him. "I can manage from here."

"I am visiting my aunt, Miss Campbell, so I'll do myself the honour of seeing you home."

Thomas was surprised to hear himself say so. He'd intended to steer clear of his aunt and her poisonous husband, despite his attraction to the niece. Unusual for him to be attracted to a little mouse; though, he had to admit, she had backbone, sneaking books into the house under the old man's nose. There was more to her than met the eye.

But she was all wrong for Thomas—Protestant, and puritan at that. This New Zealand venture would establish his fortune, and he'd return home to San Francisco to look for a wife—a good, Catholic girl like Mary Rourke, the daughter of his partner. Ben had hoped... and Thomas had started seriously thinking about it, but he had thought too long, and came back from a trip to Canada to find the girl betrothed—to a local farmer, of all things.

Miss Campbell was nothing like Miss Rourke. Slender, where Miss Rourke was prettily plump, quiet and contained, while Miss Rourke was vivacious and outgoing, wary, when Miss Rourke expected the world to shape itself to her command. Miss Rourke was all colour—red hair, rosy cheeks, blue-green eyes, bright gowns and shawls and bonnets. Miss Campbell was shades of brown—light hair the shade of a mouse pelt; soft, brown eyes, lightened with gold flecks; skin a pale olive, lit at the moment by the bright colour that rose so easily to her face; and her drab, serviceable, beige dress cut too large and untrimmed.

She should be dressed in green or red or a warm, rosy pink; something that would give her colour, instead of draining it. If she were his, he'd buy her colours.

Protestant, he reminded himself. Not for him.

"Why does your uncle call you 'Laura'?" he asked, to turn his mind from the subject.

"He does not like my other name," she explained.

"Rose Laura?" He tried it on his tongue. "Or Laura Rose?"

"Laura Rose, but my papa always called me Rose. Uncle says it is a Pap... Uncle does not like it."

Thomas could easily supply the word she caught back: *Papist*. Another reminder that they occupied separate worlds. "Rose is a very pretty name," he said.

She smiled, and the grim spring day became unexpectedly brighter.

"What business keeps you in Dunedin, Mr O'Bryan?"

"Mining supplies, Miss Campbell. My firm, Rourke and O'Bryan, sells supplies to miners, and I am here in New Zealand to set up supply lines and open stores in the main fields."

"Food, you mean?"

"And pans and shovels and blankets and buckets and clothing and tents… My father and his partner began the firm in California thirteen years ago, when I was a wee bit of a boy, and Ben Rourke took me into the firm when my father died."

"I am sorry for your loss, Mr O'Bryan. Is it… recent?"

"Three years ago, but I cannot seem to realise it, somehow. I was in South Australia, and by the time I received the letter telling me he was ill, he had already gone to his reward."

Thomas shook his head, grimacing. He'd returned home on the first ship that could give him passage, but arrived in Vancouver six weeks past the funeral.

His sister, Mary-Elizabeth, and her family had moved into the fine, new house his parents had built, so his mother would not be alone. But when he was home, Thomas constantly expected to be told it had all been a mistake, to see, at any moment, his father walking in through the front door, kissing his wife, tickling his grandson, and making a joke about the removal of his favourite chair to the attic, since Mama could neither bear to look at it, nor give it away.

Thomas shook off the mood. The whole family had offered Masses for the repose of Papa's soul, and Thomas had performed all the requirements for a plenary indulgence at Christmastide, on Papa's behalf, these past three years. Papa was a good man, and surely in Purgatory at least, if not in Heaven already.

"What of your own family, Miss Campbell? How do you come to be living with your aunt and uncle?"

Miss Campbell wilted, all the vitality sinking out of her, and Thomas felt an almost overpowering urge to give her a hug and bring some warmth back into her face.

"Never mind," he said, hastily. "You need not talk about it, if you do not wish."

If they turned now, they would be at the Campbell's cottage before he was ready. He deliberately continued straight ahead, and she followed meekly along, her thoughts far away.

"I do not mind," she said, breaking the silence. "The story is a short one. My mother died shortly after I was born, and my father raised me. Then, five years ago, he left me with his brother and went off to Australia. He said the gold fields were no place for a growing girl. A few months later... he drowned, Mr O'Bryan. A flash flood, they said, several miners swept away."

Thomas led her into a small patch of uncleared trees, hidden from those passing, so she need not be embarrassed by the tears pouring silently down her cheeks. He put a comforting arm on hers, and she leant into his hug, shoulders heaving as she tried to contain her sobs.

"Cry away, Miss Campbell," he told her. "I have two sisters who have cried on me more times than I can count, and no one else will ever know."

Miss Campbell shook her head, and took several deep, shuddery breaths.

"Uncle Campbell would not like me to return home red-eyed. He says my father is burning in Hell for a sinner, and I should not mourn such a man. But he was a good man, Mr O'Bryan. Always humming and telling jokes and hoping for the best. God would not be so cruel as to keep him from Heaven, just because he played the piano at dances and sometimes missed a church service. He would not, would he?"

Thomas was not qualified to give an opinion on the salvation of heretics. He hedged. "Didn't Jesus say we don't know? That some who think they are saved won't be, and some who think they are not, will be? Love counts, I think. And kindness." He hoped so, anyway, and the thought cheered Miss Campbell, who pulled back from his arms and set about tidying the bonnet she'd knocked askew against his shoulder.

How pretty she was, even with her eyes slightly puffy.

They continued walking, and to change the subject, he began telling her about the clerks he had hired and the warehouse he had rented and the store he intended to build in Hartley

Township, in the Dunstan gold fields. She asked intelligent questions, entering with enthusiasm into discussion of his plans, and by the time they arrived at the Campbell's cottage, all physical signs of Miss Campbell's grief had faded.

Thomas sat through an awkward visit with his aunt, who made no effort to conceal her surprise at seeing him again, bur reluctantly offered him tea, which he drank at the kitchen table while Aunt Agnes, the maid, and Miss Campbell bustled about preparing an evening meal.

Aunt Agnes was visibly relieved when he finished the cup of weak tea and refused to stay for dinner. "Mr Campbell will be sorry to have missed you," she said.

Thomas met the lie with one of his own, sending the old bully his best wishes.

He had no more wish to sit at his aunt's meagre board than she to have him there. So why, when he took his coat and hat from Miss Campbell, did he bend closer and say, "I will do myself the honour of calling again when I am in Dunedin, Miss Campbell"?

Chapter Three

Mr O'Bryan's visits were the highlight of the month, and Dunedin felt wetter, windier, and colder after he left. Rose struggled with snail depredations and weeds in the vegetable garden, did the shopping, cooked, cleaned, sewed in the evenings, and woke earlier and earlier with the lengthening day, to read a little in the dawn light before another day of unrelenting work.

From time to time, but perhaps not more than a dozen times a day, she wondered how Mr O'Bryan was faring in Dunstan and whether he would, indeed, call on them when he returned to Dunedin.

Then, suddenly, in early December, he was there again, falling into step beside her as she walked from Knox Lane to George Street on her way shopping.

"Good morning, Miss Campbell. May I carry your basket?" He was taking it from her as he spoke, his impish grin robbing the gesture of any offence.

"You're back," Rose said. What a foolish thing to say, but her wits had taken flight at his presence.

"I am. And do I find you well?"

She stammered something, trying to collect her scattered thoughts.

"And did your business prosper, Mr O'Bryan?" she managed.

"It did, thank you. The first cartloads of goods sold before they reached Dunstan. I've taken on two more assistants for the tent store and a building to house Rourke and O'Bryan is going up in Hartley Township, as we speak. All is going well there, and so I've come to attend to business at this end of the trail."

Rose looked around her, wondering what business he found in this mainly residential area, and he must have guessed her thoughts, because he said, "Today, I am taking an afternoon's holiday. I was on my way to visit you when, behold, here you are walking toward me. Dare I hope to escort you the entire afternoon, Miss Campbell?"

She smiled her consent, all at once feeling giddy. But someone might see them and report to her uncle! Well, what of it? She would still have the memory of the afternoon—a little treasure to take out and enjoy when he was gone, and she was alone.

He threw himself into the shopping with enthusiasm, debating the merits of various meats, solemnly inspecting vegetables, giving his view on the best threads to match and contrast with the cushion cover she was decorating.

When she hesitated over some bonnet trimmings, yearning for a confection of silk flowers and feathers, he offered to buy them. She blushed at the scandalous suggestion, but was not as displeased as she should be.

"No, indeed, Mr O'Bryan. My uncle would never allow me to wear any bonnet they would make. I will have three yards of the brown ribbon, please," she told the assistant.

Mr O'Bryan subsided, but his next suggestion was that they should take tea at the Empire Hotel. Rose hesitated. Anyone might walk together when out shopping, but to take tea with a man at his hotel was surely a wanton act. Or so her uncle would say, in any case.

At that moment, they passed Hackerton's Emporium, and even from the footpath, she could hear the man her uncle intended her to wed berating an unfortunate employee.

"Very well, Mr O'Bryan," she said. Another memory to cherish. Why not?

She had passed the tea rooms at the Empire on several occasions, but never thought to enter. She felt very grand sitting at one of their white-linen-covered tables, with a tiered cake plate of toothsome delicacies and a dainty china cup full of fragrant tea. And a handsome, charming, attentive escort, who kept her entertained with stories of people in the burgeoning boomtown at the Dunstan.

She was very much in charity with him as they made their way back up Princes Street and through the Octagon, skirting the muddy centre, where the churning population of miners briefly settled, before heading up the Dunstan trail to Central Otago.

In the next moment, her contentment took a knock.

"Mr O'Bryan!" The speaker was a tall, striking-looking woman with bold, dark eyes and porcelain skin, set off to perfection by her black dress and bonnet. In the next moment, Rose realised that the veil, currently pushed back from the perfect oval of the woman's face, marked her a widow. She was older than Rose had thought at first, too—older than Thom... Mr O'Bryan, that was certain.

"Mr O'Bryan, I want to thank you, Sir. The money has been— I cannot tell you. All those sharks that hovered after the money Arthur owed them..." The woman shuddered.

"Payment for services rendered, Mrs Moffat, and for those you have promised me. And how is little Mary? Better, I hope? Oh, but I forget my manners. Miss Campbell, allow me to present Mrs Moffat, who works for me. Mrs Moffat, Miss Campbell is my cousin."

The woman gave Rose a distracted nod and a brief curtsey before hurrying on, "I must get back to her. I just popped out for a few groceries and left young Arthur in charge, and Mary will not mind him when she is fretful. But I am grateful for it, Mr O'Bryan, for if she is fretful, she is on the mend, so the doctor says. And we will be in Hartley Township in the new year, I promise you that, Sir."

"Whenever the little girl is well enough, Mrs Moffat. You are not to be anxious about it."

The widow said her farewells, repeating her thanks, and hurried off, with Rose looking thoughtfully after her.

"A sad case, Miss Campbell. Her husband managed the warehouse I am leasing here in Dunedin, or so I thought. But a fortnight ago, he walked off the end of the wharf and drowned, leaving a wife and seven little ones."

"Oh, how terrible!" Rose was berating herself for her uncharitable thoughts.

"When I arrived, I found the warehouse humming along nicely, and it transpired that Mrs Moffat has been running it all along, while Moffat drank his income. I'd leave her in charge, but some of the ships' captains won't deal with a woman, so I offered her management of the store in Hartley Township."

"That was very generous of you."

"Not really. The miners behave better with a woman than a man, and—to be very selfish about it—she is old enough and soured enough on marriage not to be stolen to the altar almost before she arrives at the fields."

"You paid her husband's debts," Rose guessed, "and probably the doctor's bill, too." She smiled at him. What a kind man he was.

And the rent through to the end of January, Thomas thought, but couldn't bring himself to say, a little embarrassed at Rose's obvious approval. *Just good business.* He needed a reliable, loyal storekeeper, and the price he'd paid to redeem Moffat's gambling debts and pay his bills was cheap, compared to bringing someone of his own from another continent.

And Miss Campbell's smile upon hearing the tale was a bonus; a lovely, joyful, open beam that transformed the dismal day into glorious summer.

Before he recovered from the mind-reeling effects of it, he found himself inviting her to the Grand Ball in January, being held by the Committee of the Widows and Orphans Institution of the Oddfellows. Just like that, the sun went out.

"Freemasonry is the work of the devil, and dancing encourages licentious behaviour," she told him, primly, but her eyes were wistful.

"It will be a subscription assembly conducted by ladies of the highest probity," Thomas assured her. "Do say you will come, Miss Campbell."

"I cannot." The wistfulness leaked into her voice. "Uncle Campbell would never allow it."

They were at Campbell's front door, and he could say no more, not wishing to draw the ire of Aunt Agnes upon her vulnerable head.

Aunt Agnes was no more welcoming than she had been the last time, making a few minutes of desultory conversation before reluctantly offering him a cup of tea, which he enthusiastically refused, claiming the pressure of other business.

"But I could not be at this end of town without paying my respects, Ma'am," he said, his tongue firmly in his cheek.

After Aunt Agnes had seen him off at the front door, he doubled back to slip between the narrow houses to the rear garden, where Rose was struggling with the wind to pull in a line of sheets and other linen.

Without a word, Thomas came to her aid, his extra height helping him reach the pegs easily and fold the sheets more quickly.

Again, he was rewarded by a softening in her fine eyes, and that bright smile. "Thank you. Mostly, it is not a problem, but when the wind gets up, I swear the washing has a mind of its own! At least it is not wet."

She folded the personal items he had politely left for her to retrieve, and tucked them under the sheets in the wash basket. How pretty she looked, embarrassment touching her cheeks with the rose of her name.

"The dance is on the sixth of January," he said.

"I know."

"I will be back in Dunedin by Christmas, or not long after. If you will trust me, Cousin Rose, I'll come and fetch you for the dance and make sure you get back safely."

"I cannot." Her eyes yearned, but her voice was firm. "My uncle would never permit it. And it would be wrong of me to disobey him while I live under his roof."

"If you change your mind, a message at the Empire Hotel will reach me," he told her. But he didn't press her any further. He should be grateful she refused him. No good could come of such an evening, however innocent.

It was an afternoon to pack away in her memories, and pull out to relive again and again. Rose had to be careful not to hum as she prepared and served dinner. Even listening to her uncle's lectures and instructions over the meal could not suppress her mood entirely, nor did facing the pile of dishes that needed to be washed before she could go to bed, this being the maid's half-day.

As she washed and dried, she imagined what it might be like to attend the Grand Ball. Now that would be a memory to treasure!

Rose packed away the dishes, scrubbed the sink, and set some oats to soften overnight for breakfast porridge, all the time, listing in her head the many reasons why accepting Mr O'Bryan's invitation would be disastrous.

She believed him when he said there would be no harm in it. Why, even in their small break-away congregation, with its strict rules about social behaviour, some of the other women were going to the event. One was even on the organising committee!

But Uncle disapproved, and so she could not think of it.

Chapter Four

But the idea would not go away, and as Christmas rushed ever nearer, Rose nerved herself to approach her uncle and ask if she might go to the ball. She did not even have time to confess to Mr O'Bryan's invitation before he gave her an indignant refusal, followed with two hours of writing, in her best hand, the admonishments from the letters of St Paul about the behaviour of women.

She had expected nothing else, but that did not prevent her despondency. She was disappointed, too, as the Christmas Octave began, and Mr O'Bryan did not appear. She scanned the streets as she shopped, negotiating the excited crowds and looking wistfully at seasonal decorations.

The Campbell household did not celebrate the feast, except with an extra-long church service. No special preparations, no decorations, no presents.

Watching Mrs Moffat and two of her children negotiating with the grocer for baking supplies, arguing about which particular treats they would make, gave her a pang. She and her father used to bake special cakes and other treats at Christmas. They had hung ribbons and greenery to decorate the house, and sung carols together each evening. Christmas day had meant a special meal, and little gifts made or purchased in secret and presented to each other with great delight. At Christmas, more than ever, she missed him.

Mrs Moffat recognised her and stopped to say hello, admonishing the children to stand still or they'd have no treats, nor presents either, perhaps. They grinned, not at all concerned, but waited patiently nonetheless, while Rose asked after the sick child. "She is on the mend, thank the Virgin and all the saints," Mrs Moffat said. "We will be following Mr O'Bryan up to

Dunstan in a few weeks; by the end of January, beyond a doubt. And have you heard from the dear man, Miss Campbell?"

Rose shook her head. "He said he hoped to be back in Dunedin before, or just after, Christmas, which is only a few days away."

"Well, if ever the world held a man who keeps his word, it is Mr O'Bryan. An angel from Heaven, he has been to me and mine. Don't think I cannot see you poking your brother, Margaret Moffat. Butter would not melt in her mouth, that one, Miss Campbell, but I have to watch her every minute. I had best be getting them off home, and leave you to do your shopping. Merry Christmas."

Rose wished the same to Mrs Moffat and the children. She expected they would have a happier Christmas than she. It would take more than the kind of miracle Mr O'Bryan had wrought for the Moffat family, to turn Aunt Agnes and Uncle Campbell into Christmas carollers.

Christmas Day was even worse than expected. No Mr O'Bryan, and too much Mr Hackerton. He came home with the Campbells after church and stayed for dinner, and Rose had to endure him and Uncle Campbell discussing her cooking and housekeeping skills, as if she were a piece of merchandise whose purchase Mr Hackerton was considering. Which, of course, she was.

As she and Maisie cleaned up after the meal, she listened to the maid's grumbles with half her attention, much of her focus on whether she could refuse Mr Hackerton's courtship, and what her uncle would do if she did.

Maisie's chatter penetrated her distraction. "… leaving at the end of the quarter, and so I told him. 'I am not your niece, to be kept from any fun and work for nothing every day of the week without a holiday,' I told him."

Maisie was leaving? "But what will you do? Where will you go?"

Maisie scoffed. "Oh, Miss, with servants taking off after gold, and all the new people, there is plenty of work for a willing girl. I don't have to stay where they won't give me a half-day at

Christmas. No, I'll see out the quarter, but come 31 December, when my wages is due, I'm taking my leave, and so I have told Mr and Mrs Campbell." She nodded, her lips pursed in satisfaction. "Yes, and you should do the same, Miss."

She should, too. The seed, thus planted, rapidly took root. Plenty of work, was there? It couldn't be harder than she did here. Indeed, the difference between the way the Campbells treated their niece and the way they treated their servant put all the benefits on Maisie's side—wages, a half-day a week off, as well as time to attend the church services of her choice.

Rose would be twenty-one on the thirtieth of January, no longer under her uncle's guardianship.

She began to question Maisie about how one went about finding a job.

Rose, full of her own plans for a future in domestic service, was completely taken by surprise when Uncle Campbell announced, a few days before the sixth of January, that he had given his approval for Mr Hackerton to escort her to the Grand Ball for the benefit of the Widows and Orphans.

She was torn. On the one hand, she had no desire to encourage Mr Hackerton's courtship. On the other, this might be her only opportunity to attend such an event. Then again, she had nothing fit to wear to a ball. But that hardly mattered, did it? She would be there to see all the beautiful gowns and enjoy the music, so what she wore was of no importance.

With all these ideas cluttering up her tongue, she could only stammer, "The Ball, Uncle?"

"Hackerton thinks it will be a treat for you, and I've said you will go, Laura, so go you shall."

Rose nodded her acquiescence, and went up to lay her Sunday-best gown out on the bed. It was brown, a soft, mousy colour, a shade or two darker than her hair. Plain, cut high to the neck and loose in the waist, it was not flattering. But it was serviceable, and it was what she had. She sighed and returned it to its hook.

When she had wages, she would buy herself a Sunday dress in green, or perhaps blue. And flowers and ribbons to trim her bonnets. As she came downstairs to answer a knock on the door, she smiled at the thought.

Maisie was right about the dearth of servants; Aunt Agnes was finding it hard to replace the maid, and would not be happy at all when Rose left. Her smile broadened at the thought, and she was grinning when she opened the door.

There on the step stood Thomas O'Bryan.

Miss Campbell met Thomas with a happy smile, and for a moment, all he could do was smile back.

She recalled him to himself, saying, "Why, it is Mr O'Bryan! Come in, Sir. Are you here to see your aunt?"

I am here to see you, Rose, he wanted to say, but he kept his peace and followed her to the parlour where Aunt Agnes sat at a narrow desk, writing out accounts.

"Turned up again, have you?" Aunt Agnes said, but though the words sounded unenthusiastic, she surprised him with a smile that was almost welcoming.

Thomas pulled out the first of the presents with which he had armed himself. "Happy Christmas, Aunt Agnes."

"We do not celebrate Christmas in this house, young man." Campbell had been sitting, unnoticed, on a chair facing away from the door. His glower followed his voice as he rose to glare at Thomas.

"Happy New Year then, Uncle," Thomas said, peaceably, handing the old man a package wrapped in brown paper and tied with string, and passing another to Aunt Agnes.

For a moment, the two hesitated, then curiosity and avarice overcame their distaste, and they both began to untie the string.

Thomas turned to give his third present—the reason he'd bothered to bring the other two—to Rose, but she had left the room, and he had to wait.

Aunt Agnes thanked him for the pretty shawl, and Campbell, with considerably less grace, grumbled his grudging appreciation of the pen-and-wiper set.

"Take a seat, if you are staying. I suppose that girl has gone to make tea," Campbell said. Thomas sat, determined to remain until he could speak to Rose.

Almost immediately, he stood again, and hurried to help her with a heavy tray.

"Thank you, Mr O'Bryan." She blushed as he took the tray from her, and would have left the room again, had he not spoken.

"Miss Campbell, I trust I see you well?"

"Yes, thank you, Mr O'Bryan."

Campbell interrupted, frowning. "No point in making calf's eyes at my niece, boy. I'm supposing it is her you have rushed to see, all the way from Dunstan."

"I came to bring you presents, Uncle, as I said. I am a few days later than I intended," Thomas apologised. "I told you I would be here just after Christmas, Aunt Agnes, and that's more than a week past. But here I am now.

"I have a present for Miss Campbell, as well." He handed Rose the wrapped parcel, and her eyes shone when she found a duplicate to the shawl he had given Aunt Agnes, but with green the dominant colour, rather than the deep, wine red he had chosen for his aunt.

Campbell looked even dourer. He clearly wanted to complain, but could not, having accepted his own gift.

"So what kept you, Thomas?" Aunt Agnes wanted to know.

"I thought I had sufficient time to visit the new fields, Aunt Agnes." He studiously did not look at Rose, for whom he intended the explanation. "Up on the Arrow and the Wakatip, they're making finds every day, and at least one new town will be needed, perhaps more. Certainly, Hartley Township is too far for the diggers to bring their gold and buy supplies." The new town would have a Rourke and O'Bryan store for those diggers to patronise. He had already purchased the land and hired the builders, though that wasn't the whole reason for the delay.

No need to tell the ladies he'd discovered a body in the river—some poor digger drowned in the winter, by the looks of it, his remains exposed as the water level dropped. Rose, in particular, did not need to know he'd had to stay up the Arrow to give evidence at the inquest.

Might as well take the bull by the horns and address his real reason for coming. "Uncle, I hoped to gain your permission to escort Miss Campbell to the Grand Ball. It is for a good cause, and will be a gentile event."

Campbell opened his mouth, but Aunt Agnes spoke first. "You are too late, Thomas. Laura has an escort. A gentleman from our congregation."

"It is a respectable event, and her escort has my approval." Campbell got to his feet. "Laura. Mrs Campbell. You'll be about your work, if you please. I'll be having a word with O'Bryan here."

The ladies, Rose looking anxiously over her shoulder, left the room, and Thomas listened politely to the not-unexpected lecture from Campbell. He was to leave Miss Campbell alone. He was the wrong religion for her, and too worldly, and altogether unsuitable. Campbell had chosen her husband, and Thomas was not to interfere in any way, up to and including visiting her, dancing with her, and speaking to her.

Thomas said very little, seeing no point in causing trouble for Rose by arguing. Besides, Campbell's objections were the same he'd raised for himself. They came from different worlds, he and Rose.

But somehow, hearing Campbell say it made him want to defend what he and Rose had in common. Whatever it was that was growing between them, if it proved to be real and true, could stand a bit of difference, surely? And he'd been in the world long enough to know that how a person acted counted for more than what church they attended.

Rose might have been raised Protestant, which made her a heretic, by his family's measure. But she was as good a woman as any he'd met. Gentle. Kind. Generous. Sweet. Pure, too.

As he walked back to his hotel, he resolved to inspect this young man of Campbell's at the Grand Ball. If he is a good man, well and good. But the kind of man Campbell was likely to support? Well, Rose should have a choice. That was all. She should be able to choose. Perhaps he could offer her a job in one of his stores? She could not be worse off than she was as Campbell's unpaid skivvy.

Chapter Five

"And you are to do as Mr Hackerton tells you, Laura," Uncle Campbell said. "You are not to dance unless he says you might. Do not drink the punch, for I do not trust those Freemasons not to put ruinous liquor into it. And you are not to dance with Thomas O'Bryan, do you hear me?"

With her uncle's admonitions ringing in her ears, Rose set off to the dance. Walking on a gentleman's arm was strange. Mr Hackerton was much shorter than Thomas, barely an inch taller than she, and the strange pull she felt when with Thomas simply wasn't there, the one that urged her to tuck herself up against his side. She kept a decorous distance between them.

Conversing with Mr Hackerton was easy enough. She had only to nod, smile, and make meaningless comments at appropriate intervals. "Oh, really?" "Well, I never." "Indeed." "How nice." After a while, she began trotting them out in order, without regard to Mr Hackerton's conversation. He did not notice, continuing to regale her with story after story of his victories over customers, suppliers, employees, and household.

She could not marry this man. She could not. He was no less a bully than Uncle Campbell, and she shuddered to think of putting herself under his thumb. Whatever the marriage bed involved, she was sure she would rather clean floors in a boarding house than submit to such intimacies with Mr Hackerton.

The new Murphy's Assembly Room, on Rattray Street, was transformed with flowers and lights and great, hanging swaths of white and gold fabric. Mr Hackerton showed their tickets at the door, and attempted to hurry her through to the main hall, but Rose hung back. "I need to tidy my hair, Sir," she told him. "I will come to join you directly."

She waited her turn at the small mirror, smoothed the hair that had been disarranged by her bonnet, and spent a few more minutes tidying and arranging her clothes, reluctant to re-join her escort.

But he was not in the entrance foyer when she emerged from the ladies' retiring room. Such a small man; perhaps she was missing him in the crowd? She began to weave between the groups of people who had stopped to greet one another, or who were lined at the door of the main room, waiting to enter. No. No Mr Hackerton.

"Are you on your own, Miss?" A strange man rested a hand on her arm, and she flinched. "Thank you, no," she stammered, backing away. He persisted, following her. "Would you care for a dance, Miss?"

Her backward progress was arrested as she came up against a solid body, and her momentary panic turned to relief at Mr O'Bryan's warm tones. "There you are, Miss Campbell. So easy to get lost when there are so many people." She looked up at him with a warm smile, and the man who had addressed her melted into the crowd.

"Have you become separated from your escort?" Mr O'Bryan asked. "May I find him for you?"

"I thought he was waiting here for me, Mr O'Bryan, but he must have gone on inside. I don't suppose that man meant any harm."

"Probably not," Mr O'Bryan agreed. But his eyes remained wary as he offered her his arm.

How different it was making her way through the shifting masses shielded by Mr O'Bryan's protective arm and cheerful quips. Once they were through the door and in the main room, the crowd opened out enough for her to see Mr Hackerton talking to several other people from the church, and she directed Mr O'Bryan in that direction.

Hackerton saw them coming and abandoned his conversation to bustle in their direction, glowering. "Miss Campbell, what are you about?"

"Mr Hackerton, may I make known to you Mr O'Bryan, the nephew of my Aunt Agnes? Mr O'Bryan was kind enough to escort me through all the people."

"O'Bryan." Mr Hackerton gave a short nod, his frown not a whit abated.

"We have met," Mr O'Bryan told Rose, returning the nod with no more affability than Mr Hackerton. "I commend Miss Campbell to your care, Hackerton. The crowd presses more roughly than a lady likes."

Two dogs circling with their hackles raised, and Rose would not be the bone between them. She murmured her thanks to Mr O'Bryan and left the two gentlemen to their dispute, passing them to greet Mr and Mrs MacTavish and their adult children.

Mr Hackerton followed her a moment later, but by then, she was admiring Miss Minnie MacTavish's gown and Miss Molly MacTavish's fine Indian shawl, and having her own shawl— Thomas's beautiful Christmas gift—admired in turn.

"Virtue is a woman's best adornment," Mr Hackerton proclaimed, offending Mr MacTavish, who complained. "Ye are no' sayin' that me Minnie and Molly are no' virtuous, Hackerton?"

In the interconnected web of Dunedin's merchant world, MacTavish and his carrier business were crucial. Hackerton was quick to deny any such intention, and with luck, would forget Rose's own crimes in the ensuing fuss.

After three country dances—one with Hackerton, one with the oldest MacTavish son, and one she watched from the sidelines— the band began a waltz. Rose would not dance the scandalous dance, of course, though she watched wistfully as the MacTavish girls, one after another, accepted invitations from young men approved by their father.

How lovely the dancers looked. Gentlemen in black tailcoats; merchants and clerks and carters and miners in their Sunday best, turning and circling around the floor to the music, the women in their arms like so many flowers, with their full skirts swaying, especially those whose exaggerated bells were supported by fashionable hoops.

She did not realise she was smiling and humming until Mr Hackerton touched her arm to gain her attention. "You are not listening, Miss Campbell. I said I am surprised at Mr MacTavish, allowing his daughters to participate in such a riotous activity. A country dance, yes. Some consider such levity unbecoming, but I cannot allow that the Lord frowns on all dancing, when we are told David danced. Not the waltz, however."

Rose had a sudden image of the David from the colour plate illustration she had seen at the Athenaeum, that beautiful naked youth with a slingshot over his shoulder. The man who danced before the Ark, but also had several wives at once and pursued Bathsheba even to the point of murder, would have loved the waltz, she thought.

Mr Hackerton droned on, and she listened with half an ear, so her nods and shakes—the only conversational input he required—were not totally inappropriate. The rest of her mind was on the dancing. Had Papa not died in his futile quest for riches, he would have permitted her to waltz. Papa laughed at his brother's rigid ways and enjoyed seeing his daughter in pretty dresses.

The waltz was followed by another country dance, into which Hackerton condescended to lead her. "For you are not to think, Miss Campbell, that I will forbid my wife all frivolity," he told her when they took their turn to stand aside for the other couples. "Though I cannot approve of your acquaintance with that scoundrel, O'Bryan."

"He is my aunt's nephew, Mr Hackerton," she protested, ignoring the reference to a marriage the man had not discussed with her.

"Yes, and it is a great pity," Hackerton shook his head, as if in sorrow. "Mrs Campbell is a good woman, and for her sister to marry a half-breed, and a Papist half-breed, at that! Campbell has told me all about it. Then for that young man to come here with his foreign ways and his foreign goods…"

It was their turn in the dance again, and Rose spent her time in the figures wondering why Mr Hackerton was so upset with Mr O'Bryan.

"What has Mr O'Bryan done, Mr Hackerton?" she ventured, when they stood out again.

"Why, that scoundrel plans on importing his own supplies for his stores in the fields, instead of buying from us here in Dunedin! Are our goods not good enough for him?" Hackerton continued to rave during each break, though Rose rather thought that most of what he said was jealousy.

She sat to watch several more dances, while Hackerton chatted with various business contacts. Mr O'Bryan did not sit out a dance, though he did not dance twice with the same partner.

She was watching him promenade his latest partner up between the couples in a line dance, one hand gracefully on his hip, and the other holding the lady's high between them, when she felt a sharp pinch on her arm.

"Miss Campbell!" Hackerton frowned at her startled yelp. "You will not embarrass me by panting after that whelp."

"Mr Hackerton!" Rose rubbed her arm furiously. How dare he pinch her? And how dare he accuse her of... of inappropriate thoughts about Mr O'Bryan?

"I expect propriety at all times, Miss Campbell, and you will do well to keep that in mind. My wife must be beyond reproach. Beyond reproach, I say."

"I am not your wife, Mr Hackerton. Nor have you asked me to take that role."

Mr Hackerton waved off the objection. "No, that is all organised. Your uncle has agreed. The banns are to be called this Sunday." Sensing, perhaps, that this was not to her liking, he grabbed her hand in one of his pudgy fists and patted it. "You will find me a generous husband, if you are an obedient wife, Laura, my dear."

Suddenly, Rose was furious, being misnamed the last straw. "Mr Hackerton, you are much mistaken if you think I will be your wife, obedient or otherwise. It is my agreement you need, not my uncle's, and I do not give it."

Mr Hackerton smiled indulgently. "There, there. It is all understood. You must trust your uncle to know what is best for you, my dear, Laura."

"I am not called Laura. Nor have I given you permission to be so familiar. Nor shall I."

"Miss Campbell, you forget yourself." Mr Campbell was becoming annoyed. "Campbell has promised me your hand, and we will be wed before the end of the month."

"No, Mr Hackerton," Rose insisted, "we will not."

"Is this man annoying you, Miss Campbell?" Concentrating on her altercation with Hackerton, she had not heard Mr O'Bryan approach.

"This is between me and my betrothed, O'Bryan, and nothing to do with you," Hackerton bellowed.

O'Bryan's eyes shifted to Rose, doubt clouding them.

"He is not my betrothed," Rose said, her voice louder than she intended, and was startled to hear a hiss. Looking around, she realised they were the focus of attention in this corner of the room, and several people from the church congregation were frowning at her.

She shrank towards Mr O'Bryan, and he rose to the occasion. "Will you honour me with a dance, Miss Campbell?"

"You will not." Hackerton, too, had noticed the interest of the bystanders and lowered his voice accordingly. "Miss Campbell, you will not dance with this man. And a waltz, at that!"

Rose ignored him, though her hand trembled on Mr O'Bryan's arm as he led her onto the floor. She would not faint. She would not be ill. She would sail around the room in Mr O'Bryan's arms, and if she were a poor, brown sparrow against the colourful flowers that had sailed there before, she would make the most of her opportunity. She would, for certain, pay the price when her uncle found out, but she would have the pleasure first.

Miss Campbell slowly relaxed into the dance, and as she gave herself over to the music and the movement, Thomas let the tension drain out of his own muscles. Still, he kept an eye on Hackerton, until he saw the man push his way to the front door and leave.

Thomas had tried to do business with Hackerton when he first arrived in Dunedin, but soon realised the man was a bully and a coward, and a poor businessman, at that. Thomas had found other suppliers for the local products he couldn't easily ship in. Hackerton had not been pleased.

He hoped Miss Campbell was telling the truth when she said she was not betrothed to Hackerton. The thought of this timid, little mouse in the hands of that brute made him firm his grip, pulling her a little closer, and he was thrilled to his core when she came willingly, trustingly, looking up into his eyes, smiling as he swung her around a turn in the dance, then reluctantly let her out again to the socially acceptable distance.

He could dance with her all night, hold her in his arms for a lifetime, protecting her from any chill wind that shrivelled that sweet trust... He tried to remind himself she was wrong for him—wrong faith, wrong country, wrong in every way. He needed a strong woman who would be an asset in the business, not a shy, wee lassie that needed to be sheltered and cosseted.

Though she was a hard worker, he would give her that. And she stood up to Hackerton, right enough. He chuckled. Hackerton had not expected that. Thomas had thought the man would explode.

Rose, oblivious to his thoughts, chuckled with him. "This is such fun, Mr O'Bryan. Lovely to watch, but even lovelier to do!"

"You've never waltzed before?" He could not believe it. She followed his steps as if they had practiced together half their lives.

But she shook her head, vigorously. "Not in company. My father taught me the steps, but I have never been to a ball before."

"You dance beautifully," he assured her, looking down into her laughing eyes. How lovely she was. And stronger than she knew, with her ability to put the nastiness with Hackerton aside and simply enjoy the moment.

"Will you be in Dunedin long, Mr O'Bryan?"

"I return to the fields tomorrow, Miss Campbell. I need to supervise the store until Mrs Moffat arrives, and then I will move to the new store in Arrow."

He told her his plans for the second store, barely listening to what he was saying, only knowing how good it felt to dance with her, talk to her.

The music was ending. The dance was over, and he had to let her go. He swallowed, abruptly breathless with longing to keep her in his arms forever.

It was difficult to speak past the yearning, but he managed to sound calm as he asked, "What do you wish to do now, Miss Campbell? Is there someone else I can take you to? Do you wish me to stay with you?"

"I am sure the MacTavishes will see me home."

But when Thomas escorted her to the people she pointed out, the younger members of the family turned their backs, and the mother said, "You have chosen this outsider over one of our own, Miss Campbell. Let him see you home. If, indeed, you dare to return to your uncle's house, after showing such ingratitude."

Without a word, Miss Campbell turned and walked stiffly away, two high spots of cover on her cheeks, and Thomas, after tossing the woman a scowl that should have shrivelled her where she stood, hurried after her.

Miss Campbell said nothing until they had collected their coats and were walking through the silent streets, their breath condensing into small clouds as they walked. "She lets her own daughters waltz," she burst out. "And she would not marry them to Mr Hackerton, either!"

"Is your uncle...? Will your uncle make you marry?" He would marry her himself, rather than leave her to that fate—a solution that seemed sweeter to him the more he thought about it.

"He cannot. This is the nineteenth century. A woman cannot be married against her will."

She sounded very firm, but wills can be suborned. He pulled her into the recess of a shop doorway, so they could continue the discussion out of the wind.

"Will he be cross, Miss Campbell? Should I talk to him?"

She shook her head, decisively. "That would make it worse, I do not doubt, though it is kind of you to offer. But what can he do, Mr O'Bryan? Shut me in my room to think over my sins, beyond a doubt, but he will let me out when there are chores to be done."

She believed in her own safety. Looking into her eyes in the half-light, he could see the certainty there. Without conscious thought, he laid his hand gently along the side of her face, stroking her cheek with his thumb.

"If you have any doubt, Rose, and think Campbell might hurt you, or do something else to force you to his will, you do not have to go back."

She opened her mouth, already shaking her head, and he hurried on to say his piece before she could object. "You could marry me. I don't flatter myself that I am a prize, but I am a better bet than Hackerton. Marry me, and let me care for you, Rose." He bent, curving low to capture her mouth. It was as soft and full as it looked though, at first, stiff and unresponsive.

But she followed his lead in this as she had in the dance, and what had begun as an impulsive gesture to prevent her from saying no became a luxurious vortex that spun him out of space and time until he was oblivious of everything except the giving, the taking, the sharing of their lips, their tongues, their mouths.

She looked dazed when he drew back. Well, good. *He* was dazed. He gathered her against his chest and rested his cheek on her hair. "Marry me, Rose," he repeated.

"I cannot, Thomas. You will be gone tomorrow. And we barely know one another."

"You could travel with one of the families, and we could be married when we arrive at the fields. I know we haven't known one another long, but I know you are brave and true. I know you feel like Heaven in my arms. I know I can talk to you for hours about anything under the sun."

"Oh, Thomas… I wish…" She gathered herself, pulling away a little, so she could look up at him. He took heart that she stayed within his arms.

"If you are still of the same mind next time you come to Dunedin, Thomas, I would be proud to be your wife." She blushed, casting her eyelashes down onto her cheeks. "Proud," she repeated.

Later, locked in her room, lying, bruised and bleeding, on her bed, after the worst beating her uncle had ever given her, she regretted that choice. She should have gone with him, in her Sunday best, leaving behind her meagre belongings. But would he have taken her? And wouldn't he have regretted it?

Aunt Agnes had screamed at her, but Uncle Campbell had been silent in his fury. Mr Hackerton, who had been at the house when she arrived home, had declared himself released from his contract by her outrageous behaviour. So, one good thing had come from all the fuss.

Even days later after she was able to drag herself from her bed, she was not permitted to leave the house. Instead, the new maid was sent on errands, and Rose was set to scouring the floors and emptying the chamber pots.

She endured. Surely they would not keep her prisoner forever? Indeed, after the third time the servant came home with no change, having overspent on meat and vegetables that were old and tired, and resigned from her post when scolded, Rose was once more sent out to press every coin until it squeaked, though her time was closely monitored, so she dared add nothing to the errand on which she was sent.

Thomas would return for her, as he had promised. Or, she would find a position and make her own way.

While she waited, life fell back into a normal pattern, except that members of the congregation turned their backs to her when they saw her on the street, or even in church. It was not important. She had only to endure until she finished healing, or until Thomas returned.

Mr Hackerton came first.

Chapter Six

"He is prepared to take you despite your behaviour," Aunt Agnes crowed. And Uncle Campbell was gleefully discussing the supply contract the marriage would, apparently, seal.

At first, neither heard Rose's quiet "No."

Aunt Agnes was the first to notice. "No? What do you mean, 'No'?"

"No, Aunt Agnes. I will not marry Mr Hackerton. I would not marry Mr Hackerton, even if I had not promised to wait for Mr O'Bryan."

The storm broke, as she had expected, and she bowed her head and ignored them both. They could lock her up, beat her, starve her, but they could not force her to marry against her will.

"…And you need not think I'll continue to house such an ungrateful Jezebel. You disgraceful harlot, consorting with the Whore of Babylon. I'll not have it, I tell you. Obey me or leave my house, Laura Rose Campbell."

"Very well, Uncle. I will leave."

Rose was nearly as surprised as her uncle to hear the words coming from her mouth.

She packed her few bits and pieces while Aunt Agnes watched to make sure she took nothing that wasn't hers. In silence, her aunt by marriage escorted her down the stairs and out the front door.

When Rose was out on the public walk, Aunt Agnes looked over her shoulder, a quick, furtive glance back into the house. "Wait there, girl. Just for a moment." She disappeared back into the house and was back in moments.

"You have been a good girl, Laura, on the whole. I will miss you. Here." She pressed something into Rose's hand: a purse, with a few shifting lumps that must be coins. "Thomas is a good boy, for all he is a Papist. He has written to you. Campbell made me read the letters and burn them. He will make an honest woman of you." A quick, awkward hug, and a brush of papery lips on Rose's cheek, and she was gone, the front door closed between them.

Rose raised her empty hand to her cheek in wonder. Who knew Aunt Agnes had a heart? She had never shown any signs of it before.

The front door flew open again, and Rose was just in time to hide the purse in the folds of her skirt, before her uncle was screaming in her face.

"Go then, if you are going. Don't litter my doorstep, you foul tramp!" He caught her a buffet that knocked her into the road.

Perhaps he would have hit her again, but a man passing in the street stopped to ask, "Are you all right, Miss?"

"Thank you. I am just leaving." Rose picked up her bag and walked away without a backward look, her heart rising with every step. Thomas had written. Thomas still wanted her. And even if he didn't, surely she could find work, respectable work with a wage and roof over her head?

Right this minute, she knew exactly what to do. At the O'Bryan warehouse, she asked for directions to Mrs Moffat's house. She only hoped the woman had not yet left for the gold fields.

Thomas stood in the door of his store, admiring the bustle as the crowds passed. This late in the day, many of the area's hopeful, would-be millionaires were coming into town to while away their evening, but they were mostly a cheerful lot. Some would drink every grain of gold dust they'd found, and there would be fights and loud singing, but the New Zealand gold fields enforced a strong ban on guns, so most injuries would be minor.

Soon, Mrs Moffat would arrive, and then, after another week to make sure his new manager could keep the store as well as Thomas did, he could return to Dunedin for Rose. The bonnet trim he had purchased the day after that December shopping expedition sat on the table in his bedchamber, a constant reminder of all the gifts with which he wanted to shower her.

He had wondered, even as he proposed, if her charm would fade with separation. Instead, he wanted her more every day, dreamed of seeing her bright smile over breakfast, imagined her reaction every time he heard a funny conversation or an interesting fact, fantasised about holding her again in his arms, and feeling her burrow trustingly close.

Perhaps, though, she had changed her mind? She had not replied to his letters, sent faithfully on every mail coach. But the Campbells, that poisonous old pair, would not let her reply, he supposed. He held on to that belief, and would, in any case, test it by calling on her. Soon. He could leave soon.

A burst of noise and movement at the other end of the street caught his attention. A wagon train coming into town, full of eager miners and, he hoped, his new shop manager.

There she was, a child on either side, driving a cart laden high with what he assumed were the goods he'd ordered up from the wharves. The others must be walking and, sure enough, at least three children flanked the cart, including one hand in hand with… he caught his breath. Surely, it couldn't be Rose?

But he would know her anywhere, and his legs had not waited for his brain to catch up, but were already carrying him down the street at a stride, and then at a run.

Rose, his Rose, dropped the child's hand and pushed her towards one of the older girls with a quick word, then started towards Thomas, her dear face shining with welcome.

In a moment, he had her in his arms, oblivious to the laughing, cheering crowd of bystanders.

"You came," he said.

"Thomas."

A swollen, ugly, fading bruise disfigured one eye, but she was still the most beautiful sight he had ever seen. He brushed it tenderly with the back of his fingers, before cupping her cheek.

"Marry me, Rose," he asked again.

Her smile answered him before her shy words. "Yes, please, Thomas."

THE END

Connect with Jude Knight

Jude Knight writes stories to transport you to another time, another

place, where you can enjoy adventure and romance, thrill to trials and challenges, uncover secrets and solve mysteries, and delight in a happy ending. Meet strong determined heroines, heroes who can appreciate a clever capable woman, villains you'll love to loathe, and all with a leavening of humour.

Follow Jude on Twitter
Like Jude on Facebook
Subscribe to Jude's blog
Subscribe to Jude's newsletter
Follow Jude on Goodreads

Jude's books are available in print and as ebooks at all major eretailers. Find links, blurbs, excerpts, and special features on
http://judeknightbooks.com/books

Regency books

Candle's Christmas Chair (A novella in *The Golden Redepennings* series)
They are separated by social standing and malicious lies. How can he convince her to give their love another chance? (in this volume)

Gingerbread Bride (A novella in *The Golden Redepenning* series)
Mary runs from an unwanted marriage and finds adventure, danger and her girlhood hero, coming once more to her rescue. (in this volume)

Farewell to Kindness (Book 1 in *The Golden Redepenning* series)
Love is not always convenient. Anne and Rede have different goals, but when their enemies join forces, so must they.

A Raging Madness (Book 2 in *The Golden Redepenning* series)
Their marriage is a fiction. Their enemies are all too real. The truth will need all the trust Ella and Alex can find.

A Baron for Becky
She was a fallen woman. How could the men who loved her help set her back on her feet?

Revealed in Mist
As spy and enquiry agent, Prue and David worked to uncover secrets, while hiding a few of their own.

Lord Calne's Christmas Ruby
Lalamani prefers her aunt's quiet village to fashionable London, its vicious harpies, and its importunate fortune hunters. Philip wishes she wasn't so rich, or he wasn't so poor. (In this volume.)

A Suitable Husband
A chef from the slums, however talented, is no fit mate for the cousin of a duke, however distant. But Cedrica can dream. (first published in *Holly and Hopeful Hearts*, a Bluestocking Belles collection. In this volume)

The Bluestocking and the Barbarian
How can a viscount under a cloud win the proper English maiden who holds his heart? Why would a handsome barbarian want a bluestocking past her prayers? (In *Holly and Hopeful Hearts*, a Bluestocking Belles collection.)

Lunch-length reads: story collections

Hand-Turned Tales and *Lost in the Tale*
A double handful of short stories and novellas. Hand-Turned is free from most eretailers. Try the range of Jude's imagination one bite at a time, in a lunch-length read.

Victorian books

Never Kiss a Toad (with Mariana Gabrielle)
Caught together in her father's bed, Sally and Toad are wrenched apart, to endure years of separation. But neither distance nor malice can destroy true love. (Being published episode by episode on Wattpad)

God Help Ye, Merry Gentleman (with Mariana Gabrielle)
In this prequel novelette to *Never Kiss a Toad*, Sally wants to discuss The Scrapbook, a collection of forbidden materials Toad has been sending her. Will Toad survive Christmas?

Forged in Fire (novella in the Bluestocking Belles collection *Never Too Late*)
Burned in their youth, neither Tad nor Lottie expected to feel the fires of love. Until the inferno of a volcanic eruption sears away the lies of the past and frees them to forge a new future.

Contemporary books

A Family Christmas (novella in the Authors of Main Street collection *Christmas Babies on Mainstreet*)
She's hiding out. He's coming home. And there'll be storms for Christmas.

Post-apocalyptic fiction

A Midwinter's Tale (novella in the Speakeasy Scribes collection *Resist and Rejoice*)
Verity Marchand is an orphan of time, her family tavern under the ice that grips Boston. When Verity's dreams lead her into a nightmare, she'll need a miracle—or the family cat—to save her.

www.ingramcontent.com/pod-product-compliance
Lightning Source LLC
Chambersburg PA
CBHW031029120726
47905CB00007B/2111